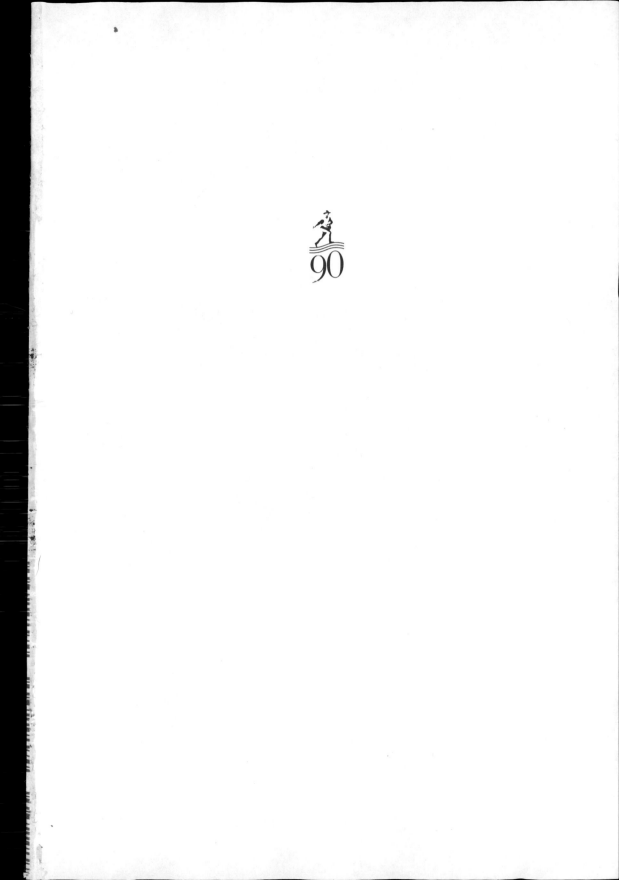

90

We Are Not Ourselves

Matthew Thomas

Simon & Schuster

New York   London   Toronto   Sydney   New Delhi

Simon & Schuster
1230 Avenue of the Americas
New York, NY 10020

First Simon & Schuster hardcover edition August 2014

SIMON & SCHUSTER and colophon are registered trademarks of Simon & Schuster, Inc.

"Touch Me." Copyright ©1995 by Stanley Kunitz, from *Passing Through: The Later Poems New and Selected* by Stanley Kunitz. Used by permission of W. W. Norton & Company, Inc.

For information about special discounts for bulk purchases, please contact Simon & Schuster Special Sales at 1-866-506-1949 or business@simonandschuster.com.

The Simon & Schuster Speakers Bureau can bring authors to your live event. For more information or to book an event, contact the Simon & Schuster Speakers Bureau at 1-866-248-3049 or visit our website at www.simonspeakers.com.

Interior design by Nancy Singer
Jacket design by Christopher Lin
Jacket photographs: houses © Kim Sohee/ Getty Images; sky © Mark Owen / Arcangel Images

Manufactured in the United States of America

10 9 8 7 6 5 4 3 2 1

Library of Congress Cataloging-in-Publication Data
Thomas, Matthew.
  We are not ourselves : a novel / Matthew Thomas.
    page cm.
  1. Irish Americans—Queens (New York, N.Y.)—History—20th century—Fiction. 2. Ireland—Emigration and immigration—History—Fiction. 3. Queens (New York, N.Y.)—History—20th century—Fiction. 4. Domestic fiction. I. Title.
  PS3620.H63513W4 2014
  813'.6—dc23
                                                            2013044414

ISBN 978-1-4767-5666-0
ISBN 978-1-4767-5668-4 (ebook)

Darling, do you remember
the man you married? Touch me,
remind me who I am.
　　　　　—Stanley Kunitz

We are not ourselves
When nature, being oppressed, commands the mind
To suffer with the body.
　　　　　—*King Lear*

To Joy

We Are Not Ourselves

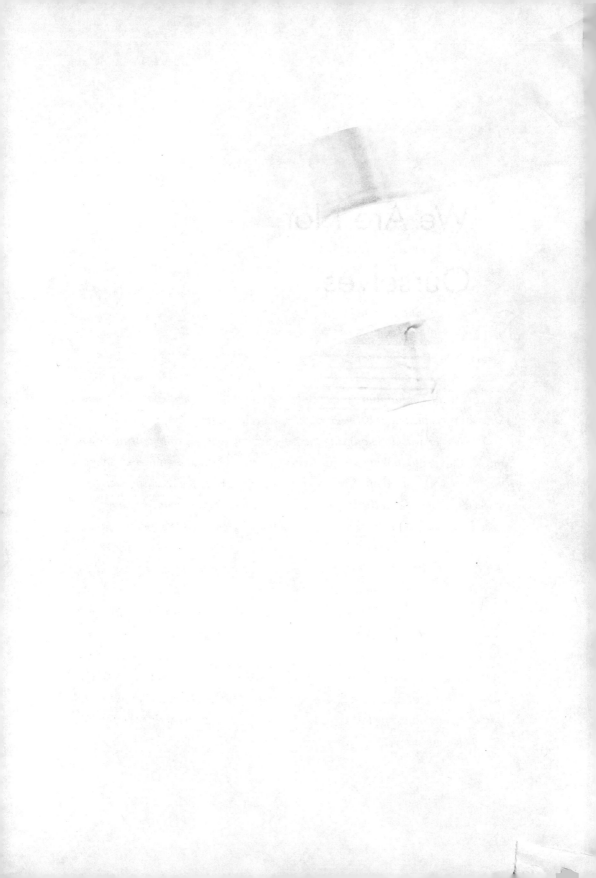

His father was watching the line in the water. The boy caught a frog and stuck a hook in its stomach to see what it would look like going through. Slick guts clung to the hook, and a queasy guilt grabbed him. He tried to sound innocent when he asked if you could fish with frogs. His father glanced over, flared his nostrils, and shook the teeming coffee can at him. Worms spilled out and wriggled away. He told him he'd done an evil thing and that his youth was no excuse for his cruelty. He made him remove the hook and hold the twitching creature until it died. Then he passed him the bait knife and had him dig a little grave. He spoke with a terrifying lack of familiarity, as if they were simply two people on earth now and an invisible tether between them had been severed.

When he was done burying the frog, the boy took his time patting down the dirt, to avoid looking up. His father told him to think awhile about what he'd done and walked off. The boy crouched listening to the receding footsteps as tears came on and the loamy smell of rotting leaves invaded his nose. He stood and looked at the river. Dusk stole quickly through the valley. After a while, he understood he'd been there longer than his father had intended, but he couldn't bring himself to head to the car, because he feared that when he got there he'd see that his father no longer recognized him as his own. He couldn't imagine anything worse than that, so he tossed rocks into the river and waited for his father to come get him. When one of his throws gave none of the splashing sound he'd gotten used to hearing, and a loud croak rose up suddenly behind him, he ran, spooked, to find his father leaning against the hood with a foot up on the fender, looking as if he would've waited all night for him, now adjusting his cap and opening the door to drive them home. He wasn't lost to him yet.

Part I

Days
under Sun
and Rain

1951–1982

1

Instead of going to the priest, the men who gathered at Doherty's Bar after work went to Eileen Tumulty's father. Eileen was there to see it for herself, even though she was only in the fourth grade. When her father finished his delivery route, around four thirty, he picked her up at step dancing and walked her over to the bar. Practice went until six, but Eileen never minded leaving the rectory basement early. Mr. Hurley was always yelling at her to get the timing right or to keep her arms flush at her sides. Eileen was too lanky for the compact movements of a dance that evolved, according to Mr. Hurley, to disguise itself as standing still when the police passed by. She wanted to learn the jitterbug or Lindy Hop, anything she could throw her restless limbs into with abandon, but her mother mother hadn't let go of Irish dancing instead.

Her father liked to tout that he'd applied for his citizenship on the first day he was eligible to. The framed Certificate of Citizenship, dated May 3, 1938, hung in the living room across from a watercolor painting of St. Patrick banishing the snakes, the only artwork in the apartment unless you counted the carved-wood Celtic cross in the kitchen. The little photo in the certificate bore an embossed seal, a tidy signature, and a face with an implacably fierce expression. Eileen looked into it for answers, but the tight-lipped younger version of her father never gave anything up.

When Eileen's father filled the doorway with his body, holding his Stetson hat in front of him like a shield against small talk, Mr. Hurley stopped barking, and not just at Eileen. Men were always quieting down around her father. The recording played on and the girls finished the slip jig they were running. The fiddle music was lovely when Eileen didn't have to worry about keeping her unruly body in line. At the end of the tune, Mr. Hurley didn't waste time giving Eileen permission to leave. He just looked at the floor while she gathered her things. She was in such a hurry to get out of there and begin the wordless walk that she waited until she got to the street to change her shoes.

When they reached the block the bar was on, Eileen ran ahead to see if she could catch one of the men sitting on her father's stool, which she'd never seen anyone else occupy, but all she found was them gathered in a half circle around it, as if anticipation of his presence had drawn them near.

The place was smoky and she was the only kid there, but she got to watch her father hold court. Before five, the patrons were laborers like him who drank their beers deliberately, contented in their exhaustion, well-being hanging about them like a mist. After five, the office workers drifted in, clicking their coins on the crowded bar as they waited to be served. They gulped their beers and signaled for another immediately, gripping the railing with two hands and leaning in to hurry the drink along. They watched her father as much as they did the bartender.

She sat at one of the creaky tables ur f   l   pleated skirt and collared blouse, doing her homework but also training   ther's conversations. She didn't have to strain to hear what they told him because they felt no need to whisper, even when she was only a few feet away. There was something clarifying in her father's authority; it absolved other men of embarrassment.

"It's driving me nuts," his friend Tom said, fumbling to speak. "I can't sleep."

"Out with it."

"I stepped out on Sheila."

Her father leaned in closer, his eyes pinning Tom to the barstool.

"How many times?"

"Just the once."

"Don't lie to me."

"The second time I was too nervous to bring it off."

"That's twice, then."

"It is."

The bartender swept past to check the level of their drinks, slapped the bar towel over his shoulder, and moved along. Her father glanced at her and she pushed her pencil harder into her workbook, breaking off the point.

"Who's the floozy?"

"A girl at the bank."

"You'll tell her the idiocy is over."

"I will, Mike."

"Are you going to be a goddamned idiot again? Tell me now."

"No."

A man came through the door, and her father and Tom nodded at him. A draft followed him in, chilling her bare legs and carrying the smell of spilled beer and floor cleaner to her.

"Reach into your pocket," her father said. "Every penny you have stashed. Buy Sheila something nice."

"Yes, that's the thing. That's the thing."

"Every last penny."

"I won't hold out."

"Swear before God that that's the end of it."

"I swear, Mike. I solemnly swear."

"Don't let me hear about you gallivanting around."

"Those days are over."

"And don't go and do some fool thing like tell that poor woman what you've done. It's enough for her to put up with you without knowing this."

"Yes," Tom said. "Yes."

"You're a damned fool."

"I am."

"That's the last we'll speak of it. Get us a couple of drinks."

They laughed at everything he said, unless he was being serious, and then they put on grave faces. They held forth on the topic of his virtues as though he weren't standing right there. Half of them he'd gotten jobs for off the boat—at Schaefer, at Macy's, behind the bar, as supers or handymen.

Everybody called him Big Mike. He was reputed to be immune to pain. He had shoulders so broad that even in shirtsleeves he looked like he was wearing a suit jacket. His fists were the size of babies' heads, and in the trunk he resembled one of the kegs of beer he carried in the crook of each elbow. He put no effort into his physique apart from his labor, and he wasn't muscle-bound, just country strong. If you caught him in a moment of repose, he seemed to shrink to normal proportions. If you had something to hide, he grew before your eyes.

She wasn't too young to understand that the ones who pleased him were the rare ones who didn't drain the frothy brew of his myth in a quick quaff, but nosed around the brine of his humanity awhile, giving it skeptical sniffs.

She was only nine, but she'd figured a few things out. She knew why her father didn't just swing by step dancing on the way home for dinner. To do so would have meant depriving the men in suits who arrived back from Manhattan toward the end of the hour of the little time he gave them every day. They loosened their ties around him, took their jackets off, huddled close, and started talking. He would've had to leave the bar by five thirty instead of a quarter to six, and the extra minutes made all the difference. She understood that it wasn't only enjoyment for him, that part of what he was doing was making himself available to his men, and that his duty to her mother was just as important.

The three of them ate dinner together every night. Her mother served the meal promptly at six after spending the day cleaning bathrooms and offices at the Bulova plant. She was never in the mood for excuses. Eileen's father checked his watch the whole way home and picked up the pace as they neared the building. Sometimes Eileen couldn't keep up and he carried her in the final stretch. Sometimes she walked slowly on purpose in order to be borne in his arms.

• • •

One balmy evening in June, a week before her fourth-grade year ended, Eileen and her father came home to find the plates set out and the door to the bedroom closed. Her father tapped at his watch with a betrayed look, wound it, and set it to the clock above the sink, which said six twenty. Eileen had never seen him so upset. She could tell it was about something more than being late, something between her parents that she had no insight into. She was angry at her mother for adhering so rigidly to her rule, but her father didn't seem to share that anger. He ate slowly, silently, refilling her glass when he rose to fill his own and ladling out more carrots for her from the pot on the stovetop. Then he put his coat on and went back out. Eileen went to the door of the bedroom but didn't open it. She listened and heard nothing. She went to Mr. Kehoe's door, but there was silence there too. She felt a sudden terror at the thought of having been abandoned. She wanted to bang on both doors and bring them out, but she knew enough not to go near her mother just then. To calm herself, she cleaned the stovetop and counters, leaving no crumbs or smudges, no evidence that her mother had cooked in the first place. She tried to imagine what it would feel like to have always been alone. She decided that being alone to begin with would be easier than being left alone. Everything would be easier than that.

She eavesdropped on her father at the bar because he didn't talk much at home. When he did, it was to lay out basic principles as he speared a piece of meat. "A man should never go without something he wants just because he doesn't want to work for it." "Everyone should have a second job." "Money is made to be spent." (On this last point he was firm; he had no patience for American-born people with no cash in their pocket to spring for a round.)

As for his second job, it was tending bar, at Doherty's, at Hartnett's, at Leitrim Castle—a night a week at each. Whenever Big Mike Tumulty was the one pulling the taps and filling the tumblers, the bar filled up to the point of hazard and made tons of money, as though he were a touring thespian giving limited-run performances. Schaefer didn't suffer either; everyone knew he was a Schaefer man. He worked at keeping the brogue her mother worked to lose; it was professionally useful.

If Eileen scrubbed up the courage to ask about her roots, he silenced her with a wave of the hand. "I'm an American," he said, as if it settled the question, and in a sense it did.

By the time Eileen was born, in November of 1941, some traces remained of the sylvan scenes suggested in her neighborhood's name, but the balance of Woodside's verdancy belonged to the cemeteries that bordered it. The natural order was inverted there, the asphalt, clapboard, and brick breathing with life and the dead holding sway over the grass.

Her father came from twelve and her mother from thirteen, but Eileen had no brothers or sisters. In a four-story building set among houses planted in close rows by the river of the elevated 7 train, the three of them slept in twin beds in a room that resembled an army barracks. The other bedroom housed a lodger, Henry Kehoe, who slept like a king in exchange for offsetting some of the monthly expenses. Mr. Kehoe ate his meals elsewhere, and when he was home he sat in his room with the door closed, playing the clarinet quietly enough that Eileen had to press an ear to the door to hear it. She only saw him when he came and went or used the bathroom. It might have been strange to suffer his spectral presence if she'd ever known anything else, but as it was, it comforted her to know he was behind that door, especially on nights her father came home after drinking whiskey.

Her father didn't always drink. Nights he tended bar, he didn't touch a drop, and every Lent he gave it up, to prove he could—except, of course, for St. Patrick's Day and the days bookending it.

Nights her father tended bar, Eileen and her mother turned in early and slept soundly. Nights he didn't, though, her mother kept her up later, the two of them giving a going-over to all the little extras—the good silver, the figurines, the chandelier crystals, the picture frames. Whatever chaos might ensue upon her father's arrival, there prevailed beforehand a palpable excitement, as if they were throwing a party for a single guest. When there was nothing left to clean or polish, her mother sent her to bed and waited on the couch. Eileen kept the bedroom door cracked.

Her father was fine when he drank beer. He hung his hat and slid his coat down deliberately onto the hook in the wall. Then he slumped on the couch like a big bear on a leash, soft and grumbling, his pipe firmly in the grip of his teeth. She could hear her mother speaking quietly to him about household matters; he would nod and press the splayed fingers of his hands together, making a steeple and collapsing it.

Some nights he even walked in dancing and made her mother laugh despite her intention to ignore him. He lifted her up from the couch and led her around the room in a slow box step. He had a terrible charisma; she wasn't immune to it.

When he drank whiskey, though, which was mostly on paydays, the leash came off. He slammed his coat on the vestibule table and stalked the place looking for things to throw, as if the accumulated pressure of expectations at the bar could only be driven off by physical acts. It was well known what a great quantity of whiskey her father could drink without losing his composure—she'd heard the men brag about it at Doherty's— and one night, in response to her mother's frank and defeated question, he explained that when he was set up with a challenge, a string of rounds, he refused to disappoint the men's faith in him, even if he had to exhaust himself concentrating on keeping his back stiff and his words sharp and clear. Everyone needed something to believe in.

He didn't throw anything at her mother, and he only threw what didn't break: couch pillows, books. Her mother went silent and still until he was done. If he saw Eileen peeking at him through the sliver in the bedroom door, he stopped abruptly, like an actor who'd forgotten his line, and went into the bathroom. Her mother slid into bed. In the morning, he glowered over a cup of tea, blinking his eyes slowly like a lizard.

Sometimes Eileen could hear the Gradys or the Longs fighting. She found succor in the sound of that anger; it meant her family wasn't the only troubled one in the building. Her parents shared moments of dark communion over it too, raising brows at each other across the kitchen table or exchanging wan smiles when the voices started up.

Once, over dinner, her father gestured toward Mr. Kehoe's room. "We won't have him here forever," he said to her mother. As Eileen was struck by sadness at the thought of life without Mr. Kehoe, her father added, "Lord willing."

No matter how often she strained to hear Mr. Kehoe through the walls, the only sounds were the squeaks of bedsprings, the low scratching of a pen when he sat at the little desk, or the quiet rasp of the clarinet.

They were at the dinner table when her mother stood and left the room in a hurry. Her father followed, pulling the bedroom door closed behind him. Their voices were hushed, but Eileen could hear the straining energy in them. She inched closer.

"I'll get it back."

"You're a damned idiot."

"I'll make it right."

"How? '*Big Mike doesn't borrow a penny from any man*,'" she sneered.

"There'll be a way."

"How could you let it get so out of hand?"

"You think I want my wife and daughter living in this place?"

"Oh, that's just grand. It's *our* fault now, is it?"

"I'm not saying that."

In the living room, the wind shifted the bedroom door against Eileen's hands, making her heart beat faster.

"You love the horses and numbers," her mother said. "Don't make it into something it wasn't."

"It was in the back of my mind," her father said. "I know you don't want to be here."

"I once believed you could wind up being mayor of New York," her mother said. "But you're satisfied being mayor of Doherty's. Not even owner of Doherty's. *Mayor* of Doherty's." She paused. "I should never have taken that damn thing off my finger."

"I'll get it back. I promise."

"You won't, and you know it." Her mother had been stifling her shouts, practically hissing, but now she sounded merely sad. "You chip away and chip away. One day there won't be anything left."

"That's enough now," her father said, and in the silence that followed Eileen pictured them standing in the mysterious knowledge that passed between them, like two stone figures whose hearts she would never fathom.

The next time she was alone in the house, she went to the bureau drawer where her mother had stashed her engagement ring for safekeeping ever since the time she'd almost lost it down the drain while doing dishes. From time to time, Eileen had observed her opening the box. She'd thought her mother had been letting its facets catch the light for a spell, but now that she saw the empty space where the box had been, she realized her mother had been making sure it was still there.

A week before her tenth birthday, Eileen walked in with her father and saw that her mother wasn't in the kitchen. She wasn't in the bedroom either, or the bathroom, and she hadn't left a note.

Her father heated up a can of beans, fried some bacon, and put out a few slices of bread.

Her mother came home while they were eating. "Congratulate me," she said as she hung up her coat.

Her father waited until he finished chewing. "For what?"

Her mother slapped some papers on the table and looked at him intently in that way she sometimes did when she was trying to get a rise out of him. He bit another piece of bacon and picked the papers up as he worked the meat in his jaw. His brow furrowed as he read. Then he put them down.

"How could you do this?" he asked quietly. "How could you let it not be me?"

If Eileen didn't know better, she would have said he sounded hurt, but nothing on earth was capable of hurting her father.

Her mother looked almost disappointed not to be yelled at. She gathered the papers and went into the bedroom. A few minutes later, her father took his hat off the hook and left.

Eileen went in and sat on her own bed. Her mother was at the window, smoking.

"What happened? I don't understand."

"Those are naturalization papers." Her mother pointed to the dresser. "Go ahead, take a look." Eileen walked over and picked them up. "As of today, I'm a citizen of the United States. Congratulate me."

"Congratulations," Eileen said.

Her mother produced a sad little grin between drags. "I started this months ago," she said. "I didn't tell your father. I was going to surprise him, bring him along. It would have meant something to him to be my sponsor at the swearing in. Then I decided to hurt him. I brought my cousin Danny Glasheen instead."

Eileen nodded; there was Danny's name. The papers looked like the kind that would be kept in a file for hundreds of years, for as long as civilization lasted.

"Now I wish I could take it back." Her mother gave a rueful laugh. "Your father is a creature of great ceremony."

Eileen wasn't sure what her mother meant, but she thought it had to do with the way it mattered to her father to carry even little things out the right way. She'd seen it herself: the way he took the elbow of a man who'd had too much to drink and leaned him into the bar to keep him on his feet without his noticing he was being aided; the way he never knocked a beer glass over or spilled a drop of whiskey; the way he kept his hair combed neat, no strand out of place. She'd watched him carry the casket at a few funerals. He made it seem as if keeping one's eyes forward, one's posture straight, and one's pace steady while bearing a dead man down the steps of a church as a bagpiper played was the most crucial task in the world. It was part of why men felt so strongly about him. It must have been part of why her mother did too.

"Don't ever love anyone," her mother said, picking the papers up and sliding them into the bureau drawer she'd kept her ring in. "All you'll do is break your own heart."

2

In the spring of 1952, Eileen's mother made the amazing announcement that she was pregnant. Eileen had never even seen her parents hold hands. If her aunt Kitty hadn't told her that they'd met at one of the Irish dance halls and found some renown there as a dancing pair, Eileen might have believed her parents had never touched. Here her mother was, though, pregnant as anyone. The world was full of mysteries.

Her mother quit her job at Bulova and sat on the couch knitting a blanket for the baby. When she tied off the last corner, she moved on to making a hat. A sweater followed, then a pair of bootees. Everything was stark white. She kept the miniature clothes in a drawer in the breakfront. The crafting was expert, with tight stitches and neat rows. Eileen never even knew her mother could knit. She wondered if her mother had made clothes for her family in Ireland, or to sell in a store, but she knew enough not to ask. She couldn't even bring herself to seek permission to rub the bump on her mother's belly. The closest she got to the baby was when she went to the drawer to examine the articles her mother had knitted, running her hands over their smoothness and putting them up to her face. One night, after her mother had gone to bed, she picked up the knitting needles, which were still warm from use. Between them swayed the bootee to complete the pair. Eileen tried to picture this baby who would help her populate the apartment and whose cheeks she would cover in kisses, but all she saw was her mother's face in miniature, wearing that dubious expression she wore when Eileen went looking for affection. She concentrated hard until she stopped seeing her mother's face and saw instead the smiling face of a baby beaming with light and joy. She was determined to have a relationship with this sibling that would have nothing to do with their parents.

Eileen was so excited to get a baby brother or sister that she physically *felt* her heart breaking when her father told her that her mother had miscarried. When a dilation and curettage didn't stop the bleeding, the doctors gave her a hysterectomy.

After the hysterectomy, her mother developed a bladder infection that nearly killed her. She stayed in the hospital on sulfa drugs while it drained. Children weren't encouraged to visit the sick, so Eileen saw her mother less than once a month. Her father rarely spoke of her mother during this period that stretched into a handful of months, then half a year and beyond. When he intended to bring Eileen to see her, he would say something vague like, "We're going, get yourself ready." Otherwise, it was as if she'd been erased from their lives.

It didn't take long for Eileen to figure out that she wasn't supposed to mention her mother, but one night, a couple of weeks into the new order, she brought her up a few times in quick succession anyway, just to see how her father would react. "That's enough now," he snapped, rising from the table, evidence of suppressed emotion on his face. "Clean up these dishes." He left the room, as though it were too painful for him to remain where his absent wife had been invoked. And yet they spent so much time fighting. Eileen decided she would never understand the relations between men and women.

She was left to handle the cooking and cleaning. Her father set aside money for her to shop and go to the Laundromat. She rode her bike to one of the last remaining farms in the neighborhood to buy fresh vegetables, and she developed her own little repertory of dishes by replicating what she'd seen her mother make: beef stew with carrots and green beans; London broil; soda bread; lamb chops and baked potatoes. She took a cookbook out of the library and started ranging afield. She made lasagna just once, beating her fist on the countertop when it turned out soupy after all that work.

After doing her homework by the muted light of the end table lamp, she sat on the floor, building towers of playing cards, or went upstairs to the Schmidts' to watch television and marvel over the mothers who never stopped smiling and the fathers who folded the newspaper down to talk to their children.

At school she usually had the answer worked out before the other girls put up their hands, but the last thing she wanted was to draw any kind of attention to herself. She would have chosen, of all powers, the power to be invisible.

One day, her father took her to Jackson Heights, stopping at a huge cooperative apartment complex that spanned the width of a block and most of its length. They descended into the basement apartment of the super, one of her father's friends. From the kitchen she looked up at the ground level through a set of steel bars. There was grass out there, blindingly green grass. She asked to go outside. "Only as long as you don't step foot on that grass," her father's friend said. "Not even the people who live here are allowed on it. They pay me good money to make sure it stays useless." He and her father shared a laugh she didn't understand.

A frame of connected buildings enclosed a massive lawn girdled by a short wrought-iron railing. Nothing would have been easier than clearing that little fence. Around the lawn and through its middle ran a handsome brick path. She walked the routes of the two smaller rectangles and the outer, larger one, wending her way through all the permutations, listening to the chirping of the birds in the trees and the rustling of the leaves in the wind. Gas lamps stood like guardians of the prosperity they would light when evening came. She felt an amazing peace. There were no cars rushing around, no people pushing shopping carts home. One old lady waved to her before disappearing inside. Eileen would have been content to live out there, looking up into the curtain-fringed windows. She didn't need to set foot on that grass. Maybe someone would bring her upstairs and she could look down on the whole lawn at once. The lights were on in the dining room of one apartment on the second floor, and she stopped to stare into it. A grandfather clock and a beautiful wall unit gazed down benignly at a bowl on the table. She couldn't see what was in the bowl, but she knew it was her favorite fruit.

The people who lived in this building had figured out something important about life, and she'd stumbled upon their secret. There were places, she now saw, that contained more happiness than ordinary places did. Unless you knew that such places existed, you might be content to stay where you were. She imagined more places like this, hidden behind walls or stands of trees, places where people kept their secrets to themselves.

When the soles of her shoes wore through, her father, in his infinite ignorance of all things feminine, brought home a new, manure-brown pair Eileen was sure were meant for boys. When she refused to wear them, her father confiscated her old pair so she had no choice, and when she complained the next night that the other girls had laughed at her, he said, "They cover your feet and keep you warm." At her age, he told her, he had been grateful to get secondhand shoes, let alone new ones.

"If my mother were well," she said bitterly, "she wouldn't make me wear them."

"Yes, but she's not well. And she's not here."

The quaver in his throat frightened her enough that she didn't argue. The following night, he brought home a perfectly dainty, gleaming, pearlescent pair.

"Let that be an end to it," he said.

Mr. Kehoe came home late, but he never seemed drunk. He was unfailingly polite. Despite the fact that he'd been there since she was two years old, it always felt to Eileen as if he'd just moved in.

She took to cooking extra for him and bringing a plate to his room. He answered her knock with a smile and received the offering gratefully. Her father grumbled about charging a board fee.

Mr. Kehoe had a smear of black in a full head of otherwise gray hair. It looked as if he'd been streaked by a tar brush. When he wasn't wearing his tweed jacket with the worn cuffs, he rolled his shirt sleeves and kept his tie a little loose.

He started battling through fitful bouts of coughing. One night, she went to his door with some tea; another, she brought him cough syrup.

"It's just that I don't get enough air," Mr. Kehoe said. "I'll take some long walks."

Even through severe coughing fits he managed to play the clarinet. She'd stopped trying to hide her efforts to listen to it. She sat on the floor beside his door, with her back to the wall, reading her schoolbooks. In the lonely evenings she felt no need to apologize for her interest. Sometimes she even whistled along.

One night, her father sat quietly on the couch after dinner with a troubled look on his face. Eileen avoided him, occupying her usual spot by Mr. Kehoe's door. Heat rattling through the pipes joined the clarinet in a kind of musical harmony. She looked up and was unnerved to find her father looking back at her, which he never did. She concentrated on her beautifully illustrated copy of *Grimm's Fairy Tales*. The day before, when she'd told him that Mr. Kehoe had given it to her, her father had grown upset. She'd seen him knock on Mr. Kehoe's door a little while later and hand him some money.

She was absorbed in "The Story of the Youth Who Went Forth to Learn What Fear Was" when her father startled her away from the door. She barely had time to step aside before he had thrown Mr. Kehoe's door open and told him to quit making that racket. Mr. Kehoe apologized for causing a disturbance, but Eileen knew there had been none; you could barely hear him playing from where her father had been sitting.

Her father tried to snatch the clarinet from Mr. Kehoe's hands. Mr. Kehoe stood up, clutching it, until its pieces started coming apart and he staggered backward, coughing wildly. Her father went out to the kitchen and turned up the radio loud enough that the neighbors started banging on the ceiling.

When she came home the next day, Mr. Kehoe was gone.

For almost a week, she didn't speak to her father. They passed each other without a word, like an old married couple. Then her father stopped her in the hall.

"He was going to have to leave," he said. "I just made it happen sooner."

"He didn't have to go anywhere," she said.

"Your mother is coming home."

She was excited and terrified all at once. She'd started thinking her mother might never come back. She was going to have to give up control of the house. She wouldn't have her father to herself anymore.

"What does that have to do with Mr. Kehoe?"

"You can move your things over there tonight."

"You're not getting another lodger?"

He shook his head. A thrilling feeling of possibility took her over.

"I'm getting my own room?"

Her father looked away. "Your mother has decided that she's moving over there with you."

3

On the Wednesday after Easter of 1953, eight months after she'd left, her mother came home from the hospital. The separate rooms were as close as her parents could ever come to divorce.

Her mother got a job behind the counter at Loft's, a fancy confectioner's on Forty-Second Street, and started coming home late, often drunk. In protest, Eileen let dirty dishes stack up in the sink and piles of clothes amass in the bedroom corners. When she got teased in the schoolyard for the wrinkles in her blouse, she saw she had no choice but to continue the homemaking alone.

Her mother began drinking at home, settling her lanky body into the depression in the couch, in one hand a glass of Scotch, in the other a cigarette whose elongated ash worm would cling to the end as if working up the nerve to leap. Eileen watched helplessly as the malevolent thing accumulated mass. Her mother held an ashtray in her lap, but sometimes the embers fell into the cushions instead and Eileen rushed to pluck them out. Her mother fell asleep on the couch many nights, but she went to work no matter her condition.

That summer, her mother bought a window air-conditioning unit from Stevens on Queens Boulevard. She had the delivery man install it in the bedroom she shared with Eileen. No one else on their floor had an air conditioner. She invited Mrs. Grady and Mrs. Long over and into the bedroom, where they stood before the unit's indefatigable wind, staring as though at a savior child possessed of healing powers.

When both her parents were home, an uneasy truce prevailed. Her mother closed the bedroom door and sat by the window, watching night encroach on the street. Eileen brought her tea after dinner. Her father stationed himself at the kitchen table, puffing at his pipe and listening to Irish football. At least they were under the same roof.

She hated thinking of her mother riding the trains. She saw her mother's body sprawled in dark subway tunnels as she sat at the kitchen table for hours watching the door. As soon as she heard the key shunting the dead bolt aside, she rose to put the kettle on or wash dishes. She wouldn't give her mother the satisfaction of knowing she was worried about her.

One night, after she had cooked the dinner and washed the pots and pans, she nestled exhausted into the couch, where her mother sat smoking a cigarette and staring ahead. Tentatively, she laid her head in her mother's lap and kept still. She watched the smoke pour through her mother's pale lips and the ash get longer. Other than a few new wrinkles around the mouth and some blossoms of burst blood vessels on her cheeks, her mother's skin was still smooth and full and porcelain white. She still had those dramatic lips. Only her stained teeth showed evidence of wear.

"Why don't you give me hugs and kisses like the mothers on television?"

Eileen waited for her to say something sharp in response, but her mother just stubbed out the butt and picked up the pack to smoke another. There was a long silence.

"Don't you think you're a little old for this?" her mother finally asked. Eventually she moved Eileen aside and rose to pour herself a tall drink. She sat back down with it.

"I wasn't like your father," she said. "I couldn't wait to escape the farm. I remember I was packing my bag, I heard my father say to my mother, 'Deirdre, let her go. This is no place for a young person.' I was eighteen. I came looking for Arcadia, but instead I found domestic work on Long Island. I rode the train out and back in the crepuscular hours. *Cre-pus-cu-lar.* You probably don't know what that word means."

She could tell her mother had begun one of those sodden monologues she delivered from time to time, full of edgy eloquence. Eileen just sat and listened.

"I used to daydream about living in the mansions I cleaned. I liked to do windows, everyone else's least-favorite job. I could look out on rolling lawns. They didn't have a single rock, those lawns. I liked to look at the tennis courts. Perfectly level, and not a twig out of place. They suggested . . . what?—the taming of chaos. I liked the windswept dunes, the spray of crashing waves, the sailboats tied to docks. And when I went out to run the rag over the other side, I looked in on women reclining on divans like cats that had supped from bowls of milk. I didn't begrudge them their ease. In their place, I would have planted myself on an elbow from the moment I rose in the morning until the time came for me"—her mother made a languorous gesture with her finger that reminded Eileen of the way bony Death pointed—"to be prodded back to the silken sheets."

"It sounds nice," Eileen said.

"It wasn't *nice*," her mother said sharply after the few beats it took her thoughts to cohere. "It was—*marvelous*, is what it was."

A few days before Christmas, her mother told her to take the train in to Loft's a little before the end of her shift. When Eileen arrived, her mother looked so effortlessly composed that one would never know she'd become a serious drinker. Eileen walked around the store in stupefaction, gaping at the handcrafted, glazed, and filigreed confections.

When her mother was done, she gave Eileen a box of truffles to take home and walked her over to Fifth Avenue and down to Thirty-Ninth Street, to the windows of Lord & Taylor, which Eileen had seen only in pictures in the newspaper. The scenes behind the windows, with their warmly lit fireplaces and silky-looking upholstered miniature furniture, gave her the same feeling she'd had when she'd stood before that great lawn and peered up into the perfect world of the garden apartments. Gorgeous drapery framed a picture she wanted to climb into and live in. Brisk winds blew, but the air was not too cold, and the refreshing smell of winter tickled her nose. In the remnant daylight, the avenue began to take on some of the enchanted quality visible behind the windows. It thrilled her to imagine that passersby saw an ordinary mother-daughter pair enjoying a routine evening of shopping together. She checked people's faces for evidence of what they were thinking: *What a nice little family.*

"Christmas gets the full treatment," her mother said in the train on the way home. "Mind that you remember that. It doesn't matter what else is going on. You could be at death's door, I don't care."

That night, her mother tucked her in for the first time since she'd gone into the hospital. When Eileen awoke in the middle of the night and saw the other bed empty, she stumbled out to find her mother sitting on the couch. For a terrible instant, Eileen thought her mother was dead. Her head hung back, mouth open. Her hand clutched the empty tumbler. Eileen drew close and watched her chest rise and fall, then took the ashtray from her lap and the tumbler from her hand, careful not to wake her, and brought both to the kitchen sink. She took the blanket from her mother's bed and spread it over her. She slept with the door open in order to see her from where she lay.

The package she received in the mail contained a book on how to play the clarinet and, beneath it, Mr. Kehoe's own clarinet. A note on legal stationery said that he'd died of lung cancer and left it to her in his will. She slept beside it for several days until her mother found it one morning and told her to stop, calling it ghoulish. She tried to play it a few times but grew frustrated at the halting noises it produced. With an undiminished memory for its muffled, sensuous sound through the walls, she thought of Mr. Kehoe. She could hear whole songs when she shut her eyes and concentrated, as if the music were waiting to be extracted from her by a trained hand. She could never even string together a couple of familiar-sounding notes. Eventually she took to laying out its pieces and looking at them awhile before fitting them back into the soft pink felt that lined the case. She didn't need to play Mr. Kehoe's clarinet to appreciate it. Its parts were sleek and expertly wrought, their burnished metal protuberances shining with a lustrous gleam. They filled her hand with a pleasant weight. She liked to press the buttons down; they moved with ease and settled back up with a lovely firmness. The mouthpiece where Mr. Kehoe had pressed his lips came to a tapered end. She liked the feel of it against her own lips, the pressure against her teeth when she bit down.

The clarinet was the nicest thing she owned, the nicest thing anyone in her family owned. It didn't belong in that apartment, she decided. When she was older she would live in a beautiful enough home that you wouldn't even notice the clarinet. That was what Mr. Kehoe would have wanted. She would have to marry a man who would make it possible.

When she was thirteen, she started working at the Laundromat. The first time she got paid, after kneading the bills awhile between her thumb and forefinger, she spread them on the table before her and did some math. If she kept working and saved every dollar she could, she wouldn't need anything at all from her parents once she was done with high school— maybe even before. The prospect excited her, though excitement gave way to sadness. She didn't want to think of not needing anything from them. She would save her money for them.

Her mother drank harder than her father ever had, as though she were trying to make up for lost time. Eileen started tending to her needs in a prophylactic rather than merely reactive way. She made coffee, kept a constant supply of aspirin waiting for her, and lay a blanket over her when she fell asleep on the couch.

One night, Eileen came into the living room and saw that her mother's head was bobbing in that way it did when she fought sleep to hold on to a last few moments of conscious drunkenness. Sitting with her was easiest then. She was too far gone to say something tart and withering but could still register Eileen's presence with a tiny fluttering of the eyelid.

Eileen took a seat next to her and felt wetness under her hand. At first she thought her mother had spilled her drink.

She was terrified to change her mother's clothes, because there was a chance her mother might realize what was going on, but she couldn't just let her sit there in that sopping spot all night. She managed to remove her wet clothes and wrap her in a robe. Then she lay her back down on the dry part of the couch. Getting her to bed would be much harder.

Eileen sat on her haunches next to the couch and guided her mother's head and shoulders from her lap to the floor, then dragged the rest of her down. Once she had her there, she slid her along by hooking her arms up under her mother's armpits. Her mother was making murmuring noises.

When Eileen got her to the bed, though, she couldn't lift her up into it. Her mother had stirred to more wakefulness and was trying to stay on the floor.

"Let me get you up, Ma," she said.

"I'll sleep right here."

"You can't sleep on the floor."

"I will," she said, the end of the word trilling off. Her brogue came back when she was drunk or angry.

"It's cold on the floor. Let me lift you up."

"Leave me be."

"I won't do that."

Eileen tried for a while and then gave up and lay on her mother's bed to rest. When she awoke it was to the sound of her father coming home from tending bar. She went to the kitchen and saw him sitting at the table with a glass of water.

"Can you pick Ma up? She's on the floor."

He stood without a word and followed her. It occurred to her that, except on Mr. Kehoe's last night, she'd never seen her father enter that bedroom. In the light streaming in from the kitchen, her mother looked like a pile of dirty sheets on the floor.

Eileen watched him pick her mother up with astounding ease, as if he could have done it with one hand instead of two. One of his arms was cradling her head. Her long limbs hung down; she was fast asleep. He took his time laying her in the bed. He looked at her lying there. Eileen heard him say "Bridgie" once quietly, more to himself than her mother, before he pulled the blanket over her and smoothed it across her shoulders.

"Go to bed now yourself," he said, and shut the door behind him.

"Imagine all of Woodside filled with trees," Sister Mary Alice was telling her eighth-grade class. "Imagine a gorgeous, sprawling, untouched estate of well over a hundred acres. That is what was here, boys and girls. What is now your neighborhood, all of it, every inch, once belonged to a *single family* that traces its roots back to the very beginnings of this country."

A garbage truck in front of the school emitted a few loud coughs, and Sister paused to let it pass. The rolled-up map above the blackboard swayed slightly, and Eileen imagined it unfurling and hitting Sister in the head.

"The grandson of one of the early Puritan founders of Cambridge, Massachusetts, built a farmhouse near this spot, on a massive plot of land he'd bought." Sister started walking around the room with a book held open to a page that contained pictures of the house. "His heirs converted that farmhouse into a manor house. This *manor house*"—Sister practically spat the words—"had a wide hall leading to a large front parlor. It had a back parlor with a huge fireplace, a grand kitchen, a brass knocker on the door. It had an orchard to one side." The insistent way Sister counted off the house's virtues made it sound as if she was building a case against it in court. "After a few generations, they sold the estate to a Manhattan-based merchant from South Carolina to use as a weekend retreat. Then, in the latter half of the last century, when the train lines expanded, a real estate developer saw an opportunity. He cleared the estate's trees, drained its swamps, laid out the streets you walk on today, and carved it into nearly a thousand lots that he distributed by random drawing. He opened the door to the middle class, letting them pay in installments of ten dollars a month. Houses were built. The last vestige of the estate, the manor house, was razed in 1895 to make room for the church, and, eventually, the school you're sitting in right now."

Eileen was watching the frowning white face of the clock at the front of the room when Sister came up to her with the book. Her gaze drifted lazily to the pictures, but once she saw them she couldn't take her eyes off them, and when Sister moved down the row, Eileen asked her to come back for a second.

"The Queensboro Bridge was completed in 1909, and then the LIRR East River tunnel the following year, and they began laying out the IRT Flushing line—the seven train to you—station by station, starting in 1915. The Irish—your grandparents, maybe your parents—began coming across the river in droves, seeking relief from the tenement slums of Manhattan. They wound up in Woodside. Imagine ten people to an apartment, twenty. Then, in 1924—providence. The City Housing Corporation began building houses and apartments to alleviate the density problem." Sister had

made it back to the front of the room. The faint outline of a smile of triumph crept onto her lips as she addressed her final arguments to the jury.
"This is the way the Lord works. To those who have little, he gives. Isn't it
nice to think of all of you here instead of it just one privileged family in a
mansion in the woods? Wouldn't you agree, Miss Tumulty?"

Eileen had been daydreaming about the demolished mansion she'd
just seen the picture of. Sister's question snapped her to attention. "Yes,"
she said. "Yes."

But all she could think was what a shame it was they'd knocked that
house down. A big, beautiful house in the country with land around it—
that wasn't a bad thing at all.

"And think of this," Sister Mary Alice said in closing. "Not a single one
of you would be here if that estate were still around. None of us would. We
simply wouldn't exist."

Eileen looked around at her classmates and tried to conceive of a reality in which none of them had come into being. She thought of the little
apartment she lived in with her parents. Would it be a loss if it had never
been built?

She pictured herself on a couch in that mansion, looking out a window at a stand of trees. She saw herself sitting with her legs crossed as
she flipped through the pages of a big book. Someone had to be born in a
house like that; why couldn't it have been her?

Maybe she wouldn't have been born there, but she'd have been born
somewhere, and she'd have found a way to get there, even if the others didn't.

Some nights she went up the block to see her aunt Kitty and her cousin
Pat, who was four and a half years younger than her. Her uncle Paddy, her
father's older brother, had died when Pat was two, and Pat looked up to her
father like he was his own father.

Eileen had grown up reading to Pat. She'd delivered him to school an
early reader, and he could write when the other kids were still learning
the alphabet. He was whip-smart, but his grades didn't show it because he
never did his homework. He read constantly, as long as it wasn't for school.

She sat him at the kitchen table and made him open his schoolbooks.

She told him he had to get As, that anything less was unacceptable. She said there was no end to what he could do with her help. She told him she wanted him to be successful, and rich enough to buy a mansion. She would live in a wing of it. He just rushed through his work and read adventure stories. All he wanted to do when he grew up was drive a Schaefer truck.

Her mother's morning powers of self-mastery, so impressive in the early days, began to dry up, until, when Eileen was a freshman in high school—she'd earned a full scholarship to St. Helena's in the Bronx—they evaporated overnight. Her mother went in late to Loft's one day, and then she did so again a couple of days later, and then she simply stopped going in at all. One day she passed out in the lobby and the police carried her upstairs. After the officers left—her father being who he was meant nothing would get written up—Eileen didn't say a word or try to change her mother into clean clothes, because her mother would be embarrassed, and Eileen still feared her wrath, even when her mother was slack as a sack of wheat, because the memory of her mother taking the hanger to her when she misbehaved as a child was never far from her mind.

The next day, when they were both at the kitchen table, her mother smoking in silent languor, Eileen told her she was going to call Alcoholics Anonymous. She didn't mention that she'd gotten the number from her aunt Kitty, that she'd been talking to others in the family about her mother's problem.

"Do what you want," her mother said, and then watched with surprising interest as Eileen dialed. A woman answered; Eileen told her that her mother needed help. The woman said they wanted to help her, but her mother had to ask for help herself.

Eileen's heart sank. "She's not going to ask for help," she said, and she felt tears welling up. She saw her mother's darting eyes notice the tears, and she wiped them quickly away.

"We need her to ask for assistance before we can take action," the woman said. "I'm very sorry. Don't give up. There are people you can talk to."

"What are they saying?" her mother asked, pulling the belt on her robe into a tight knot.

Eileen put her hand over the receiver and explained the situation.

"Give me that goddamned phone," her mother said, stubbing out her cigarette and rising. "I need help," she said into it. "Did you hear the girl? Goddammit, I need help."

A pair of men came to the apartment the following evening to meet her mother. Eileen had never been more grateful not to find her father home. She sat with them as they explained that they were going to arrange for her mother to be admitted to Knickerbocker Hospital. They would return the next evening to take her in.

That night, as soon as the men had left, her mother took the bottle of whiskey down off the shelf and sat on the couch pouring a little of it at a time into a tumbler. She drank it deliberately, as if she were taking medicine. They'd told her mother to pack enough clothing for two weeks, so Eileen filled a small duffel bag for her and slipped it under the bed. She would explain things to her father once her mother was in the hospital.

Eileen spent the school day worrying that, with so many hours left before the men returned, something would go awry. Her mother seemed okay, though, when Eileen got home. All in the apartment was still. The kettle sat shining on the small four-burner stove, the floor was swept, the blinds were pulled evenly across the windows. Eileen cooked some sausage and eggs for them to eat together. Her mother ate slowly. When the men arrived, shortly before six o'clock, both wearing suits, her mother acquiesced without denying she'd agreed to go. The strangely tender, sorrowful look she wore as she shuffled around the apartment gathering the last of the things she needed—toothbrush, wallet, a book—made Eileen's chest ache.

Eileen rode with them to the hospital. At the end, the two men drove her back. When they reached the apartment building, the driver put the car in park and sat motionless while the man in the passenger seat came around to open her door. She stood outside the car, thinking she might like to say something to express her gratitude, but there wasn't a way to do it. The man took his hat off. A strange, knowing silence filtered into the air around them. She was glad these men weren't the kind that said much. He handed her a piece of paper with a phone number on it.

"Call if you need anything," he said. "Any hour." Then they drove off.

Her mother stayed in for nine days. When she reemerged, she attended meetings and took a job cleaning grammar schools in Bayside. She complained about being beholden to the Long Island Rail Road schedule, but Eileen figured what actually bothered her was all the time she had to herself on the train to consider how she hadn't gotten very far in the years since she'd made similar trips.

Eileen dreamed of taking a dramatic journey of her own. When she learned about Death Valley in geography class, how it was the hottest and driest spot in North America, she decided to visit it sometime, even though she wouldn't be able to leave her alabaster skin exposed there for long without suffering a terrible burn. A vast, desert expanse like that was the only place she could imagine not minding the absence of company.

4

In the fall of 1956, when Eileen was a sophomore, another round of relatives started coming over from Ireland. How she loved it! Sure, at times the apartment was like a sick ward, teeming with newly landed, sniffling relations who commandeered a bit of the floor or even her own bed, but still: with all those people crowded around, her father came alive, charming them like a circus animal keeping a ball aloft on the tip of its nose, and her mother worked alongside her to keep the peace in cramped quarters.

Over a dozen people passed through their little space: her mother's youngest sister Margie, who was only a few years older than Eileen and whom her mother had never met; her aunts Ronnie and Lily; her uncles Desi, Eddie, and Davy; her cousins Nora, Brendan, Mickey, Eamonn, Declan, Margaret, Trish, and Sean. Two or three or even four would stay with them at a time, until that group found an apartment in Rockaway or Woodlawn or Inwood and the next moved in. Nothing came close to the feeling Eileen got when they gathered at the table for meals, and when she awoke in the night and heard the gentle snoring and the shuffling sound of their rolling sleep, she was sure she'd never felt happier.

Uncle Desi, her father's youngest brother, was the first to arrive. He moved into the room with her father. The first time her father wasn't around, Eileen peppered Desi with questions. It wasn't hard to get him to talk. It was as if he'd turned a faucet on and the words came pouring out.

"Your father loved Kinvara," Uncle Desi said. "He was the happiest fellow you could imagine. A smile from ear to ear all day long. Then we were made to move to Loughrea when the Land Reform laws came. We went to better farmland, but I believe he never got over the sting of leaving those fields and that house he'd helped to build as a lad."

The apartment and neighbors and outside noises seemed to succumb to Desi's charms. All went hush as he rubbed his bristled chin.

"I was much younger than him, seven or so when we moved, so I had a grand time building the new house. We pulled it up out of the land. We boys and our father dug clay, dragged timbers from the bog, and harvested the thatch for the roof. I tell you, it was plumb and solid, still is. Everyone was satisfied but your father. He said that if they could take one house from you against your will, they could take another. He never settled into it. The sky was his ceiling, I suppose. One thing: he never had to be asked twice to work. Jesus, he never had to be asked once. He was always working. The stone walls he built—you would have thought they were a mile around.

"All he ever wanted was a little money to play cards. There'd be poker games that would last five days. That, and a chance to work in the fields. When I tell you he had strength enough to bend a hammer, I don't know if you'll believe me. The only thing he wanted it for was to pull up stubborn vegetables. Then, in 1931—your father must have been twenty-four—my eldest brother Willie, he was a beat cop in Dublin, well, he developed a cataract. He went blind in that eye and had to come back to the farm. The plot wasn't big enough to support two men and my father, and there wasn't a job to be found on the entire godforsaken island, not even for a man like your father."

He raised one brow and clicked his tongue dramatically, as if to suggest that the failure to find room for his older brother spelled doom for the country he had left behind.

"The best our father could do for him was buy him a ticket over. It was Willie who'd wanted to emigrate, not your father, but that was out of the question. This country didn't admit the infirm.

"Our father gave him three months. Your father spent the time plowing, harrowing, and sowing, barely stopping to eat or sleep. A man could be forgiven for wondering if he were trying to die in the fields. His friends threw the biggest good-bye party in memory; it lasted three days and nights. What a time! At the end, your father went directly from the revelry to the crops. People tried to get him to go in and sleep, but he wouldn't listen. He worked through the night. Our father went out in the morning, the ticket in his hand; I followed behind. He found him ripping out weeds. I'll never forget what he said."

Desi paused. He stood up to act out the scene.

"'Michael John,' he said, handing it over." He stretched an imaginary ticket toward her. "'You have to go. And that's that.' Then he turned back to the house." Desi faced away, took a couple of steps and looped back. "I stood there for a while with your father in perfect silence. Our mother took him to the boat."

He sat back down and eyed his empty teacup. She got up to refill it for him.

"I remember the first letter from your father," Desi said as he chewed some shortbread. "He said the hardest part about leaving was knowing that Willie had no idea what to do with the crops he'd planted, that he'd let them linger in the earth too long. And that's exactly what happened. He wrote that the whole way over, he saw, in his mind, the crops moldering there, sugaring over, their rich nutrition going to waste. He said he was never planting another seed. My brother Paddy—your cousin Pat's father, God rest his soul—was here already a couple of years. Paddy referred your father to Schaefer Beer. As soon as they got one look at him, they put him to work hauling barrels."

She knew how much pride her father took in being able to write, since not everyone he grew up with could, and she watched with interest whenever he slipped on his reading glasses to sign his name to checks and delivery slips, but the idea of him sitting down to write a letter—especially one that revealed his thoughts and feelings—simply baffled her. The closest he got to expressing a feeling was when the foolishness, idleness, or venality of certain men moved him to indignation.

She'd always understood that her father had been young once, but she'd never really considered what that meant. Now she saw him as a young man crossing a sea to start life anew, a courageous man carrying a kernel of regret and heartache that he would feed with his silence. There was more in him than she'd grasped. She wanted to find a man who was like him, but who hadn't formed as hard an exterior: someone fate had tested, but who had retained a little more innocence. Someone who could rise above the grievances life had put before him. If her father had a weakness, that was it. There were other ways to be strong. She wasn't blind to them.

She wanted a man whose trunk was thick but whose bark was thin, who flowered beautifully, even if only for her.

Maybe having all those relatives around had given her father a reason to settle in, or maybe it was the power of a management salary to keep a person in line. Whatever it was, when her father was promoted from driver to manager of drivers, something extraordinary happened: he stopped going out and began to do his drinking at home, where she'd never seen him put a glass of alcohol to his lips. There was such a self-possession about the way he drank at home, such an air of leisure and forbearance, that rather than signal chaos as it had in her mother's case, it suggested urbanity, balance, a kind of evolution.

He bought nice glasses and stacked them with ice cubes and sipped a finger of expensive whiskey once or twice a night with whichever relative was there, as if it were no more than a salubrious activity to pass the time, an efficient way to filter the sludgy residues out of the engine of his planning. He bought new furniture, a dishwasher, a handmade Oriental rug. He bought a television; in the evenings they all watched it together. The only time the spell of Eileen's happiness was broken was when she sneaked a look at her mother's face at a moment of great drama in the program, expecting to see her squeezed along with the rest of them in the tightening grip of a tense plot, and saw her intently focused on the drink in her husband's hand, like a dog watching for a scrap to fall from a table.

She went to Anchors Aweigh in Sunnyside with Billy Malague. Billy was a year older. After he'd graduated from McClancy, he'd approached her father for help getting a job at Schaefer. Apparently he'd been in love with Eileen for years, or so her friends said. She wasn't interested in him; she only went out with him to be able to say she'd given him a chance. A lot of girls would have thrown themselves at Billy. He had thick locks of blond hair that looked strong enough for a person to suspend from. He was rugged and charismatic, and well liked by other men. She could see the appeal in him, but she couldn't be with a man who didn't have his sights on anything higher than driving a truck for thirty years.

Anchors Aweigh was dark and a little musty. A band was playing when she and Billy first arrived, but they soon packed up their fiddles and the jukebox came on. A lively energy emanated from the crowd, which was a healthy mix of generations.

She'd never taken a drink before. She scanned the menu and ordered a zombie, figuring she might as well dive in headfirst. Billy raised the ends of his mouth in an appreciative grin.

"I remember my first day. Your father called me a narrowback. He calls anyone born in America a narrowback. I tell you, it feels like an honor coming from him." She couldn't avoid noticing the way Billy rattled the ice around in his tumbler, the way he wiped his mouth with the hairy back of his hand after he took a sip. "He gave me a route that went into Staten Island. That means extra zone pay. My first day, an upstart kid like me, and he's making sure I get some money in my pocket. He said, 'You have twelve stops. You'll be done in six hours. You should stay out ten.' I didn't understand. I didn't want him to think I was a shirker. I said, 'If it takes six hours, sir, I'll try to get it done in five.' He looked at me like I was a stone-cold idiot. 'If you get back here in less than ten hours,' he said, 'don't come back.'"

He was so excited talking about her father that she wasn't sure which of them it was he was supposed to be in love with. She surprised herself by how quickly she drained the tall glass, sucking the sugary drink up through the straw. It made her nervous to look at the empty glass and feel herself begin to lose control, her brain tingling slightly, her lips taking their time to come together when she spoke, her head a little heavier on her neck. She wondered if she'd taken the first step on the road away from her dreams. What scared her was how easy it had been to do it. All she had to do was get the contents of the glass into her stomach. To chase her agitated thoughts, she ordered another drink immediately. The chatter in her head quieted down as she sat drinking and trying to return Billy's insistent gaze. All she could focus on were his strangely doughy cheeks and protruding ears. She imagined him a couple of feet shorter, in a T-shirt with horizontal stripes, and a bowl haircut. In the middle of a little story he was telling, she laughed to think that what was evidently a boy before her somehow struck the rest of the world as a full-grown man. The bartender, whose age wasn't in question—he must have been a year or two shy of her father—gave her a look that Billy didn't see, in which there seemed to be pity for the boy. The first drink had been too syrupy sweet, but she liked the second one so much that she ordered three more after it.

It was after midnight when Billy carried her in, begging her father, she later learned, to spare his life, explaining that she'd been possessed, that she'd smacked his face whenever he'd tried to get her to leave, that he hadn't wanted to give anyone the wrong idea and get escorted out and have to leave her there with those animals.

Her father woke her early in the morning. She spent a couple of hours on the tiled floor of the bathroom, leaning her head on the rim of the bowl and sitting up straight when the urge to throw up possessed her. When she'd emptied her guts completely, her father told her to take a shower. Then he walked her to Mass at St. Sebastian's.

"You're no different from the rest of us," he said. "You don't get a special dispensation."

The air conditioning in the new church cooled her sweat and set her to shivering. Once, she had to get up to go to the sacristy bathroom. When she fell asleep, her father elbowed her awake. When communion came, she had to choke down the host. For a terrible moment up by the altar, she feared she'd have a retching spell. She took deliberate steps and deep breaths all the way back to the pew, and she ended up missing a day of school.

That Friday night, after dinner was over and the kitchen was clean and her mother had retired to her room, her father sat her down on the couch.

"If you're going to be fool enough to do this," he said, "you can't go about it half-cocked."

He went to the liquor cabinet and brought over a couple of tumblers and set them down on the coffee table. Then he went back and returned with a number of small bottles of different types of whiskey.

"What's this?"

"You'll be getting a lesson."

"I can't," she said.

"You will," he said.

"I've learned my lesson already."

"This is a different lesson," he said. "We'll start with the good stuff."

He told her he would take her methodically through everything there was to drink and everything there was to avoid. Then he poured a couple of fingers of whiskey into her glass. What struck her more even than her revulsion at the idea of taking a drink was that her father had come up with a plan, that he'd thought ahead about all this. He seemed to have bought the bottles for the occasion, as if he'd plotted the lesson out like an actual teacher.

She took a small sip; it burned her throat. He told her to take a bigger one. It smelled like charred wood and tasted like ashes. He poured a drink from each bottle and made her drink it in turn. She could tell there was a difference in quality, but only barely. When he got to the fourth, he poured some for himself and told her to drink with him slowly. It went down easily and left no trace except a warmth in her belly that spread out and seemed to heat her body a part at a time.

He put the whiskey bottles away and brought out several small bottles of vodka. She hated every one. He didn't drink any. He was wearing his reading glasses. There was something scholarly in it. She couldn't tell if it was supposed to be a master class or a form of house arrest. Then he brought out several varieties of gin. He took the wrapping off each and poured a small amount in her tumbler for her. He had stopped drinking after the whiskey. She wondered if by boring her with a scientific approach he was trying to take away whatever fascination attached itself to alcohol in her mind.

He went to the refrigerator and brought back a bottle of Schaefer.

"Drink this," he said.

"I don't like the taste of beer."

"Drink it down and get it over with."

He took the cap off and handed it to her. She took a few small sips and tried to push it back toward him.

"Finish it," he said.

When she'd finished, he told her she wasn't to be seen drinking any other beer. Then he brought out bottles containing drinks that were fruitier and more colorful than anything she'd imagined him permitting in his house. Cointreau. Crème de menthe. Crème de cassis. Grand Marnier. He made her taste each in turn. She liked the taste of the crème de menthe and he shook his head and poured a full glass.

"Enjoy it, then," he said.

"I don't want to drink that much."

"If you want to stay under this roof, you'll finish that glass." He took out another tumbler and filled it. "And this one when you're finished with that."

He came in when she was done and poured out another glass.

"What's going on?" she asked, feeling woozy.

"Drink this."

She woke in the morning with a headache, grateful it was Saturday.

"You will never again drink anything you can't see through," her father said when he saw her in the kitchen, leaning on the counter after taking an aspirin. "You will never pick up a drink again after putting it down and taking your eye off it."

"Okay," she said.

"Drink whiskey," he said. "Good whiskey. Not too much. That's the long and short of it."

"I don't think I'm ever drinking again."

She thought she saw a trace of a smile cross his lips.

When New Year's Eve came around, he raised a glass to her, and everyone else gathered did too.

"Here's to my Eileen for making the honor roll again," he said to a loud cheer. "God bless her, we'll all be working for her one day." He paused. "And let me tell you, there must be something right with her if she can stand after half a dozen zombies. She's definitely my daughter."

She's definitely my daughter. She heard a lifetime of unexpressed affection in the words. She imagined she could go for years on it, like a cactus kept alive by a sprinkling of rain. Still, she was so embarrassed that she decided never to drink anything but whatever the most boring girl in any group she was in was drinking.

5

From the moment students entered the doors of St. Catherine's Nursing School, on Bushwick Street in Brooklyn, until the day they graduated, the one bit of knowledge instructors seemed most concerned to impart was that they'd be thrown out for poor performance, but Eileen was used to those tactics after thirteen years of Catholic education, and she knew that even if nursing wasn't the field she'd have chosen, she'd been training for it without meaning to from an early age. There was nothing these veterans could throw at her that life hadn't thrown already, and they somehow knew this themselves. There were times she could feel them treating her with something like professional courtesy. She couldn't help thinking this was what it felt like to be her father, to be praised for something you'd never had any choice about, to wonder if there was a way out of the trap of other people's regard.

Martyrdom was never her aim, the way it was for some of the halo polishers she went to school with. They might as well have joined the nunnery for all the secret satisfaction she heard in their voices when they complained about the exhaustion and thanklessness of it all. But they wouldn't have lasted five minutes at a nunnery. They lacked the mental fortitude.

She'd never dreamed of being a nurse. It was just what girls from her neighborhood did when they were bright enough to avoid the secretarial pool. She would've preferred to be a lawyer or doctor, but she saw these professions as the purview of the privileged. She didn't know how she'd ever have gotten the money to pursue them. She thought she might have had the brains for them, but she was afraid she lacked the imagination.

• • •

After St. Catherine's she went on scholarship to St. John's for her bachelor's, enrolling in the fall of 1962. Her plan was to take summer classes, finish in three years instead of four, get through grad school, and begin the path to administrator pay. She earned spending money—and savings for the nursing administration degree tuition to come—as a dress model at Bonwit Teller. Women came to look at dresses and she showed them how they could look if they lost a few inches from their waist, or were taller, or had neat divots by their clavicle, or a galvanizing shock of black hair, or smooth skin, or arrestingly heavy-lidded, owlish emerald eyes. What they had on her was money and the insolent ease that came with it. Despite herself she became the preferred girl in the showroom. She didn't try to push dresses on potential buyers by slinging a hand at the waist and jutting an elbow out. She simply put a dress on and stood there. She didn't smile or not smile; make eye contact or avoid it; speak to customers or remain silent; she did whatever came naturally to her. If her nose itched, she scratched it. She turned to show them the dress at all angles when they asked her to, and when they were done looking at it, she went back to the dressing room and took it off. The other girls seemed to linger more, attempting to convince themselves of what they hadn't convinced the customers of.

She daydreamed that the next person who walked in would be a rich man looking for a dress for his girlfriend, who would see her and change his mind about the drift his life was taking. He would let her forget about nursing, fly her around the world, care for her parents' needs. She could sleepwalk through life, never changing a dirty bedpan, never batting away an exploratory hand when she leaned over a man in his senescence, never pressing through a fog of halitosis to take an old lady's temperature, never working another day, never thinking another thought. She would come back to this store and sit in the chair and put the girl through her paces. She'd make it seem as if she was going to leave without buying anything, that she'd wasted everyone's time, and then she would order one of everything to remind them that they had no idea how women like her really lived. But the only people who showed up were women a little older than her, or teenaged girls with their mothers. They said how radiant she looked, but she could hear them thinking of themselves.

One afternoon in April of 1963, a girl about Eileen's age came in looking for dresses for her bridesmaids. The girl made apparently random selections, projecting a nervous aura. She looked familiar—alarmingly so; only after Eileen had modeled a handful of dresses did she realize the girl was Virginia Towers, who'd left St. Sebastian's in seventh grade to move to Manhasset. Eileen prayed she wouldn't recognize her, but while Virginia was examining the seams she started patting excitedly on Eileen's shoulder.

"Eileen?"

"Yes?"

"Eileen! Eileen Tumulty!"

Virginia's voice was all heedless abandon. Eileen raised her brows in silent acknowledgment, perturbed to be addressed so familiarly in a place where she'd worked to keep her distance from the other girls.

"It's me, Ginny. Ginny Towers."

"Virginia, my goodness," she said mutedly.

Kind, sincere Virginia had been the only kid in her class with an investment bank executive for a father. Her father was also a Protestant, though her mother was a Catholic who'd grown up in the neighborhood. No one teased Virginia, even though she'd been shy and fairly awkward; it was as though her family's means draped a protective cloak across her shoulders.

"What are you doing here?" Virginia asked.

There was no answer that wasn't awkward, so Eileen gave the dress a demonstrative little tug in the chest and raised her hands in amused resignation.

"Right!" Virginia said. "Dresses." She had two in her hands and three more draped across the armoire, none promising. "Well, hell. Do you like any of these?"

If Eileen had the money to buy bridesmaids' dresses this expensive, she would buy different ones entirely—sleeker ones, less vulgar, more versatile. She was convinced she had nicer dresses hanging in her closet than Virginia did. She owned only half a dozen, but each was perfect. She would never buy five dresses for twenty dollars each when she could snag one truly gorgeous one for a hundred. She went out infrequently enough that she never worried about being seen too often in any of them.

"I think the one I tried on a couple of dresses ago is quite nice," Eileen said.

"The lavender one? I knew it! I liked that one too. I'll just have them order that one then."

Standing in the billowing dress, Eileen felt like one of those men in sandwich boards advertising lunch specials.

"Eileen *Tumulty*," Virginia said, as though it were the answer to a quiz-show question. "I'm guessing this is just your day job."

"I'm doing my bachelor's," she said. "I went to nursing school."

"I figured you'd be on your way to being a doctor or something. You were always the smartest one of us."

She felt her face redden.

"I'm finishing at Sarah Lawrence this year. And I'm getting married! But you knew that already. He's a Penn man. Very square—he makes me giggle he's so square. My father has set him up with interviews at Lehman Brothers. We're going to live in Bronxville. I'm going to walk to school my last month!"

She knew of the town; it was a wealthy bedroom community in lower Westchester County. "That sounds just lovely."

"And I know you won't guess what I'm doing next year."

"What's that?"

"I'm going to law school. At Columbia."

"You were always intelligent," Eileen said, stifling her surprise.

"Not like you. You were a whip."

"You're very kind."

"You were more of an adult than the rest of us," Virginia said. "I often think about that day in sixth grade when you took me to Woolworth's and made me buy a notebook for every class. Do you remember?"

She remembered, but she didn't relish recalling what an excess of energy she'd had then for grand improving projects, as though she'd thought the moral balance of the world could be restored by a regimen of directed efforts.

"I remember you weren't the most organized girl, but I don't remember going to Woolworth's, no."

"I think you'd had enough of watching me never be able to find anything when I needed it. You made me separate my notes. That was one of the most helpful things anyone's ever done for me."

"I'm glad," Eileen said, feeling a churning in her gut.

"You should come to law school with me. We could be study partners. I'd get the better end of that deal."

It was as if Virginia was speaking to her from the outside of a circus cage, clutching a bar in one hand as she absently held a lamb chop in the other. Eileen had to get away before she said something she'd regret.

"Maybe in my next life," she said, and the awkwardness she'd kept at bay came rushing back at once. The dress's low cut left her feeling exposed. A new customer had arrived, and the other girl was busy with someone else, so Eileen asked Virginia if she was sure about the lavender dress and left her with the woman who arranged the accounts.

"Please look us up," Virginia said on her way out. "Give us a couple of months to settle in. Bronxville, don't forget. We'll be in the phone book. Mr. and Mrs. Leland Callow. We'd absolutely love to have you over. There's nothing so valuable in life as old friends."

Her mother told her to save her money, to buy used if she had to have a car, but her father was the one to go with her to the showroom.

The new Pontiac Tempest was on the floor, the 1964 model.

"It's most of what I have saved," Eileen said.

"You'll make more. You'll save again."

"It's a bad investment."

"It's an investment in life," her father said. "If this is what you want, this is what you're getting. It beats the piss out of a beer truck, I'll say that. Maybe I'll get one myself. Or I could get one of those convertible types over there. What did he call that one? The GTO? I could drive your mother around in it. Do you think she'd take to it?"

For a moment, he sounded serious, and Eileen wanted to say, *Daddy,*

I think she would, but instead she just said, "Now *that* is a *terrible* investment," and asked him whether cherry red or navy suited her better.

She could buy used and save for the future, or she could make a statement about where she thought her life was heading, and shape the perceptions of others about that trajectory, and maybe sway the future by courting it.

"What the hell do you think I'm going to tell you?" her father said.

She went with cherry red.

She was at the table when her mother got in from work.

"Studying again?"

Eileen barely grunted in reply. In shedding herself of her effects, her mother had dropped her keys on Eileen's splayed notebook. There were so many keys packed onto the interlocking rings; each represented a room, or several, that her mother had to clean. Eileen slid them off the notebook as if they were coated in pathogens.

"Why don't you put those books aside for five minutes," her mother said. "You can drive me and my friends."

"Drive where? Which friends?"

"My meeting friends."

Meeting friends, Eileen thought crankily. *She almost makes it sound pleasant.*

"Take my car," she said, not looking up from her book.

"I'm nervous to drive it."

Her mother had only had her license for a year, and she was shaky on the road. The Tempest was still brand-new.

"I've got a test."

"We started a car pool," her mother said. "I said I'd pick everyone up this week."

"And how had you planned on doing this, exactly?"

"Come on," her mother said. "It's getting late."

The first stop was in Jackson Heights. She was surprised to pull up outside one of the co-ops; she'd always imagined that people of means were spared some of the sadder aspects of man's nature. As soon as her mother left the car, Eileen took out her textbook. She was planning to study at every stop, even with others in the car. There wasn't time for the squeamish propriety of small talk; the fact that she had submitted to this depressing task was enough.

When her mother returned, there was a brightness in her voice.

"Hiram," she said to the man getting in the backseat, "this is my daughter, Eileen."

"So I guess you're Charon tonight."

"*Eileen*," she said.

"Charon. The ferryman. On the river Styx."

"Oh," she said. "Right."

"Shuttling the dead."

He had bumped his hairpiece on the doorframe in getting in; instead of adjusting it with a furtive hand, he had taken it off completely and was resetting it with such nonchalance that it seemed he wore it not to disguise his baldness but to bring it out in the open.

"You're very much alive, Hiram," her mother said, beginning to titter. "Though I can't say the same for that rug you're wearing."

"I'm supposed to give you a tip," he said. "How about this: avoid men in borrowed hair."

"Sound advice," Eileen said.

"Tell it to my wife. Not that I had this when she met me. You should have seen the locks. I was Samson."

In the rearview mirror she watched him look contemplatively out the window. He returned her gaze alertly, as if he was used to being watched.

"Beware of women bearing scissors," he said, chuckling. He was in on some private joke that made even the heaviest things weightless. "Beware of three-drink lunches."

"One-drink lunches," her mother said.

"Well, if we're going to hell, at least we're doing it in style. This is a beaut."

"Thank you," Eileen said.

"You've got it backwards," her mother said. "We're leaving hell."

"Yes, yes," he said agreeably. "We're in purgatory, but we're hopeful. Or if we're not hopeful, at least we're not succumbing to despair. Or if we're succumbing to despair, at least we're in this beautiful car."

Her mother was buoyant as she rang bells and led her meeting friends to the car, where she peppered them with chatter to put them at ease. Eileen couldn't bring herself to open the book even when it was only Hiram in the car. She ended up having a marvelous time. In even a few minutes with some of them she could see they radiated hard-won perspective. She made three trips; then she parked up the block and watched in the mirror as her mother and the final quartet, a spectrum of widths and heights, disappeared down into the church basement.

On the way home, after they'd dropped everyone off, her mother blew smoke through the cracked window and talked with a quick and ceaseless fluency. Upbeat as her mother seemed, Eileen saw that the corners of her mouth were being pulled down, as though by a baited hook. She could tell that her mother didn't entirely believe in her own forgiveness. Eileen wasn't sure she believed in it herself, even though she'd been the one to grant it, through tears, after her mother had sat her down at the kitchen table and unearthed mistakes Eileen had successfully buried and said how sorry she was for them. Her mother had worked hard to kill the past, but it clung to life in Eileen's mind, in the thought that this apparently solid form might dissolve back into the liquid that had seeped into every corner of her childhood, bringing disorder and rot. The smell of the past, that irrepressible smoke, was spoiling the air between them, where, in the absence of others to filter it, an acrid cloud now hung.

"Roll that down further, please."

Without a word, her mother did as asked. She stared straight ahead, smoking and avoiding Eileen's gaze as she used to at the height of her drinking days. Eileen pulled over and got out to roll down the rear windows. She stood briefly outside the car gazing at the back of her mother's head, which for a strangely exhilarating moment looked as if it belonged to someone else. Whatever her mother was going through, Eileen would allow herself to care only so much about it. She had her own life to worry about. Life was what you made of it. Some of the houses she'd dropped these people off at would have been enough for her, so why couldn't they be enough for them? If she lived in one of these houses, she wouldn't need to get into another woman's car and head to a damp lower church for a meeting. She could look at her fireplace, her leather sofa, her book-lined drawing room; she could listen to silence above her head; she could peer in on empty bedrooms lying in wait for fresh-faced visitors, pleasantly useless otherwise. It would all be enough for her to put a drink down for. And yet there these people were. The fact that they were there, that everything they owned wasn't enough somehow, disturbed her, suggesting a bottom-lessness to certain kinds of unhappiness. She shook the thought from her head like dust from an Oriental rug and decided that a house would have to be enough.

6

She spent the entire fall of 1963 trying to convince her cousin Pat to apply to college. Then December rolled in and the application deadlines were around the corner, and many of them had already come and gone. She went to him to make one final appeal.

"I'm not college material," Pat said, his big feet up on the coffee table in her aunt Kitty's apartment, where Eileen sat with her knees together under the pressed pleats of her cotton skirt.

"Bull."

"I've never been big on school." He leaned over and tapped ashes into a coffee cup, stretched back again.

"You could have been a great student. You're smarter than all those boys."

"You need to give up on this idea of me as a Future Leader of America."

The truth was, she already had. He was smart enough to make it to his senior year without doing a lick of homework, and he possessed an intuitive ability to make men champion his causes that reminded her of her father's own. He was pissing away his apparently unbearable promise at underage bars, but she didn't care about that anymore. All she wanted was to keep him safe.

"You could get As in your sleep," she said, "if you gave it a tiny bit of effort." She crossed her legs and played with the pack of cigarettes. She resisted blowing away the smoke that was traveling in her direction.

"I can't sit and study. I just get restless."

"I'll do the applications for you."

"I need to *move*. I can't be cooped up." He snubbed out his cigarette and folded his hands behind his head.

"You'll have plenty of chances to move in Vietnam," she said bitterly. "Until you're in the ground, that is."

He turned eighteen that February, 1964, and she tried to get him to marry the girl he was dating, but he wouldn't do it. When he graduated in June and received the notice to report for his physical, she was terrified, because he was a perfect specimen, big and strong and almost impossibly hale, with 20/10 vision, practically, and great knees despite the family curse, so there was zero chance of his getting declared 4F. She tried to get him to enlist in the National Guard to avoid a dangerous posting, and then after the Gulf of Tonkin resolution in August she was *sure* he'd find some college to enroll in, but instead a couple of weeks later he went to the recruiter for the Marines.

He'd been on the winning side of every fistfight he'd ever been in, so he might've thought he could simply stare down whatever trouble was to come. He went to Parris Island for basic, got further training as an antitank assaultman, and was assigned to Camp Lejeune, where he stayed until June of 1965, when he volunteered to go over after the first waves of the ground war had landed in South Vietnam.

He called before he left. She couldn't picture him in a crew cut at the other end of the phone, wearing that one outfit they all seemed to wear, a polo shirt and chinos, as if they all shopped in the same store. All she could see in her mind's eye was him standing in his St. Sebastian's blazer, five grades behind her, shifting impatiently from foot to foot while she fixed his tie. He was the closest she'd ever had to a brother.

"You'd better stay alive," she said.

"There are some scared-looking fellas I could hand the phone to if you want to give them a little pep talk. This is Pat you're talking to. Pat *Tumulty*. I'll see you in a while."

"Fine."

"Tell your father I'll make him proud," he said.

Her father had filled her cousin's head with so much patriotic rhetoric that he thought he was embarking on a noble adventure.

"Don't you even *think* about trying to impress him," she said. "He'd never say so, but he's scared to death that something's going to happen to you."

"He told you that?"

"He doesn't have to say it for it to be obvious. He just wants you home in one piece. The bullshit around that man is piled so high you can't even see him past it."

"He'd take my place if they'd let him."

"Even if that's true, it doesn't mean a goddamned thing. The only thing he's ever been afraid of is regular life. Come home and live a regular life and impress *me*. Forget about my father."

She could almost hear him straighten up.

"Tell him I'll make him proud," he said.

She sighed. "Tell him yourself. He'll be where you left him, in that damned recliner. He doesn't go anywhere. Everybody comes to him."

"I will."

"Good-bye, Pat," she said, and then she thought, *Good-bye, Pat*, in case she was really saying it. She waited to hear him hang up.

7

She began to look forward to the day when she would take another man's name. It was the thoroughgoing Irishness of Tumulty that bothered her, the redolence of peat bogs and sloppy rebel songs and an uproar in the blood, of a defeat that ran so deep it reemerged as a treacherous conviviality.

She'd grown up around so many Irish people that she'd never had to think much about the fact that she was Irish. On St. Patrick's Day, when the city buzzed like a family reunion, she felt a tribal pride, and whenever she heard the plaintive whine of bagpipes, she was summoned to an ancient loyalty.

When she got to college, though, and saw that there was a world in which her father didn't hold much currency, she began to grasp the crucial role the opinions of others played in the settling of one's own prospects. "Eileen" she couldn't get rid of, but if she could join it to something altogether different, she might be able to enjoy her Irishness again, even feel safe enough to take a defensive pride in it, the way she did now only on those rare occasions when her soul was stirred to its origins, like the day just before her nineteenth birthday when President Kennedy was elected and she wept for joy.

She wanted a name that sounded like no name at all, one of those decorous placeholders that suggested an unbroken line of WASP restraint. If the name came with a pedigree to match it, she wasn't going to complain.

It was mid-December 1965. She was in a master's program in nursing administration at NYU after getting college done in three years, as she'd planned. Between classes, she met her friend Ruth, who worked nearby, under the arch in Washington Square, to head to lunch together. It was an unusually mild day for December; some young men had on only a sweater and no jacket.

"Well, it's not that he *needs* a date, necessarily," Ruth was saying as they walked toward the luncheonette on Broadway. "He just doesn't have one."

Eileen sighed; it was happening again. Everyone always believed they'd found her man for her, but more often than not he was a blarneying, blustering playboy who'd charmed her friends and the rest of the bar and whom she couldn't ditch fast enough.

"I'm sure one will turn up," she said. "Tell him good things come to those who wait."

The men that stirred her—reliable ones, predictable ones—were boring by other girls' standards. She didn't meet enough of these men. Maybe they couldn't get past the guys who crowded around her at bars. If they couldn't at least *get* to her, though, they weren't for her. She'd rather be alone than end up with a man who was afraid.

"You are *impossible!*" Ruth said. "I am trying to look out for you here. No—you know what? Fine. That's just fine." Ruth fastened the buttons on her coat.

Eileen could feel Ruth burning. In front of the luncheonette, Ruth stopped her. "Here's the thing," she said. "Frank asked me to do this favor, and we just started, so I want to come through for him. I don't care what you do on New Year's. You want to miss the fun, that's fine by me. You want to be alone the rest of your life, that's fine too. I've tried. I even set you up with Tommy Delaney, and look what you did with that."

"You think you're safe with a West Point man," Eileen said, as though to herself. "You think he'll have a bit of class." She watched a cab stop at the corner and a man with a newspaper tucked under his arm pay his fare.

"Tommy's a *fine* man," Ruth said.

"Oh, I'm sure he's swell," Eileen said. "I have no way of knowing. He couldn't sit still long enough to say two words to me. He spent the whole time making sure every back in the place got slapped."

"Tommy has a lot of friends."

"He bought everyone a round and said I didn't know it yet, but he was my future husband. There was a big cheer. The *nerve!*"

The man with the newspaper got out of the cab. He was tall and handsome, with dark cropped hair and striking eyeglasses. She imagined he was a visiting professor, Italian or Greek. She took her eyes from him before he turned in her direction.

"He liked you. He wanted to make an impression."

"An impression!"

"Look, this one is different," Ruth said lamely. "He won't be trying to win you over. He doesn't want to be there any more than you do."

"What's the problem with him? Is he queer?"

Eileen didn't know why she was still resisting. She would normally have done her friend Ruth this small favor, but she wasn't in the mood for disappointment, not on New Year's Eve. She watched the taxi launch off from the curb, only to stop again up the block to let a young couple pile in. The sun came back out from behind a cloud. Ruth unbuttoned her coat.

"He's a grad student at NYU. A scientist. Frank's in an anatomy class with him. He's obsessed with his research. He never leaves the library. Frank is worried about him. He wants to get him out."

Eileen didn't say anything. She was trying not to believe in the promising picture she was forming in her mind, for fear of disappointment.

"So what Frank told him is that I was nagging him to find a date for my friend for New Year's."

"Absolutely not!" Eileen said. "I will not pretend to be somebody's charity case."

"He's a gentleman. He couldn't resist a woman in need. It's the only thing that would have worked."

"Ruth!"

A pair of girls pushed past them into the luncheonette. Eileen could see the counter seats filling up and could make out only one empty booth.

"Would it help if I told you he's handsome? Frank even said it himself. He said all the girls they know think he's very handsome."

"Let them have him," she said, not meaning it. She couldn't believe she was feeling defensive about this man.

"Just do this for me and I'll never bother you again," Ruth said, putting her hand on the door to open it. "You can go become an old maid after this."

"Fine. But I'm not going to pretend to be grateful he went out with me."

In the interval between the setup and the date, she'd convinced herself that this was nothing more than a good deed she was doing. When the bell rang at Ruth's, though, she was seized by nerves. She ran to the bedroom and locked the door.

"Come on! I have to answer the door."

"I'm not going. Tell him I got sick or something."

"Come *out* and say *hello*!" Ruth whispered forcefully as the bell rang again.

She heard Ruth invite them in. She liked his voice: it was soft, but there was strength in it. She decided to open the door, but not before resolving to give him the hardest time she could. She wasn't going to have any man thinking she needed him there, certainly not some spastic recluse she'd have to lead around the room by the sleeve.

Before she had a chance to say anything sarcastic, Ed rose to his feet. He was indeed handsome, but not too pretty; neat and lean, with clean lines everywhere, including those in his face that gave him an appealing gravity when he smiled.

He leaned in and whispered in her ear. "I realize you didn't have to do this, and I promise to try to make it worth your time."

Her heart kicked once like an engine turning over on a wintry afternoon.

He could dance like a dream. When he pressed her close, his substantiality surprised her. The glasses, the neatly combed hair, the chivalry on the sidewalk and at doors made an impression, but the back and shoulders let her relax. The girls at their table thought him the most polite man they'd ever met. When she first heard him speak in his articulate way that was oddly devoid of accent, she thought he was like the movie version of a professor, but without the zaniness that emasculated those characters. Still, he was refined in a way that might have raised eyebrows among the men of her set. He could discuss things they didn't understand. He didn't so much drink a beer as warm it in his hand as an offering to the gods of conversation. She fretted over how he'd get along with her father, and so she brought him around earlier than she would have otherwise, in case she had to cut him loose, but something in Ed's carriage disarmed the big man. Eventually she had to feign annoyance at how well they got along. She shouldn't have been entirely surprised. He'd been a neighborhood kid, the kind who knew how to throw a punch when a friend was in trouble and could talk everybody's way out of it before it started—the kind men listened to because the way he spoke suggested he wasn't telling them anything he thought they didn't know already.

He was a natural athlete. They went to the driving range with her old friend Cindy and her husband Jack, who was into golf. Ed teed up and smacked the ball so soundly that when she saw it next it was a tiny pea at the end of its parabolic journey.

They headed out to Forest Hills one weekend to see her friends Marie and Tom Cudahy. There was a tennis court near the Cudahys' townhouse. They borrowed tennis whites from their hosts and the four of them hit the ball around in doubles, no keeping score or serving, just volleying. Ed returned shots he shouldn't have been able to get to in time. At the end, Tom asked him to play him solo, and Eileen turned and saw the embarrassed look on Marie's face. They both knew what was coming. Tom had been a letterman at Fordham and had a powerful serve, and though he mostly kept his competitiveness in check during mixed doubles, he liked to throttle his counterpart for a while afterward.

The two men took their positions and Tom fired a blistering smash. The ball raced up Ed's body off the bounce, as if it was trying to hit him more than once. The second serve came in on Ed's hands. He flicked his wrist at the last second and deposited the ball just over the net. Tom hustled but the ball died, bouncing again before he got to it. They traded points and games. Ed's serve was careful and reliable, his returns determined and vigorous. She liked the way he whipped his racket across his chest, dismissing offerings with sudden ferocity. He tucked the ball into corners and moved it around the court. Tom won the set, but Ed made the contest closer than anyone in their circle had.

They walked back to the Cudahys' to shower and change. She had one hand in Ed's, while the other held down the hem of Marie's mod minidress. On the court she'd felt protected by all the activity, but off the court she felt almost naked in it. Ed looked terrific in Tom's spare whites, as if he was born to wear them.

"When did you get so good at tennis?"

"I'm not that good."

"You looked pretty good to me."

He bounced a ball as he walked. "I cleaned up trash one summer in Prospect Park. I stuck around after work a few times and played at the Tennis House. I was always running after shots, trying to catch up to them. There was a pro who gave me some free advice. 'Go where you think the ball's going,' he said. 'Beat it there.'"

"I have a good strategy too," she said. "I don't move at all. I let it go past me to you."

He laughed. "I noticed."

"I'm flat-footed."

The smell of honeysuckle wafted up at them from a garden. Ed put the ball in his pocket. "Well, we can't exactly have you sweating through this white dress." He pulled her to him and gave her hip a squeeze. "This *little* white dress." They took a few stumbling steps together. "It just wouldn't be decent."

"The term is *tennis whites*, Tarzan," she said, shoving him playfully. "And they're very proper. So behave yourself."

Tom was walking ahead with Marie, his racket slung at his shoulder like a foxhunter's spent rifle. His clothes were casually disheveled, his shirttail hanging out in a way that suggested he'd never had to worry about money, but Eileen knew he was wearing a costume, trying to blend in. He worked for J. P. Morgan, but he was from Sunnyside, his father was a laborer like hers, and Fordham was Fordham, but it wasn't Harvard, Princeton, or Yale.

When the waiter came over, Tom wrinkled his nose up and pointed at something on the wine list, and she knew it was because he didn't want to mispronounce the name. He ordered for the table without asking what anyone wanted to eat. Ed gave her hand a little squeeze, and it felt like a pulse passed between them. For a moment she knew exactly what he was thinking, not just about Tom, but about her, and himself, and all of life, and she liked the way he saw things. She could spend her life tuning into the calming frequency of his thoughts.

He wasn't a stiff, and he wasn't a weakling either. What was the word for it? *Sensitive* was the only one that came to mind, amazing as that was to consider; he was a sensitive man. He soaked up whatever you gave him.

His name was Leary, as Irish as anything, but she decided she could marry him anyway.

8

E d's family had been in New York since just before the Civil War, but their sole claim to distinction was that his great-great-grandfather had had a hand in building the USS *Monitor*. Ed said his father liked to suggest by a looseness in his wording that his ancestor had been some sort of naval architect, but the truth was he'd punched the clock with the grunts at the Continental Iron Works in Greenpoint, where they fashioned the hull.

Ed's mother, Cora, had a soothing voice and a velvety laugh. Friday nights, Eileen sat with her and Ed, drinking tea and eating oatmeal cookies in the kitchen Ed grew up in, in a railroad flat on Luquer Street in Carroll Gardens, near the elevated F tracks. Cora kept the window open on even the coldest days, to drive off the steam heat. Eileen liked to watch the lacy curtains kick up in the breeze. Cats stalked the adjacent lot, curling into old tires. When they hopped onto the windowsill, Cora swished them away with a dish towel. Trains rumbled by at intervals, marking the passage of time. Whenever she rose to leave, Eileen found herself pulled into Cora's bosom for a hug. She never got over her surprise at receiving maternal affection, and she returned the hugs awkwardly, with an abstracted curiosity, though she welcomed them all the same.

Ed's father, Hugh, had been dead for a few years. Eileen knew little about him; Ed released that information in a trickle, and Cora never brought him up. The only evidence of him in the apartment was a framed picture, on one of the end tables, of him wearing a hat, an overcoat, and a slightly furtive half smile. Eileen knew he'd played the piano to accompany silent movies; that he'd sealed up paint cans in the Sapolin factory, once earning a small bonus when he suggested they paint a giant can on the water tank on the roof; that he'd worked as a liability evaluator at Chubb; and that World War II had given him his only real feeling of purpose.

Ed seemed to feel safest talking about his father's experience during the war years, though he had no memory of that time. It was all just stories he'd heard.

"You could get him going for hours if you asked about the war," Ed said.

The government had urged civilians to pursue activities essential to the war effort, and Hugh landed on the docks, in Todd Shipyard, sticking bolts in steel plates in the bulkheads and hulls of damaged ships. The work itself wasn't stimulating, save for the mild danger of hanging out over the water, but he liked toiling under the sun alongside other men, breathing in the salt air and thinking of what his labor led to—never mind the irony that after three generations in America, the Leary line was still working on ships.

Ed said his father and the other men modified ships from regular freighters into tankers, adding a second layer to the hull. They converted luxury liners to barracks for troop transport. The peak of their activity, in terms of both industry and importance, was working on the *Queen Mary*. They stripped her of her furniture and wood paneling, replaced her bars and restaurants with hospitals, painted her a dull gray to confuse rising submarines, and gave her smoke suppression. She could go as fast as a destroyer, reaching speeds of thirty knots where an average submarine could only go ten. At the height of the conflict, in 1943, she carried sixteen thousand men from London to Sydney without a gunboat escort.

One night, Eileen stayed late at Ed's house. Cora had gone to sleep. They were sitting on the couch, which was worn along the seam by its skirt, some of the filling rupturing through. Eileen picked the picture of Hugh up off the end table.

"What was he like?"

"I suppose he was like a lot of fathers," Ed said. "He went to work and stayed out late. He wasn't around a lot."

"What about as a man? All I see when I try to picture him is this coat and hat."

A pair of end table lamps provided the only illumination in the room, which was like a parlor in a shabby club. Cora had installed cute statuettes in every corner, but personality only went so far in making an apartment feel like a home. Eileen had a new appreciation for how her mother had kept things neat and in working order, how her father had paid to replace the furniture whenever it got run down. Ed had grown up with less.

"He liked to laugh," Ed said. "He told raunchy jokes. He always had a cigar dangling from his mouth. It made him look like a dog hanging its tongue out on a hot day. He was always hustling, working angles."

"What else?" she asked, putting the photo down. She sensed he was on the verge of candor. "Tell me more."

"He liked to drink," Ed said. "It wasn't pretty when he did."

"I know a little about that," she said, and they shared a moment of quiet understanding.

"I'm sorry," he said. "You deserved better."

She felt her emotions catching in her throat. "You can tell me any-thing, you know."

"I wouldn't know how to say it if there were anything to say."

"Just say what comes to mind."

He was silent, and she worried she'd pushed him too hard. In her ner-vous state she had picked off the material that covered the sofa's arm, and now she tried to fit it back into place with one hand while keeping her eyes on Ed. She should have left him alone, rather than risk angering him and making him shut down, but she didn't want to revert to the surface-level interactions she'd had with other men. She had never wanted to talk to anyone more than she wanted to talk to Ed. She wanted to tell him things she'd never told anyone, and to learn more about him than she'd learned about anyone else. She used to think a bit of mystery was a prerequisite to her feeling attracted to a man. For the first time, her attraction didn't diminish the more she knew, but actually grew.

"You remember Charlie McCarthy?" Ed said after a while. "Edgar Ber-gen's dummy? My father used to say I looked like him."

Eileen folded her hands in her lap and held her breath, trying not to look too eager to hear what he had to say.

"I figured out early on I could make him laugh if I did a Charlie Mc-Carthy impression. So I practiced. I got to the point where I could do the voice pretty well. When my father got in from the bar, I'd hop up on the couch and twist up my mug for him." Ed showed her, forming a rictus and opening his eyes wide, looking from side to side with an eerie, doll-like blankness. "Sometimes he laughed. Sometimes he told me to cut it out and said I looked nothing like that doll. I never knew which it was going to be. I remember the last time I did it. He laughed and laughed. Then he smacked me in the mouth, *whack!*"—Ed brought his hand down on the coffee table—"and told me to stop embarrassing myself."

Their hands migrated toward each other on the couch. After their fingers sat intertwined for a bit, she clasped his hand in both of hers, pulled it to her, and gave it a little kiss, then shifted closer to him.

Ed said he and his mother had never discussed his father's drinking, but it was his understanding that his father hadn't been a drinker before the war. "If the war had gone on forever, or if he'd been a park ranger or done something outdoors, maybe things would have been different."

When peacetime returned, Hugh went back to Chubb and sat at a desk all day. He didn't have any hobbies. "I think the only way he knew how to drive off the anxiety in him was to go to Molloy's," Ed said. "Everybody raised a glass when he walked in. They laughed at his jokes. They let him buy rounds."

By the time Ed was nine, he said, his mother was sending him by train on pay Fridays to pick up his father's check. If he didn't get there in time, they were stuck for the week. If he did, his father wasn't necessarily stuck. With his beautiful singing voice, he could make twenty-five dollars, or two-thirds of his weekly salary, as the cantor at a single funeral Mass at St. Mary's Star of the Sea. Ed only knew his father did this because he served funerals during the school day as an altar boy.

"The first time he sang," Ed said, "I walked out of the sacristy with the cross to start the funeral and there he was, standing off to the side with this sheepish grin on. When the time came, he walked up to the lectern. He gave me a nervous look, like I'd caught him in something. Maybe one of his friends knew what kind of voice he had and set him up with the gig. I remember *knowing* he'd been drinking beforehand. It's just something you can tell."

She nodded.

"Then the organ started up, and he started singing, and it was like he was surprised by the sound of his own voice. Like he was hearing it for the first time. I couldn't believe how good he was. He sang his heart out. There were tears on some faces in the pews."

"My father can't sing," she said. "But he thinks he can."

Ed gave her a warm smile. "He came to collect the cash afterward. I was in the rectory changing out of my alb. He put his finger to his lips. 'Don't tell your mother.'" Ed's face took on an intense expression. "I already knew enough not to say anything, you know?"

She nodded again. Sometimes, she thought, life makes you grow up early. And some people never grow up at all.

"He started showing up often. I don't know how he did it without getting fired at Chubb. It was a pretty decent round-trip on the train. He must have been gone two, three hours at a time. He did it for years. I doubt a penny of that money made it home to my mother. To think that he was a block away from her all that time. She would have loved to have lunch with him."

Once Ed started talking, the dam broke. They went out once a week to eat in Manhattan, and the conversation turned often to their early years. She found out that in grammar school Ed was a model student, but by the time he reached high school he'd turned his back on his studies. After he was kicked out of his second school, Cora used her influence in the parish to get him admitted on probation to Power Memorial in Manhattan. The long train rides settled him down enough to get him graduated. He took a job mixing paints and dyes at the Kohnstamm factory on Columbia Street, a short walk from home. He brought his paychecks home to his mother.

At Kohnstamm's, Ed said, he found someone to look up to—the scientist who directed the mixers. The chemical processes awoke a scholarly impulse in him that had lain dormant. He got to know the chemicals so well that soon other men began coming to him instead of checking the manuals. He moved over to Domino for a better paycheck, turning slag into sugar, paying attention to the reactions, the reagents, the products. He began taking night classes at a community college, then quit Domino to enroll full-time at St. Francis College, where his younger brother Phil was a student. Cora paid both their tuitions with the money she'd saved from what Ed brought home.

Their flat had no hallway. To get from the kitchen to the living room, you had to brush against the foot of every bed, one of which Ed shared with Phil until he was twenty-one, when his sister Fiona got married and moved to Staten Island. Until the day Hugh brought a desk home from his office, Ed and Phil studied together at the kitchen table, the only good surface to spread out on. Cora never had to call them to dinner; she only had to tell them to put their books away.

Friday nights, when his friends were out, Ed waited for the bartender's call. He would pull up in front and honk, and Hugh would keep him waiting while he had another. Ed wouldn't go in, because he didn't want to watch his father drink. Once, he waited so long that he woke up slamming the brakes, thinking he'd nodded off while driving and was about to plow into the car in front of him. He started beating on the horn; a few guys came out to see what was the matter. Hugh joined them and stared as if it were somebody else's crazy kid. Ed kept slamming on the horn. When he finally stopped, his father screamed at him. After that, Ed said, when he drove up he gave a quick toot and shut the car off.

Ed was named to the Duns Scotus Honor Society, like Phil the year before. They were the first pair of brothers in St. Francis's history to receive the honor.

They were at Lüchow's on Fourteenth Street, eating Wiener schnitzel and sauerkraut, when Ed told her about the day his father died.

"A few days before I graduated," he said, "my father had a heart attack on the couch. I drove him to the hospital. I must have flown through every light. I had my arm on him to keep him from slumping forward"—Ed pressed it against her to show her—"like I did when I picked him up at the bar. I was burning through intersections. When I got there, I saw that he'd died. I slapped his face a few times. Then I threw him over my shoulder and ran him in."

Only after Ed had heard definitively that his father was gone, while he sat weeping in the waiting room area, did he realize he'd wrenched his back. As he alternated in spasms of grief and pain, he understood that he loved all the things he'd always thought he'd hated about carrying his father's body home all those nights: the weight of him hanging on him, pulling at the sockets of his arms; the drunken heat that came off him; the roughness of his beard against Ed's neck; the soft sound of his voice as he mumbled; the sickly sweet smell of whiskey.

"There are things you feel that you can't explain," Ed said. "You know other people won't understand them."

"I know just what you mean." She was thinking she was referring to how she'd felt at times about her own parents. Then she realized she was feeling something like it just then for Ed. You had to hope the love you felt would get recorded in the book of time. "You don't have to say another word," she said.

9

S he wanted to buy her husband-to-be a luxurious wedding gift. It happened that her father's best friend, in addition to regularly occupying the stool next to him at Hartnett's—where her father had shifted from Doherty's when he'd started going back to pubs—was a vice president at Longines, which distributed LeCoultre in North America. For six hundred dollars, Eileen purchased a prototype of the next line of LeCoultre watches. It was slung with a beautiful eighteen-karat gold band and would have retailed for two thousand dollars. She paid in three installments.

She tried to think of a creative inscription that would encapsulate her feelings for him, some intimate notion to commit to posterity, but everything she came up with sounded too fanciful by half. In the end she settled on his full name, middle included, and hoped he'd hear a rough sort of poetry in the lack of embellishment and a tenderness in the identification of him as her man.

They went to Tavern on the Green a week before the wedding. They emerged from the subway and took a horse and carriage up to the entrance. She had never been to the Tavern before. She loved the banquet tables, the big picture windows, the austerity of the trees in winter.

She presented the watch to Ed after the salad course. He undid the bow, neatly removed the green foil wrapping, opened the box, and held the watch.

"It's beautiful," he said. Without trying it on, he put it back in the box. "I can't take it, though. I'm not the kind of man who's ever thought of wearing a gold watch. You should return it to the store."

In an astonished instant she'd gone beyond words, beyond anger, to a disappointment so deep it made her stomach ache.

"It's a prototype, Ed. I can't." She refolded the napkin in her lap, smoothed down the silk of her dress.

"Why not?"

"It's unique."

"I'm sure they'd listen—"

"It's *engraved*, goddammit."

Ed was still talking, but she didn't hear him. Quickly, dispassionately, she ran through the mechanics of how she would exit the restaurant. She wouldn't say a word. She would of course leave the watch on the table. She would go home and tell her parents that the wedding was off. She was disappointed that she wouldn't get to see her father in a top hat and tails. A busboy stacked and removed the salad plates, and now another stopped to replenish their water glasses, taking his time to keep too many ice cubes from tumbling out of the pitcher. His conscientious presence was the only reason she hadn't risen yet.

"Maybe you could have them take off this gold band and put a leather one on it for me instead, if you don't want to take it back," this man to whom she'd sworn her devotion was saying in lordly ignorance of how far from him she'd flown in her mind, how almost absurdly vulnerable he was to her at that moment. "I'm a regular guy. I don't know how to wear a watch like this."

She saw how unfathomably easy it could be for her to walk out on her own life. She was awash in sudden sympathy for Ed. Then the cloudburst passed, and she sat in a little puddle of resentment over how benighted and pinched her future husband was.

They endured a tense dinner, even managed to make it through dessert. After they'd risen to leave, a surge of spite compelled her to fish the watch out of her pocketbook and make him read the engraving on its back.

He looked at it quietly. For a moment, it occurred to her that he might be moved enough to change his mind, and she grew unaccountably nervous. Then he handed it back.

"I'll give you love and devotion and work hard all my life," he said.

"And I appreciate your getting this for me, more than I could say. It's the nicest thing I've ever gotten. But I know I'm not going to wear it. If you take it back, we can put that money in an account to send our kids to college. I'm sorry. I can't help the way I am. I wish I could. It'd be easier sometimes to be someone else. Right now, for instance. You look so beautiful tonight. I hate that I've disappointed you."

A couple of days later, her father saw Ed and asked where the watch was. When Ed told the truth—it was home in the box, he didn't feel comfortable putting it on—her father didn't react with the fury she'd anticipated. Ed's answer put him in a contemplative mood.

Later that night, her father called her into his room. "There's a reason he can't accept nice things," he said. "His family's been in this country a hundred years, but they never owned a house. That's a sin. If you're not in a house by the time I'm dead, I'll haunt you from my grave."

They got married a little over a year after they met. They spent a honeymoon weekend in Niagara Falls. It wasn't what she'd dreamed of—France, Italy, Greece—but Ed was researching a paper that would synthesize part of his dissertation work, and they couldn't afford to go away for long.

The *Maid of the Mist* didn't run in the off-season, so they had to experience the falls from the viewing areas. Large blocks of ice had gathered in sections of the falls, and the cold spray made it hard to stay long. They went to restaurants and took scenic walks.

On their final day, as she stood in the Prospect Point Park observation tower wrestling with the thought that all bodies of water were part of one larger body, Ed announced that when they returned home, there would be no time to go out while he did his research, which would take the better part of a year. She didn't take this threat too seriously. She figured he *believed* he needed that kind of sequestration, but more likely he was just trying on the role of head of household—making a show of arranging his affairs with an exaggerated masculine correctness. He'd been doing the same research in the run-up to the wedding, and pretty much the whole time they were courting, and he'd managed to make himself available to her. True, they'd only seen each other on the weekends, but she'd been busy with work herself.

They got back in late March 1967 and moved from their parents' apartments into the second floor of a three-family house on Eighty-Third Street in Jackson Heights. She was elated that part of the dream she'd conceived for her existence had been fulfilled. For years, the neighborhood had exerted a powerful pull on her imagination, and now it was the one she came home to and slept in at the end of every day. The details were familiar, but they burned with a new intensity. Flowerpots at intersections announced the birth of new life, and the smell of spring through the windows lingered in the pillowcases.

She was happy to put the turmoil of life in her parents' apartment behind her. She wanted to be conservative, if not in politics—her father would disown her if she made that shift—then in comportment, in demeanor. She'd always behaved a little older than her age, but now she found herself making extremely prudent choices, like dumping expired milk down the drain, even when it didn't smell, and driving more slowly on curves or in the rain. She bought Ed a beautiful new tweed jacket and made him get rid of all his old shoes, replacing them with wing tips and oxfords.

There was still a little lingering restlessness in her spirit, though. It hadn't been her dream to live in an apartment like the one she and Ed had ended up in, sandwiched between two ends of a family. The Orlandos, the owners, lived on the first floor, and Angelo Orlando's older sister Consolata took up the third by herself. Angelo worked for the Department of Sanitation, and Lena was a housewife. They had three children—Gary, ten; Donny, nine; and Brenda, seven. The Orlando home was full of the sort of ambient noise she associated more with apartment buildings than houses. She had convinced herself that moving into a house, even a multifamily one, meant diving into a pool of blessed silence. The Orlando boys played tirelessly in the driveway with a small army of neighborhood kids. When it rained, they roughhoused indoors for hours, crashing into walls, and Lena's voice rang out in shrill rebukes. The insistent murmur of a radio rose at night from Brenda's room, which was below Ed's office. Ed wore earplugs and possessed advanced powers of concentration, so the radio didn't faze him, but it incensed Eileen. And Angelo and Lena's fights, though infrequent, were of the screaming, door-slamming variety. The noise came at her from both sides. Most nights, Consolata made a restless circuit of her apartment, pounding between rooms with oddly heavy steps for a woman so thin, turning the television off in one room and on in another, leaving it on until programming ended and sometimes beyond, so that the rasp of a lost signal harassed Eileen to sleep.

Three months into the marriage, Eileen was astonished to realize that she hadn't entered a bar, restaurant, or party with her husband. She'd grown tired of making excuses to her friends; when they called and she had to say she couldn't go, she wanted to hand the phone to Ed to have him explain. She showed up alone if she went at all when they got together at each other's houses, and after she'd faced enough inquisitions about where Ed was, she decided it wasn't worth it to go. She'd envisioned playing euchre with him at the Coakleys', or watching him save Frank McGuire from grilling disasters, or seeing his entertainer side come out at the piano after everyone downed a couple of banana daiquiris at Tom Cudahy's place. She'd envisioned her own dining room, which was finally appointed hospitably after Ed had agreed to let her spend the money on furniture, thronged with friends around the table, Jack Coakley clapping his hands and dramatically sniffing the roast chicken's lemon-pepper aroma as she carried it proudly past him, but instead what she had for company were the dog-eared pages of novels as she sulked in the armchair. The only reason she even had that damned chair was that her mother had shamed Ed into buying it so she'd have somewhere civilized to sit when she came over. Her mother flatly refused to sit on their ratty couch, which they'd inherited when Phil left for Toronto. As long as Ed had a place to rest his head—and it could have been the floor for all he cared—he was content to go about his work as though the body's needs were nuisances and the soul's demands, illusions. The only thing he seemed to consider authentic was his work—not work in the abstract, because he hardly listened when she spoke about her day, but *his* work, his precious, important work that was going to make a contribution to science. She would pause in the doorway for a moment before she headed out for solitary walks around the neighborhood, looking at his back hunched over his infernal notebooks, his hand not even rising to give her a perfunctory wave good-bye.

She walked the path her youthful self used to tread on dates, when Jackson Heights was the neighborhood to be seen in. She'd pass Jahn's, where she used to have a burger and a shake after the movie, and remember how whatever hopeful young man she was with would escort her up and down both sides of Thirty-Seventh Avenue before returning her home on the train. Sometimes she'd take them on detours onto side streets, not to find an alley to make out in—though she did that too—but because she liked to look at the co-ops and houses and imagine a future in which she lived in that privileged setting.

Sometimes, she would feel that sense of possibility reenter her chest, and then she'd keep walking until it had worn off and the blocks looked strangely unfamiliar. She would stop at Arturo's and gaze in at the couples dining in neat pairs, or the families passing plates around, and wonder when things would settle down long enough for her to enjoy some of that hot bread with him, buttered to perfection, a glass of red wine warming the stomach, the two of them in no hurry to get anywhere, choosing from an inviting menu. There needed to be time for that kind of leisure, or she didn't see the point in living.

One day, the heat was unusual for early spring, and Ed was at his desk in his underwear and T-shirt. She'd begun to resent that desk, beaten up around the legs and stained a dull brown. She knew she'd never be free of it, that it would follow her wherever she went.

Getting that desk, Ed had told her, had been one of the few happy times he'd shared with his father as an adult. His father walked in from work one day and told him to get up and come with him. They drove into the city; his father wouldn't say what it was about. They went to the Chubb offices. "The place looked like it had been cleaned out," Ed said. "He led me to a storage closet. There was a desk and chair in it—his desk and chair. He'd had a handyman buddy hold them for him. They were getting new furniture for the whole office the next day. 'Sit down,' he said. 'Pull out the drawers. Pretend to work.' It was strange to have him watching me. My mother was the one who peeked over my shoulder when I worked. 'Can you get your work done at it, or what?' he asked. I said, 'Who couldn't get work done at this desk? It's beautiful.' My father, being my father, said,

'Good. Now I can read the paper at the table.' But I knew he was glad to do something nice for me."

The story had touched her when she'd first heard it, but now the ugly desk seemed a symbol of how little her husband would ever be equipped to see beyond the limits his biography had imposed on his imagination.

She watched him work, his pasty legs sticking out absurdly from his briefs, and waited for him to swivel in his chair to face her, to be a normal man for a moment. Angry, disappointed, she walked over and turned the air conditioner on. Ed rose without a word and turned it off again, then went back to work. He didn't even look in her direction. They went back and forth like this several times. She couldn't believe she'd signed on to live with a man so committed to his own pointless suffering. They weren't poverty-stricken by any means; they were even able to put aside a bit of money from every check for a down payment on their future house. But Ed thought even minimal indulgences were best lived without.

When they were courting she'd seen his eccentricities as a welcome change. There was a bit of continental flair about him. Certainly he was more charming than the doctors at work. He was as smart as any of them; he only hadn't gone to medical school because he was too interested in research to stop doing it. There was something romantic about that, but living with him made his eccentricities curdle into pathologies. What had been charmingly independent became fussy and self-defeating.

The heat broke her. She told him she'd had enough and started walking to her parents' apartment in Woodside. She sweated through her blouse, her resentment spurring her forward. Ed could have all the heat he wanted in that apartment by himself. She wouldn't be cooped up for another minute with him.

When her father came to the door and saw her fuming and drenched, he knew what was up. "That's your home now," he said. "Work it out with him."

In her rush to leave Ed, she had neglected to bring her purse. She asked for change for the bus.

"You walked here," her father said. "You can walk back."

By the time she got home, she had grown so angry at her father that she'd forgotten all about being angry at her husband. Ed didn't say anything when he saw her, but after she showered she emerged to an apartment bathed in the cool of a churning air conditioner.

They made love for what felt like forever that night. She didn't mind the sweat at all.

She was in Woodside visiting her parents when she saw a sign taped to the window of Doherty's: "Big Mike Tumulty vs. Pete McNeese in a footrace. Friday, July 21, 7:00."

She knew Pete, and she'd never much liked him. He was tall and skinny, and he always seemed to speak a little louder than came naturally, as if he were imitating another man's voice.

"What's this about a race?" she asked her father as she walked into the kitchen. He was sitting sideways at the table with a cup of tea, looking out the window. He wore a new white undershirt and slippers.

"He was running his mouth off about how fleet of foot he was."

"You're almost sixty years old."

"So what?"

"Pete is barely thirty." Her father put the kettle back on.

"So he's half my age," her father said. "He's also half the man."

She thought the whole thing ridiculous, but on the race's appointed day, she couldn't help dropping by Doherty's on the way home from work. The bar was fuller than usual, almost visibly crackling with static energy, as if a prizefight was about to take place instead of an absurd pissing contest. Happy shouts rose over the din, and everywhere she looked, men huddled and clapped their palms to the backs of each other's necks. Someone asked her father how he planned to beat Pete. "I'll blind him with the tobacco juice," he said through a cheekful of chaw, to a round of hearty laughter. Guys were taking final book. "Two dollars on Big Mike," she heard one say proudly, and she imagined that if all the money her father's adherents were willing to lose to support him were piled on the bar, it would be enough to buy the establishment from the owners, or do something worthwhile.

The course was set: they would start in the bar, at the back, run out to the sidewalk, circle the block once, and return to the bar. It wouldn't be easy to watch. Pete and his horse-long legs would come around the corner upright and easy, and her father would follow with his cheeks puffed, his face carmine red, his legs churning. Everyone gathered would watch an era end.

"Give me a glass of Irish whiskey," her father said, gently rapping his knuckles on the bar. "I'm warming up." He took his shirt off, then his undershirt. He resembled a bare-knuckled fighter. Pete tried to smirk, but he looked unnerved. Her father put his foot up on a stool. There were packs of muscle shifting under his skin, and when he leaned over to tie his shoe, his back looked broad enough to play cards on.

"Jimmy," he called out with mock sharpness. "Get those kids out of the street. I don't want to run any of them down."

Guys laughed, exchanged looks. Her father and Pete toed a line in the back of the bar. The bartender counted down from three and they headed through a crowded gauntlet on either side, reaching the door at the same time. Her father shifted his massive body laterally like a darting bull and crushed Pete in the doorframe. They never made it outside. Pete staggered, out of breath before he'd even begun.

"They broke at the gate," her father said as he returned to his stool, heat radiating visibly off his naked skin, a slight glower to him, a hint of violence in his eyes, the pride of a clan chieftain in his heavy step. She watched his friends retrieve their money and felt their eyes on her long, lean body, which her work suit clung to in the summer evening heat. They regarded her appreciatively, with a slightly wistful longing. She was the chieftain's daughter, and she'd married outside the clan.

They hadn't won anything, but they hadn't lost anything either— neither money nor their idea of Big Mike. Her father had played Pete's game, but by his own rules. It was a Solomonic solution, and she thought sadly of the difference he would have made with his gift for inspiring men if he'd been born into another life.

10

Ed was an expert on the brain. His subspecialty within the field of neuroscience was psychopharmacology, specifically the effects of psychotropic drugs on neural functioning. While doing his dissertation research, he ran an experiment in the aquaria of the Department of Animal Behavior at the American Museum of Natural History, studying the relationship between the neurotransmitter norepinephrine and learning in the black-chinned West African mouthbrooder fish, whose female laid eggs and whose male spat sperm at them and gathered them, then healed them under its tongue. Ed housed them individually in small aquaria in a greenhouse whose temperature was maintained at 26°C, and performed experimental tests in a separate room at the same temperature, injecting them with drugs that either enhanced or depressed action. The fish saw a red light, and if they didn't jump over a barrier in five seconds, they received a shock. He was testing the effects of drugs on an organism's ability to augment its decision-making abilities—in short, to learn.

The subject of learning fascinated him. He told Eileen it was because it had happened almost by accident in his own life. "If I hadn't run into that chemist at Kohnstamm's," he said, "I don't know what would have become of me. I think about that narrow escape."

He experimented on the fish faithfully six days a week for almost a year, going in even when it was supremely inconvenient to do so, missing family functions and dinners with friends, leaning on colleagues for favors when she put her foot down and demanded a sliver of his time. He never slept enough, he seldom ate enough, and his back always hurt because he sat too long at his desk, but the way the work was coming together gave him so much energy that he glowed as he neared the end, so much so that she went shopping without him and put a coffee table, two couches, a pair of end tables, and some lamps on the American Express, thinking he'd be too happy to complain. Still, she was so nervous about the cost that a few weeks later, on the Saturday when the furniture was supposed to be delivered, she still hadn't told him it was coming. She was relieved when he left early for his lab to gather data, and after the men delivered the pieces and hauled the old couch to the backyard until the Monday pickup, she sat on one of the couches, fretting over what she'd say. When the front door finally opened, she leapt to her feet, ready to spar, but Ed stepped in from the vestibule wearing that tranquil expression he wore when he was deep in his work, that made it look as if he'd just come from meditating. As he took in the room, she waited to see his face fall and readied to say she'd send it all back, but all he did was sit on the couch and say how nice and firm the pillows were compared to the lumpy ones they'd been living with. She'd never even thought he'd registered the lumps.

He was about two weeks shy of having gathered all the data he needed when the heating plant broke down and the aquaria froze, killing his specimens.

He didn't smash equipment or hurl insults at the plant manager. He didn't come home and make life miserable for her. He ate a quiet dinner and lay on the floor in the living room, between the glass-topped coffee table and one of the couches. She lay on the other couch reading to keep him company. She understood he didn't want a pep talk. When it was time to turn in, she leaned over him and saw in his eyes not sadness but extreme fatigue. She knew enough not to tell him everything would be fine. She gave him a kiss on the lips, told him to come in soon, and shut the light off. He remained behind in the silent dark. He came to bed very late, and the next day he began again from the beginning, with new fish, because he needed a full set of data.

When he finished a year later, he had worked on the fish for so long that the species' scientific name had changed twice, from *Tilapia heudel-otii macrocephala* to *Tilapia melanotheron* to *Sarotherodon melanotheron melanotheron*.

"You never get anywhere worthwhile taking shortcuts," he said when she asked how he'd gotten through that difficult time. She couldn't have agreed more. Not taking shortcuts—not settling for someone inferior— was the only reason she'd been free to marry him.

They started going out again. Ed got them a membership at the Metropolitan Symphony Orchestra. Once, when they were heading to the symphony, he picked a wounded fledgling off the sidewalk and carried it in his handkerchief for a few blocks, until he bowed to her protestations and deposited it in a planter. He gave her the silent treatment until they got home. When she was shutting off the light she said, "Good night, St. Francis of Assisi," and he laughed despite himself and they made love and fell asleep.

In December of 1970 she headed to the city with Ed to see the window displays on Fifth Avenue. She was excited to see them, despite how corrosively ironic Ed had been about them the year before, when at one point in his jeremiad he'd called them "altars to consumer excess." She wasn't about to let his grousing spoil her enjoyment of a tradition she'd observed whenever she could since she'd first gone with her mother as an eleven-year-old.

Ed refused to pay for a parking garage. It took them half an hour to find a spot, and they ended up on Twenty-Fifth and Seventh, almost a mile from Lord & Taylor. He refused to let them take a cab, even though she was wearing heels and it was twenty degrees out, with a wind that whipped up the avenue. The sun was setting, and store gates were being pulled down as if in protest of the cold. The sidewalks of Seventh Avenue were unusually empty. She noticed that most of the cabs that passed were occupied.

As they neared the store, the sidewalks grew more crowded, the bells of the Salvation Army collectors jingling on each corner. They saw a pack gathered in front, which quickened her step and made Ed sigh and slow down.

She had been delighting in the scene of a golden retriever pulling at the corner of a wrapped gift when Ed—who had been munching his way toward the bottom of a little bag of roasted nuts—broke the spell.

"These things seem here for the purpose of entertainment," he said, "but really they're here to get you to come in and part with your money."

He spoke in a breezy, careless way that suggested he believed a new understanding had sprung up between them. "They're like organisms that have evolved elaborate decorative mechanisms to lure you in. People fall for it. It's fascinating, actually."

"Listen to yourself."

"The bee orchid, for instance, has flowers that look like female wasps. Males try to mate with it, and in the process they get pollen on their feet and spread it around. It's not about the window. It's about pulling you into the store. It's about getting you to leave with something."

She was attempting to concentrate on the little animatronic girl whose hand was traveling slowly to cover her mouth, which had fallen open at the sight of Santa Claus's ebony boots disappearing up the chimney.

"It's a stupefying, hypnotic loop. It puts you in a suggestible state."

"Do you have to be so heady about everything? Do you have to analyze everything to death?"

"What's amazing is that they're exactly the same every year."

"That's an *ignorant* remark," she spat. "They're not the same at all. They put a lot of work into these. Months of planning."

She wouldn't have minded his objections so much if he hadn't insisted on drawing her into a dialogue about them. Was it too much to ask to share a moment of joy?

She looked around at the other husbands. They didn't look any happier to be there, but they stood back dully, hands folded behind them or scratching their noses. They couldn't have been as cleverly cruel about it as Ed if they'd tried.

"And the battling of tourists," he said. "Every year it gets worse. The jostling, the jockeying for position. They're descending on the imperial city for their bread and circuses. I wish we didn't have to do this."

She started walking to the train. A couple passing in the other direction gave her curious looks, as though they could see the intensity of her disgust in her expression. She found herself unaccountably smiling at one man, giving him a manic sort of grin full of the slightly breathless ecstasy of being unmoored, and he returned it with a delighted blush. By the time she felt a tug on her elbow, she was at the next corner.

"Don't be hysterical," Ed said. "I was just making a few observations."

"The world isn't a lab."

"Come on," he said. "Let's go back and look."

In his worn jacket with the frayed sleeve ends, he looked like a war veteran about to ask for change for the subway.

"You've ruined it."

"Don't say that. Listen, I can't help myself sometimes. I don't know what's wrong with me."

"I do," she said. "You didn't have enough fun as a kid."

He pulled her arm, but she wouldn't budge. She watched steam rise from a manhole cover and felt in her chest the rumbling of a passing bus. She was keenly aware of the limits of the physical world. She wanted to be in one of those scenes in the windows, frozen in time, in the faultless harmony of parts working in concert, fulfilling the plan of a guiding, designing hand. It would be lovely not to have to make every decision in life, to be part of a spectacle brought out once a year, for the safest of seasons, and put to work amusing people who stared back in mute appreciation. The real world was so messy, the light imperfect, the paint chipped, the happiness only partial.

"One of these years," she said, "we will come here and you will enjoy it and not make me feel miserable about it. I dream of that."

"Let's let that be this year," he said. "Let's go back and look at those windows. Please, honey. Let me make it up to you."

"It's too late," she said.

"It's never too late," he said. "Don't say that."

She hadn't been looking at him; now she stopped to. Streams of people flowed past in either direction, rushing toward obscure destinations. This was her life right here, petty as it seemed at the moment, and this was the man she'd chosen to spend it with. He was holding his hat in his hand as if he'd taken it off for the purpose of beseeching her, and she saw that he would always have flaws, that he would always be a little too intense in his objections, a little too unbending when it came to the decadence of the world. She thought, *We can't all wear a hair shirt all the time.* But there he was, trying to pull her back to the scene he despised, and she saw that he couldn't live in a way other than the one he thought was right, and when he saw what the right thing was, like now, he cared about it as if it were the only thing that mattered. Everyone else around seemed as insubstantial as the air they moved through, the shopping bags they carried the only things anchoring them to the ground.

"Did I tell you I love what you did with your hair?" he said, and she let herself be mollified, because she'd thought he hadn't noticed. She took his hand. They retraced their steps, the street around them thrumming with life. She saw that there was something perfect about the imperfection of her husband—her mortal, living husband with his excessive vigilance about the effects of capitalism and his unmistakable pair of bowed legs that she watched carry him forward. She kept her eyes on his shoes hitting the pavement and let him guide her wherever he was going.

11

Shortly after getting his PhD, Ed came home with the news that he'd been sought out by an executive at Merck, who'd read an article of his in a journal. Eileen was in the kitchen cutting vegetables for stew.

"He said I could have my own lab, with state-of-the-art equipment, everything top of the line. I'd have a team of assistants."

"Did he say how much you'd be paid?" She pushed the peppers into the stewpot and rinsed the knife in the sink. She could smell something fried and sickly sweet coming up from the Orlandos' apartment below.

"He didn't have to. More than I'm making now. Let's just say that."

"How *much* more?" She began to cut the beef into cubes. It was a thick cut with veins of fat. Ed would not have approved of how much she had spent on it.

"We'd be very comfortable."

He didn't appear terribly enthused to be able to make such a statement.

"Honey!" she said, hearing herself squeal as she put the knife down. "This is amazing!" She threw her arms around him.

"We'd have to move to New Jersey."

"We could live anywhere we wanted," she said, letting him go to take a few steps and get the motor started on her thoughts. She was already envisioning a house in Bronxville. "If not New Jersey, then Westchester County, for instance."

"That's too far to commute."

"Then we'll move to New Jersey."

"Not me," he said.

"How do you want to do this, then? What would make you comfortable?"

"Staying where I am," he said.

She looked at him. He was seriously considering not taking the job. If she had to say, he had already made up his mind. She picked up the knife and cut the last slab.

"You love research. Think of the lab you'd have. I'd have to drag you home."

"It's not research. It's making drugs." Ed paced toward the living room and back.

"Drugs that *help people*," she said, pushing the meat into the pot.

"Drugs that make a lot of money," he said.

This opportunity looked like their destiny. There had to be a way to get him to listen to reason. She added salt and pepper and two cups of water and turned the burner on. "You research drugs already. What's the difference?"

Ed stood in the arched doorway between the kitchen and living room. He stretched his hands up and flexed his muscles against the doorway. "Researching drugs and making them are not the same," he said. "On my own I can be a watchdog. For them I'd be a lapdog. Or an attack dog."

"What about when we have kids?" She put the caps back on the oil and the spices. "Don't you want to be able to provide for them?"

"Of course I do. I guess it depends what you mean by *providing*." He gave her a meaningful look, let down his hands, and peered through the glass lid of the stewpot. He switched the radio on and played with the antenna to relieve the static. The kitchen filled with the violins and flutes of a classical orchestra.

"I could make you do it," she said. "But I won't."

"You could not."

"I could. Women do it all the time. I could find a way. But I won't."

He straightened up. "You're not like that."

"Lucky for you, that's true," she said, though what she was thinking was that she was more like that than Ed understood. If her husband wasn't going to fight to secure their future, someone had to. "I just want *you* to know that *I* know what I'm not doing here. What I'm not *making you* do."

"Don't forget I'm on the fast track to tenure," he said, and she could tell it was a done deal in his mind.

Ed was an assistant professor at Bronx Community College, where he'd started teaching while in graduate school at NYU. One day soon he would be an associate professor, and then, probably soon after that, a full professor.

"There's nothing fast about the track you're on," she said bitterly, looking at him in the window's reflection in order not to have to look right into his face. "I don't care how quickly you get there."

Five years into their marriage, when Eileen was thirty-one, they decided to stop using birth control and try to conceive a child. At Einstein Hospital, where she worked, she had established a reputation as a head nurse and was confident she'd be able to return to the field after a short absence. She would have to go back to work eventually, something she wouldn't have had to do if Ed had said yes to Merck.

Seven months passed with no results and she started to worry. She wasn't too old yet by any means, but she also knew the time for rational calculations had arrived. They'd been going about it haphazardly, having sex when they felt like it and leaving it to chance. She decided to make getting pregnant a conscious project, turning her attention to managing it as she'd managed so many others. She drew up ovulation charts and held Ed to a schedule. They both went in for tests. Ed's sperm count was normal, his motility strong. Nothing was wrong with her ovaries. Every month, she cried when her period came. Every month, Ed reassured her.

Then, finally, after another six months had passed, she got pregnant. A new lightness entered her spirit. Things that had once annoyed her hardly registered with her anymore. She laughed more easily, gave Ed more rope, and was practically a pushover with the nurses she supervised. She surprised herself with how serene she felt. She never thought she'd be one of those egregious earth mothers, but there she was, tired all the time and yet still making meals and keeping the place in order and smiling through it—laughing, even, at the comedy of being alive. She didn't get angry at the evening news. When she got cut off on the highway, she shrugged her shoulders and shifted over a lane and hoped everybody arrived safely where they were going.

Her mother was over at her apartment, reading the newspaper. She grunted in appreciation and handed it to Eileen.

"Here," she said. "Read this. You might learn something."

It was an article about Rose Kennedy; one paragraph discussed how the Kennedy children used to hide the coat hangers so their mother couldn't deploy them on their backs. Eileen seldom thought anymore about her mother using the hanger on her, both because the memory was so unpleasant and because it was woven so thoroughly into the fabric of her childhood that it barely merited conscious thought, but even this many years later, as she pictured her mother cracking her with that little metal whip, she could almost physically feel it on her body.

"See?" her mother said proudly when Eileen handed it back. "I'm not the only one. If Rose Kennedy can do it, I can too. You should do it yourself, but you won't. You're too soft."

If Eileen hadn't been pregnant, she might have said something about how all that money doesn't necessarily buy you class, you can still act the same as a cleaning lady from Queens, because it would have cut to the quick, but she just said, "I guess it takes all styles," and decided then and there that she would never lift a hand in anger at her child.

A few months into the pregnancy, she suffered a miscarriage. The sadness she felt was ruinous, unspeakable. Almost worse was the awakening in her of a dormant foreboding that went back, perhaps, to her mother's own miscarriage and the effect it had had on both their lives. She'd never acknowledged it consciously, but in the blind alleys of her mind she'd feared that if she ever did manage to get pregnant, she'd have difficulty bringing the child to term.

She tried not to let Ed see how distraught she was. She needed to keep him on task trying to get her pregnant again, and she didn't want him thinking it would be gallant to take the pressure off her for a while. Another year passed with no results. She started having an extra glass of wine at restaurants. She took to suggesting wine with nearly every home-cooked meal. She began buying cases of wines she liked and storing them in the basement to have something on hand when company came over, and because buying in bulk was cheaper. She felt she was acquiring a little more insight into the way her mother's life had played out. She was still in control, though; she kept going to work every day, kept depositing money into her savings account.

Ed no longer made efforts to reassure her. He seemed to have resigned himself to not having children. At times she wondered if he weren't relieved. Despite his protests to the contrary she imagined he wouldn't terribly mind preserving for himself some of the time that fatherhood would claim. Once, when he said he was too tired on a night they were scheduled to try, she accused him of sabotaging their plans. She knew she was being hysterical, but she couldn't help herself.

Her friends ran into no trouble having babies. Cindy Coakley had three girls in five years until she finally delivered Shane to Jack. Marie Cudahy followed up Baby Steven with the twins, Carly and Savannah. Kelly Flanagan's Eveline was born with a cleft lip, but then Henry came out a couple of years later looking like the Gerber baby. One after another, the calls came in with the cheerful news, and the cards arrived celebrating fecundity. The only holdout among her close friends was Ruth McGuire, who had raised the last two of her seven younger siblings herself. When Ruth told her she was done raising kids, Eileen felt herself drawing even closer to her. They would greet the childlessness together.

Whenever they gathered around to watch whichever of her friends' kids was celebrating a birthday open presents, Eileen bit her nails down to the quick. She was sure everyone could read her thoughts in her mortified grin. She always spent too much money and bought too many gifts. She felt a nervous expectancy whenever the kid began to tear the paper open. She needed to have gotten the essential gift, the inevitable gift.

Having no kids freed Ed to pursue his professional interests without the burden of nighttime feedings or diaper changes or pediatric visits. He did important work on neurotransmitters, gave talks at conferences, and was named full professor faster than his peers.

She stopped thinking of each menstruation as a referendum on her femininity. She threw herself into her work with a compensatory vigor and was promoted several times. She sensed that her bosses and coworkers saw her as one of a new breed of women—it was 1975—willing to sacrifice motherhood on the altar of career. The men deferred to her and the mothers hated her, and there was an opportunity here if she was willing to pursue it fully.

Still, the miscarriage haunted her. She had dreams of sitting on the toilet bowl and hearing an unusual plop and finding in there a tiny baby who'd open its eyes at her—she couldn't tell its sex—and look at her angrily, blinking slowly, and she would wake with a start and shake Ed awake. She avoided looking into the bowl when she went to the bathroom. Eventually, she and Ed settled into the rhythms of a childless life, which offered undeniable compensations: they could go out with other couples without having to arrange for child care; they could indulge in the leniency reserved for aunts and uncles; and they were free to nurture their careers in the way they might have nurtured offspring. Maybe this was why she was so upset when Ed was offered the chairmanship of the department and turned it down to devote more time to teaching and research. It was as if he was telling her he didn't love their child.

To make up for the money he'd left on the table in passing up the chairmanship, Ed started teaching night anatomy classes at NYU. He'd pop home for dinner and head into the city by train. On dissection nights, he came home smelling like a pickled corpse himself. She couldn't stand to have him touch her after he'd been handling dead bodies, and when he teasingly ran his hands over her anyway, she squealed and squirmed out of reach.

A tenure-track position opened in NYU's biology department. One of Ed's advisors was on the search committee. He said Ed would be given serious consideration if he applied.

She urged him to do it. NYU would be an obvious bump up in prestige.

"They need me at BCC," he said. "Anyone can teach at NYU. What's important to me is having my students leave knowing they got a real education. I want to help them get into NYU. I want them prepared to meet the demands that will be placed on them when they do." There were other reasons to stay: the city had an airtight pension plan and great health benefits; there was no guarantee of tenure at NYU; he had a pretty good lab at BCC and could do the same research there that he'd do at NYU; there were grants out there to be procured. "It's all about having the right ambition," he said.

In the end, he never applied. To all the people she'd excitedly told about the NYU possibility, Eileen defended Ed's choice by saying that when the opportunity arose, which was bound to be sooner rather than later, he would be a natural choice for dean of the college. That prospect, she said, wasn't something you just flushed. That was the sort of career experience that could be parlayed into a parallel administrative position in a more prestigious institution.

He kept teaching the night classes. Now when he came home stinking of embalming fluids, not only wouldn't she let him near her in bed, she made him shower before she'd even hug or kiss him hello. Dinner and dishes would intercede after that, and often she could get to bed without having to touch him at all. She didn't feel bad withholding herself from him. He had made his choice. He shouldn't have expected to have everything he wanted, not if she had to give so much up to keep him happy.

The tall tree in the backyard, whose crown eclipsed the apex of the Orlandos' gabled roof, blocked much of the light in their bedroom. They were into their midthirties, and hints of seniority crept into their thoughts; they held them off by making love. Sometimes the activity was tinged by anger. Neither of them was going anywhere, even if in the middle of fights that lasted for days she entertained thoughts of divorce and suspected he did, though neither raised its specter aloud. They knew they would never sever their union, and this knowledge opened a door to the basement of their psyches. They became familiar enough to each other to begin to feel like strangers in bed, which infused their love life with a new potency. She wondered whether her friends had wandered down similar alleys, but she never had the courage to ask.

When she was thirty-five, after she'd long since given up worrying about it, she conceived a child and carried the pregnancy to term, delivering at dawn a couple of days before the ides of March, 1977. She and Ed had been struggling for weeks to come up with something to call the baby if it happened to be a boy, and by morning of the second day they were no closer to an answer, to the consternation of the girl with the birth certificate paperwork. Ruth took the train in to visit and accidentally left her book behind on the hospital nightstand. When the girl came around again on the morning of the third day and said Eileen could always take a trip down to City Hall to file the documents herself, Eileen's gaze landed on the name of the author of Ruth's book, *Mrs. Bridge*, which she had never heard of. She had a distant relative named Connell, but the real reason she chose it was that it sounded more like a last name than a first name, like one of those patrician monikers the doctors she worked for often bore, and she wanted to give the boy a head start on the concerns of life.

When Connell was a couple of months old, she realized, as though she'd awoken from an extended slumber, that his coming into the world had been a matter of grave importance. She had escaped a trap without knowing she'd been in it. For a while, she pushed Ed to conceive another child, until she stopped for fear of what misbegotten creature might result if she succeeded at her age. She would build the future on the boy.

It surprised her how much she enjoyed bathing her baby. She suspected it would have surprised anyone who knew her. As soon as she put the stopper in and opened the tap to fill the sink, a remarkable calm settled over her. She held his neck and head with one hand, her inner forearm cradling his body, and cleaned him with the other, pressing the cloth into the little creases in his skin. He smiled mutely at her and she felt a terrible unburdening of pent-up emotion. A little water splashed up in his face and he coughed and resumed his uncanny placidity. When he grew bigger and could sit up in the sink, she handed him a sopping washcloth to grip and suck on while she washed him with another, and she delighted in the sound of his draining it, the sheer vital pleasure he took in pulling it in his little teeth.

When he was old enough to be bathed in the tub, she loved the sight of him leaning over its lip, standing on tiptoe as he reached for the water with his swinging hand, his little back muscles shifting in the effort. In his enthusiasm he nearly fell in headfirst. He splashed waves out of the tub with a succession of quick slaps at the water's surface. He giggled and gurgled and pulled at his penis with exploratory joy as she rubbed shampoo into his black hair. He grabbed the rinse cup and took a long draft of the soapy water before she could seize it from him. She loved to wrap the towel around him when she was done, powder his little body, secure the diaper, and work his limbs into pajamas, sensing the calm and ease he felt when snug in the garment's gentle pressure. Snapping the buttons gave her an unreasonable pleasure. She would breathe his baby smell and wonder how she could ever have lived without it. Her heart swelled when she bathed him, when she dressed him for bed, when she combed the last wetness out of his washed hair, when she gave him the breast, when she gave him the bottle, when she lay him down, when she went to check on him at night and felt his chest rise and fall under her hand and his heart beat through her fingertips. She thought of him as she lay awake, and though she was always exhausted, and though there were nights she imagined she'd rise in the morning and the enchantment would have worn off, the well of her affection filled up in her sleep and she plucked him from the crib and pressed him to her, kissing his soft neck. There were some things that couldn't be communicated, and this was one—how much pleasure a woman like her could take in the fact and presence of her beautiful baby boy. She knew it wouldn't be like this forever; soon she'd make demands on him, expect the world of him. She was going to enjoy this part. She was going to fill up her heart with it enough for years.

12

After Eileen's mother got sober, sitting idly took more out of her than working long hours, so she continued to haul herself out to Bayside to clean up after grammar school kids even into her midsixties, long after Eileen's father had taken the watch and pension and tossed the truck keys to the younger bucks. When her employer lost its contract with the schools, though, her mother didn't look for another job. She had talked for years of putting money down on a beach home in Breezy Point, but Eileen suspected she'd realized she couldn't make a vaulting leap forward in the time she had remaining. She started reading the *Irish Echo* instead of the *Daily News* and making trips to Ireland using the savings she'd accumulated. The line of her allegiances began to blur, as if her time in her adopted homeland had been an experiment whose hypothesis had proved unsound.

Eileen had long been able to tell her mother about the fights over Ed's career and know that she would click her tongue and shake her head in censure of his lack of drive. Some change was occurring in her mother, though, to make her less pragmatic. She seemed less bothered by her station in life. She stopped complaining about politics, or the idiots on the subway, or the ugliness and stench of city life. She read novels and met with a group to discuss them. Eileen couldn't help feeling a little betrayed. She figured part of this transformation was her mother trying anything to avoid taking a drink. "Negative thoughts back you into a corner," her mother said to her, smiling, one afternoon after returning from a picnic with the baby in Flushing Meadow Park. "They multiply and surround you. Don't think of what you don't have. Try to focus on the simple pleasures." It was rich, this spouting of shibboleths, this late-stage wisdom-mongering. It was the tactic of a woman who'd played her hand and lost, or worse, never played it to begin with. But her mother had picked the wrong audience for her speech. It may have gone over well with down-and-outers at AA who'd wrecked their lives and slipped into a spiral of regret, but Eileen's problem wasn't negative thinking, it was too little positive thinking on the part of everyone around her. She had a vision, and she wasn't turning away from it for a second, even if her husband, and now her mother, saw some ugliness in it. At least she had her father on her side—though God bless him, he supported anything you threw your heart into. She was going to do that, no question about it. What waited ahead, if only Ed would walk the path she'd laid out for him, was a beautiful life, an American life.

"One day at a time," her mother said, and Eileen thought, *And everything all at once.*

Christmas of 1980 Eileen bought Ed a VCR. They'd looked at them together, but when he'd seen what they cost—about a thousand dollars—he had decided they could live without one. Eileen hadn't worked hard all her life to sit on her hands when she could afford to buy something. She was making decent money now that she was the nursing director at Lawrence Hospital in Bronxville. It was the perfect gift for him, considering how much he loved old movies. Starting in August, she paid for it on layaway.

When he unwrapped it, he looked horrified, as if it were a relic unearthed from a sacred burial ground that would bring a curse down upon their heads.

"How could you do this?" he asked, seething in front of the three-year-old boy. "How could you think of buying this?"

A few days later, she came in from the shower and saw him on his haunches putting a tape in the machine. She gave him a sardonic look.

"All right," he said. "I was wrong. It's a great gift."

"Save it."

"I mean it. It was thoughtful of you." He was clutching the empty sleeve of the VHS tape to his chest. "I appreciate it."

"I can't believe this."

"Look, I know I get set in my ways."

"You're telling me."

"Doesn't mean I can't learn a thing or two."

He wheeled the TV cart over, so that it was right next to the bed. PBS was on, the fund-raising appeal between programs. Ed patted the bed. "Get in," he said.

"I've got to brush my hair out."

"Come on," he said. "I want to make sure I get this whole thing on tape."

"Anyway, I'm happy you're using it."

"What can I say?" He threw his arms out in amused resignation. "You're good for me. I don't know what I'd do without you."

"Really?"

"Really and truly. I'd be lost without you."

Sometimes it felt like all the difficulty he put her through was worth it. It was a rare man who'd admit so thoroughly that he'd been wrong.

"Honey," she said, and she dropped her towel and stood naked before him the way he was always trying to get her to do. At first she hunched a bit, and then she stood tall, her hands at her hips, feasting on his gaze and letting him drink in her body. The movie was starting, but Ed didn't take his eyes off her. She felt herself blush. "You'd better hit record," she said. Ed didn't stop looking at her. She climbed on him and hit the button.

"We can watch it later," he said, kissing her neck. "That's the genius of this thing." He moved his hand down her back, squeezed her butt, touched her sex.

"Anytime we want," she said breathlessly.

She rolled off him and ripped the sheet away. He lowered the volume and yanked his underwear off. She reached across him to switch off the bedside lamp and he thrust up into her, flipped her onto her back. The tape whirred rhythmically. The television pulsed, filling the room with light and plunging it into darkness, outlining their bodies in the lovely deep of night.

●   ●   ●

In January of 1981, her mother was diagnosed with cancer of the esophagus.

A nurse came to the apartment, but her father did his share of nursing too. Eileen would go over after work and find that he'd given her medicine, bathed her, changed her clothes, made her a liquid meal—she could no longer eat solid foods—and tucked her in. He'd moved into her room, and slept in the other twin bed.

The day her mother entered the hospital for good—November 23, 1981—her father mentioned some pains in his chest. They admitted him and found that he had been concealing his own cancer, which had spread throughout his chest cavity, colonizing the organs. They gave him his own room, down the hall from her mother. They rolled them out to see each other once a day.

Her parents had slept in separate rooms for thirty years, but a few days before Christmas, when the doctors rolled her mother away from her father for what would turn out to be the last time, she called to him from down the hall.

"Don't let them take me away from you, Mike, my Mike!" she said, for all on the floor to hear.

What they didn't hear was what she asked Eileen later that night, with the tubes in her.

The curtain was drawn. The lights were off except for the one above her bed. Eileen had filled two cups with ice water, but both were left full and the ice had long ago melted.

"Was it worth it?"

Eileen leaned in to hear her better. "Was what worth it, Ma?"

"I didn't touch a drop for twenty-five years. Did it make a difference?"

She felt an uncomfortable grin forming on her face. She wasn't at all happy, but she couldn't keep this ghoulish smile away. She didn't want to show her mother how much she was hurting. Through the open door, she heard the distant beeps of call buttons and voices in intercoms. She had worked in a hospital for twenty years, but somehow she felt she was in a place she'd never been before. Under the green glow of the fluorescent lamp, her mother looked like a wraith, her skin so thin you could count the veins.

"How can you ask that?"

"I'm asking you." Her mother shifted her head on her pillow with great effort. Her cheeks were two smooth hollows beneath large, alert eyes. "Was it worth it?"

Eileen had thought of the time since her mother had gotten sober as the happiest of both of their lives. There had been a quiet thawing of the glacier in her mother's heart, with occasional louder crackings-off of icebergs of emotions, until, after Connell was born, it had melted so thoroughly that all that remained in an ocean of equanimity were little islands of occasional despond. Her mother appeared almost joyful at times. But perhaps it had been a performance.

"Of course," Eileen said, taking her hand.

"I wish I hadn't stopped." Her mother didn't look at her but gazed at the folds of the curtain, her other hand palm down on the blanket.

"Think of all the things you wouldn't have had. Think of all the lives you touched. We had some great years."

Her mother pulled her hand back, folded it into her other one. "I would have given it all away for a drink."

"Well, you didn't."

"I still would."

Eileen took her hand again and held it with force. "It's too late. You did all that. You can't take it back. You had a great life."

"Fair enough," her mother said, and in a little while she was dead.

Her father died two weeks later. In going through the papers, Eileen learned that he had cashed in the bonds and sold the life insurance policies decades before. Maybe that was how he'd gotten her mother's ring back from the pawnbroker. Or maybe he'd incurred bigger debts than she'd ever suspected. She knew he'd always played the horses, but it had never occurred to her that he'd had an actual gambling problem. If so, he'd been good at keeping the consequences from her. She remembered something

she'd witnessed when she was ten, at her friend Nora's apartment after
school. Nora opened the door to a man in a dark suit and hat who told
her to give her father the message that he should pay what he owed. Eileen
was standing behind her. "You kids will pay if he doesn't," the man said,
pointing at Nora and herself. "Tell him." Eileen went home frightened, and
when she told her father what had happened, he said, "He didn't mean you.
He thought you belonged to that girl's father. But you don't. You belong to
me." It was impossible to imagine any man having the courage to show up
at her father's apartment that way, not when her father counted every Irish
policeman in the city as an ally, and many of the non-Irish too. But that
didn't mean he wasn't in someone's debt. Maybe that explained why they'd
never lived in a house. And maybe it explained why he'd been so adamant
that she own one herself. In any case, she had to dip into her savings to pay
for her parents' funerals.

The wakes were so close together that she worried few relatives would
be able to return for her father's, but those who'd flown in for her mother
flew back, and if they hadn't there would still have been standing room
only at the parlor.

She was staring at his coffin trying to understand how he could fit into
that little box when a black man about her age came over and introduced
himself as Nathaniel, the son of Carl Washington, her father's longtime
driving partner. Nathaniel asked if she knew how their fathers had come to
drive together. With all the stories told about her father over the last couple
of days, she was amazed there was one she hadn't heard.

"My father was the first black driver Schaefer ever hired," Nathaniel
said. "The first morning my father showed up for work, none of the other
drivers were willing to be paired with him. There were rumblings of a
walkout. My father wondered if he was going to have to go find another
job. Your father walked into the warehouse after the others and took one
look at everyone back on their heels with their arms across their chests and
said, 'Get in this truck with me, you black son of a bitch.' Then he hopped
up in the truck without another word."

She cringed, but Nathaniel was smiling.

"His language could be rough," she said.

"My father heard worse," he said. "Your father wouldn't drive with anyone but my father after that. For twenty years. I don't know if you remember, but he used to hold a Bronx route."

She nodded.

"Once he had my father with him, he insisted on being switched to the Upper East Side."

"I remember when he switched."

"'There's enough blacks in the Bronx,' he told my father. 'Let them see a black face in that neighborhood for a change.'"

She put a tissue to her eyes and handed him one as well.

"Big Mike this, Big Mike that," Nathaniel said. "Growing up I heard your father's name around the house more than the names of people in my own family."

He waved his wife and children over and she greeted all of them in turn.

She was embarrassed to learn that Mr. Washington had died a few years before. She was even more embarrassed to see in Nathaniel's face, when she said, "I wish I'd known," that he never would have dreamed she'd show up at his father's funeral.

13

In February of 1982, Bronx Community College announced that the dean would be stepping down at the end of the semester. They offered Ed the job and even mentioned the possibility of his becoming president someday. She felt like a chess master who had seen several moves ahead. Taking the deanship would mean the end of Ed's teaching career, but there was no question of his refusing: he would strap the boy and herself to his back and carry them further up the ladder of respectability.

Working at Lawrence had opened her eyes to how people lived on a higher rung of that ladder. She found herself walking or driving around Bronxville after work, to marvel at the manicured shrubbery, the gorgeous houses set back from the street, the shining plate-glass windows behind which every table looked set for Christmas dinner. From time to time her car was in the shop and she had to take the Metro-North, but it was almost a pleasure to do so, because the Bronxville station was quaintly beautiful, with no graffiti in sight and the lambent glow of the station house and cars idling amiably as they dropped people off. She waited in the strange serenity of the platform's airy expanse, and when the train came around the bend, it bore the dignity of another era. Drowsing riders slipped past sleepy towns on the way to Grand Central Station. She began to dwell on the idea that she could finally begin to really live her life if she came home to an enchanted place like that, but they would need more money to live there. Ed's job offer had come just in time.

She thought she'd made her feelings clear to Ed, and that he'd understood and agreed, but one day he came home and told her he'd turned the deanship down. "The classroom is too important," he said. "I want them getting the education they'd get at elite schools, and I know that, at least in my classroom, that's what they're getting. I can control that much."

This about-face infuriated her—the caprice in it, the self-indulgence. This wasn't the sober man she'd thought she'd married. Sure, he had his arguments: his ambition had never been for fancier titles and fatter pay-checks; he was after something unquantifiable, philosophical, the kind of aim never properly rewarded in earthly terms. She grew increasingly impatient with his disquisitions, but she found herself parroting them to her friends, wrapping herself in the chastening rhetoric of sacrifice and duty.

She wanted Ed's idealism to trump her pragmatism, and for a couple of weeks it did, until one night at dinner she said that she was tired of living in their apartment, and that after fifteen years it was time for a change, time, even, to own a house. Ed made his case for the low rent the Orlandos charged and the fact that they were socking away money for Connell's education and avoiding the expenses and headaches of owner-ship. Another day Eileen would have let herself be appeased, turned the temperature down on the conversation, but now she allowed her anger to boil up at Ed and his unbecoming lack of courage. She felt herself on the verge of screaming one of those unforgettable phrases that could alter the dynamic of a relationship forever, and so she told him to put the boy to bed and slammed the door on her way out the room.

After work the next day, when that regular crowd that were never in a rush to get home to their families went to a bar in the vicinity of the hospital, Eileen for once accepted the invitation to join them. She was de-termined to stay out until God knew what hour, even with the young boy at home, and do whatever these people did as they watched their numbers dwindle to a determined few, but she was only halfway into her first glass of wine when a memory rose up of one particularly lugubrious episode during the period when her mother went out after work. She reached for her wallet to settle up, but the others wouldn't let her pay. As she drove home, she decided that she couldn't just pretend to Ed that nothing had changed. She felt a timer ticking on the way they were currently arranging their lives. She was getting restless. She had thought they were walking a mutual path toward greater stakes in a shared dream, but the more he insisted on staying in their apartment, the harder it was for her to see him as a fully vested partner in her future. She needed him to be her partner, because she loved him terribly, despite the difficulty of living with him sometimes, and so she was going to save him from himself, and save their marriage if that was what it was coming to, by insisting that they leave. He had always been good at listening to her. As he got older and more fixed in his fears and habits, she had to shout a little louder to be heard, but once he heard her, if he could stomach what she was asking for, he did what she asked. She did what she could do for him as well. He needed a real home no less than she did. His mind had grown smaller as he'd bunkered himself in his ideals. He needed space for his thoughts to breathe. He needed to regroup, to see new possibilities, to think bigger than ever. If there was anything she could help him with, it was thinking big.

She'd almost reached her landing with the basket of folded clothes when she heard the doorbell ring. Ed was teaching his night class. She groaned in frustration and elbowed the door open, hustling to the front stairs to get down there before the bell rang again. The boy had always been a light sleeper, but in the months since he turned five he'd seemed to awaken at the mere suggestion of activity. This constant up and down—two flights to the laundry room, a long flight to answer the door—was driving her crazy.

When she saw Angelo standing there, she wondered if she'd forgotten to slip the rent payment under the door. She found the whole exercise so humiliating every month—stooping in subservience, struggling to slide the envelope past the stubborn insulating lip—that she might unconsciously have followed her desire to forget about it and see how long it would be until they said something.

"Is this a good time to talk?"

"Sure, come in."

She was in a form-fitting sweat suit, which made her a little self-conscious walking up the stairs in front of him. When they got upstairs, she asked him to have a seat at the dining room table, but he chose to stand in the doorway, leaning against the doorjamb, holding the knit cap he'd taken off his head.

"Can I get you some coffee? Water?"

"No, thank you."

She sat.

"I've run into a little financial trouble," Angelo said.

"I'm so sorry," she said, and because she didn't want to hear the details, she began to worry the upholstering on the chairs.

He inhaled deeply, cracked his swollen knuckles. "I don't want to burden you with the whole story. Long story short, I'll have to sell the house."

"All right," she said.

"I wanted to see if you had any interest in it."

Recently, she and Ed had begun to seriously discuss the possibility of buying a house. She'd campaigned to sway him to the virtues of home ownership by appealing to his practical side. Owning would mean an added financial burden, but they'd be building equity instead of flushing rent money, and they had already put enough aside for a down payment. The only things holding them back were his conservatism about expenses and general fear of change. She hadn't been thinking multifamily, but the rental income would offset part of the mortgage, and it struck her that it wasn't going to get any easier to convince Ed to buy a house than telling him she wanted to buy the one they were already in. They wouldn't even have to get a moving truck. This was her best chance to capitalize on his recent softened stance; the longer they waited, the more time he'd have to convince himself that they shouldn't tie their money up in a home. And when he heard that Angelo was in trouble, he would want to help him out.

It didn't hurt that her father, who had promised to haunt her until she and Ed owned a house, would be appeased. She'd been thinking of her father's curse more and more lately. She could make the case that she'd been in a house long before he was dead, and that it was just a matter of signing a few papers to make it officially hers. He would appreciate the neatness of such a solution.

"This is all very sudden," she said.

"I'd sell it to you at a discount," he said. "I'd only ask that you keep my family on at an affordable rent."

"I'll talk to my husband about it."

"Please do," he said. "I'm going to have to move quickly, one way or the other."

Her mind was churning. She didn't like being on an upper floor, especially after Ed's cousin's kid in Broad Channel, playing Superman, had climbed out onto a second-story roof, jumped, and broken an arm and a leg. And she was tired of not having a driveway of her own. She used to consider herself lucky that Angelo allowed her and Ed to park in the driveway at all, but that gratitude had worn off, and now it nettled her to have to walk around the house to get to her door, or to have to ring Angelo's bell when she was blocked in.

"There's one thing I would want," she said.

"You name it."

"I would want to switch apartments. I would want to be on the ground floor."

"It's your house," he said.

"And one other thing."

"What's that?"

"I would ask you to park your car on the street," she said. "I would want the driveway clear for our use."

He seemed to chew on what she'd said. His mouth rose at the corners in a forlorn smile at the concessions his situation—she realized that she didn't care to know the first thing about it, not the first thing—had forced upon him.

"No problem," he said, regaining the momentum he'd briefly lost. "There's plenty of parking around here. Worst case, I walk a block or two."

"And we'd need the garage cleaned out."

"Everything will come out of there."

"And the cedar closets in the basement. You can have the ones we use now."

She thought she heard him whistle. She couldn't tell if he was taken aback or impressed by the bargain she was driving. "All of these details can be arranged," he said. "We can work together on this."

"I just needed to get these things out in the open."

He picked up her keys from the bowl on the mule chest and let them twirl in his fingers. "I got you."

"I'll talk to Ed."

"And you'd keep us on?"

"Yes."

He dropped the keys and straightened up. "At affordable rents?"

"I wouldn't charge an arm and a leg," she said. "You folks are like family now."

"Even if I die?"

"Angelo! My God."

He gave her a look that suggested he saw her not as a woman but as another man. "I'm asking: even if I die?"

"Even if you die. Of course."

"I just want to know my family is taken care of," he said. "I'm not looking to break the bank. I just want to take care of my people." He backed toward the stairs.

"I understand," she said, stepping toward him.

"Why don't we find out how much houses like this are going for, and then you can give me less than that."

"I need to talk to my husband," she said again. "We'd have to qualify for a mortgage."

"Don't worry." He had taken a step downstairs and he turned, smiling fully now, so that he almost appeared mirthful. "People like you, with all your affairs in order—you can have anything you want in this country."

Part II

The

Salad Days

Thursday, October 23, 1986

14

E ileen was understaffed again, so she had to stay late filling out charts and writing notes, and when she went around to dispense a final round of meds in little paper cups, one patient crashed his fist into his mouth in that way stupid people did when trying to look cool taking pills or eating peanuts, and he missed and sent the pill skittering across the linoleum floor. Pharmacy wasn't picking up the phone, and she was out of that medication, so she got down on all fours and searched for it. A quarter of an hour later she found it covered in dust under the far bed. She reached her arm up with it from under the bed in a gesture of mutual victory, but as she crawled out backwards on her hands and knees, she saw that he was staring idiotically at her rear end, which she'd left hovering as she focused on the task at hand. She wanted to cram the pill in his mouth and slam his jaw shut, cracking his teeth, but she wasn't about to let a useless fool like this defeat her poise, so she just placed it back in the little cup. In her chosen profession (in fact she felt it had chosen her, in a kind of malevolent possession) even administrators weren't spared feeling like pieces of meat.

It was almost six thirty when she hit Eastchester Road. The Hutch was moving, thank God, and the Mets were in Boston, so maybe it wouldn't be so bad on the other side of the bridge. The traffic during the playoffs had been a nightmare: mindless, endless, pointless; very nearly proof of the randomness of the universe. Her sciatic nerve was throbbing and her feet were going numb, and she didn't have it in her to sit there inching along.

As she approached the Whitestone and the road sloped up toward the start of the cables, she felt her mood lift. Her time on the bridge was the only part of her commute she didn't mind. She loved the way the cables shot up in a triumphant curve as the first arch neared and then plunged down immediately afterward. Sometimes—it was happening now—the music on the radio matched the rhythm of the bridge. The cables climbed toward the second arch, and she felt herself in the uncanny presence of beauty. Nothing else in her day stirred her to the contemplation of abstract ideas. The bridge was making an argument for its own soundness as she drove over it. High above the East River, the sharp focus of ordinary life gave way to hazy impressions as the eye worked to contain the vastness it beheld. Then the cables rolled into anchor, the landscape resumed a human scale, and that hopeful notion she'd conceived for the evening at the peak of the span began to recede.

At least the traffic was flowing. She'd be home by seven at this rate. She had called at five to say she expected to be quite late and to ask Lena to feed Connell, and then she'd called again before she left and said not to feed him. Lena had assured her it was no trouble, and Eileen had heard the touch of sharpness in her own voice when she'd said she wanted to have dinner with the boy herself. She had put chicken in the fridge to defrost it, and if she didn't cook it, it was going to go bad.

That morning, she'd decided that they were going to have a family meal, even though Ed wouldn't be there with them. If he was forcing her to compromise on her ideal of family time by continuing to teach these night classes, then a compromise was all she could stand anymore, not the complete capitulation she'd made lately on nights he taught, when she let Lena feed the boy and took a restless bubble bath before she went up to get him. She and Connell were enough to make up a family; in fact, they were plenty. In some families, mother and child was all there was. She didn't need Ed to be happy.

She was angry at Ed for the class that met two nights a week, and she was angry at him for staying late another night to attend to his research. If he was going to be away this much, at least he could be making good money doing it. His turning down the job at Merck still bothered her, and the fact that he'd spent these years taking on extra instruction only served to make him seem more irresponsible somehow.

At the exit for Northern off the Whitestone Expressway, she took pleasure in seeing Shea Stadium empty. Soon enough—it couldn't come soon enough—this endless season would be over. At 114th Street, she headed over to Thirty-Fourth Avenue, because she didn't like driving through Corona on Northern. It depressed her to live next to a neighborhood that run-down, though things closer to her end of town weren't all that great lately either. Some of the reliable old stores were becoming junk shops, and the number of signs with Spanish in them was on the rise.

She wasn't looking forward to fetching Connell from the Orlandos. It used to be, when he was in kindergarten or first grade, he'd come running when she appeared at the back door, but lately she'd had to fight to get him out of there. They always had the television going, that was part of it, and the place was comfortable in a way that appealed to a kid, with knick-knacks everywhere and interesting clutter. Brenda's four-year old daughter, Sharon, was usually there. The number of Orlandos present never seemed to dip below three. It reminded her of her apartment during the happy period in her teens when a new wave of relatives came over from Ireland. There were differences, of course: the Orlandos were louder, more physical, certainly more affectionate. She'd dealt with smoke as a kid, but there were more smokers in the Orlando house; everyone but Sharon seemed to have lit up at some point in Eileen's presence. She suspected that whatever fun Connell had up there paled in comparison to the afternoons she'd enjoyed with all her cousins around, but he didn't know the difference. Or maybe it was like when she went up to the Schmidts' apartment to watch television as a girl. She always felt she was escaping the reality of her life. Was that how Connell felt? If so, he had no reason to. She and Ed provided a calmer home than she'd ever had. Still, these days he never wanted to come down. She had to admit that for the first few minutes after they got downstairs, until she put the kitchen radio on and started cooking, her house felt empty by comparison.

She parked and went inside, took her shoes off, and changed quickly out of her stockings. She put her slippers on and went up the back stairs. Lena answered the door in a smock and said, "Come in, come in," with the carefree informality of a woman perfectly comfortable in her own home. Behind her, Angelo sat at the table in the dining room that had once been Eileen's own, smoking a cigarette and flipping through the *Post*. He still had his Sanitation Department shirt on, unbuttoned and untucked, with an undershirt beneath it. His hands were thick, and his fingers were stained from cigarettes, but there was an elegance in the way his hair was cropped and the longer strands on top were slicked back. He gave her a warm smile and welcomed her with a small gesture of the hand. The only books in the house were a few dusty volumes in the glass case behind him, and he hadn't finished high school, but still he gave the impression he could summon up reliable answers to almost any question put to him. She watched him luxuriously turn the pages of the newspaper, licking his finger and sliding his hand behind the page to flip it as though it were a leaf in an illuminated manuscript. Since Consolata's death a few months back, he was less quick to yell, and he sat at the table and talked to Connell more, which the boy delighted in. The family was still paying the rent for Consolata's apartment, presumably out of whatever small inheritance she'd left them. Lena and Angelo were planning on moving upstairs with Gary, to give Donny, Brenda, and Sharon room to breathe. The kids were grown, but it was evident they wouldn't be striking off on their own anytime soon.

Gary and Brenda were on the couch, Sharon between them, resting her head on her mother's lap while her uncle held her feet. Donny was in the easy chair. Connell had the smaller couch to himself. They were watching *Jeopardy*. Connell barely looked up when Eileen walked in. Donny waved; Gary looked embarrassed to be noticed. He was wearing corduroy pants and a T-shirt that was too tight in the gut. He wasn't fat so much as the shirt was a shrunken relic of his youth.

The question at hand was about which president served the shortest term in office, thirty-two days. Eileen couldn't remember the name.

"Harrison," Gary called out, just before the contestant buzzed in with "William Henry Harrison." Connell said "Yes!" with gusto and Donny grinned proudly at his older brother. The next question in the category asked for the name of the man who shot James Garfield at the Baltimore and Potomac Railroad Station.

"Charles Guiteau," Gary said quietly, and a moment later the contestant did too.

It was easier for her when Gary stayed in his room. She didn't like
to think about him. He was the oldest of the siblings, but he'd never held
down a job. He had an air of resignation about him, as if he'd already given
up on life. At the same time, he had a good deal of intellectual ability. She
didn't like to acknowledge that people with real ability might not arrive at
comfortable stations in life. Her cousin Pat had been a bad enough disappointment; she didn't want to consider the possibility that Connell might
fall through the cracks like Gary. She certainly didn't like to think that
something similar had happened to her too, on a smaller scale. She had
achieved professional status, but her existence wasn't ideal, and hard as
she tried to hack her way through the thicket of middle-class living, she
couldn't find a way out to the clearing. It would have been easier to see
Gary as a savant with an overdeveloped capacity to absorb trivia, but the
truth was he was a complex, intelligent individual. She'd heard him discussing issues of the day and couldn't help agreeing with him, even being
enlightened by observations she couldn't have made herself. And yet there
he was, living in the margins, talking to a television, dying half an hour at
a time. A claustrophobic sensation swept over her. She needed to forget
that people like Gary existed, to forget even the possibility of failure. She
needed to spirit her son away or Gary would suck him into the black hole
of his life.

Connell rose and slapped Donny five across the coffee table. Then he
looked up at her.

"It's time to go," she said. "I'm making dinner."

"Can I come down when it's ready?"

"*No*," she said sharply, then collected herself. "You're coming down
now. They've had enough of you up here. Let the Orlandos have their evening in peace."

"He's no bother," Angelo said over his newspaper. "He can stay as long
as he wants."

"Thank you, but he's going to help me get dinner ready." She hadn't
had any intention to ask Connell for help, but she needed a good excuse.

"We were discussing politics before," Angelo said. "He said you wanted
him to be a politician. I asked him if he knew what a politician was."

Eileen offered up a little embarrassed laugh. "What I mostly want is for him to get downstairs right now," she said, loud enough for Connell to hear.

She said her good-byes and walked to the door. Connell lagged behind, standing and watching the show. Gary got another question right, and Donny and Connell broke into hysterics.

"*Connell*," she said. "Come *on*."

He took his time getting his schoolbag and followed her down the stairs. She got him set up chopping lettuce while she grilled the chicken. She was going to make salad for dinner, with the chicken spread over it. She'd given in to pizza too often recently, and the nights Ed cooked it was grilled cheese in a lagoon of butter, or cheeseburgers, anything with cheese. The boy was too chubby for her liking. It was true that he hadn't hit a big growth spurt yet, but it was also true that the tendency toward physical largeness on her family's side could edge into overweight if it wasn't watched scrupulously. In the absence of worldly cares, Connell stuffed his face with candy and ice cream. She hadn't had time to get fat as a kid. When she was only a few months older than he was now, she was planning meals, shopping, keeping the house—things she couldn't imagine him doing. When she sent him to the store, she had to write a list, and he still inevitably forgot something on it.

She was going to start mapping some order onto his life. Ed wasn't a big help in that area. He loved the boy so much, was so permissive, seemed delighted by everything he did. Connell brought home a ninety-five and Ed beamed; she was always the one forced to ask where the other five points went. She resented the way Connell walked around oblivious of how carefree his existence was, how little responsibility he had.

She put some cherry tomatoes in the salad and cooked the chicken quickly in the pan. She grabbed some dressing, tossed it all together, and told him to sit down. She served him salad and put the chicken over it.

"This is dinner?" he said.

"You need to eat more leafy greens. *Some* leafy greens."

It was seven thirty. Ed was just half an hour into his class, with an hour to go. She spent a few moments of pique in wondering if she and Connell were crossing his mind at all. Connell was eating too fast, as usual. He

didn't even like salad, and yet he was rushing to eat it. There was something irrepressible in the way he ate. Maybe he was trying to speed through
dinner so he could get to dessert. He knew the rules: no dessert until his
plate was clean. It had been a couple of years since she'd had to stage one
of those nightlong sit-ins to get him to eat his meal. She'd figured out what
to avoid, and he'd stopped trying to slip it in the garbage when she wasn't
looking and just ate what he was served. Dessert held that power over him.
She always kept something in the house, for herself as much as for him, but
she took only a little portion, nothing like the heaps he wolfed down. He
was going to have to learn restraint if he ever wanted to make a success of
himself among serious people. It was unseemly to behave with that kind
of abandon. She told him to slow down and he nodded at her and kept on
eating at his pace. "Slow *down*," she said, annoyed. "You're going to choke."
She got up to refill her water glass. She stood at the sink drinking it and
filled it again. When she turned around she saw him waving his arms, his
fork on his plate, and then she saw him leap to his feet, his hands on his
throat. She told him it wasn't funny, and then she saw his face and began
screaming, "Are you choking?" but she already knew he was. It had happened a few times when he was a toddler, but it had always been a mere
scare, some dense foodstuff, tuna fish or peanut butter, compacted in his
esophagus, and he'd been able to breathe through it, but now he wasn't
making a sound. It was time to grab him coolly and dislodge the food with
one fist to his abdomen and the other shoving up, but she couldn't do it.

   She'd dealt with choking a number of times in her career. You got your
hands in the midsection and gave the diaphragm a healthy shove and out
the food popped. A couple of seconds and it was over. You had more time
than people thought, a lot more, four full minutes until brain damage set
in. But this was her son and she had no room for error.

   She had him by the shoulders. She began to panic. She knew she
shouldn't panic, but she couldn't help herself; she loved the boy so much.
She was thinking *Please don't die, please don't die* and she started screaming
for help, and then she was shoving him out the door and pulling him toward the back stairs. She got to the stairwell and screamed, "Angelo! Angelo!
Angelo!" and ran upstairs and banged on the door and screamed, "Come

down!" and then she ran back down, because she had left the boy alone. Her hands were shaking. "He's choking!" she screamed. Connell was turning blue. She heard someone flying down the stairs, and then Donny was shoving her aside, and then he was standing behind Connell, giving him a muscular approximation of the Heimlich, and then something flew out of Connell's mouth onto the carpet. He started coughing and wailing a terrified wail that sounded more like a cat's than a child's. It was a cherry tomato. He must have swallowed it whole. She picked it up and crushed it angrily in her hand. She sat him at the dining room table. Angelo, Gary, and Brenda came in. Connell kept coughing, though the wailing subsided. She went to get him a glass of water. In the kitchen she saw the plates and slammed them into the trash with their contents. She could feel the feelings rising up, getting ready to wash over her, take her over. He took the water down quickly. She would never get angry at him for eating fast again. It was Ed she was angry at, for not being there, for exposing Connell to this danger by his absence. She was grateful the Orlandos were reliably present in the evenings, and mortified that she, a nurse, hadn't been able to save him herself.

"Are you going to slow down now?" was all she could think to say when she went back to the dining room. Then she burst into tears. Connell seemed too dazed to cry.

"If you'd been Gary," Donny said, "I would have let you choke. What do they call that, Gary? Euthanasia?"

Connell gave a little chuckle through his coughs.

"Don't you do that again," Angelo said. "I don't need another heart attack. Two is plenty."

"You good?" Brenda asked, putting her hand on Connell's shoulder. He nodded. "Slow down. Your food's not going anywhere."

"Well, my work here is done," Donny said. "I better go find a phone booth to change in."

"Why don't you go pick up your dirty drawers from the bathroom floor instead," Brenda said. "I don't think the hamper's made of kryptonite."

The laughs were welcome, but she could see that Donny had been affected by the brush with disaster. He was wide-eyed and shaking his head. The whole Orlando family seemed unnerved. Connell spent the afternoons

up there, but it had never occurred to Eileen that they might in some way
have thought of him as being part of their family too.

"*Wheel of Fortune* is on," Gary said. They made their way up the stairs.
She sat at the table with Connell.

"Are you okay?"

He nodded.

"Shaken up?"

He nodded again. "I couldn't breathe," he said.

"I know."

"I couldn't talk."

He couldn't know how hard on her he was making this.

"Horrible," she said. "I froze up."

"Donny saved me."

"I don't know what happened. I've done it before. I guess it never
meant as much to me."

"Thank God they were here," he said.

"I would have done it eventually," she said. "My training would have
kicked in. I think because I knew they were here, I didn't have to go into
lifesaving mode."

"He saved my life," the boy said thoughtfully.

"Let's not go overboard," she said. "You were going to be fine. We had
time."

He looked like he was in shock. She went to the freezer and scooped
some ice cream into a bowl for him.

"Here, have this," she said. "I don't think you can choke on this. Maybe
you'll find a way."

Ordinarily at this time of night she would have made him sit down
with his homework, but she didn't say anything about it. At the moment
she didn't care if he never did his homework again. Maybe this was how
Ed felt all the time.

She told him he could take the ice cream to the couch—another first—
and she went to get the television for him. The only set in the house was the
little black-and-white one in their bedroom. They had been wheeling it out to
the living room during the playoffs and the World Series. She cleaned up the

pan from the chicken while he watched *Entertainment Tonight*, and joined him when she was done. The games usually started at eight, or before eight, but when he got up to change the channel to NBC, *The Cosby Show* was on. It took only a moment to understand that preempting *The Cosby Show* would have cost the network ad revenue. They lay on separate couches. It wasn't easy to see the set from that far away. The girl, Vanessa, was trying to wear makeup to school, against her mother's wishes. The boy, Theo, was attempting to organize his family to do a fire drill. It could have been *Leave It to Beaver*, except that everyone was black. The world was changing fast. It was hard to fit her son's America into her memory of how the world had been ordered when she was a child. She felt like a member of an in-between generation, straddling sides in a clash of history. Her life was as remote and ancient to Connell as the stories of the pilgrim settlers had been to her when she was his age.

The Cosby Show ended and the game was about to come on. She told him she was going to the bedroom to lie down, and he gave her a stricken look.

"You're not watching the game?"

She could tell he was disturbed by what had happened to him, that he didn't want to be alone. "I'll watch for a little while," she said, relenting.

She didn't blame him. Over and over she had been reliving in her mind the moment when she'd watched Donny pop the tomato out. She wanted to sit next to Connell, to hold him close to her, but she had no idea how to do it. She had no interest in watching another of these games she'd had to sit through so many of in the run-up to the playoffs, so after a few minutes she rose to get *Lonesome Dove*. She flipped through it distractedly, reading and rereading the same page several times. The Mets fell behind early, and by the end of the fifth inning they were down 4–0.

She knew she wasn't the softest mother in the world. She worked a lot. She worked, period. Other mothers stayed home, baked cookies, talked to their kids all the time, knew everything their kids were thinking. It had never occurred to her to try to be Connell's friend. She did her best to encourage meaningful conversations at dinner, the three of them talking as a family, and not only because it would be constructive in lubricating Connell's future advancement among people who judged a person by how he spoke, but also because she liked to hear what he was thinking. She had worked hard to give him a comfortable life. That was as valuable as providing emotional sustenance. Life wasn't only about expressing feelings and giving hugs. Still, she couldn't figure out how to break through the defenses her son had put up, and it bothered her, an intellectual problem as much as an emotional one.

She placed her bookmark in the page and held the book in her hands. "I'm thinking of turning in," she said.

"Can you stay here and read?"

So, he needed her there. He couldn't say it in so many words, but he had more or less admitted it. She opened her book again and started in on the first page of the chapter she'd been reading.

Ed walked in before ten. They heard the door, and then they heard him hanging his coat in the vestibule, and then they heard him dropping his briefcase on his desk in the study before he came into the living room.

"Still four–nothing?" he asked when he walked in.

Connell nodded. "Gooden got smacked around."

"They were saying on the radio his velocity is down."

"El Sid has been great in relief. But the bats are ice cold."

"Something happened," she said, interjecting. "Connell choked."

"What?" Ed turned to her, then back to him. "What happened, buddy?"

"I was trying to concentrate on not choking, and then the next thing I knew I was choking."

He looked at her. "*Really* choking?"

"It was in his windpipe."

"What was?"

"A cherry tomato."

"You got it out?"

"Donny did."

He pointed upstairs. "You ate with the Orlandos?"

"Donny came down," Connell said.

"To eat with us?"

Her blood ran cold at the thought of discussing the particulars around the boy, who would see on her face how unsettled she still was.

"I'll explain later," she said.

"Come here," Ed said, and he sat on the couch and put his arm around Connell, who leaned into the lapel of his father's tweed jacket. It was so easy for Ed to connect to him. She always had to be the scold. Maybe Connell had hardened his heart to her. He leaned in further, so that his chubby belly pressed against the waistband of his sweatpants. He had his face in Ed's flannel shirt and started sobbing. Ed kissed the top of his head and rubbed his back. Connell kept his face buried there for some minutes. Ed was looking to her for a mimed narrative of what had happened, but she kept waving him off. After a while, Connell lifted his head.

"Will you do what your mother has asked you to do a few times now, if I'm not mistaken," Ed said in a firm but gentle voice, "and try to slow down when you eat? Can you do that for me?"

Connell nodded.

"Good."

And then, without another word, they had transitioned out of that conversation and were watching the game. She stopped reading *Lonesome Dove* and directed her attention to them. It was something to behold, Ed's physical comfort with the boy, who had his leg draped over his father's. She'd been affectionate with Connell when he was very young, up until he was about three, but then something had interceded to make it subtly harder for her to connect to him. She knew Ed could do it, so she'd never spent much time worrying about the boy being deprived, but now she had the sensation that she was on the other side of something important. She wasn't angry so much as hurt and darkly fascinated.

The Mets scored a run in the top of the eighth inning, and then, in the ninth, after Ray Knight grounded out and Kevin Mitchell popped out—she'd sat through so many playoff games of late that she knew the players' names by now—Mookie Wilson doubled, and then Rafael Santana singled him in. Ed said this team had a knack for getting two-out hits. Lenny Dykstra came to the plate as the tying run, but a few pitches later he struck out swinging and the game was over. The Mets were down three games to two in the World Series. Another loss and their season, which seemed to have united New York for a while and which even someone like her, who paid little attention, knew had been an extraordinary success, would be over.

"Complete game for Hurst," Ed said. "Impressive."

"They couldn't get to him," Connell said.

Ed rose and shut the volume off but left the screen on, and they watched the Red Sox players celebrate as the credits rolled and the news came on. Then he shut the television off and pulled the plug on it to prepare to roll it back into the bedroom.

"Clemens is up next," Connell said, foreboding in his voice.

"Yes, but they're in New York."

"They have to win two."

"They'll do it."

"It's Roger Clemens."

"What did Tug McGraw say?" Ed asked Socratically.

" 'Ya gotta believe,' " Connell answered.

"Well, then."

It was after eleven thirty, much later than Connell's bedtime. They said quick good nights and the boy headed off. Ed wheeled the television in front of him as if he was piloting a projector cart. She got into bed, and Ed came in a few minutes later, after he'd tucked Connell in. She told him the story of how the boy had choked and how she'd responded to it, or failed to respond, and Ed nodded and said it was over now and everything was fine, and it calmed her to hear it; Ed was good at putting her at ease. He gave her a kiss and she rolled over and lay thinking about what had transpired, with a clarity of thought the clamorous broadcast hadn't allowed. Why had she frozen? As Connell had stood there not even gasping for air, but silently motioning toward his throat, a feeling for him more intense than love and more mysterious had risen up from the depths of her mind. She felt that he was part of her own flesh again, as he'd been once, and that she was on the brink of dying along with him. Nothing would be the same if he died. She would go on, but her life would lose its meaning and purpose. This kid who annoyed and infuriated her so often was walking around with her fate in his hands. She didn't trust him with it. She felt fragile, exposed. She was going to make him be more careful going forward.

At one thirty in the morning, she was awakened by Connell nudging her, asking if he could come into the bed. She was too sleepy to object. She moved aside and let him slide into the space between them. She couldn't remember the last time he was in bed with them. She had policed that boundary well when he was younger, not wanting to become one of those couples whose marriages were held hostage by a child in the bed every night. Forget about sex: she just wanted to get a good night's sleep. Eventually Connell had stopped trying to join them.

She began to groggily recall the events of earlier, and it made sense that he was there. She could hear him nudging Ed awake, the two of them talking.

"I almost died," Connell said.

"You're fine," Ed said.

"I was scared. I'm still scared."

Ed rolled over. "You are completely fine. You're safe. You have a long life ahead of you. A long life."

"I didn't want to die," Connell said.

"Well, now you have to remember that feeling. Go out there and make the most of life."

"You really think they're going to win?"

"The Mets? Yes."

"Both games?"

"Both. You'll see."

"You're sure?"

"Have faith," Ed said. "They'll pull it out. Now go to sleep."

As she listened to them talk, she was taken back to the row of beds she slept in when Mr. Kehoe was still living in the other room. She had no memory of any conversations taking place among the three of them once the lights were out. Both her parents faced away from her. She remembered wondering what it would have been like for the two of them to sleep in the same bed. Now she wondered whether she'd have had the nerve to crawl between them and feel their heat radiating on either side of her. Maybe if they'd slept in the same bed, she would have grown up as the kind of girl who had that nerve. Maybe your imagination stopped at the boundaries that contained it. She had taken comfort in the placement of her bed between theirs. Maybe you took what you could get. She could have reached out and touched their backs. That had been enough for her. It wouldn't be enough for her son. She was glad, on this night when she hadn't been able to save him herself, to have one bed they slept in and to be able to give him this opportunity. She hadn't had it as a girl, but that didn't mean he shouldn't have it. She wondered if he'd lost some of his trust in her tonight. So much of life was the peeling away of illusions. Maybe she'd only hurried that along. Maybe that wasn't the worst thing. He was going to have to fend for himself at some point.

She felt Connell roll away from Ed and nuzzle up to her in a way that she hadn't anticipated him doing. His forehead was pressed against the top of her back. Within a minute, he was asleep. She couldn't move without waking him, but she also couldn't sleep without moving him. She decided to wait. She felt oddly touched having him there. Still, it was going to be a long night, and she'd be exhausted in the morning, so she'd eventually have to move him off her.

She lay there thinking, *I almost lost him. I'm never serving goddamned cherry tomatoes again. Ed better be right about the Mets, or this kid is going to be more disappointed in his father than he is in the Mets. Then again, he has to learn that things don't always work out the way you want them to.*

She went back and forth between thinking it would be nice if Connell got the outcome he wanted and thinking it would be character-building for him not to get it. Fatigue from a long day at work and the effects of adrenaline withdrawal must have been enough to overcome her need for space, because she felt herself drifting off, even though he was still attached to her.

The kid would be thrilled, she thought. *Let them win.*

The next thing she knew she was waking up. Somehow in the night she had gotten herself to face the boy, who was still sleeping, and Ed behind him on his back, out cold. Connell breathed in and out softly. His lashes were long like his father's, and in the muted sunlight peeking through the blinds his cheeks looked sweet and full. As if he could sense her looking at him, he opened his eyes and blinked a few times in that half-conscious, slightly perturbed way he used to as a toddler when he hadn't yet fully come to. He gave her a slumber-drunk smile; then he was back asleep. She didn't know what to do with everything she was feeling for him, even for her husband, so she got up to take a shower and left the two of them to wake up and find each other there.

Part III

Breathe
the Rich Air

1991

15

After Connell turned in, Ed surprised her by not moving to the study to grade lab reports or read journal articles. He lay on the couch with the newspaper listening to Wagner. She didn't have to know music to recognize that it was Wagner, because the swelling crescendos and singer's deep voice gave it away. Ed often listened to Wagner when he was in a contemplative mood.

She sat on the other couch with her book, happy to share with him the beaten-back chill of a February night, which made itself known in the frost on the windows. She switched the light on in the artificial fireplace, pausing briefly to rattle the glass coals and hear them clack against each other. It pleased her that the man she'd married, in addition to possessing an erudition that impressed even worldly friends, read the sports section in its entirety. At one point he rose and went to the study, and she thought she'd lost him for the night, but he returned with a pen to do the crossword. She loved the carefree way he called on her for help when flummoxed by a clue. It suggested an abiding faith in the soundness of his intellect that he could meet head-on those swells of ignorance that might capsize another man's confidence; they were wavelets lapping against his hull.

"I've done everything I can do," he said, as he lay the quarter-folded newspaper on the coffee table. "I want to be realistic. Maybe it's time for me to relax."

She glanced up from her book to catch his eye, but he was looking at the ceiling.

"I'm not sure what you mean," she said.

"I'm turning fifty soon. I'm slowing down. I've earned a rest."

"Nonsense," she said.

"I'm going to become one of those guys who come home and call it a night. Maybe I'll watch some TV."

"I'll believe that when I see it."

"I can start right now."

Her heart leapt a little. It was pleasant to imagine him spending more time in their bed. He had finally given up the night classes, thank God, but he still worked so hard, often coming in from the study long after she was asleep.

"I don't know how long you could keep that up," she said. "You'd get bored."

"I'll be fine."

"Well, if it makes you happy," she said.

He'd already moved to the stereo to change the record. He plugged his headphones in and had them on before she could hear what he was listening to. He lay back down and closed his eyes.

She waited for him to acknowledge her gaze. He liked to lie like that and slip into a reverie, but he usually opened his eyes between movements to give her a little review with his raised brows. She wondered if he were sleeping, he was lying so still, but then he began tapping his foot rhythmically. When the side ended, he lay there, arms crossed across his chest, impassive. She shut off her light and stood to head into the bedroom. She called his name, but he didn't reply. She watched for some kind of acknowledgment of her departure, but he only shifted his glasses. She went to him and stood over him. He must have imagined he could outlast her in this game, but she was starting to grow disturbed by it. She leaned in to kiss his cheek good night; before she reached it he had opened his eyes and was staring back at her in a kind of horror, as if she'd interrupted him in a reflection on something monstrous.

"I'm heading to bed," she said.

"I'll be right in."

After a few bouts of fitful sleep—she never slept well without him beside her—she headed to the living room. She found the end table lamp on and Ed still wearing the headphones. A record was spinning, and he'd set up a stack to be played by the autochanger. She shut the stereo off and called his name. He put a hand up to silence her.

"I'm just going to lie here a minute," he said.

"It's four in the morning." She switched off the lamp, but ambient light still filtered into the room from the coming sun. "You need good, quality sleep. You're always saying that. Don't lights interrupt sleep? You need REM sleep. *Restful* sleep. Come on inside. You have to teach in a few hours."

"I think I'm going to cancel class," he said. "I'm not feeling it."

"Huh?"

He hadn't missed a class in twenty years. They'd had fights about it. *You can miss a single class*, she would say when something came up. *They can't fire you for it. They can't fire you, period.*

"I think I've earned a day off," he said.

"Well, either way, just come to bed. It's late."

She stood over him until he got up. They shuffled down the hall together. In the morning when she woke he was sitting at the foot of the bed.

"Maybe you'd better call for me," he said.

After she'd made the call, she showered and dressed. When she headed to the kitchen, she saw him lying on the couch again, as if he hadn't moved from the night before, the only difference being the cup of tea on the table.

"You're taking this whole 'taking it easy' thing pretty seriously," she said.

"I'm just gathering my energy," he said. "I'll be all right tomorrow. I'll go in tomorrow."

He let himself be kissed good-bye. She went to work. When she returned she was surprised to find him in the same spot, wearing the same clothes. She hadn't really believed he'd stay home all day; it was unlike him. His record of never missing work was a matter of somber pride. Connell's bag and jacket were slung over a chair in the dining room.

Ed's eyes were closed. His feet beat the time. She stood over him, tapped him on the shoulder. As she spoke, he motioned to the headphones to indicate he couldn't hear her. She mimed pulling them off her ears.

"I'm listening to music," he said.

"Plainly."

"How was work?"

"Work was fine," she said. "Did you stay there all day?"

"I got up to eat."

"So this is the new thing?"

"I'm trying it out. I'm feeling enormously refreshed."

"I'm glad to hear that," she said.

"I've been meaning to spend more time attending to my needs," he said. "This is step one. I've had a cloudy head for a while. I'm trying to get back to basics."

"What about work?"

"I'm going to need you to call in again for me tomorrow."

In the big mirror in the other room she saw herself in the coat she'd been meaning to replace. She had once thought of thirty as a terribly old age, but now she was turning fifty at the end of the year, and thirty seemed impossibly young.

"How long do you plan to do this?"

"I hadn't formulated a plan."

"Shall I expect you to eat with us tonight?"

"Of course," he said, waving her off and putting the headphones back on.

As she began to prepare dinner, she reflected on what this thing could be. It was clearly some kind of midlife crisis. Something was spooking him: getting old, probably. She was confident it wasn't another woman. They were coconspirators in a mission of normalcy. A stronger deterrent to infidelity even than love was the desire to maintain a stable household, a stress-free life. She knew he was reliable, and not only because he wasn't going to miss work to sleep off a drunk, or gamble his paycheck at the track, or forget their anniversary. He was, in a subtler way, reliably knowable. Some women yearned for a hint of mystery about their men; she loved Ed's lack of mystery. It had shade, depth, texture; it was just complex enough. His heart contained too little passion for him to attempt a grand affair, and too much for him to endure a scurrilous one. He was too preoccupied with his work to love two women at once; he lacked that tolerance for superficial interaction every successful adulterer wielded.

A few days later he returned to work, but the headphones ritual persisted in the evenings. One night he returned to his study, and she felt relieved. She assumed he was grading lab reports, but when she went in to bring him a plate of cookies she found him writing in a notebook, which he took pains to block from her view. When she went back later that night to look for it, it was gone.

Their dinners began to feel strange to her. Ed looked away when she tried to meet his gaze, and he never wanted to talk about his work—or about anything, really, but Connell's day and the happenings at school.

"And then," Connell said, "they lifted him up to grab the rim, but they didn't give him the ball to dunk. Somebody pulled his shorts down. And then they pulled his underwear down! He just hung up there until Mr. Cotswald ran over and got him."

"Ha!"

Ed laughed with just a bit too much gusto. She'd expected him to condemn the boys' behavior. It was as if he hadn't really absorbed what Connell had said. Something in the warmth in his voice, the distraction that flickered in his eyes, made her wonder if she'd been too hasty in ruling out an affair. A listlessness had come over him lately that seemed at times like a species of dreaminess.

"Well." Ed pushed back his chair. He gave Connell a perfunctory pat on the head and retired to the couch and the privacy of his headphones. Connell looked embarrassed, as if he'd extended a hand for a shake and been rebuffed. She knew enough not to compound it by speaking to him.

She went to bed feeling frowsy. She squeezed the deposits of fat at her hips and wondered how they had managed to sneak up on her. She knew the doctors at work still turned to look at her in the halls, but if Ed didn't see her that way, then the interest of other men felt less a vote of confidence than a shabby habit that in its mindless lack of differentiation—she saw the way they looked at so many of the girls—called into question whether she had ever been beautiful at all.

Ed came in after midnight. He stood over her, gazing oddly. She could feel herself stiffen.

"Anything you want to tell me?"

"Not really," he said.

"What are you listening to, anyway?"

"Wagner's *Ring Cycle*. I have so many records I haven't even cracked the plastic on. It makes me anxious to see them all sitting there. I'm working my way through them."

She was surprised by how relieved she felt to hear this. It was sufficiently particular to actually be plausible. It was the kind of thing she imagined people did when they came to a point where the roads to the past and the future were equally muddy—retreat to the high ground of a major project.

She had long measured a meal's success by the range of colors arrayed on the plate, but it felt hopelessly middle-class now to conceive of food in this fashion, and she looked askance at orange carrots, bright green beans, white mashed potatoes, the dark pile of meat and onions, picking at it with her fork in the way she resented in her child.

She used to love to sit at her kitchen table and watch the drapes kick up in the wind, to look through the window across the little divide and see the Palumbos gathered in their dining room, but now the house next door felt far too close. She hated its plain brick face and the shabby décor visible within. She had long tolerated this vulgarity because she felt privileged to have a house at all, but now she found it too disappointing to bear.

Lately she couldn't stop thinking about Bronxville. When she'd left Lawrence in 1983 for the nursing director job at St. John's Episcopal in Far Rockaway, she'd missed going to Bronxville every day. When she returned to Einstein a couple of years later to be head of nursing, she'd begun to think the timing might finally be right to move to Bronxville. The commute would be shorter for both of them, she was making good money now, Ed had gotten into a decent pay class himself, and they'd made a few good investments. They had put eight thousand dollars into oil shale stock on the advice of one of Ed's colleagues, a geologist at NYU, and it had climbed to forty-four thousand. But then in '85 the shale oil company went bankrupt. That year, they also lost twenty grand on a penny stock scam with First Jersey Securities. The final nail came in 1987, when her boss left for a government appointment, and the new head of the hospital fired those he could and appointed his own leadership team. Though she landed on her feet at North Central Bronx, she had to take a pay cut to do so.

She couldn't look across at the Palumbos' just then, with their dreadful chandelier glowing like margarine and the two of them looking all their years as they sat down to a cheerless meal, so she got up to close the drapes. Ed took her rising as a cue that the meal was over and headed for the couch.

When she and Ed moved in, the neighborhood was Irish, Italian, Greek, and Jewish, and they knew everyone on the block. Then families started to trickle out, and in their place came Colombians, Bolivians, Nicaraguans, Filipinos, Koreans, Chinese, Indians, Pakistanis. Connell played with the new kids, but she never met the parents. When an Iranian family—they called themselves Persian, but she couldn't bring herself to refer to them as anything but Iranian—bought her friend Irene's place up the block after she moved to Garden City, the son, Farshid, became a classmate of Connell's at St. Joan of Arc and started hanging around the house.

It wasn't hard to feel the pull of the suburbs, because the neighborhood was half suburb already, arranged around mass transit but also around car travel. There were driveways next to every house, and gas stations and car dealerships at regular intervals along Northern Boulevard. LaGuardia Airport was a short drive away, and Robert Moses's highways, and the massive parking lots at Shea, and the husk of the World's Fair, which had left detritus like a glacier.

Most of the stores she loved were gone, replaced by trinket shops, T-shirt shops, fireworks black marketeers, exotic hair salons hidden behind heavy curtains, over-the-counter purveyors of deadly martial arts paraphernalia, comic book stores, karate schools, check-cashing places, Korean-run Optimo-branded cigar and candy stores that sold cheap knockoffs of popular Japanese toys, taxi depots, sketchy bars, fast food, wholesalers of obscure cuisines, restaurants suggestive of opium dens, bodegas stocked with products she would never consider eating. The Boulevard Theatre on the corner was now a Latin dance hall with neon lights flickering late into the night and an insistent beat that hectored the remaining old guard to leave. Cars piled up outside it and the cops were always breaking up fights. The gloomy little Irish bar was the last stand against the invasion, but she couldn't take some specious pride in it now after avoiding it all these years.

The memory of wealth haunted the nearby garden apartment buildings. She imagined gaunt bachelors presiding over dwindling fortunes, long lines coming to a silent end. There were remnants of the way it had been, like Barricini's Chocolates and Jahn's, but stepping into them only reminded her how few of the old places were left.

She knew it was possible to see the changes as part of what made the city great, an image of what was to come, the necessary cycle of immigration, but only if you weren't the one being displaced. Maybe even then you could, if you were a saint. She had no desire to be a saint, not if it meant she'd have to blunt the edge of her anger at these people. It certainly wasn't saintliness that led her to attempt to get past her resentment at the break-in that occurred a couple of years back, while they were on a cruise in the Bahamas. Rather, it was a desire to continue living in the neighborhood without boiling over into outright vitriol whenever she stepped into the grocery store, where anyone she laid eyes on, worker or customer, unless they looked respectable, could have been one of the offenders. She had returned from that cruise to find her jewelry box rifled through and her drawers turned inside out. Luckily, she'd long ago overridden Ed and spent the money to rent a safe deposit box at Manufacturers Hanover, where she stored Ed's LeCoultre watch and her mother's embattled engagement ring. All the bonds were in the box as well. She took a certain satisfaction in thinking of how little the thieves had made off with; for once it seemed an advantage that Ed had never been the sort to buy necklaces and bracelets for her birthday or their anniversary. The degenerates had pinched Ed's stereo, that was true, but he'd needed a new one for years, and this was an excuse for her to buy one for him. She was angry too at the Orlandos, who'd been home at the time. She couldn't imagine how they hadn't heard anything, or done anything if they'd heard. What kept her awake some nights, though, fantasizing about revenge, was the fact that they'd taken Mr. Kehoe's clarinet from the bedroom closet. What could they possibly have wanted with a clarinet? How valuable could such a thing have been on the secondhand market? There was no way they were keeping it for themselves, because the swine wouldn't know what to do with such a delicate instrument. She pictured them back in their sty of an apartment, surveying their loot, sniffing it, looking at the clarinet's pieces in stupefaction and dropping them into a garbage can.

She couldn't blame everything on the latest waves of immigration. Her immediate neighbors had been there longer than she had and both had fallen on tough times. Both houses used to look respectable, if a little dull, with dingy lace curtains in the windows and bleached paint on the trim, but now a rusted-out car sat on blocks in the Palumbos' backyard, next to a rain-filled drum, and Gene Cooney's house was under permanent construction, with ugly scaffolding marring the facade and a garden box full of crabgrass and construction debris. Gene stalked the perimeter all day with an edgy intensity, wearing a tool belt around his waist. Wild rumors had sprung up about him and his family, spread by newer residents. He was said to be an IRA arms smuggler lying low. There were whispers about his daughter, who wore short skirts and fishnet stockings and kept nocturnal hours. Eileen knew the truth: he'd gone off the rails after his wife had been killed on Northern Boulevard by a hit-and-run driver, and his daughter wasn't a prostitute but a girl who had fallen victim to the fashions of the Hispanics she'd grown up around—though one could be forgiven for confusing some of them with hookers.

When she'd first moved onto the block, the garden boxes in front of the houses were lush with flowers in bloom and respectable attempts at horticulture, but many had since returned to the wild, with giant weeds poking up over their walls. She was committed to making hers an oasis against decay, although she hadn't inherited her father's sympathy with all manner of vegetable life. Angelo had helped her keep things alive, and she'd picked up a bit of knowledge working alongside him, but ever since his third heart attack had killed him a few years back, she was constantly buying new plants to replace the ones that wilted in the middle of the night.

She overspent on furniture. She had the rugs cleaned and the walls painted every two years. She'd found a beautiful crystal chandelier on sale on the Bowery. The house wasn't fancy, but it had a certain luster. The one thing she couldn't escape was the sound of the Orlandos' footsteps above her. The fact that she owned the whole building didn't make it any more pleasant to hear them.

Ed was seated at the table as she fixed the tea. His back was to her, possessed of that solidity that so delighted her the first time she put her arms around him. Now she wanted to pound on it. He was hunched over and rubbing his temples. She put a hand on his shoulder and he flinched at her touch. She thought, *Who the hell does he think I am?*

She considered flinging herself on him before he could get the headphones plugged in. She thought of ripping the plug out once he'd settled into his pillow and filling the room with sound, screaming over the music the invectives she'd held in. But she didn't do that. She sat in the armchair and read a book until she headed to bed.

She wondered whether she was being hard on her husband. He had, after all, more than earned a rest after teaching for so many years. She hadn't heard anything from Connell yet about it, and she expected that the boy, who was becoming a more sullen presence in the house as he slunk into adolescence, would be oblivious enough to his father's new routines to allow her to conclude that it was all in her head.

Connell noticed, though. "So what's with all the record listening?" he asked one night, snapping his gum in that insouciant way that usually annoyed her. Now she saw that the attitude gave him the courage to speak.

Ed looked up but didn't respond.

"What's up with the headphones?" he asked again, stepping closer to his father.

Given the strange way Ed had been behaving lately, she thought he might fly into a rage, but he simply took the headphones off.

"I'm listening to opera."

"You listen to it all the time now."

"I decided I didn't want to die not having heard all these masterpieces. Verdi. Rossini. Puccini."

"Who's dying? You've got plenty of time."

"There's no time like the present," Ed said.

"You don't have to use those," Connell said, pointing to the headphones.

"I don't want to disturb anyone."

"You don't think you're disturbing anyone this way?"

Another night, when she picked him up from track practice, Connell asked her in the car if his father was unhappy.

"I wouldn't say that," she said. "I think he's quite happy."

"He always says, 'You have to decide in life. You deliberate awhile, you think of all the possibilities on both sides, and then you make a decision and stick to it.'"

She'd never heard this particular line of reasoning from Ed. This must've been one of those things he and the boy talked about when she wasn't around. She could almost feel her ears pricking up.

"Like with girls. He says, 'When you're getting married, you make a decision and that's it. Things aren't always perfect, but you work at them. The important thing is that you decided.'"

Her stomach tightened.

"But what I don't get is, if it's such a chore, if you're talking about having to stick to it because you decided it, why do people do it in the first place?"

"They do it because they're in love," she said defensively. "Your father and I were in love. *Are* in love."

"I know," he said.

It occurred to her that perhaps he didn't know. Overt affection had always been uncomfortable for her, but in front of the boy it felt impossible. Ed used to squeeze and kiss her when Connell was a baby, but she would wriggle out of it. Certainly she didn't reach for him herself, but he knew when they married that he'd have to take the lead. She wasn't like the women a few years younger who wore miniskirts. What she offered instead was the negotiated submission of her fierce independence. She was different in bed with him than she was anywhere else, but this wasn't something her son could have any idea about.

"Your father is happy," she said. "He's just getting older, is all. You'll understand someday. The same exact thing will happen to you."

It didn't feel like the best explanation, but it must've been good enough, because the boy was silent for the rest of the ride.

16

His father was always on the couch now, but that morning he came to Connell's room and told him he wanted to take him to the batting cages. They drove to the usual place, off the Grand Central Parkway, in back of a mini-mall.

Connell picked out the least dinged-up bat from the rack and tried to find a helmet that fit. His father came back from the concession stand with a handful of coins for the machines. Connell headed for the machine labeled Very Fast. He put the sweaty, smelly helmet on and pulled his batting glove onto his right hand. He took his position in the left-handed batter's box and dropped the coin in. The light came on on the machine, and then nothing happened for a while, until a ball shot out and thumped against the rubber backstop. Connell watched another one pass and wondered if he was going to be able to hit any of them. They were easily over eighty miles an hour, though they weren't the ninety miles an hour they were presented as.

The next pitch came and Connell timed his swing a little too late and the ball smacked behind him with a fearsome *thwack*. The next pitch he foul-tipped, and the one after that he hit a tiny grounder on, and then the next one he sent on a line drive right back at the machine. It would have been a sure out, but it was nice to hit it with authority. His father let out a cheer behind him, and Connell promptly overswung on the next pitch, caught the handle on the ball and felt a stinging, ringing sensation in his hands and hopped in place, then swung through the next pitch entirely.

"Settle down, son," his father said. "You can hit these. Find the rhythm."

The next pitch, which he foul-tipped, was the last, and he stopped and put the bat between his legs and adjusted his batting glove. There wasn't a line forming behind him, so he could take his time. Balls pinged off bats in nearby cages and banged off piping or died in the nets. His father had his hands on the netting and was leaning against it.

"You ready?"

"Yeah."

"Go get 'em."

He put a coin in and took his stance. The first pitch buzzed past him and slammed into the backstop.

"Eye on the ball," his father said. "Watch it into the catcher's mitt. Watch this one. Don't swing."

He watched it zoom by.

"Now time it. It's coming again just like that. Same spot. This is all timing."

He took a big hack and fouled it off. He was getting tired quickly.

"Shorten your swing," his father said. "Just try to make contact."

He took another cut, a less vicious one, more controlled, and drilled it into what would have been the outfield. He did it again with the next pitch, and the one after that. The ball coming off the bat sounded like a melon getting crushed. The whole place smelled like burning rubber.

When the coins ran out, he held the bat out to his father. "You want to get in here?"

"No," his father said. "You have fun."

"I don't mind."

"I don't think I could hit a single pitch."

"Sure you could. You're selling yourself short."

"My best days are behind me," his father said.

"Why don't you take a few hacks? Come on, Dad. Just one coin."

"Fine," his father said. "But you can't laugh at me when I look like a scarecrow in there."

His father came into the cage and took the helmet from him. He took the bat, refused the batting glove. He was in a plaid, button-down shirt and jeans that fit him snugly, and Connell thought that he actually did look a little like a scarecrow. His glasses stuck out from the helmet like laboratory goggles. Connell stepped out of the cage and positioned himself where his father had been standing. His father dropped the coin in and took his place in the batter's box, the lefty side, Connell's side.

The first pitch slammed into the backstop. The next one did as well. His father had the bat on his shoulder. The next pitch came crashing in too.

"Aren't you going to swing?"

"I'm getting the timing," his father said.

The next pitch landed with a thud, and the following one went a little high and came at Connell. His father didn't offer at any of them.

"You have to swing sometime," Connell said. "Only three left."

"I'm watching the ball into the glove," he said. "I'm waiting for my pitch."

"Two left."

"Okay," his father said.

"*Dad*. You can't just stand there."

The last pitch came and his father took a vicious cut at it. The ball shot off like cannon fire and the bat came around to rest on his father's back in textbook form, Splendid Splinter form. The ball would have kept rising if it hadn't been arrested by the distant net, which it sank into at an impressive depth.

"Wow!"

"Not bad," his father said. "I think I'm going to quit while I'm ahead."

Connell went in and took the helmet and bat from his father, who looked tired, as if he'd been swinging for half an hour. He dropped the coin in and found the spot in the batter's box. His father's hit must have freed his confidence up, because he made solid contact on all but one of his swings, and then he put another coin in and started attacking the ball, crushing line drives.

"Attaboy," his father said.

He hit until he was tired, and they drove to the diner they liked to go to after the cages. Connell ordered a cheeseburger and his father ordered a tuna melt. They shared a chocolate shake. Connell drained his half and his father handed him his own to drink.

"That's okay, Dad."

"You drink it," his father said.

The food came and his father didn't really eat. Instead he seemed to be looking interestedly at Connell.

"What's up?" Connell asked.

"I used to love to watch you eat. I still do, I guess."

"Why?"

"When you were a baby, maybe two years old, you used to put a handful of food in your mouth and push it in with your palm. Like this." His father put his hand up to his mouth to show him. 'More meatballs!' you used to say. Your face would be covered in sauce. 'More meatballs.' You had this determined expression, like nothing was more important in the world." He was chuckling. "And you ate fast! And a lot. You used to ask for more. 'All gone!' you said. I used to love to watch you eat. I guess it was instinct. I knew you would survive if you ate. But part of it was just the pleasure you took in it. A grilled cheese sandwich cut into little squares. That was the whole world for you then. You getting it into your mouth was the only thing that mattered. You couldn't eat it fast enough."

His father was making him nervous watching him. He hadn't eaten any of his sandwich.

"You going to sit there and watch me the whole time?"

"No, I'm eating."

His father took a couple of bites. Connell called for more water and ketchup.

"I wish I could explain it to you," his father said after a while.

"What?"

"What it's like to have you. What it's like to have a son."

"You going to eat those fries?"

"They're all yours," his father said. Connell took some. "Eat as many as you like." His father slid the plate toward him. "Eat up."

17

She decided to scrap the intimate dinner they'd agreed upon for his fiftieth birthday and throw a full-scale surprise party instead. One thing it couldn't fail to do was get him off the couch for a night, but she wanted more than that: she wanted to wake him up, set him on the course to recovering his lost enthusiasm. He'd spent so much time alone lately that it would be good for him to be forced to mix with others.

Until she was drawing up the list for the party, she'd never noticed how weighted toward her side their social group was. So many of the friends they'd lost touch with were Ed's. When she considered her friends' husbands, she saw the same thing—a withdrawal, a ceding of the social calendar to the wife. It was her responsibility to ensure that her husband didn't get domesticated entirely. She would go beyond the usual crowd. She decided to track down some of the guys who were his regular buddies when they first got married and reach out to the cousins he never saw. She would remind him how much there was to look forward to.

She gave her garden box a full makeover, even though she knew the early-March chill would kill everything right after the party.

As she finished patting the soil down around a rosebush, a car zoomed past at a murderous clip bound for Northern Boulevard, salsa music pounding from its four-corner speakers. If she were a man she would have spat in disgust. She hated the driver; she hated the drug cartel he likely worked for; she hated worrying that people taking the train to the party might run into some kind of trouble. God forbid any of them got propositioned by the prostitutes that had begun to walk Roosevelt Avenue. One of them had approached Ed while Eileen and he were coming off the stairs holding hands.

She hoped that the NCB executives she'd invited wouldn't judge her for her current situation. Her career depended on their seeing her as the kind of person who belonged in their midst. How could she ever explain to them the way Jackson Heights used to be?

She didn't think of herself as racist. She was proud of her record of coming to the aid of black nurses who'd been unjustly targeted by superiors. She enjoyed an easy rapport with the security guards at NCB, most of whom were black.

She loved to tell the story of her father's stepping forward to drive with Mr. Washington when no one else would. She also enjoyed recounting the tale of how, when none of the old Irish guard would shop at the Chinese grocer up the block, and the new store was on the verge of failure, her father had paid the man a visit to take his measure. Satisfied that the man, Mr. Liu, was a hard worker and an honest proprietor, her father had stood for a few evenings on the corner near the grocer with the suspect vegetables and stopped people and said, "Go spend some money at the chink son of a bitch's place," and they'd listened. Now the whole of Woodside was Chinese grocers. She wondered if the newer generation would do for an Irish immigrant looking to make an honest living the same thing her father had done for one of their own years before. She wondered if some of the black nurses she'd helped along the way would lift a finger for a white woman in need. She'd watched the Bronx spiral downward over the years, and she hadn't flinched. The security guards marveled at her driving into the neighborhood alone every day. They never let her walk to her car unescorted at night.

No, she couldn't be called racist. That didn't mean she had to like what they were doing to her neighborhood. They were making it into a war zone.

The day of the party, her house had never seemed so small. An hour before Ed was supposed to arrive, there was barely room to pass in the halls; she had to ask her cousin Pat to carry a side table down to the basement. Still, as soon as people began assembling in the kitchen, she felt their presence as a kind of armor around her. She tended to the ham and the broccoli casserole in the stove and the separate duty of each pot on the stovetop. She had made nothing to offend anyone's palate, and so she presented it without anxiety. When the caterer arrived with trays containing more food than could possibly get eaten, she told herself it was safe to begin to relax.

When Connell called from a pay phone and said they were ten minutes away, she was surprised to find herself seized by terror. She passed the news to the living room, which filled with that clamor particular to a crowd silencing itself. A quiet grew louder than the din that had preceded it; she could almost hear her pulse in its murky depths. She moved through the wall of people to be near enough for him to see her when he entered.

As Ed stepped into the room, Eileen closed her eyes, obeying a strange compulsion not to look at his face. A frenzied chorus rang out around her. When she opened her eyes, she saw him beaming and being passed from person to person, shouting as he encountered every new face—shouts like war whoops that could have been either exultant or lunatic. He was red with excitement, and sweat was gathering on him. As she moved close to hug him, she heard him whoop the way he had for the others, as though he hadn't seen her in years. His whoops went on; they wouldn't die down. He greeted each successive person with the same ecstatic disbelief.

She was afraid to leave him, afraid to stay. She saw him engulfed in friends' arms and ducked into the kitchen to get him a drink. When she returned he was miming his own shock for them over and over. She didn't want anyone else to notice the unconvincing mirth in his performance. She shouted to Connell to cue the stereo. Ed was ushered into the dining room. In the mirror she tried to look at other people's reactions but was inexorably drawn back to her husband's expressions. When he saw his brother Phil in from Toronto, he let out a howl that sounded like that of a dying animal. She reached for a tray of hors d'oeuvres to pass. The food smells were mingling successfully; no trace of dust came off any surface she touched; nothing was out of place. The only messes were the ones guests were making themselves—someone bumped into the punch bowl and sent a couple of crystal mugs crashing to the floor—and for those she had great patience.

She poured herself a glass of wine and drifted into the living room, where she gave herself over to conversation. Behind the timbre of any individual voice lay the lovely murmur of the group, but she couldn't distract herself from the thought of her husband's frenzied surprise, and she went in search of him.

She went out on the stoop with Pat and the smokers and the kids, but no one had seen him come outside. The bathroom was locked, but after a little while her aunt Margie came out. She went down to the basement and searched its recesses, where she found no sign of him.

When she got back up to the landing at her back door, instead of heading inside she called up the stairs. There was no response, but she had an instinct to proceed upstairs anyway, and she found him sitting on the flight between the second and third floors, just sitting there, looking directly at her as she approached, in a way that unnerved her, as though he'd been waiting for her to find him. The music and talking muffled through the intervening flight rose and fell in waves, following the rhythm of its own respiration. There had been no dip in the revelry yet.

"Frank wants to take your picture," she said. "Fiona just got here. I don't know if you saw her."

He sat in silence, though he didn't look away.

"Pat's only here to see you. He doesn't go to parties anymore. You should have heard him when I finally got him on the phone. 'For Ed?' he said. 'Sure. Anything.'"

"Keep him away from the bar," Ed said.

"He won't even come inside," she said, chuckling. "He's on the stoop."

She could feel her eyes watering, though she wasn't consciously sad. "We're having a real party downstairs," she said. "It'd be even better if you were there."

He patted the spot beside him. The gentleness of the gesture touched her, and being moved when she was also angry confused her, so that she wanted to go back down alone, but she gave in, gathered her skirt under her and sat.

"I'm getting old," he said. "I can feel my body breaking down."

"You just feel that way because it's your birthday," she said. "Everyone gets old."

"I didn't expect to see all these people. I thought we'd have a quiet night."

She looked at him wryly. "Haven't we had enough quiet nights lately?"

"I don't even know half these people."

"You know almost every single one of them," she said. "There are maybe four people that you've never met."

"Then I don't remember them."

"Of course you do. I'll go around with you and start conversations and you can hear who they are that way."

He looked away.

"You love parties," she said. "You grumble and complain that I entertain too often, but once the party's going, no one enjoys it more than you. Those people are here to see you. I don't know what to tell them when they ask where you are."

"Tell them you saw me a second ago in the other room."

"What's wrong with you?"

"I'm tired. I can't tell you how tired I am. I'm tired of standing in front of a bunch of people and being the center of attention. Do you have any idea how much energy that takes? You're never off. *Never.* You can never have a bad day. I feel like I've been trying to keep all these juggling balls in the air, and I can't let them hit the ground or something bad will happen. I'd love to just lie down right now."

"Well, you can't. Everyone's here. We have to make the best of it. I'm sorry I did this."

"You don't need to be sorry."

"I am. This was a stupid idea. Stupid, stupid."

"I just need the school year to end," he said. "That's it. I can't tell you how much I'm looking forward to vacation. No summer classes for me this year, that's for sure. I'm just going to stay put."

Another day, she might have hissed at him to get off his ass and get down there, but something prevented her. She was about to say she'd come back and get him in five minutes when he slapped his knees and stood.

"Okay," he said. "Let's go."

Before they reentered the party, she ran down to the basement to grab a bottle from the rack.

"Wave this around when we get in there," she said. "In case anyone noticed you were gone."

Frank McGuire had the camera around his neck and called Ed over, as relieved as a retriever reassembling the pack. She watched him arrange the guys in a row in the dining room, the group waiting for him to focus, and then a moment of stillness that seemed to expand and breathe. She tried to memorize the scene—not the visual details, which she could recall later by looking at the photograph, but the mood, the nimble camaraderie, the way they clutched each other, the hint of annoyance at having to pose, the way afterward they laughed off the brush with intimacy. Every picture of men in a row, she thought, ended as this one did, with them expelled as if by force, dispersing into separate corners to get a drink, a plate of food, to smoke a cigarette. Ed looked vulnerable standing there in the lee tide. She decided not to leave his side for the rest of the party, and ushered him around with a subtle steering of her arm. He was a perfect sailboat, responding to the slightest tug on the line, tacking when she wanted him to tack, coming about when she wanted him to come about. She could feel him relax with her there, and soon she was having fun again. She had to resist her impulse to leave him and head to where the good conversations were taking place. She'd always considered it a luxury that she could count on her husband to entertain himself at parties. From across the room they would check in with each other with a wave, a nod, a wink, and a charge of desire would run through her as she watched the way women's eyes danced when they were near him. It was hard to see him as well up close; something was lost in the foreshortening.

Cindy Coakley brought the cake in. They sang "Happy Birthday" and Eileen put her hand on his back as he blew out the candles with a remarkable lack of wind, so that a few stray flames survived his second and even third attempts. The lights came on and Cindy passed him the knife. He stood for a moment brandishing it before him, and Eileen couldn't help finding something menacing in the image. She put her hand over his in what she hoped would look like an evocation of the gesture of unity with which they'd cut their wedding cake, and she pressed his hand down into the thin layer of frosting and the forbidding brick of ice cream beneath it. When she released her hand he struggled to free the knife from that frozen denseness and, failing, threw up his palms in defeat and took a step back from the cake. She laughed with an expression she hoped said something universal and vague about the uselessness of men and took his face in her hands and gave him a big, unrestrained kiss. To do so in front of all those people went against every ounce of culture she'd ever absorbed. He stiffened at first, but then he relaxed and let her kiss him. People began hooting and cheering. She let him go and pulled the knife from the cake and started serving little slices.

She hated to wake up to a messy house; it felt like paying a bill for something consumed without being savored. Still, when the last guest left, she went straight to bed. Ed slept on his back, inexorably flat. It was nearly her favorite thing about him. She'd read that it took confidence to sleep on one's back, because it exposed the internal organs. He'd always been confident in bed. She loved how small he made her feel, how she could nestle up to him and be enveloped in his reach. She thought of the first time they'd danced, her surprise at his size, which he had hidden in his overlarge jacket. He had a rangy athleticism that put him at ease in the company of men who made their living with their hands. He allowed her to bridge two worlds, the earthbound one she'd come from and the rarefied one she aspired to. And he was the only man in whose arms she'd ever been able to fall asleep.

In the morning, she fixed herself tea and got to work dispatching the pots and pans. When she'd cleaned the countertops and cabinet doors, she ran the mop over the kitchen floor, but her usual feeling of pride at the glossy shine and the piney scent didn't come. How had she tolerated the floor's permanently dingy linoleum this long? The wallpaper had bubbled up in places, and the joints in the window frames were so slack that the glass shifted like a loose tooth when the window was lifted. In the dining room she felt better for a while as she ran the rag over those stately pieces and breathed in the easy astringency of Murphy's Oil Soap, but soon the tarnish along the bottom edge of the wall-length mirror was all she could see. In the bathroom, she noticed places where the enamel had worn away in the tub, exposing the black beneath it.

She began to obsess over the details of her guests' attentions. Had they seen the stains on the rug under the ottoman? The evidence of rot on the vanity? She imagined them picking up objects and finding a layer of dust beneath.

She moved to the basement to clean the laundry room. She would have to have a talk with Brenda about the dryer sheets she always found in the machine and the empty detergent boxes she ended up throwing out herself. These little quality-of-life infractions added up to a diminishment of her happiness on the planet. When she was done, she moved to the storage shelves to organize those and decided she'd have to talk to Donny about keeping his tools better organized. Then came the cedar closets. This time she chided her own inattention, because a few of her favorite sweaters had been eaten through by moths. Then she went upstairs and started to give the grout between the bathroom tiles a proper scouring. When she looked up, Ed was standing in the doorway, Connell behind him. They were wearing their Sunday best.

"What are you doing?" she asked.

"We're going to Mass," Ed said. "Isn't that what we do on Sundays?"

"What time is it?"

"Four forty-five," Connell said.

She had missed every Mass except the five o'clock service. She felt them regarding her strangely and looked down at rubber gloves on hands that seemed to belong to someone else, one of which held a crumbling green sponge.

"Wait for me," she said, as she peeled them off and closed the door to freshen up.

18

Connell dreaded when the teacher left the room, because in that vacuum of authority he was subject to a tribunal of his peers. And so when Mrs. Ehrlich went to the bathroom during geography class and brought Laura Hollis up to the board to take names, Connell knew the general contours of what was coming. That day, Pete McCauley ran up to the blackboard and grabbed an eraser, missing badly when he threw it at him. Somebody in the rear made up for this errant toss by throwing a pencil, then another, the latter of which hit him in the back of his impassive head. The laughter in the room clattered like shutters in a howling wind. Even his nerd friends chuckled a little. Laura wrote nothing down, as Juan Castro stood by the door keeping the real watch. Pete retrieved the eraser and ran over and stamped it on his back. He couldn't get the chalk splotch off his blazer, though he rubbed at it the rest of the day.

He used to hang out with these kids. Most of them lived in apartments, so his backyard made him useful. They'd meet there, drop their bikes off. He'd go with them to Woolworth's to steal Binaca. He never stole it himself, but he went on the expeditions and spent the whole time fretting that he'd be grabbed by a guard. When they were just outside the front door, they'd pull it out conspicuously and spray it into their mouths like it was some kind of drug. They said they needed it for their girls. Shane Dunn and Pete McCauley claimed to have already had sex, and Connell had no reason to doubt them. Every summer at CYO camp there was at least one pregnant seventh- or eighth-grade girl riding the bus.

Then, in the spring of fourth grade, something happened that changed his life. One day they rode over to Seventy-Eighth Street Park because of some dispute Juan's older brother had gotten into. Connell found himself walking with his classmates and a bunch of older kids in a line, toward another group coming at them. He saw one of the kids on his side take out a knife, but he kept walking forward as though powerless to do anything else, and he was sure he was going to get stabbed in the melee to come. Then he heard sirens and everything slowed down and he could see it would end with him in the back of the squad car, his future ruined. The lines atomized in all directions. He ran with his friends to the bikes. They rode down Thirty-Fourth Avenue to his house. He pedaled furiously, his heart pounding in his chest, feeling like a crocodile was snapping at his heels.

After that, he hung out with the nerds in his special math group. Starting in fifth grade, he never got less than ninety-five on anything. He won the math bee twice, the spelling bee, the science fair. He didn't show people up when they were wrong the way John Ng did; he didn't crow about his accomplishments the way Elbert Lim did; but still he was everybody's favorite target, probably because he acted like a wooden soldier, sitting stiffly upright and barely ever turning his head. He wouldn't respond when kids tried to get his attention, because he didn't want to get in trouble with the teachers. He didn't let kids copy off his tests anymore. It didn't help that he was chubby. Starting when he was in third grade, the fat came on stealthily, as though in his sleep. Now, in eighth grade, he'd grown several inches, and the fat was hardening into muscle, but that didn't matter: he was the fat kid. Being the only one in his class to get into the best Catholic high school in the city made matters even worse. It felt like it'd be years before he ever got to kiss a girl. It was like the other kids smelled something on him. He used to talk to his father when he'd had a bad day. Now he just went to the basement and started lifting weights.

At lunchtime, he served a funeral Mass. He'd started serving funerals whenever he could, to avoid the cafeteria. He wasn't eating lunch anyway. When he did, sometimes he threw it up afterward. He wanted his muscles as tight as the skin on action figures.

The church was tall and long, and dark everywhere except the altar, which had spotlights and floodlights on it, especially the tabernacle. He liked to look at the faces in the pews. He was the best altar boy they had. He arrived early and knew the ceremony as well as the priests. He didn't sway the way other kids did when they stood holding the big book. He was a human podium. He offered the cramps in his legs and arms up to God.

Gym was his least favorite class, despite the fact that his athleticism made him a temporary asset to whoever his teammates were on a given day. Changing for gym was a nightmare. Someone sadistic had decided that they should wear their gym clothes under their uniforms and shed their outer layers in a proto-striptease. They peeled their uniforms off in front of each other, girls on one side of the auditorium, boys on the other. He made sure not to look across at the girls, because the fallout of being caught doing so by one of the other boys would be unspeakable. He couldn't look down or to the side either, because then someone might call him a fag. So he looked at the high ceiling, almost as tall as the one in church, and the high windows up at the ground level, which were always open and which made the outer world seem tantalizingly near.

There were a couple of minutes of milling around before Mr. Cotswald blew the whistle to start class. He kept to himself the way he had ever since the day he'd allowed himself to be hoisted up to the basketball hoop by Pete and Juan, who'd interlocked their fingers to make a step for each of his feet. Other kids had been getting lifted up there and getting the ball passed to them, and then dunking and dropping off, and since it looked like fun he'd let his guard down when Pete and Juan waved him over. Instead of passing him the ball, Shane had pulled his shorts and underwear down. He still felt weird about telling his parents it had happened to someone else. He still had no idea why he hadn't just dropped off the rim when they'd done it.

At the end of the day he sat in homeroom waiting for the bell. He wanted to spring to his feet when it rang, but he knew better than to let that happen again. Last week he jumped the gun on the okay-to-rise sign and the class erupted in laughter.

Mrs. Balarezo gave the signal for everyone to stand. Then she gave a second go sign to John Ng to lead the ordered procession out. Connell was at the head of the second row. He slid in behind Christina Hernandez and waded out into the sea of kids heading down the stairs. Thank God Ms. Balarezo sat him up front. It gave him a fighting chance to escape. It was the one good thing that had come of being singled out. A while ago she'd switched his and Kevin's desks. She didn't have to say why she was doing it; everybody knew he was getting murdered back there.

He got down the stairs and out to the street, no lingering, no talking to anyone. Passing through the gate he exhaled deeply. He loosened his tie, undid the button. He couldn't relax entirely. It was a long couple of blocks, each house feeling slightly safer than the last. The route was a fist slowly releasing its clench.

The first block was the avenue that ran along the school. It was a short stretch before he turned at Eighty-Third, and it should have been the safest one, with all the cars and adults around, and the church on the corner, but it wasn't; it was the worst. He walked past the rectory. Somehow they had all gotten there first, as if by teleportation, and were sitting on the steps. He felt them deciding his fate: Tommy, Gustavo, Kevin, Danny, Carlos, Shane, Pete. Danny lived on his block; that meant something—after school, anyway. At school, Danny was like everybody else. When they cracked jokes, he laughed louder than the others. He never hit Connell, though. He'd push him, but he wouldn't fight.

As Connell passed the church, his mind was afire. Did he do anything today to get their notice? Did he talk to a girl? Did he talk to anyone at all? Did he offend anybody by *not* talking? Anything was possible. He wanted to be invisible. If he could get to the corner unnoticed, and across the street, the chances of their following him home dropped, but then it was one and a half long side-street blocks, narrow ones, less busy, and he had to hurry. If they wanted to get him in that stretch, he was a man in the desert without a horse.

He crossed the avenue. Out of the corner of his eye he could see them following him. When he reached the other side, they were upon him. They surrounded him quickly, a phalanx closing its gaps. There was a moment of indecision, in which the fact of their outnumbering him seemed to hang in the air like a question. He thought they looked vulnerable in this in-between moment, as though they saw something absurd in the ritual of his submission. He imagined them calling the whole thing off, Danny saying, "Hey guys, let's forget about it," and then the group breaking up and walking home.

Sometimes lately he looked at them, even at times like this, and saw not bullies but lost children and, down the road, lost adults. He didn't know why he thought all this stuff, why he did laps around the block after dinner, saying hello to strangers and waving at old ladies perched on their stoops.

The hiccup of indecision passed. As though propelled by an electric wind, one kid shot out of the circle. Today it was Carlos Torres, quiet Carlos, disappearing Carlos, and the role was bigger than him, so he puffed himself up to fit it. He approached Connell awkwardly, jabbing at the air. Connell did his best to avoid the blows. He felt his shirt riding up on him, the buttons straining as he darted around. It was only a matter of time. The circle grew smaller and smaller. A stinging slap landed on his ear and he heard a deafening pop. The one thing he needed to do was hold on to his bookbag; God forbid they should get that from his grasp. Another smack landed hard on his face. The kids gaped in a kind of amazed half respect as they watched him take the blows. Then it turned to anger: why wouldn't he defend himself? He wondered too. He was bigger than them, stronger too. Maybe it was the fact that some of them carried knives to school. He saw them show them off. One recent graduate, whose older brother was in the Latin Kings, had become a legend for bringing in a gun. It would be nice to have an older brother, Connell thought sometimes: to be in a band of brothers that took on the world, instead of getting his solitary ass beaten to a pulp. It wasn't always fear that he felt, though, when he didn't fight back. It was something else, something mysterious.

His hands went up to cover his face and he felt a thud in his side. He was winded, and he focused on keeping his feet. If he fell he would have to cover his body with his arms, leave himself to their mercy and hope they didn't kick him in the head. Something about his keeping his feet kept them civil. He staggered around, Carlos screaming at him, growing in confidence with every blow he landed.

"Fight back!"

He looked to the blurry group for help. It was the same way he always looked at them, and he sensed something like sympathy in the way some of them looked back, but they were also revolted, and they joined Carlos in hectoring him.

"Fight, *maricón!*"

They pushed him into Carlos.

"Oh, snap, Carlos, you gonna take that?"

He kept his hands up.

"You wanna fight, huh? You wanna fight?"

"No," Connell said. "No."

He felt a fist explode in his gut and he doubled over. His stomach was burning, but the tears didn't come. He wasn't afraid for them to come. He had wanted to cry for a while, but he just couldn't.

Carlos was grinning maniacally. For a second he looked like he was sharing something with Connell, letting him in on a joke. "Fight back!" he screamed. "Faggot!" Connell saw the hatred in his eyes, tried to watch his hands. Carlos smacked him so hard that Connell could actually hear it resound, as though it had happened to someone else. The kids were startled. Connell staggered, and an adult, a stranger, came to break up the fight. Everyone scattered.

Connell let himself in with his key. He collapsed on the couch and awoke to the sound of his father coming home. He could hear him in the study, where he always stopped to drop his briefcase. Soon he would move to the living room. Connell didn't want to be on the couch when he walked in. He didn't want him to see any marks or bruises and start asking questions, but more importantly, he didn't want to deal with the weird negotiations that could ensue if he were there, his father hovering over him, waiting for Connell to move so that he could resume his headphoned isolation.

He thought of how he used to tell his father anything. His father knew how to make him feel better about things. He would hang on his father and cover his face and neck in kisses. It embarrassed him to think of it. He knew it wasn't as long ago as he liked to pretend.

He stood up. "I'm going out," he said to his father's back, which was bent over the desk. His father nodded wordlessly. He started walking up the block. He turned up Northern, heading toward Corona. He had started taking longer trips into areas he didn't feel safe in, but it didn't matter. He would walk until it was time go home and eat. He could feel the fat on him burning up with every step.

They sat through another dinnertime silence, every clinking fork magnified as though by a set of speakers. His parents' former banter had given way to remorseless, efficient eating, like that of lions after a hunt. A vague unease hung in the air, localized for Connell in the spot above the doorway where a pair of plaster doves sat perched on a heart, locked in a kiss. The doves were a wedding present from friends his parents had since lost touch with. They hung loosely on the nail and were dislodged by the slightest bump or bang. A year ago, one of those falls broke off a chunk of the heart. His father had Krazy-Glued it back together, and there were white cracks in the broken places. Connell wanted to take it off the wall, thrust it up under their noses, and say, "You see this! This is supposed to be you two! Lovebirds!"

The silvery clinks grew more frequent as the meal progressed, as though his parents were hurrying to dispatch the business of eating so they could return to the more complete nourishment provided by their private thoughts. His mother hadn't noticed that he'd slipped most of his fatty steak into the napkin in his lap. He would deposit it into the garbage when she wasn't looking.

His mother slapped her hands on the table. "Since when does this family have nothing to say to each other?" His father kept chewing, so Connell did too. They had a nice little solidarity going. His father was looking down at his plate. Connell tried to do the same, but he could feel his mother's eyes on him.

"Fine," she said. "I'll start. What about school? Any interesting assignments?"

Lately he'd felt called upon to drive the silences away. Never before had his comings and goings generated so much fodder. He felt perpetually on the verge of blurting out something embarrassing.

He shook his head.

"Okay," his mother said. "I've had enough of the both of you." She stood up to clear her plate.

"I'm writing an essay about Uncle Pat," he said. He hadn't wanted to mention it, because he resented the responsibility of keeping conversation alive in their family, but the assignment was real, and if it could bring his mother back to the table, it would take some pressure from his father.

"Why Uncle Pat?" his mother asked, resuming her seat.

Uncle Pat wasn't really his uncle. He was his mother's first cousin. He put Connell on stools in dark saloons and introduced him as "the Dude." He had a scar on his face from the time he stopped the mugging of an old lady. Wherever they went, Uncle Pat knew everyone.

"I have to find someone in my family with an interesting job," Connell said. "Go where this person works if possible, and write five hundred words about it."

"I'll tell you who has an interesting job. Your father does. You can watch him teach."

His father put down his knife and fork and looked up. "He doesn't want to watch me teach," he said firmly. "Let him follow Pat around the cages. He can learn some valuable lessons."

"Ed," she said.

"He can ask him why he's cleaning up canary poop after owning one of the most successful bars on the North Fork. He can ask him why we had to write a check to pay his state taxes last year."

"I'd rather you watched your father," his mother said.

"I can't watch Dad," he said. "It's due tomorrow."

"*Tomorrow*," she said, snorting. "That's just great. And when exactly were you planning on getting out to the Island?"

"I've seen the farm," he said. "I can just make it up."

"No, you can't. I won't let you avoid the research."

"Jeez."

"I'll call the school in the morning and say you're sick. You'll turn it in a day late."

"Cool! I'll take the train out to Uncle Pat."

"You're dreaming," his mother said. "You're going to the college with your father." She threw her napkin on her plate. "I'm going for a walk. I cooked, you two can clean."

He and his father exchanged glances as the front door slammed. His father didn't notice him emptying the napkin into the garbage.

Normally he needed a raging fever to stay home. People died on his mother's gurneys; a guy once died in her arms.

"Tomorrow's your lucky day," his father said flatly. "I don't teach until eleven."

Connell did a victory dance. He expected his father to laugh, but his father kept his head down and his hands plunged in the filmy water.

Connell awoke to the odd sensation of a motherless house and stumbled out to the study to find his father leaning over his desk writing something. He started to speak, but his father put up a hand to cut him off.

"Get in the shower."

He hadn't finished his cereal when his father told him to start the car. Connell loved to sit in the driver's seat when the engine was running. The rumbling under him spoke of power and freedom, as well as great potential for danger. If he shifted the gears incorrectly, he could go crashing through the new garage door, or back into a pedestrian on the sidewalk.

"Move over," his father said. "This isn't the time. And keep that thing off." He snapped at the radio knob before Connell could.

"Let me tell you about my students," he said after some silence. "They're tough." He had that look in his eye that he got when he was moved by something. "They're proud. They can spot a faker a mile away. They don't tolerate being treated like children. There's too much at stake for them."

Connell had no idea what his father was getting at.

"When we get to the lecture room, I'm going to introduce you, and I want you to sit in the back and listen. I don't want you to distract anyone.

I won't be able to talk to you, so you can't ask any questions. Please don't interrupt me, because I have to concentrate."

They arrived at the campus and parked in the garage. His father shut the engine off and sat still. He had his eyes closed and was taking deep breaths. Connell waited for something to happen. His father started rubbing his temples. After a while he opened his eyes and looked at him.

"You ready?"

"Yeah," Connell said.

His father reached to the back seat for his briefcase. "I was just doing a little relaxation ritual I have before I go in to teach."

It was hard to believe his father needed such a thing. He'd always projected such easy command, and there were plaques on the wall attesting to his excellence as a teacher.

He was looking for something in his briefcase, not finding it, and growing agitated. He pulled a pile of papers out in a panicked frenzy and rifled through them. In the close quarters of the front seat, Connell could almost hear his father's heart pounding. When he found what he was looking for, a legal pad, the heaving in his chest and the kinetic fury of his hands settled into an eerie stillness that overtook his whole body. Connell had no idea what to say. His father was staring straight ahead.

"It's nothing," his father said. "It's that you're here. I want everything to be perfect."

They walked through the campus, passing people his father knew. His father introduced him quickly, barely stopping to do so, even though the people sported those deliberate expressions of instant delight that all people, however curmudgeonly, were required to produce upon meeting the progeny of their colleagues. He was walking so fast that Connell had a hard time keeping up with him, and eventually he broke into a little trot, which prevented Connell from taking in the sights as he would have liked. It looked like one of those fancy campuses in movies, with buildings with august columns and stonework, not like a place for people hanging on by a hair.

"This is nice," Connell said.

"This campus was designed by a famous architect named Stanford

White," his father said automatically. "At one time, it was the Bronx satellite of New York University." His voice sounded distant, as though he were delivering a lecture. "When NYU built this campus, their chancellor said he wanted it to look like the American ideal of a college. In the early seventies, after it had gotten too expensive to maintain, NYU sold it to the State of New York, and we moved over here from the old Bronx High School of Science."

"Dad," he said.

"Yes?"

"Are we late?"

"No."

"Then why are we running?"

Something in his voice must have given his father pause, because his father stopped and put a hand on his shoulder.

"This isn't how I would have wanted this to go," he said. "Believe me. There's a lot here I wanted to show you. There's a beautiful overlook point called . . ." He rubbed his nose. "The Hall of Fame for Great Americans," he said after a few seconds. "You can see for miles up there. It has a lot of statues arranged in a circle around you. Maybe if everything goes well I can take you there after class."

They arrived at the building, but instead of marching directly into the lecture hall to a throng of expectant students, as his father's pace suggested they might have to do, they headed to his lab, where he closed the door behind him. His father told him to absorb himself in whatever he might find interesting, so long as he didn't break anything. He waved at a human skeleton suspended in the corner, a row of rat cages along the far wall, and a lonely assemblage of beakers and petri dishes. Then he took out his legal pad and paced back and forth, quietly reading aloud.

Connell left the beakers huddled in their fragile little gathering. He avoided the accusing eyes of the rats and hurried past the hollow ones of the skeleton. Finding nothing more promising, he circled back to tap on the glass of the rat cages and listen to what his father was reading.

"You can feed them if you want," his father said, gesturing to the rats, which almost seemed to listen along over his shoulder. "There's a bag of pellets in the drawer behind you."

"I'm okay," Connell said.

"I'm trying to focus," his father said, "and it would help if I didn't have to worry about you listening to every word."

His father searched around. "Here, take this," he said, tossing him an issue of *Scientific American*. Connell didn't like that magazine; they had a lot of them at home. His father was always drawing his attention to articles on black holes or glaciers or acid rain, but Connell stuck to *Sports Illustrated* and the "People" page in the back of *Time*.

"Why don't you sit outside and I'll come get you when I'm done?"

Connell wanted to tell him he didn't have to come to his stupid class at all if he wanted him gone that badly, but he held back. He did have to write the report. But something else told him not to make a big deal of it. "I'll just go to the class and wait for you," he said.

"Great," his father said, visibly relieved. "Two flights up. Room four forty-three. Introduce yourself."

As Connell left, his father was splashing water on his face in one of the sinks at the end of the long tables.

He took the stairs three at a time. The classroom door was open; he walked past it as casually as he could. The room was more full than he'd expected. How was he supposed to introduce himself to a room full of college students? He could barely get up in front of kids his own age without worrying about his voice betraying him with squeaks and squawks.

He mimed absorption in a bulletin board, then doubled back, passing the room again. The floor sloped upward from the front, so that the people at the back stared down from a lofty perch. A box on the wall taunted him: In Case of Emergency, Break Glass. The words took on a sudden poignancy; he would've been helpless even with an axe in his hand. He was beginning to see the wisdom in his father's having prepared a speech.

He stepped into the room and hustled to one of the empty seats in the back. He waited for the thumping in his chest to subside. They could figure out who he was for themselves if they cared so much.

When his father walked in, he didn't look up but headed for the podium and started reading from his pad.

"Today we are going to begin our discussion of the central nervous system," he said. "I have quite a bit of material to cover, and it is crucial that you assimilate this material for the final exam, so I would ask you to take careful notes, because I will not be able to repeat myself or interrupt the lecture to answer questions. Should you happen to find yourself confused at any point, please write your questions on a sheet of paper to hand to me at the end of class, and I will provide you with a written response when we meet on Thursday. Additionally, I am sorry to report that, due to the demands of a long-term research project, I will be forced to cancel office hours for the remainder of the semester."

The room erupted in incredulous groans. His father didn't look up but only held his finger on the page and waited for the furor to die down.

"At the end of each remaining class session, I will collect your questions. After I do so, I will pass out the detailed responses I have written to your earlier questions. Writing these responses will come at the expense of a considerable amount of my time, so I hope you will rest assured that any lost office hours will be more than adequately compensated for in this fashion. If on occasion I appear sluggish or distracted, or seem to need a second to compose myself, be aware that I am likely exhausted from the busy schedule I am keeping.

"One other point of note. Beginning today, I will be reading exclusively from prepared lectures and leave off answering or posing questions. In recent class sessions, we have covered comparatively less material than we did in the earlier part of the course, as you are all no doubt aware."

There were murmurs of acknowledgment, though his father didn't stop to notice them.

"I ask your forgiveness for the relatively inert nature of my presentation of the material from now on, but I assure you that a certain briskness is vital to your being adequately prepared for the final examination. And so, without further ado, I would like to begin."

When his father walked in, an indignant chatter had percolated throughout the room. At the beginning of his speech, a few students scanned the room for the reactions of others, but now several who didn't have notebooks out before took them out, and many pens were poised over pages.

He began.

"The central nervous system," he said, "represents the largest part of the nervous system. It consists of the brain and the spinal cord. Along with the peripheral nervous system, which we will learn about later, the central nervous system plays an essential role in the control of behavior."

All around Connell, people were writing down everything he said.

"The central nervous system is contained within an area known as the dorsal cavity, which can be broken down into two subcavities, the cranial and the spinal. The cranial cavity contains the brain, while the spinal cavity contains the spinal cord."

A few hands went up; it was evidently a hard habit to break immediately. If his father saw them out of the corner of his eye, he didn't give any indication. He flipped pages in his pad as he read.

"The central nervous system is protected by an elegant, two-tiered system. First, both the brain and the spinal cord are enveloped in a sheath of membranes known as the meninges. The meninges are three continuous sheets of connective tissue. From the outside in, these sheets are known as the dura mater, the arachnoid mater, and the pia mater."

The students seemed confused. Most had stopped writing. They were looking at each other and adding their hands to the gathering chorus in the air.

"The second tier of protection of the central nervous system is provided by bone. The brain is protected by the skull, while the spinal cord is protected by the vertebrae."

Now most of the class had its hands raised. His father had said he didn't want questions, but Connell was sure that if he knew how many hands were up, he would want to clear up the point so everyone could move along.

"The brain receives sensory input from the spinal cord as well as from its own nerves—which we will name and discuss later. It dedicates most of its capacity to processing sensory inputs and instigating motor outputs."

He had to think of something. His father obviously couldn't hear the grumbling that had overtaken the class. He was in some kind of zone. No one was taking notes anymore. Connell didn't want to anger him, but he knew his father would thank him later if he helped him solve this problem now.

His fingers tingled as he stood and felt everyone turn to face him. All he wanted to do was get his father to look up from the page. He cleared his throat.

"Dad!" he said sharply.

His father must not have heard him, or if he did, he must not have understood the seriousness of the situation. Connell wanted to sit back down, but now he couldn't. He felt short of breath.

"The spinal cord serves three main functions," his father went on. "It conducts sensory information from the peripheral nervous system to the brain. It conducts motor information from the brain to various effectors. And it serves as a minor reflex center."

"Dad!" he said again, this time more emphatically. "Dad!"

His father looked right at him. It felt as if they were the only two people in the room. All the hands in the air fell at once. His father looked around at the faces staring back at him. Everyone seemed to wait to see what would happen next. His father bent over the pad again. As he did so, hands shot up all over the room. Voices called out.

"Professor Leary!"

"Professor!"

But he didn't hear them. "The second tier of protection of the central nervous system," he said, to a round of groans, "is provided by bone." One man hopped in his seat, as if he were about to run up and tackle him away from the lectern.

"The brain is protected by the skull . . ."

Connell knew he had heard this already.

"What is this shit?" the hopping man asked.

"Hello!" shouted a lady a few rows up. "You can't just *ignore* us here."

Connell had seen his father determined before. When he wanted to do something, when he really wanted to do it, he put his head down and got it done.

A growing outcry was filling the room, so that you could barely hear him reading.

"Dad!" Connell shouted. "*Dad!*"

His father stopped again. This time he backed away from the pad and the lectern. Connell saw the pages he'd folded under the bottom flip back onto the pad. His father looked at him again in that uncanny way, as if Connell was the only other person there. He backed up to his briefcase and squeezed the handle as though to keep it away from someone trying to snatch it from him. Then he seemed to recover a bit and approached the podium again. Connell sat down.

"Today we are going to begin our discussion of the central nervous system," he said. He stopped talking and looked around at the room. They were eerily quiet. Connell was desperate for someone to say something. He knew he couldn't do it himself.

After a few seconds, his father gestured to a woman in the front who had been taking notes through the chaos.

"Karen," he said. "Karen? Is that right?"

"Yes, Professor Leary."

"Karen, if you don't mind, would you tell me where I left off?"

"You had just finished telling us that the spinal cord serves as a minor reflex center."

"Okay," he said. "That's good. That's good. Thank you. That's exactly what I needed. The spinal cord as a reflex center."

He flipped through the pad furiously. When he had gone through all the pages, he flipped back through them again so hard that it looked like he might rip them off.

"You see," he said. "I'm tired. I've been working hard. And there's a lot on my mind. In fact, there's something specific on my mind that's distracting me, and I hope you'll forgive me for letting it get in the way today. If you'll all turn and look, you'll see my son at the back of the room."

Connell could feel the blood rush to his cheeks.

"My son came along with me, as you can see," his father said. "Today is an important day for him." His father was looking directly at him. "Isn't it, son?"

He was going to make him talk about the project.

"Yes," Connell said.

"Today's his birthday," his father said.

Everyone was staring at him. It had been almost a month since his birthday. He could see it all: the metal bat, the batting gloves, the high-end tee, the netting, the boxes of balls, the bucket to keep them in; heading out into the cold and the whipping wind after dinner and setting up at the back of the driveway; under the moon, in the quiet of the evening, slamming balls into the net and delighting in the *ping* produced by a ball squarely struck.

The faces smiled. He heard a volley of clucking. One lady near him asked him how old he was.

"I'm fourteen," he said.

"Fourteen today," his father said. "And he's been such a good kid, waiting for me. You see, we're going to the Mets game right after this class. Opening Day. And I've had that in the back of my mind. I've been worried about the traffic. We're going to be cutting it a little close. So I apologize for not being all here today. Really, if I'm being honest with myself, I should ask you all if you wouldn't mind if we just ended class early and made up for it next week. I realize some of you have come from far away. Would you forgive me if we canceled today's class and made it up next time?"

The students looked around at each other. Some grumbled; one man slapped his desk in frustration, yelled "Bullshit!" and walked out. Others shrugged.

"Good. Good. That's great," his father said. "Then we'll end class now."

They started packing up their stuff. "I'll draw up a handout explaining in depth what I was going to go through today, and I'll spend a little time at the beginning of next class taking you through it point by point." He picked up the briefcase from the floor and began gathering his things. "Thank you all," he said, over the rustle of bags and jackets. "This is kind of you. I apologize for imposing on your time like this."

Some of them wished Connell a happy birthday as they left. His father waved them out the door. Connell remained seated until everyone had gone. He walked up to the front of the room. His father stood facing the blackboard, his hands on the chalkwell. Connell could see his shoulders rising and falling.

"I have to pee," Connell said, though he didn't really have to.

In the bathroom, he looked in the mirror. He lifted his shirt up, then took

it off and flexed with both arms. There was more mass and definition. He brought his fists to his ears and squeezed his muscles like Hulk Hogan. He smiled a big, crazy smile with lots of teeth. He drew close to the mirror, leaned his forehead against it. His breath collected on it and evaporated. He slapped at the little bit of baby fat still on his stomach, hard enough to leave a red mark.

"Go away," he said. "Go away!" Then he started to worry that someone would walk in on him.

He put his shirt on and went back out. They walked to the car in silence.

"I don't have tickets to the game," his father said after they'd been driving awhile. "We can still go. We can try to get in."

"We don't have to."

"It might be hard to get tickets."

"Yeah."

"I was thinking we could go watch some planes."

Connell turned the radio on and the volume up a few clicks. He watched his father's face for flickers of anger, but his father didn't seem to notice the change in volume. Connell turned it up even more. His father's hand shot to the knob.

"That's too loud," he said. "Not too loud."

It was lower now than it had been before he raised it the first time, but he didn't want to chance it. He looked out the window.

"Hey, Dad?"

"What?"

"What was all that about?"

"I just didn't feel like teaching today."

"Why did you say it was my birthday?"

He could see his father's face reddening, his hands gripping the whee tighter.

"Don't you think I know my own son's birthday? It's March thirteen' His father took a deep breath. "I just wanted everything to go perfec wanted you to have good material for your project."

"You seemed confused."

"I was fine!" he shouted. "That's the end of it! I wanted thing

well while you were there. I've never had you in the classroom with me before. End of discussion!"

The pitch in his voice rose along with the volume, and his words became a kind of shrieking. Then he stopped and his breathing settled down.

"I didn't want to be cooped up inside today," he said.

They drove in silence.

"I'm sorry about your project," he said. "Maybe you can come back and watch me sometime."

"It's all right," Connell said. "I can make it up. I already know what kind of teacher you are. You teach me every day."

They drove back to Queens, heading to the strip of grass they'd come to call their own, along a road that led to LaGuardia Airport. When they parked, his father turned to him.

"Can you do me a favor? Can you not tell your mother about this?"

"Coming here?"

"No. The other thing."

"Sure. Sure."

"She won't understand it the way you do."

They walked to the fence near one of the landing strips. In the distance, Connell could see planes coming in in a line, separated by long intervals. Planes took off around them; engines roared. They stood there dwarfed by arrivals and departures. His father's arm was around him, and his own fingers clung to the chain-link fence.

They listened to the game on the way back. When they got home, instead of putting a record on and breaking out the headphones, his father put the game on the radio and they sat on the couch listening to it. The Mets beat the Phillies by a run, Gooden throwing eight solid innings and Franco nailing down the save.

He thought about telling his mother how weird it had been, but so much about his father was weird that it was hard to say where the weirdness began and ended. It wasn't a generation gap so much as a chasm that had opened up and swallowed a whole lifetime. Instead of hanging out with the flower children, his father had haunted laboratories and listened to

a disturbance." He took one arm out of his jacket slowly, then the other. He had cut the entire rear panel from what looked like an expensive shirt. The sleeves clung to the shirt's outline like windsocks in a strong gust. His skin was a blank, ridiculous canvas flecked by freckles and scraggly hairs. For a moment, the room seemed suspended in time.

"Is this what you wanted?" he asked. "To see this? Does this make you happy? Behold, then!"

Then Jack let out a bark of laughter so loud and sudden it could have been a death rattle; another followed to punctuate it; then his laughs came quick and plentiful, like the little skips a stone makes on the water's surface after the first big few. The laughter was passed around the room like a contagion.

"Sit down at this goddamned table and eat some of my turkey, you goofy son of a bitch," Jack said after he'd composed himself. The look on Jack's face said he'd charge into battle for Connell's father if he had to. Connell had seen people give his father that look before. Maybe you had to be an adult to really appreciate him.

That fall, he had made Connell do a project on habituation for the science fair. They tapped a bunch of roly-poly bugs a number of times with a pen. Some stopped rolling up quickly; the rest just kept getting annoyed. Eventually they all quit responding. This was supposed to be extremely significant, the fact that they could learn to ignore millions of years of inherited instincts after five minutes of pointless irritation. Connell gathered the data; his father helped him draw up the findings on a couple of poster boards—charts, graphs, everything low-tech. When he arrived at the auditorium, Connell knew he didn't stand a chance. Other kids were setting up huge working volcanoes, radio-controlled cars, and full ecosystems with convoluted loops that ran the length of two tables. He didn't even have a box full of bugs. When the teachers came around for the presentation, he started sweating. He explained the way they—*he*—had gone about it, as best as he understood it, which was less than he should have.

In awarding him first prize, they cited the project's elegant simplicity and its careful application of the scientific method. Other parents hooted and hollered when their children's names were announced. His father kept

Bing Crosby. He loved foreign languages and corny puns. How often, when Connell reached for another helping at breakfast, did his father stop his hand and ask him in mock earnest if one egg wasn't *un oeuf*?

Who could forget the events of that past Thanksgiving? They went to the Coakleys. The Coakleys used to live a few blocks away in a three-family house like their own; now they lived on Long Island, in a house with plush carpets and a low-lit den that had a couch on all sides and a large television perfect for watching the game. Cindy Coakley had been his mother's friend since first grade at St. Sebastian's.

His parents were getting ready in their bedroom. Connell was lying on his bed reading. The radio was on in the living room; his parents must have thought he was out there listening to it, because his mother started laughing in a girlish way that made him feel as if he was hearing something he wasn't supposed to be hearing. He crept to his door.

"Oh, Ed," he heard her say. "Don't do it!"

"Why not? I think it's a great idea."

"It's a *terrible* idea," she said, but the delight in her voice said otherwise. "I insist—no, I *demand*—that you not do this."

"I'm doing it," he said. "Here I go."

"Ed!" she squealed. "That's brand new!"

It wasn't strange to hear them laughing, but this was different; this was playful. Around him they laughed like parents, with a certain restraint. He had never heard his mother sound so young.

"How does that look?" his father asked.

"You are not going to show that to anybody. Do you hear me?"

"You're afraid the women won't be able to handle it," he said. "You think they'll swoon."

A few seconds passed in silence. He went right up to their closed door, his heart pounding in his chest. He heard some muffled sounds.

"We don't have time," his mother said, but she sounded as if she was saying they had all the time in the world.

She made little moaning noises. Connell's blood ran cold. He had never seen them kiss on the lips, and yet there they were, kissing and doing God knew what else. He thought of all the times he'd watched Jack Coakley pull Cindy to him in brute affection, the times he'd silently urged his father to sweep his mother up in his arms in front of everyone.

"We'd better get going," his mother said. He heard the sound of the zipper on her dress.

"Maybe I'll give Jack a laugh. He needs a laugh."

Connell dashed back to his room. When his parents emerged, he watched for some sign of the mischief he had heard them discussing, but there was nothing.

They drove in a pleasant silence to the Northern State Parkway and the Coakleys. The men watched football in the den while the women talked and transferred food from pots to serving dishes. The dining room table was set with good silver and wineglasses, salt and pepper in sterling silver shakers, and two layers of tablecloths. As everyone trickled in, Connell was already at the table, looking forward to the painful bloat about to overtake him. After the meal, he would sit on the couch with the rest of the men and pat his swollen belly, burping quietly.

Jack carved the turkey. Everyone began passing dishes.

"Ed," Jack said. "Why don't you take your jacket off? Join us awhile." Everybody knew what was coming.

"I can't," Connell's father said. "There's no back to this shirt."

A little wave of laughter passed over the table. Connell felt his face redden. They played this routine out every year. Connell didn't care if everyone else was amused by the line; why did his father have to be so weird? He was the only one in a suit; everyone else wore sweaters and khakis. Even on the hottest days of summer he wore long-sleeved shirts and pants. Connell didn't care about his warnings about skin cancer and the shrinking ozone layer. All he knew was his father looked like a dork.

"You know, Ed," Jack said. "You always say that. What does that mean? What are you trying to tell me?"

Jack was six-four, two-fifty, an ex-Marine. When they watched the game in Jack's den, it wasn't hard to imagine Jack on the field protecting the quarterback. In a booming voice, he told stories that ended in uproarious laughter; Connell's father spoke gently and people leaned in to hear him. Jack's face lit up whenever Connell's father talked, but Connell always

wanted his father to finish quickly; he was nervous that Jack would see how strange his father really was.

"Just that the shirt I'm wearing happens not to have a back, and so I can't take my jacket off."

"Now why would a shirt not come with a back?"

"It's cheaper this way," his father said. "Less material."

"I don't think anyone here would have a problem with seeing your back," Jack said with an odd edge in his voice. He turned to Frank McGuire. "Do you have a problem with seeing Ed's back?"

Frank looked back and forth between Connell's father and Jack, like he didn't know what the right answer was. He broke into nervous laughter. "Come on, guys," he said. "He wants to wear his jacket, he wants to wear his jacket. It's Thanksgiving."

"I realize he wants to wear his jacket, Frank. But I'm asking him to take it off. He's making me nervous."

"Is that what you want? You want me to take my jacket off?"

Jack was giving Connell's father a hard look. Cindy, who had only belatedly caught on to the tension in the scene, as though it were occurring on a frequency only dogs could hear, put a hand on Jack's arm in a silent plea.

"Yes," Jack said. "That's what I want."

"Well, it is your house."

"Last time I checked it still was."

"Jack!" Cindy said.

Even Connell's mother, who had been smiling at the outset, l[...] concerned. Connell wasn't supposed to know what his parents bot[...] which was that Jack's airline was planning major cuts and Jack [...] ried about getting laid off. At night Connell stood in the dark[...] of his room, listening down the hall to his mother on the p[...] kitchen.

"It's okay, Cindy," Connell's father said. "This jacket is re[...] you, huh?"

"Nobody else has a jacket on."

"Okay," his father said, rising. "I understand. I'm so[...]

his seat and gave him a cool little nod and pumped his fist. Connell was never more impressed by him in his life. It was as if his father had known all along that they were playing a winning hand.

When his mother got home, she pulled him aside. "What was it like at Daddy's school?" she asked. "How was he?" Her expression was strangely intense, and she was practically whispering. Connell was so unnerved that he almost said something. Then he remembered his promise.

"Dad was Dad," he said. "I didn't understand a word he was saying."

19

An article in a nursing journal said that a fixed routine had a deleterious effect on the mind of a person prone to depression and that shaking up elements of a depressive's environment could be a productive way to introduce treatment. She didn't know for sure that Ed was technically depressed, but she knew she'd never be able to get him to a psychiatrist to find out.

What Ed needed—what they all needed—was to climb out of a rut. She started to wonder whether a move to another house might not be just the thing to jolt him out of his torpor. The timing was right: Connell was starting high school next year and could commute into the city from almost anywhere; the value of their home, given the encroaching neighborhood decay, would only go down. In a few years, they'd be trapped.

A house could make all the difference. Things improved for the Coakleys after Jack got promoted to director of cargo for SAS and they moved out to East Meadow. Jack had shown some signs of depression himself when they were still in Jackson Heights, but in East Meadow he started making furniture in his big garage and got into gardening and landscaping. He established an idyll in their backyard for all to enjoy: the echoing pool, the radio raised to drown out the rattle of distant mowers, wet footprints drying on hot concrete, the ubiquitous smell of sunblock.

It had been five years since she'd raised the rate on the already far-below-market rent she charged the Orlandos, and even then she'd raised it only a pittance. The knowledge that her son was safe had always offset in her mind the revenue she'd lost by floating the Orlando clan. Connell went up to one or the other of their apartments after school and stayed until she and Ed came home. Now that he was getting old enough to take care of himself, though, the protection they offered meant less than it once had.

"I've been thinking about this house," she said. Connell was having dinner at Farshid's, and they were alone at the dinner table. Ed didn't respond. She'd gotten used to these one-sided exchanges. She'd learned to read different meanings into his silences. That night's silence was auspicious; it lacked the heaviness of other varieties. It was like a sheet she could project her thoughts onto.

"I've been thinking that it might be nice to have a place of our own, where we don't have renters. I'm tired of being a landlord. Aren't you?" She filled a plate with chicken, potatoes, and steamed green beans and handed it back to him. It looked bland, but it was just the two of them, and Ed never seemed to care either way.

"This is our home," he said.

"I know," she said. "I was just thinking we could look for a place that would be . . . *more* ours."

"We've done a lot of work on this house." Ed cut into his chicken. Rather than cut a small bite, he sawed it in the middle until it was in two halves.

"You're happy here?"

"I am." He began cutting the halves in half, his head into his work.

"You're not happy," she said. "You're miserable. You won't get off the couch."

"I'm happy."

"We could move to the suburbs. Get a nice house."

"We have a nice house right here." He looked up at her for the first time. His chicken was arranged in a neat mosaic of bite-sized pieces, but he hadn't begun to eat.

"This neighborhood is going to hell."

"I'm a city boy," he said. "All those empty streets. All the space between houses." He gestured dismissively with his fork.

Space between houses was all she wanted in the world.

"Wouldn't it be nice to get out of here? Start somewhere else? The timing is perfect. Connell's starting a new school next year. We've saved so well."

"This place is a lot better than what I had growing up," Ed said.

"Yes," she said. "You're right about that."

She hated being made to feel churlish. She wasn't looking for a palace, just a step up from where they were. It was for him that she was thinking of all this, but how could she talk to him about it without alerting him to her line of reasoning?

"I don't want to have anyone walking over my head anymore," she said.

"We'll switch apartments with Lena. She'd jump at it. Those stairs probably kill her."

She gave him a withering look. His green beans were all cut in half now too.

"Our life is here," he said.

"Wouldn't you like to get to know another neighborhood?"

"I don't want to be isolated," he said. "I don't want to have to get used to a whole new way of life."

She bit her tongue, then said it anyway. "You already have a whole new way of life."

She watched him finally begin to move some food into his mouth and chew it slowly, as if considering the mechanics of chewing anew. It was driving her crazy. She put her knife and fork down and waited.

"We can't afford to move where you want to move," he said, but it was as if he wasn't in the conversation anymore, so caught up was he in bringing small bites to his mouth, gnashing them between his teeth, and swallowing.

"You don't know the first thing about where I want to move," she said bitterly.

She had long ago stopped concerning herself with the details of their money management. They had a common bank account that he balanced fastidiously. He also handled their investments. Since he was conservative in his portfolio choices (the First Jersey Securities investment had been her idea, based on a tip she'd gotten from a doctor at work; Ed had reluctantly agreed to it), they'd seldom suffered the effects of overexposure, and they were in a strong position relative to peers of similar or even greater income. This was one decision, however, that she couldn't afford to let him control. If she couldn't get him excited about this project, she would have to generate enough excitement for both of them.

She began searching through the listings in Bronxville.

"This place looks perfect," she said, as she showed Ed an open house notice in the newspaper.

"You know how I feel about this."

"Humor me. It's on Saturday. We'll make a day of it."

"I've got something lined up for us for then."

He almost never made plans. She couldn't help but smile at the obvious ploy.

"Do tell," she said.

"Mets tickets," he said.

"You've *bought* these tickets? It *has* to be this Saturday?"

"Somebody at work is holding them for me. I said I had to check with my wife's schedule."

Such a hopeful look came over his face, as if he really thought she hadn't seen through his ruse, that she couldn't bring herself to argue. The next night he showed off the tickets, undoubtedly purchased at the stadium on the way home from work. He'd even bought four, the unnecessary fourth there to lend verisimilitude to the bit of theater.

Saturday came. It was a sunny, mild day in early May, and, she had to admit, a perfect day for a game. With the other ticket, Connell brought Farshid. On the 7 train, adults in the infantilizing garments of fandom buzzed with an adolescent excess of energy. When the doors opened at Willets Point, she felt carried along by the buoyancy of the crowd. Instead of following the switchback ramp to the top as they usually did, though, they stopped after a single flight. When they emerged from the corridor and were flooded with light, they saw that the players looked unusually life-sized.

The boys took their seats with palpable pride at being envied from above. Batting practice was still going on, and they got their gloves out. Connell never failed to bring his glove to games and wear it for hours in an uncomfortable vigil, despite having never come close to snagging a ball; they were always in the wrong seats. On the lower level, though, having a glove was good planning.

Ed took their orders and went for refreshments. In the absence of his moderating influence, the boys fired fusillades of obscure terms at each other: *hot smash, can of corn, high and tight, round the horn, hot corner, filthy stuff, the hook.* As she listened to them speak, a meditative calm came over her. She did some of her best thinking at ball games, or while Ed was listening to them on the radio. She'd always understood the basic mechanics of baseball, and Ed had successfully explained a good deal of the more complex aspects to her, but she'd never cracked the code of the priestly solemnity her husband and son greeted the game with, in which old bats and split-leather gloves were revered like relics, as saints' fingers and spleens had been in earlier centuries. In truth, she was impressed by the range of her son's knowledge. It was an arrested form of scholarship he was practicing when he allowed his brain to soak up these facts. It was really history men craved when they fixated on the statistics of retired athletes—men who hadn't been to war, in a nation still young enough to feel dwarfed by the epochal moments of its onetime rivals. The rhetoric of baseball was redolent of antiquity, the hushed tones, the gravitas, the elevation of the pedestrian into the sublime. Connell and Ed would read write-ups of games they'd watched or listened to on the radio, even ones they'd attended. The narrative that surrounded the game seemed as important as the game itself. Ed raved about the descriptive power of some sportswriters, but she never saw what he was talking about; it seemed like boilerplate stuff, dressed up as the chronicle of an epic clash. She focused on the visceral particulars of the stadium experience instead: the smell of boiled meat, nestled under sauerkraut; the thunder of the scoreboard exhorting them to clap; the feel of her son's hand as he slapped her five.

Ed had been gone a long time. She panned around for his Members Only jacket. After some restless searching she spotted him a section over, leaning into the railing, staring around with his hand over his eyes like a lookout in a crow's nest. She had his ticket stub in her pocket, so he couldn't show it to the ushers, one of whom was trying to move him along. She could see Ed growing agitated as he swatted a second usher's hand from his shoulder. She hated making a spectacle of herself, but any second now the guards would be called, and that would create an even bigger scene. She stood and shouted his name, waving her arms. He finally saw her and broke free of the ushers, who gave no chase, seeing order restored. He made his way down the aisle encumbered by trays; she distributed the quarry to the boys.

He stood in front of his seat. "Where the hell were you?"

She stole a glance around to see who was listening. "I was right here," she said, trying to urge him toward calm. No one had cocked an ear yet, but she and Ed were on the border of a full-on commotion.

"I couldn't find you," he said sharply.

"I realize that, honey. But you're here now."

"I was looking all over for you."

"Ed," she said. "I'm here. You're here. Enjoy the game."

The boys were too caught up in the food to notice Ed. He still hadn't taken his seat but was standing looking into the crowd as if the answer to what confounded him were projected on the backs of their heads. Farshid listlessly fingered a waxy-looking pretzel. Connell wolfed down a hot dog in two bites and started in on his own pretzel. When she picked up on annoyance behind her, she tugged on Ed's sleeve and he fell into the seat and began to smooth out his pants with an insistent repetitiveness, as though trying to warm himself or clear crumbs from his lap. He had bought nothing for the two of them to eat.

"Where's the food for us?"

"I didn't get us anything."

She shook her head in disbelief. "What are we going to eat?"

"You didn't ask for anything."

"I have to *ask* to eat now?" She took a piece of Connell's pretzel.

"Hang on," he said. A hot dog salesman had entered their section, and Ed flagged him down.

"I feel like you don't *think* anymore," she said when they were settled in with their dogs. "I need you to get with it, Ed."

"Let's just enjoy the game," he said.

A couple of innings later, a Met lifted a high foul ball toward their section. She could feel it gaining on them. As it approached, time seemed to slow; an awful expectancy built. It shifted in the wind, so that it appeared to be headed elsewhere; then it was upon them. People all around reached for it, but it was headed right for Ed. He stabbed at it clumsily and it bounded out of his hand, snagged by a man behind them in the ensuing scrum.

For a moment, Connell appeared stunned. He had been brushed on the neck by the hand of destiny. His body seemed to shiver with contained nervous energy, and he hopped like a bead of oil in a saucepan.

"Wow!" he said, to her, to his father, to Farshid, to anyone who would listen. "Can you believe it?"

The victorious fan stared into empty space with a determined expression as he received the forceful backslaps of his friends. His studied lack of fanfare had the effect of holding the note of his triumph longer.

Ed was miserable. "I'm sorry, buddy," he said. "I tried to get it for you."

"No problem, Dad."

"I'm really sorry." He looked bereft. "I feel terrible."

"Maybe if you'd had a glove," Connell said sweetly, extending his own. Ed turned and asked if the boy could see the ball, which the man handed over more warily than Eileen thought appropriate. Connell held it covetously. She worried that he might ask to keep it, but after a few moments in which he seemed to communicate wordlessly with it, he gave it back, and the man secreted it into his jacket pocket. Something about these talismanic objects, spoils of an ersatz war, reduced men to primal feelings. Connell pounded his glove every time a foul ball was hit in their general direction, no matter how far away it was, and she could think of nothing to say to stop him.

20

She sat beside Connell on the top step, wondering about all the fuss people made over the constellations. The webs of light poorly described the forms they were meant to evoke, and even if she'd known what those forms were, she doubted she could have suspended her disbelief enough to see them characterized there.

On an average night the stars glimmered weakly, if they were visible at all, but that night they were unusually prominent. This was another reason to move—maybe in the suburbs he could see the stars well all the time.

"What do you see?" she asked.

"A lot of stars," he said. "What about you?"

"There's the Big Dipper," she said.

"And the Little Dipper."

"Yes."

"And the North Star."

"Yup."

They had come to the limit of their knowledge. She was relieved to have a son who didn't spew forth a stream of facts about the sky when he looked up at it. One fear in marrying a scientist had been that her children would be ill-equipped to live in the world of ordinary men.

"I like to imagine people thousands of years ago looking at the same stars," he said.

She smiled at his philosophical tone.

"And people in the future long after we're dead," he said.

A shudder came over her. She was the one who was supposed to put it into perspective for him, not the other way around. She had lived through the loss of two parents and witnessed death nearly every day at work, and yet she was spooked to hear him invoke their inevitable finality.

"Come inside," she said. "It's late."

"I want to see if the stars get brighter the later it gets."

"It's a school night." She felt her grip on her temper begin to slip. The males in her life refused to cooperate with her. "You can investigate this in the summer."

She stood in the hallway watching him trudge to his room. Then she found herself stepping back onto the stoop and looking again to the night sky, trying to divine what ancient people might have seen in it—animals, hunters, maybe kings. Nothing came into focus, except when she thought she saw a dog with a long leash around its neck. When she looked up again it was gone.

That night, when she couldn't sleep, she concentrated on the steadiness of the stars, their transcendence of human sorrow and confusion, the reassurance offered by the unfathomable scale of geologic time.

21

On Sundays, they went to one o'clock Mass. Ed was never the driving force in their church attendance. When Connell was a baby, Ed had loved to usher him out the back of the church at the first hint of a meltdown.

For someone whose responsibility it was to get everyone to Mass, she didn't feel confident of her own belief in God anymore. It had been years since she'd thought of the world as the product of a divine plan. Maybe working as a nurse was too much for belief to fight against. She'd seen people expire on the table in every way—noisily, quietly, thrashingly, completely still. Death had come to seem no more than the breaking down of an organism: the last exhalations of the lungs, the final pumpings of the heart, the brain deprived of blood.

That didn't mean she was going to stop going to Mass. She liked the moral lessons for the boy, and the good works the Church did were the most important reason to attend—God or no God. When alone with her thoughts she couldn't help detecting some frequency she was tuning into, and she prayed to that frequency after communion when she knelt alongside her pew mates, though most of the time she felt like she was talking to herself.

The previous Sunday, Pentecost Sunday, at the end of the last Mass he would celebrate at the parish, Father Finnegan, who had been there thirty years, had introduced his replacement, Father Choudhary. Everyone registered the new, dark figure up there preparing the gifts as a harbinger of the future. Over the last decade, the priests had gone from being mostly Irish to mostly Hispanic; now, apparently, they were coming from India too.

Every year, there were more Indians around her at church. A few months ago, an Indian family had bought the Wohls' house up the block, and because she'd assumed they were Hindu, she'd been surprised to see them at Mass the following week. She'd lingered a bit so she wouldn't have to walk down the block with them, something she hadn't been proud of when she lay in bed thinking of it that night. The next Sunday, she made sure to catch them on the way out and walk with them. It had felt good to make amends for a slight no one knew she'd committed, and thereafter she felt comfortable letting them walk home alone.

Ed was more open-minded about other cultures. When they walked through Greenwich Village, he marveled appreciatively at the stratospheric Mohawk haircuts of the punk rockers, while she felt only disgust. So when they found themselves at Father Choudhary's first Mass, she wasn't surprised that Ed seemed extra attentive. To her, Father Choudhary looked spooky under his stark-white vestments, with the effigy of Jesus behind him on the altar. He spoke in a trilling accent. Even the Hispanics looked around as if to say, *This guy isn't one of us.* Ed just sat with his arms folded in amusement, or tapping the church bulletin against his thigh.

During the reading, Ed was usually good for a flip to another section of the liturgy—he was more into the literature of the Bible than the sacred text aspect—but with Father Choudhary at the pulpit, he held the book open to the reading. At least she could understand Father Choudhary better than Father Ortiz, who she wished would give in and speak Spanish with an interpreter beside him.

It was a reading from the book of Proverbs, on how the wisdom of God was born before the earth was made:

When he established the heavens I was there,
when he marked out the vault over the face of the deep;
When he made firm the skies above,
when he fixed fast the foundations of the earth;
When he set for the sea its limit;
so that the waters should not transgress his command;
Then I was beside him as his craftsman,

and I was his delight day by day,
Playing before him all the while,
playing on the surface of his earth;
and I found delight in the sons of men.

When Father Choudhary closed the book to begin his homily, Ed settled in to listen. Father Choudhary began preaching about matters wholly
unrelated to the reading: the idea that if we are all made of dust, then the
same dust, cosmic dust, he called it, could be found throughout the universe; that this cosmic dust might have been created by the Big Bang; that
somehow our sharing in this dust called us to responsibility to each other.
Ed looked positively enthralled. Father Choudhary spoke of the smallness
of man in relation to the vastness of the universe, and how that smallness
was instructive, how it reminded us that part of our humanity was a sense
of humility. He exhorted everyone gathered to allow themselves to feel
wonder and awe in the face of all creation, big and small. Then he quoted
from a French Jesuit named Teilhard de Chardin: "He recognized with
absolute certainty the empty fragility of even the noblest theorizings as
compared with the definitive plenitude of the smallest fact grasped in its
total, concrete reality." She had never seen Ed more enthused at church. He
slapped his hand on the back of the pew in front of him, and for a moment,
as she watched him shift in his seat in restless indecision, she thought she
would have to reach over and keep him from standing and applauding.

After Mass, a crowd gathered outside the church. Eileen worked her
way to the curb, but when she turned, only Connell was behind her. Ed
was on the steps, waiting in the receiving line to greet the priest like a well-
wisher at a wedding. This was too much.

She reached him just as he was extending his hand for a shake.

"Great speech," he said absurdly, as though congratulating a politician.
"Where are you from?" She was mortified, but Father Choudhary seemed
delighted as he pumped Ed's hand. They talked at length, the receiving line
at a standstill.

She waited until they had gotten far enough away.

"What was all that about?"

"All what?"

Connell had produced a tennis ball from his pocket and was bouncing it to himself.

"Since when are you so interested in the lives of priests?"

"He did a good job," Ed said.

Connell lost the ball and Ed fetched it from the street, flipping it in his hand as he walked, infuriating her. In her anger she twisted the bulletin into a baton that she smacked into her open palm like a nightstick.

"You really needed to ask where he's from? He's from India."

"He's from Bangladesh."

"You needed to know that?"

"I like to learn new things. If we don't learn, we die." Ed threw the ball to Connell. "Isn't that right, buddy?"

When they arrived home, Ed stood rooted to a spot on the sidewalk in front of the house. She waved Connell inside, and the boy hesitated, then went in. Ed didn't budge. She began to climb the stairs, hoping Ed would follow.

Ed bounced Connell's ball on the ground and caught it. "I saw the paper," he said. "The houses you circled."

She tucked up her skirt and sat on the top step. She felt as if she'd been caught canoodling with a boyfriend. The ball went *thwunk* as it hit the sidewalk; Ed cradled it back into his cupped palm.

"I don't want to leave," he said. "We have a perfectly nice house. We know the neighborhood. Doesn't that count for anything? Plus, we have this new priest."

"He's *Indian*," she blurted out incredulously before she could catch herself. "Look around you. Look at what's happening to this neighborhood. What's already happened."

"It's home," he said.

"How about that?" she asked, pointing to some graffiti at the base of the big apartment building across the street.

"That too," he said.

"How about when you walked in covered in eggs on Halloween?"

"Kids horse around everywhere."

"How about when Lena got mugged?"

"You can't live in a bubble," he said.

"How about what happened to Mrs. Cooney? You want that to happen to me?"

"Of course not. But that was an accident."

"I'd say it was closer to murder."

She paused, feeling herself shift from anger to resolution. She didn't need to argue with him. She could do this without him if she had to.

"I want us to look," she said. "Just to know what's out there."

He shook his head. A tiny patch of bald was forming, but she could only see it from this angle. He stopped bouncing the ball and put his hand on her foot and gave it a squeeze. The touch electrified her, as if he had channeled all his energy into his hands.

"I can't explain why I can't give you more in this," he said. "I just really don't want to go anywhere. Have you ever felt like life was getting away from you, and people were lapping you and you couldn't catch up? And if you could just stop the world and take it all in, and nobody would go anywhere for a little while, you'd have enough time to understand it? I wish I could do that. I don't want anybody or anything to move an inch."

"People move," she said. "That's life."

"I'm lodging my protest," he said, and he put the ball in his pocket and rose to go inside, leaving her alone on the stoop.

22

The first house she saw cost nine hundred thousand, at least twice what they could afford. She had to see it, though, to have a basis for comparison.

She wore a nice gray suit, a ruffled blouse, and heels. She drove up a long driveway that turned into a circle in front of the house, along whose perimeter a few cars were parked: a BMW, a VW, an Audi. She was embarrassed to be driving a Chevy Corsica. She was glad that Ed's torpor hadn't led to an attenuation of his car-washing habit; at least she had neatness on her side.

The door was open. She entered a capacious vestibule with marble floors, oil paintings on the walls, and an enormous chandelier hanging from the vaulted ceiling. She took in the sweep of the place for only a few moments before an effervescent real estate agent descended the stairs, trailing behind her a young couple who were dressed more casually than Eileen and looked more comfortable there. She had made a mistake. She removed her jacket—it was too warm for one—as they took the final steps of what seemed an endless staircase.

"Welcome," the agent said, extending both arms as if drawing her in for a hug. The couple had to be ten or fifteen years younger than Eileen. She felt she was intruding. She wanted to turn around and head to the car.

"I saw the door open," she said.

"Of course! Of course! We were just about to look at the back patio. Join us, or take a look around yourself if you like."

"Thank you," she said. "I think I'll walk around."

She stood there while they made their way outside. She thought again about leaving but couldn't bear the idea of their talking about her after she was gone. The inevitable simmering potpourri wafted in from the kitchen. She didn't want to fall for it, but she couldn't resist the mood it put her in. She headed upstairs. In the bedroom at the top she was surprised by another couple who looked closer to her age and had two girls in tow, the younger of whom was bouncing lightly on the bed. When the mother saw Eileen standing there, she told the girl to stop. The husband was admiring the craftsmanship of the window. He took Eileen in with an appraising glance from top to toe, as though she were part of the house, and smiled. The wife ushered the girls out, but the husband lingered behind, making pronouncements about the bones of the house as though he imagined being trailed by an audience of onlookers.

After they left, she drifted to the window the man had been admiring. Her car looked like a miniature version of itself. Birds and acorns had taken a toll on its roof; it needed a paint job.

She fluffed up the pillows the little girl had leaned against. She tried to resist the impulse to sit but felt suddenly tired and didn't know what else to do in the room, which she now felt trapped in, as she didn't want to face the young couple and the agent downstairs. She heard the low murmur of voices and labored to slow her breathing. She hadn't noticed until this moment that her heart was racing. She tried to calm herself by gazing at the beautiful sunlight coming through the window and feeling the lace of the duvet, but what put her at ease eventually was the quiet of the house. There were no horns honking outside. She breathed deeply and remembered that these people did not know she was an impostor; for all she knew they were impostors themselves. Maybe no one visiting the house really belonged there—including the agent, who had to project an air of aristocracy to blend in with her surroundings, but when it came down to it was working a job like anybody else.

She had almost willed herself into equanimity when she noticed three photos, each nicely framed, standing sentry around a bedside table lamp. Nothing in the photos could have explained the twisting in the gut she felt.

She saw a tableau of a family, possibly from the holidays; a wedding portrait in black and white; and a picture of an elderly couple on horseback, the husband wearing a grin of effortless control. The house was probably being sold so they could move to an inviting snowbird locale or else as an inheritance after the death of one or both of them. It seemed they had lived a full life. The husband possessed a heartiness that belied his years. She felt a surge of nerves that verged on nausea.

What Ed didn't understand was that in a house like this she would finally be able to breathe enough to put things in order for both of them. Here, she could make herself into the kind of wife who wasn't always rushing to get lunch made before he walked out the door in the morning. She didn't even mind thinking that the next place she lived could be where she died.

She gathered the courage to head downstairs. She found the agent and the young couple outside on the patio, the husband taking in the sweep of the yard, the wife inspecting the grill. She straightened her blouse before she slid the glass door open.

"I've got to run. I don't have much time to stay and chat."

"Of course!" the agent said. "Did you pick up a brochure?"

"It's a lovely house, but it may not be exactly what we're looking for."

"Everyone has a checklist, right? Otherwise it'd all be one big house!"

"My husband and I would like to look at other properties in the area."

"Please! Take my card. Where are you now?"

"The city," Eileen said. Queens was technically the city, but she knew that wasn't what she was conveying.

"I'll be happy to show you other properties."

"Thank you." She turned to the couple. "I wish you the best of luck in your search."

"And you in yours, wherever it leads," the young man said in a grand way that struck her as ungracious.

When she got home Ed was on the couch with his eyes closed and the headphones on. She stood there waving both arms, trying to draw the gaze of his inner eye. Then she went into Connell's room.

He was lying on the floor in his baseball uniform. It touched her to see how cute he looked in it. It was small on him; he had grown a lot over the past year, and his arms were wiry and long. He had begun to fill out in the upper body. She wondered how concerned she should be about how much time he spent in the basement lifting weights. She'd heard it could stunt his growth, but there was so much else to worry about lately, and she was just glad he wasn't getting into anything really destructive.

He'd had the sense to take off his mud-caked cleats, but the rest of his uniform sported a layer of that clayey dirt that never came off in the wash.

"How did it go?"

"We lost. I stink. I walked nine guys."

He was flipping a ball to himself and catching it; it was coming close to hitting his face. One toss would have crushed his nose if he hadn't turned away at the last second.

"You'll get better."

"I threw pretty hard, though," he said, a proud smile spreading across his face.

"Just don't dent the garage door," she said. "I don't want to have to spend money on yet another one right now."

He nodded. "Dad came to the game," he said.

"Really?"

"He did something weird."

She felt herself begin to panic. "What happened?"

"He wigged out on me after the game. I had to stay and help with the ball bag and bases and stuff. Dad went to get the car. When I got in, he started screaming at me. I've never seen him like that before. He kept yelling, '*You kept me waiting! You kept me waiting!*'"

"Well, it's not good to keep people waiting," she said halfheartedly, wondering if he could hear how tenuous her solidarity with his father was at the moment.

"I couldn't leave all the bats and stuff. My coach asked me to help. And I wasn't that long, I really wasn't. He screamed all the way home."

"Your father's going through a hard time right now," she said. "You can't take it personally."

"I didn't ask him to wait for me. I didn't ask him to come."

"He loves going to your games."

"Whatever."

"Don't say that."

"Mom, you weren't there. He was crazy."

A careless toss caused the ball to roll out of reach and he sat with his hands on his knees looking like a little man, already beleaguered by experience. He was a smart kid; he knew some kids had fathers who beat them or simply weren't there. Still, it was hard to see him disillusioned. Normally she was jealous of the bond between the two of them, but now she wanted to defend it.

"Daddy has a thing about being made to wait in the car," she said. "You can't take it personally. I'm sure he's sorry."

"He made us sit in the driveway for half an hour so he could apologize."

"See," she said. "There you go."

In bed that night, though, she confronted Ed.

"Connell said you flipped out on him."

"I lost my temper."

"He's just a kid, Ed."

"That's not going to happen again."

"It had better not. I don't give a damn what your father did to you. That boy's not him."

She parked a few blocks away and walked to the realty office on the chance that the agent hadn't seen her car the first time. The ruse would be exposed eventually, but she liked being taken seriously as a contender for these places. It was like when she was younger and would ask that a certain item be placed on hold at a store. The cashier would write her name on a slip of paper, and she would be granted time for consideration. The mere idea of possessing it in that allotted limbo was sufficient to quench the desire for it and she would almost never come back to complete the purchase. Perhaps it could be like that with the expensive houses; a few minutes in them could inoculate her against the need to live in them.

The office was in the center of Bronxville, and though it was sand-wiched between two boutique shops, it had the feel of an old dentist's of-fice. There was paneling on the walls, a thin blue carpet, and a few worn desks on either side of an aisle that ran through the center. The desk chairs didn't have wheels. The office made Eileen feel she was not completely out of her realm. One other agent talked quietly in the corner.

Gloria wore her brown hair cut short, like a politician's. There were ghostly remains of blond in it. She wore a navy business suit with what looked like a silk blouse. Her teeth were bright white, and level and straight enough that they could have been caps. She was around Eileen's height.

Once again, Gloria extended both hands in greeting. Eileen wondered whether this was something she had learned in a real estate textbook. And yet, she found herself succumbing to it as she had to the potpourri. They sat at the desk.

"Why don't we start by talking about what kind of house you're look-ing to see? Is there a style you're particularly interested in?"

Eileen had no real grasp on the terms of art that governed houses. Colonial? Edwardian? Tudor? These were terms she'd heard. As much as she'd always wanted a house in the suburbs, it was an abstract desire. It was about what the house represented: polish, grandeur, seclusion, per-manency.

"I liked the house I saw last week quite a lot," she said.

Gloria looked surprised. "I thought it hadn't appealed to you."

"Well, yes, that's true. In some ways it didn't. But in many ways it was a perfect house."

Gloria looked like she was weighing whether to let her off the hook or not. Then she smiled. "It has to be a perfect house in every way," she said. "That's what I want for you."

"Thank you."

"If you don't mind my asking, was it a matter of price?"

"Not at all," Eileen said. "Money wasn't the issue."

Gloria raised her brows. "Okay," she said, clicking her pen into action. "Well, if I'm going to find your future home, I'm going to need certain guidelines."

"Of course," Eileen said.

"Why don't we just start from the top, Eileen. It's Leary, right?"

"Yes."

"And you live in the city, you said?"

"We do."

"Which part?"

"Queens."

"Parts of Queens are so lovely, aren't they? I actually have a brother in Douglaston."

Douglaston was another world entirely. Eileen paused. "We're in Jackson Heights," she said.

"One of the garden co-ops?" Gloria asked, raising her brows again in what looked like a hopeful manner. "I hear they're quite beautiful."

"We own a house," she said. "A three-family house."

"Okay." She was writing things down. "And you're looking to move to Bronxville specifically? Or is it this general vicinity you're interested in?"

"Bronxville."

She looked up from the pad, beaming. "Isn't Bronxville just beautiful? When my husband moved us here I thought I'd died and gone to heaven."

"I used to work at Lawrence Hospital," she said. "Years ago. I remembered loving it."

"So you liked the house you saw. What did you like most about it?"

"The size."

"How many bedrooms do you want? Three? Four? Five?"

"At least four," Eileen said, feeling like a drunk picking the figure in the middle.

"Okay! That's a start. Now, what's your price range?"

Eileen thought for a minute. "It depends," she said, "on whether you're asking me or my husband."

Gloria laughed. "But that's why we love them, isn't it? Men will lay their heads anywhere. I'm always trying to get my husband to consider moving to a bigger house, to tell you the truth. There's nothing wrong with living up to your means. Does your husband work on Wall Street? The train ride down is so easy."

"He's a college professor."

Another silence ensued, another appraisal from Gloria.

"So, four bedroom. Close to the train, or no? Does he teach in the city? NYU? Columbia?"

"We'll both be driving," she said flatly. "He teaches at Bronx Community College."

"Do you want to be in the school district?"

"It's not necessary. My son Connell will be going to school in the city." She paused for effect, then added, "To Regis," expecting the revelation to inflate a protective balloon of prestige around her, and indeed the agent raised her brows.

"Well!" Gloria said. "He must be a bright young man!" Then she punctured the balloon. "My husband went there. It's all he ever talks about. I get tired of hearing about it. I have all girls, but if I'd had a son, I would have sent him there myself."

Eileen had to fight to suppress her urge to correct the woman. You didn't "send" your son to Regis: your son took the scholarship exam in November and you prayed for a letter inviting him to the interview round; then, after the interview, you prayed again that he'd aced it—actually prayed, no figure of speech, even if you never prayed otherwise. Then you gathered around your son as he sat at the dining room table and opened the letter that informed him he'd been admitted, and when he said he didn't want to go to an all-boys' school that was full of nerds, you told him he was going and that he'd thank you later, and you saw a little grin flash across his face, though he was trying to pretend to be annoyed. And when you said, "Your grandparents would have been so proud," you felt something in your spirit lift, because you had a responsibility to them that you'd carried for years, and now you could hand off part of it to him. And you saw that he understood somehow what it meant for this to have happened, that he wasn't the only person involved. You imagined your father looking over your shoulder, nodding silently, and your mother, that enigma, was there too, and you could almost see her smile at the thought of what might become of the boy, of all of them, the living and the dead.

"So what's a comfortable range? Over a million? Under a million?"

She had been thinking she could afford as much as four hundred thousand. Once they sold the Jackson Heights house and paid down the taxes and commissions, they'd have enough for a good down payment, but four hundred thousand was the upper limit. It was a long way off from "under a million," but that was her reply.

"Anything else I can work with?"

"I want a house that makes an impression from the street," Eileen said. "A house that almost pulls you up into it. A big, impressive house."

Sunday after Mass, instead of taking to the couch, Ed packed a picnic lunch for the three of them and drove them to their spot near LaGuardia. She spread the blanket and they ate the strangely spartan sandwiches he'd prepared: turkey on bread, no mayo, no mustard, no lettuce or tomato; they weren't even cut in half.

It was the first hint of repose they'd had in who knew how long. She wanted to enjoy it as a family, but Connell took out the gloves, bounding around like a buck, and Ed rose to gratify him.

The sun was out after a sojourn behind some clouds. Planes glinted in the sunlight and gradually diminished in the distance, leaving a trail of noise. A light breeze took the edge off the heat. The moment struck her as perfect, in the way that quotidian moments sometimes did. She tried to freeze it in her mind: the acid sweetness of her apple, the crunch of it against her teeth, the smell of the grass. It was cheating, in a sense, to circumvent the natural sifting process of memory, but she found that those moments when she stopped and thought *I'm awake!* as though in the midst of a dream, were ones she remembered with an uncommon clarity.

Ed stood sturdily, a bit stodgily, as he waited for throws to arrive, though a surprising spring entered his step when he had to move laterally. His button-down shirt and dress slacks weren't conducive to the activity, but he adjusted gamely. Connell's accuracy suffered in his enthusiasm to return the ball almost as quickly as it landed in his glove. They started out close together. Connell seemed to want to spread out and drifted steadily back. Ed arced his throws in broad parabolas, and Connell threw on a line, though in his zeal he would sometimes overshoot and send Ed scurrying to retrieve the ball before it reached the street. A row of parked cars flanked them on either side. The last thing she wanted was for the pastoral quality of the moment to be shattered along with a window. Ed began to call Connell closer. The boy resisted at first but crept forward when Ed held the ball in his mitt and waved him toward him. They were back to a distance not much farther apart than they'd been when they first started throwing. Ed signaled to him to slow it down.

"Not so fast," he said. "We're just having fun."

"I'm not throwing that hard, Dad," Connell said.

But she could tell he was. He seemed to be reaching back and giving the throws all his strength. Ed was catching them, but he looked almost frightened at their speed.

"Slow it down," Ed said, his voice skirting anger.

"Why? Can't catch it?"

Connell unleashed a throw that came at Ed like a fist. Ed stepped aside and let it sail past. He gave the boy a look and went to retrieve it.

"That's enough," she said when Ed was out of earshot. "Your father asked you to stop throwing so hard."

"I'm not! I'm not throwing my hardest."

"Just listen to him."

"Okay," he said. "Relax, Mom."

Ed looked more defeated than angry. He was at the mercy of the Darwinian logic of an adolescent, and he stood for a minute, seeming to consider his options, then threw the ball to Connell, who snatched it out of the air midhop.

She could see it before the ball left his hand, the coiled fury in Connell's body. There was something majestic about the physical changes that turned a boy into a man, the inexorability of the need to advance, to clear away the previous generation and make room for the current one. There was also something terrifying about the impending clash between the males in her life. Neither would come out unscathed.

Maybe he was angry with his father for yelling at him in the car. Maybe he was upset that his father was having a hard time corralling his throws. Maybe it was that his father had always been a step behind some other fathers. Ed wasn't just older, he was also old-fashioned, but he and Connell had always had baseball in common. Maybe it was too much for Connell to withstand aging's incursion into his father's ability to carry out this ritual. Whatever it was, he put everything he had into the throw, so that as it left his hand she let out a little involuntary gasp.

It came so fast at Ed that he seemed to freeze in anticipation of it. He didn't even try to get out of its way. She could see, as time slowed for her observation, that sometime since she'd married him there'd been an attrition in his motor functions. His hand was no longer as fast as his mind. Even from that far away, she could see his eyes widen. The ball struck him square in the chest. He staggered and fell backward, first on his rear, then on his back.

She shouted and leapt to her feet and started running. Connell did the same. He was on his knees talking to Ed when she got there, and she pushed him aside. Ed was clutching his chest as though he'd had a heart attack. Connell was stammering apologies. He kept trying to get at Ed as she shoved him away. Then Ed was stiff-arming her as he rose to his elbows and looked at both of them.

"I'm fine, goddammit," he said. "Let me stand up."

As Ed stood, Eileen raised her hand at Connell and held it there, poised to smack him. She could feel the way the three of them were suspended in the moment as though in the relief of a sculpture. Her hand throbbed with the need to connect. Her son almost quivered in anticipation of the blow. She smacked him once, hard, on the face.

"The boy doesn't know his own strength," Ed said, taking hold of her ringing hand. He picked up the ball from the ground. "Get back out there."

"Let's go back to the blanket," she said quietly.

"We've got a few more throws left."

"We don't have to play anymore," Connell said to Ed. He wouldn't look at her.

"We're not done," Ed said.

"Ed," she pleaded, uncomfortable with every possibility she could imagine.

"Have a seat," he said, pounding his glove. "Get going," he said to Connell.

"And I can't leave. I told you."

"You can't go back in the womb, Ed."

"Don't be a bitch."

He'd never called her that in all their years together. She looked at him savagely.

"I'm sorry," he said. "I didn't mean that."

She ground her teeth. "Don't talk filth to me," she said, practically hissing. "You want to talk that way to a woman, get a girlfriend. Is that what this is about? This mooning, this philosophical mumbo jumbo? Is there a girl in the neighborhood you can't bear to leave? A *chiquita*?"

Ed rolled over. "Good night," he said.

She wasn't going to be the one to break the silence. She lay there turning her ring on her swollen finger, chafing at the discomfort of its digging into her skin. The salty corned beef she'd cooked for dinner had made her fingers expand as if they'd been inflated. She wanted the ring off, not so much because of the discomfort but just to have it off, just so that Ed wouldn't have any claim on her at the moment, even if he didn't know he didn't, but she couldn't get it past her knuckle.

"You're all wrong," Ed said after a while. She felt his hand between her shoulder blades. "There's no girl. You're my only girl. You know I adore you."

She didn't turn over. She stared at the handles on the chest of drawers. "Then why won't you do this for me?"

He slapped at the bed in frustration. She felt it shake. "I can't right now," he said. "I just want to stay in place."

"That's what the suburbs are *for*—staying in place." He didn't respond. "Honey, listen. Is everything all right with you? Really? You don't seem yourself lately."

"I'm fine. It's just been a long year."

They lay in silence again. Finally she turned to him. "We wouldn't be moving right away," she said. "It takes months to move. Maybe even more than a year."

"I just can't!" he said, pounding the pillow. "Don't you hear me?"

She fooled with the little raised flower at the front of her camisole, to disperse the humiliation she felt at being spoken to that way.

23

ileen went in Gloria's car. One house had six bedrooms, more space than she'd ever imagined in even her most lavish dreams of dinner parties and extended visits, and she wanted Gloria to leave her there to sleep on the floor in the master bedroom and wake in the night to roam the dark spaces like a watchman in an empty office building. She registered her approval of touches Gloria pointed out, the beauty of which she needed no vocabulary to understand. It was impossible not to be enchanted by the exquisite good taste of the wood running everywhere, the quiet granite of the countertops.

"I want to see as many houses as I can," she said giddily as they left. "I want to take them all in."

Gloria was a willing enough conspirator that Eileen allowed herself to relax. She'd been afraid of wasting the agent's time, but Gloria did such a good job of projecting professional aplomb that Eileen decided to believe in the durability of her patience. Gloria would tell her the price on the way and what she thought they could get them down to. Eileen could see Gloria watching her for some reaction that would establish benchmarks to strive for, and she gave her none; she merely marveled indiscriminately at the gorgeous interiors, the manicured lawns, the impeccable patios, the huge kitchen windows that might look out, in the future, on grandchildren at play. Every time, Eileen said the same thing: "Wow!" or "Gee!" or "Beautiful!" or some other blandishment that kept Gloria off the trail of what she really felt, which was terror. She dispatched that terror with manic exuberance and affirmation. They would sit in the car for a few minutes talking, then head up to begin another simulation. The afternoon passed in a haze.

After perhaps the fifth house, Gloria paused before turning the key in the ignition.

"This is fun, isn't it?"

"Enormous fun," Eileen said. "I could do this all day."

"Yes. Well, at some point we have to settle on some parameters."

"It's so hard to say. They're all so beautiful. Who could ever leave some of these houses, except to move to the others?"

"I'm pretty sure you're going to love this next one," Gloria said determinedly. "I'm not even going to give you the fact sheet. I just want you to react. I want to see what tickles you."

They drove to the house, which turned out to be the most impressive yet. It was a gray brick center hall colonial—she knew that term now—set high off the road, with a front lawn that sloped gently downward. It had long black shutters, a gorgeous front porch, and a room off to the side with floor-to-ceiling glass windows. It must have had three times the space of the floor they inhabited in their house. After they'd walked through it, Eileen studiously wide-eyed the whole time, Gloria led her to the porch.

"Do you mind sitting for a minute?"

"Not at all," Eileen said, and took a seat in one of the tall white rockers. Gloria sat on the top step and faced her. It felt as luxurious to sit on the porch as it had seemed it might from the curb.

Gloria took out a pack of cigarettes. "Care if I smoke?"

Eileen shook her head.

"I don't normally smoke around clients. Believe me, it's not easy not to."

"Please feel free."

"I feel comfortable around you," Gloria said.

Eileen looked down. Gloria was a working girl, like her. Her shoes were slightly scuffed, and Eileen could tell she painted her nails herself. She wondered what her father would have thought of this performance of hers. Her lip began to tremble.

"When I said under a million, I think I wasn't being entirely realistic."

"What's a better number?"

"You're not going to like it," Eileen said.

"I can work with any number. I just need to know where to start."

"I don't even know if I can convince my husband to move."

"Look at you. You're a beauty. He'll go wherever you want."

"You're sweet," she said. She could feel sadness gathering in her chest, as though scattered shards of it were being pulled from her extremities by a powerful magnet.

"What are we talking about? Eight hundred? Seven?"

Eileen felt anxious talking about money this explicitly; she felt as if the agent had held a bright light up to her face and could see the imperfections on her skin.

"More like four," she said. "Five at the most."

"Hoo-wee!" Gloria exhaled a deep puff and stabbed the butt out on the step. "Do you have any idea how much this house is listed at? Take a guess."

"Eight hundred thousand."

"Nine *fifty*," she said with a flourish, like she was calling out someone's weight at a carnival. Gloria laughed. "We're going to have to change our strategy."

"I'm sorry I've wasted your time," Eileen said miserably.

"Look, I'll be straight with you. We've wasted some time. But I don't really mind. I like looking at houses. I'll find you a good one. One your husband won't be able to resist."

They agreed to go looking again the following week. As she returned Gloria's hug good-bye, it occurred to her how grateful she was that this woman who weighed her fate in her hands hadn't humiliated her.

She had an electrolysis appointment scheduled at her regular place in midtown. She didn't feel like going, but it was impossible to get an appointment, and she had begun to obsess over the little hairs that poked through her top lip and dotted her jawline. She wondered if they were harbingers of greater changes to come. Lately her skin tingled and itched a little more than usual. She felt warm at odd times; she wasn't ready to call them hot flashes. Her breasts seemed slightly less full. She'd always had irregular periods, so there wasn't anything to read into those, but she did have more headaches lately, though it was hard to imagine anyone *not* having headaches under her circumstances. She wasn't going to bury her head in the sand when the change began, but she also wasn't ready to conclude that it had begun before she had firmer proof. In the meantime, she was going to fight to hold on to her beauty as long as she could.

To avoid the traffic snarl, she took the train. On the way back, the crowd on the 7 platform pressed close, and the train offered no relief. At every stop the car got more crowded instead of less, until at Seventy-Fourth Street the train bled riders making connections to other lines. The walk home from Eighty-Second Street thrust in her face the horrors of the change. The street had once been the jewel in the neighborhood's crown. The white stucco storefronts were crisscrossed with wooden planks to give it a Tudor charm—Tudor was another style she recognized now when she saw it—and the streetlamps were made of ornate iron, but now gangs clotted its great arterial expanse, and the mom-and-pop stores had given way to bodegas, check-cashing places, and dollar stores with cheap signs that obscured the old facades. The globes that used to adorn Eighty-Second Street's lamps were gone. Similar ones could still be found on Pondfield Road in Bronxville, which might have been part of why she was so drawn to the town: it was like a time capsule of Jackson Heights before the collapse.

As she made her way down the street, a group of young men in sweatshirts and baseball caps—they looked Hispanic to her, but she couldn't always tell—were heading in her direction, taking up the width of the sidewalk. One of them walked backwards in front of the others, gesturing wildly with his arms outspread as the others clapped and hooted. A collision would ensue unless she went into the street, and she wasn't about to do that; they should all be able to share the sidewalk. The one with his back to her wasn't turning around. She decided to stop and hope they would filter around her, like water around a branch lodged between rocks. She held her hands in front of her protectively. The young man reacted too slowly to the wide-eyed looks of his friends and bumped into her.

"Excuse me!" she said, more shrilly than she'd intended. He spun around in a defensive posture, as though in preparation for a karate chop. When he saw her he dropped his hands.

"Sorry, lady," he said. The others snickered. She knew she should just keep moving and not say anything. She had an instinctual fear of groups of young men like this. She'd heard stories of ugly incidents. Still, she felt a wave of righteous indignation pass over her.

"This sidewalk's for everyone, you know."

"Sorry," the young man said. "It was an accident."

She had wrung a second apology from him; she knew this was probably the time to stop. They could run off and have a laugh at the crazy white lady. Maybe they'd shout curses at her as they receded from view. The perfunctory way he'd apologized irked her, though. She was going to teach this young man how to comport himself, even if no one else was bothering to take the time to do so.

"You should watch where you're going," she said. "It's hard enough to get down this sidewalk. There was no room to get past any of you."

"Whatever you say." There was a restrained quality to him, as though he were a tiger waiting to pounce.

"It's my neighborhood too," she said. "Just because you're taking over doesn't mean I'm leaving."

One of the boys standing behind the one who had bumped her moved forward. She knew what was coming: *Fuck you, white bitch!* But the other put up his hand to restrain him. "Hold up," he said. "I'm sorry for running into you. I didn't mean to crowd the sidewalk. Nobody's taking over your neighborhood. I was born here. There's room for all of us."

His articulateness shocked her. He parted the group to make room for her and indicated with a pacific gesture that she should pass. As she hastened to leave she replayed the incident in her mind, trying to make sense of the inscrutable turn it had taken. She had expected hate to be directed at her and had almost been disappointed not to face it. The kid had been raised well, there was no denying it. She wanted to forget the encounter. It unsettled her more than a brush with violence would have. A vision of the future loitered in it, an intimation of her obsolescence.

That night, when she told the story, she substituted for the young man's oddly delicate apology a bowdlerized version of the slurs she'd anticipated hearing—which was, in any case, closer to the truth of her lived experience than this inexplicable aberration. "I wouldn't repeat some of the vile things

I heard," she said, "even if Connell weren't here." It was a venial sin, she knew, but she didn't have to labor to justify it to herself, because it was in everyone's interest that they move to the suburbs. Ed, though, offered up only a muted version of the chivalric indignation she'd expected to hear, which stoked the fire of her anger at the gang members. Within a few days, she'd begun to consider the possibility that they'd actually said some of the things she'd put in their mouths, and there was a decent chance they had, memory being such a slippery thing.

When she went back to the realty office, she parked in front this time, and Gloria greeted her in a more familiar and less overtly warm way. A bridge had been crossed, a confidence shared. There was perhaps a greater investment on Gloria's part in finding a house for her.

They began their rounds. On the way to each house, Gloria enumerated the positives in what Eileen was about to see but also addressed certain ineluctable realities, a little confidentially, as if to allow her to encounter these realities in a mood of mutual trust. Then they went inside. If the memory of the previous visits hadn't been fresh, Eileen might have found the houses appealing; they were, after all, in a neighborhood more desirable than her own. But what a falling off! Where there had been five bedrooms, there were now three; where marble, now linoleum; where wood, some sort of composite, or else actual wood in a state of such severe neglect as to necessitate its wholesale removal and replacement. Expansive atriums became foyers not much larger than the claustral vestibule in her current house. And the magisterial light that pervaded the earlier houses, born of high ceilings and plentiful windows, gave way to a darkness that was all too familiar. Eileen's expectations sank with the price of the houses.

Gloria saw the shift in mood and tried to bolster her with recitations of hidden advantages, but Eileen would have none of it. She could live down the road from the houses she coveted, she could make friends with their inhabitants, but she could not live in them, not in this life she had with Ed. She had enjoyed years of intellectual partnership, and she'd raised a happy, healthy child, and this was far more than some women ever came close to having. She felt churlish even beginning to wonder what life would've been like if she'd married someone else. And yet as she sat outside the latest disappointing house, she couldn't help thinking that these were the wages of self-respect, sitting in a car outside a house she couldn't afford anyway, turning her nose up at it.

A baleful air hung in the car. She wanted to reassure Gloria, to express her gratitude for the kindness and patience she'd been shown. "I had unrealistic expectations," she said. "I can't get what I want with the money I'm capable of spending."

"Some of these houses are pretty nice, actually," Gloria said.

"Some of them remind me of where I live now," Eileen said. "The neighborhoods are on the border. They could go either way. I'm looking for this next house to be the one I settle down in. I don't want to have to look over my shoulder. I might as well stay in Jackson Heights if I'm going to do that."

The houses Gloria had shown her were in areas like Yonkers and Mount Vernon, where poor and comparatively wealthy populations—they happened to be drawn along black and white lines—abutted each other. It wasn't that she wanted to avoid black faces. She wanted to avoid black anger, black retribution, black vigilante justice. She wanted a buffer from the encroachment of crime. She didn't want to have to watch a neighborhood go to ruin again and preside over the memory of it like a monk guarding the scrolls of a dwindling people.

"Don't give up yet," Gloria said. "Give it some more time."

"Of course," Eileen said.

24

On days Connell didn't have games or practice at Elmjack Little League, he went to Seventy-Eighth Street Park, even though it scared him to go there sometimes. They played softball there—no league, just pickup—and during the games he felt protected. The older white crew came around, guys in their twenties who wore bandanas and sweatpants, blasted classic rock on boom boxes, and played roller hockey when they weren't playing softball. They drank beer out of bottles in paper bags. Somehow they didn't have to be at work in the late afternoons. The girls his age swooned over them.

He liked to throw with the high school kids who sometimes came around, because they didn't complain if he gassed it up. He was playing catch with one of them when Benny Erazo sauntered up in a way that looked like he was carrying bricks in his pockets. Benny had gotten kicked out of St. Joan's the year before. He went to IS 145 now. Connell had helped Benny through fifth-grade math by letting him copy his homework and look at his tests. Benny's little brother José was still at St. Joan's and was sometimes in the group that jumped Connell after school.

"You need to worry about your rep," Benny said.

"My rep?"

"Your reputation on the street is that you're soft." Benny was wearing a Bulls jersey. He had a light mustache and smelled of cologne under several layers of clothes.

"I didn't even know I had a rep on the street."

"I'm just saying."

"I'm not soft," he said.

"People say shit. You need to take care of your rep."

"Thanks for telling me." Connell slapped the ball into his glove.

"Come with me and tag up later. You need to have a handle."

"I already do." He didn't know why he was saying this.

Benny looked at him dubiously. "Yeah? Really?"

"Yeah."

"What is it?"

He thought quickly. "PAV," he said, because they were the first letters that came to mind.

"I've seen that shit," Benny said.

He hadn't thought he'd stumble on a tag that easily. "Don't tell anyone it's me," he said nervously.

"What does it mean?"

He thought again. "People Are Vulnerable," he said.

Benny considered it for a second. "Deep."

"Thanks."

"Somebody hears you claiming his tag, that's it for you."

"It's mine."

"Draw it for me later," Benny said. "When I come back from my moms."

"I don't do that anymore," he said, trying to sound cool.

"Why?"

"I almost got caught once."

"You really are a pussy-ass white boy."

"No, I just have to worry about my reputation." He paused. "With my parents." He was trying to make a joke of it. Benny pushed him and he staggered back a step. The guy he'd been playing catch with walked away.

"I'm not fooling with you," Benny said. "Your rep is that you're soft. I was telling you to tell you."

Connell knew what he was about to do might look crazy, but he did it anyway. He rolled up the sleeves of his T-shirt. "You think this is soft?" he asked, flexing. Benny reached into his pocket and took out a switchblade.

"Tell me again you're not soft," Benny said quietly. "Tell me again."

Connell stood there in silence.

"Tell me you tagged up." There was menace in his voice. "Tell me, Connie." Benny switched the blade out for a second and showed it to him, then popped it back in with the heel of his palm. He kept it in his hand.

"What do you want me to say?" Connell asked, his terror confusing his thoughts.

"Say, 'I'm a pussy-ass pussy motherfucker.'"

"I'm a pussy-ass pussy," he said, and paused. He wasn't comfortable saying that word. Benny laughed like he'd read his mind.

"Motherfucker!" Benny corrected. "Pussy-ass pussy *motherfucker.*"

"Pussy-ass pussy."

Benny showed him the knife again. "*Say it!*"

"Motherfucker," Connell said, his stomach tightening.

"Say the whole thing. 'I'm a pussy-ass pussy motherfucker.'"

"I'm a pussy-ass pussy motherfucker."

Benny howled with laughter. "You want to take care of your rep, you better not go around telling people that!" He put the knife in his pocket. "Man—I wasn't going to use this shit on you." He motioned to push him, and Connell flinched. Benny laughed again. "You want to stay alive, you better not go around claiming someone else's tag. They'll end you. That's it for today's lesson."

The whole way home, Connell replayed in his head what he'd said. *I'm a pussy-ass. I'm a pussy-ass pussy.* When he got there, his father was on the couch with the headphones on. Connell stood over him and watched him. He watched his hand going back and forth, the index finger raised. His father's eyes were squeezed shut, as if he was trying to see something he needed absolute dark to see. When the dull murmur coming from the headphones rose to a crescendo, the upward thrusts of his arm lifted his body off the couch. When the symphony lulled, he lay there, eyes still squeezed shut, and his chest rose and fell with his breathing.

Connell dropped his bookbag on the dining room table and headed to the basement. He added a ten-pound plate to either side of the bar and then lay on the bench. *Lift it, pussy-ass,* he thought, but he couldn't make it budge. He took the plates off and did a couple of sets of ten.

While he was lifting, he thought of something he could have said to Benny to make him laugh. When Benny asked, "What does it mean?" he could have said, "Pussy-Ass Virgin." But he only ever thought of that kind of stuff after the fact. He even knew a French expression to describe coming up with witty things too late; *that* was the kind of pussy he was. His father had taught it to him: *Esprit d'escalier*, the spirit of the stairs; the thing you think of when you're already gone. The kids who thought of snappy things on the spot never had to worry about being fat or smart or pussies. You had to have a little meanness in you to do it. You had to be willing to embarrass other people sometimes. He didn't want to have to embarrass other people. Deep down, or not even that deep, he knew he was a pussy-ass; maybe that was why it hadn't been that hard for him to say what he'd said to Benny.

Maybe it was partly his father's fault that he was such a pussy-ass. His father was a nice guy. Not that he told Connell not to fight back. The last time Connell had come home with a swollen eye, his father had said, "You have my permission to fight back. You're not going to get in trouble with me." But Connell hadn't wanted to risk it. He hadn't wanted to get a JD card or suspended or worse. He'd been thinking of his permanent record. He hadn't wanted to ruin his chances of getting into a good high school or having a good life. He'd needed the teachers on his side, the principal. He'd wanted to get out of the neighborhood. Well, now he was going to a fancy school in Manhattan on scholarship. You couldn't get more out of the neighborhood than that. Maybe he was a total pussy-ass, but at least he wasn't an asshole like Benny.

He put the plates back on. He thought, *Lift it, motherfucker*, and then he said it aloud, like he was uttering the password to a new club. He got the bar up once; it came crashing down with a loud bang. His father didn't come running down to see whether he'd hurt himself, because his father couldn't hear anything with those headphones on.

Pussy-ass pussy, he thought. *Motherfucker*.

25

Ed had been working in the garage since she woke up. He had emptied much of its contents into the backyard, which now bore an uncomfortable resemblance to those of their immediate neighbors. It was a hot May morning, and sweat was pouring off him.

"I'm taking Connell," she said.

"Okay."

"You sure you don't want to come?"

"I'm a little busy." He gestured to the clutter. She felt bad taking the boy, who probably should have been helping him with whatever this project was, but she couldn't face those houses alone again.

In the car, Connell found Z100 and turned the volume up.

"How come you're not telling me to turn it down?"

"It's not that loud," she said.

"Dad doesn't let me turn it up when he's driving. He says he needs to concentrate."

"I don't mind." She started tapping the fingers of her free hand on the door. It was a song she'd heard while driving to work. Connell smiled at her, and she felt like the favored parent for a change. He'd always gravitated toward his father—a consequence, she suspected, of her having returned to work so soon after he was born. It probably wasn't just that she was out of the house so much; it was also the way she got on the phone with her friends after dinner as though punching the clock at a second job. But some of that, she saw now, had been the need for escape. There would be less of that when they moved. She could begin to be more of the mother he wanted.

"Your father's got a lot on his mind," she said generously.

"He's the most uptight person in the world. He grips the wheel with both hands the whole time. You can't say *anything* to him."

When they first met, he would pick her up with one elbow hanging out the window, like a cool guy in a movie.

"You don't know what it's like to be an adult," she said. "There's a lot to think about all the time."

"He wants me to have the change ready for the tollbooth about a mile in advance. He gets all weird about it. He freaks out if I don't have it in my hand, counted out. And then he throws it in that bin with all this force, like he's throwing a baseball. It's so awkward. What's up with him? Why is he so weird?"

She had been a passenger of Ed's herself. It was as if he was doing brain surgery instead of driving a car. "Fathers are just weird sometimes," she said. "Don't think too much about it."

"It's so embarrassing."

A song came on that he liked and he bobbed his head up and down and tapped his hands on the dashboard.

"I want your input," she said. "I've been looking at all these houses and I can't tell what I think anymore."

"What about Dad? What does he say?"

"Your father and I have a difference of opinion right now about whether we should move," she said. "I'm going to have to ask you to be a man about this. I might need you to keep quiet about it for a while if we find a place we really like."

"Sure."

She felt her foot falling heavier on the gas pedal as they hit the Grand Central Parkway. A new spirit entered the car. She had a conspirator. She could feel it making a difference already. She felt freer than Ed as she drove. She was cool enough to appreciate her son's music, to pick up a little speed on the highway, to let the coins wait until they got right up to the booth. She had enough energy to make important changes in her life, to pull her husband out of a pit, to yank her whole family out of the maw of a neighborhood that threatened to swallow them whole.

• • •

Gloria gave Connell the full open-armed treatment. She seemed inor-
dinately glad to meet him. At first Eileen thought it was a salesperson's
come-on, but then it occurred to her that by existing, Connell might have
been confirming that his mother wasn't a fantasist.

"I've found the perfect place for you," Gloria said. "It's gorgeous. It's
slightly out of your price range, but only slightly. I want you to consider it.
It's as close as you can get to your perfection with the money you can spend."

They drove up Palmer Road toward Yonkers, past the stately com-
plexes of condos and leafy gardens, but turned off it before they'd gone
too far. She had studied the area enough to know that this was an outpost of Bronxville with Bronxville post office boxes and Yonkers schools.
But the schools wouldn't matter with Connell heading into the city in the
fall. A sign announced—either proudly or defensively, it was hard to tell
which—"Lawrence Park West."

The area was promising. It was a mixture of old and new homes,
but the road was curvy and lined with enormous oaks, and between the
wooded plots, she caught glimpses of stucco Tudors with carriage houses,
and even what may have been a tennis court. They turned onto a wider
street and the road flattened and the houses were all easy to spot but ma-
jestically elevated above the road. They stopped in front of a gray colonial
with overgrown hedges and columns that linked the porch on the first
level to one on top. Stone pillars flanked the driveway, and next to the
front walk was a jockey holding a lantern. His red coat had been chipped
and bleached to pink in the sun. The house looked as if it had been built
sometime in the first half of the century, but built well, and it was twice as
large as the houses she'd seen the week before. She was hopeful.

Gloria led them up the driveway to a staircase at the back entrance. A
patio of moss-covered brick, framed by a stone wall and a terrific amount
of growth, resembled an English garden gone to seed. It opened up onto
the craggy slope, which contained an enormous stone blanketed by ivy.
Atop the hill were houses accessed by another street.

The kitchen looked like it had been despoiled by squatters. Cabinet
doors didn't close right, the wallpaper bubbled, and the brick floor was
coated in a thick, dingy skin of polyurethane. Everything on the rear side

of the house—the kitchen, the den, the dining room—was dark as a catacomb, but she could tell that light would penetrate its depths on a good day, particularly if she trimmed some of the bushes, and while the dining room had a matted rug and a rickety-looking chandelier, she could envision the grand meals she'd serve there, and the living room was practically bleached by light. Next to it was the brick-floored foyer and the entrance proper, and a flight of banistered stairs leading to the second floor. Off the landing at the bottom of the stairs was a little flight down into what could be a reading room, next to what would be Ed's study, with a bay window and built-in bookshelves.

Gloria went to the two front doors and threw them open with a flourish. Light flooded in. Looking left from the front porch, which was fringed by a rotting wooden fence, Eileen could see where the road curved and headed down to Palmer Road, the main artery into the town that lent this house its respectable mailing address.

Eileen stood on the porch, imagining people opening the big metal gate at the bottom and making their way up the gently winding path. The thought of their approach thrilled her, the moments of anticipation, the embraces, the handing off of wine bottles, cakes, presents. And then she turned and saw Connell looking out the window in the living room, an ethereal light flooding against him, so that he resembled a figure in one of those portrait paintings of the children of nobility from centuries past. These days and years would act as a crucible in which his fate was distilled. The closing down of possibilities had begun, almost imperceptibly. She had to act quickly to preserve her image of the life she imagined, in which Ed toiled happily in his study, turning over ideas until they yielded fresh hypotheses, and she was a grand hostess and the matriarch of a respected clan. This house would be the backdrop to the second act of their lives together. It was Connell's contemplative gaze that gave her that assurance.

"What do you think?" Gloria asked rhetorically as she drifted into the room. She was a maestro of timing: there was no need to respond. She led them up the stairs like a groom guiding his bride to the bower.

"I'll show you the other bedrooms first," she said, "and then the master suite."

She led them to a room so massive it could have swallowed Connell's current bedroom whole, along with the spare, with room left over.

"This could be your bedroom," Eileen said.

"Sweet!" He darted into the room and walked its perimeter like a cat marking its territory. He opened and closed the closet doors and then lay in the center of the room and stretched his arms and legs as far as he could. She laughed out loud at his exuberance.

"Come on," she said. "Get up now."

"It's okay," Gloria said. "He can be excited."

"You could land a plane in here," he said.

"Maybe a helicopter," Gloria allowed.

"There's no doubt it's a big enough house," Eileen said cautiously. How "slightly" out of her price range was this house? This might be another tease, only this time she wouldn't have done it to herself.

"You haven't even seen the master bedroom."

"I'm a little worried about the price."

"You're prepared to spend four hundred thousand," Gloria said. "Five at the most."

"The uppermost," Eileen said.

They were in the hallway now, their voices low.

"This house is five sixty."

"That's a big difference." Eileen tried to hide the panic and disappointment that had already set in.

"Not when you think about the fact that when it's fixed up, it's a three-quarter-of-a-million-dollar house. Minimum. *Minimum*." Gloria spoke coolly, a little impatiently, as if they were discussing an artwork she didn't want to sully with considerations of money. "There are some catches, though."

"Catches," Eileen said.

"Not necessarily deal breakers. How handy is your husband?"

She thought of Ed at home in the garage, tools strewn around him in a blast-radius circle, trying to make the house presentable enough to entice her to stay in it. Everything he knew about home improvement he'd learned from how-to books. Whenever he made a study of something, though, he could do it at least passably well. "If I can earn a PhD," he'd said when they'd had a short in the hallway light, "I can figure out how to fix some faulty wiring." And he had. The handiness came at the expense of great effort. Doing a big project around the house always left him exhausted.

"He's pretty handy," she said. "Why?"

"This house was on the market for over a year, then taken off and relisted. They just dropped the price."

"What's wrong with it?"

"It's suffered some water damage. It's a twofold problem. It's at the bottom of a hill, so there's always runoff. And it's built on a rock, with a rock behind it, so everything just flows into it. On top of that, the pipes burst this winter. There's a lot of damage in the basement. A lot of it needs to be ripped out and rebuilt. Plus there's no guarantee the water won't come back. You're going to need a new roof in a couple of years. It's an expensive proposition to fix this place, but it's a steal if you can do any of the work yourself."

"My husband can do it," she said.

It would be good for him. He could sweat this thing out through manual labor. She could see him drinking a beer in jeans and a T-shirt, wiping his brow and holding a baseball cap at his hip.

"Let's make our way to your room," Gloria said. They left Connell and stopped briefly at each of two average-sized bedrooms and a bathroom with matching sinks below bulb-lighted mirrors like those in dressing rooms. A toilet hid demurely behind French doors.

The master bedroom suite contained a closet as large as her current guest bedroom. She pictured a sitting area in the corner of the bedroom proper. The same light poured in as below but unencumbered by tree cover. It would be impossible to dwell on sad things in that light.

In recent years, a tentative mood had obtained in their bedroom. They fumbled over each other's bodies. It was as if they'd entered a new phase of life and had to get reacquainted. She needed light for play, discovery. Something could be gained if they saw each other naked in the bright light of day.

The wallpaper was all seams and bubbles, and something would have to be done about the stain on the ceiling in the corner of the room. There would be time and money to worry about such particulars in the proper order.

She made her way to the window. She'd heard all about suburban ennui, but she couldn't imagine feeling it in a house like this. If the abundant space and light failed for a moment to confirm for her how far she'd gotten from what she'd left behind, and a shadow of uncertainty drifted over her, she needed only to throw open the curtains on this window, gaze out onto the empty street, and wait for a car to drive down the block, and then another. In the substantial interval between them, she would feel a calm settling in: there was no reason to be there unless you had someone to see; there was no way to stay there long unless you had a reason to stay.

"I think you like it," Gloria said.

"I do," she said quietly. "I like it a lot. I'm trying to figure out how I can afford it."

She was in the middle of the sort of reverie that invented the future by imagining it. The spell would be broken in a moment, but she lingered in it, telling herself to remember the details.

They wouldn't be able to put as big a percentage down. They'd have a much higher monthly payment. They might not be able to immediately do all the renovations she had in mind. They'd have to work in stages. They'd have to live lean, not go to restaurants or shows.

"What about you?" Gloria asked Connell.

"Can we put a hoop in the driveway?"

What a simple thing, Eileen thought. *What a different set of concerns he has.*

"I don't see why not."

"Yes!" He pumped his fist.

"Someone's excited," Gloria said.

"I'm excited too," she said, "but the person we need to convince is his father. Provided the structure is sound and the repairs are possible and the finances are in order, I think this might just be the perfect house for us."

Gloria clapped her hands. "That's the spirit," she said. "You wouldn't get this house at this price except under some very specific circumstances. Now, having said that, why don't we go take a look at those circumstances."

They headed downstairs. Gloria pointed out some flood marks that

Eileen hadn't seen earlier, and then she took them into the house's bowels. Eileen passed her eyes over everything Gloria pointed to, but she did her best not to register it. Connell poked at a section of rot. When he pulled a piece off, she barely mustered enough indignation to scold him. She heard, as though from underwater, the litany of troubles the house had endured. She nodded when she needed to nod and pulled long faces to demonstrate concern. She even heard herself sigh when Gloria showed her a section of foundational wall in the garage that had been soaked through and was threatening to collapse. She was determined to let these subterranean details remain subterranean. They could be handled in due time. The issue now was preserving her vision. The base of the house might be rotting, but the visible portion was commanding enough to chase any qualms away.

"It's not an inconsiderable amount of work," Gloria said.

"We could make it work." Eileen turned to Connell. "You and Daddy could take this on, don't you think?"

"No way."

"He just doesn't want to have to do anything around the house," she said to Gloria. "But they could handle it. I'm confident."

"If you say so, Mom."

"Maybe we'll pay you like a contractor. Maybe it's time you earned your allowance."

"There are things he can't do. There's the roof, as I said. You've got a little time on that. The electrical wiring is old. You might not have enough amp service. You might blow some fuses. Some of the outlets don't work. Am I scaring you yet?"

"I'm just listening."

"There's asbestos around the plumbing and ductwork. That could make it hard to resell. So could the underground oil tank."

"I'm not worried about selling it. I'm worried about buying it."

"Water gathers in the fireplace. Some of these are expensive jobs. Thankfully there's no mold from the flooding. That we know of."

"It sounds like we need a plumber. And a roofer."

"And a general contractor," Gloria said. "And an electrician. And a willing husband."

"I can live without a few outlets for a while. I don't know if I can live without this house."

They stopped for gas on the way home. When she went in to pay, she bought a couple of scratch-off tickets, something she'd thought she'd never do, and scarfed a pair of Twinkies while she rubbed a quarter on the tickets. She didn't win, and she bought five more. Then she got two more with the free tickets she'd won, and those were losers too. She bought five to take home with her and another package of Twinkies to split with Connell and headed out to the car, where the boy sat oblivious of the turmoil she was in.

She drove with an anxious feeling in the pit of her stomach, fidgeting with the button for the electric window. When they pulled in, she saw one of her good sheets strewn like a makeshift tarp over whatever tools Ed had left in the driveway. Cinderblocks held the sheet down at the corners, and the garage door was closed. The stark whiteness of the sheet put a chill in her.

Ed was sitting at his desk. The vestibule abutted his office, a glass-paneled door between them. He had a pleasant habit of wheeling around in his chair whenever he heard her come home, but he didn't turn this time. "We're home," she said. When he didn't respond, she went over and stood behind him. He was calculating his semester grades. His desk was cluttered with tests and lab reports; little piles of them abounded. He jotted notes on a legal pad as he did his calculations. She'd never seen him do his grades with such elaborate exactitude. He had written the last name of each student, along with the roman numerals from the test sections, in a long row. She watched him meticulously check each number against those he'd written on the exams. It was double work, and moreover it was the kind of task he usually dispatched in his head.

When she placed a hand on his shoulder, he almost leaped out of his seat. He didn't turn around to her.

"What's the matter with you?" he exclaimed.

"I didn't mean to frighten you."

"Don't bother me when I'm doing my grades."

"Since when?"

"I want to get these right. It's a big class, and I've graded a lot of assignments in the last few days, so I feel a little fuzzy, as you can imagine. I don't want to make any mistakes in my calculations. When I look at this stuff long enough, I feel like I'm seeing double."

"What's up with the sheet?"

He took off his glasses, the way he sometimes did when he was going to give thoughtful consideration to a question, but then he just dropped his shoulders.

"Sheet?"

"Outside," she said. "The bed sheet."

"I wanted to leave things there."

"Why did you use a good sheet?"

"Good sheet?"

"There were other sheets you could have used."

He slammed his pencil down. "What's the difference?"

"You used one of the sheets I put on the bed. There are about ten old sets in that linen closet that you could have used."

He spun around in his chair. She backed away from him instinctively. His face was red and his mouth contorted. "I took the first sheet I could find!" He was on his feet now. "I didn't have time to work out which sheet was which. I just grabbed a sheet!" He had begun to shout. "I took the first sheet!" He had his hand in front of his face, as if to strike her or bite it. "People walk by the house all day long, peeking back there. I needed to cover everything up!"

She had intended to let it go, but now she had to ask. "Why did you leave it out in the first place?"

"I didn't want to have to set it up again," he said. "Is that okay with you? God damn it! God damn it!"

She was quiet. She wondered whether Connell could hear.

"I'm sorry," he said. "There's a lot of pressure on me to get these grades right. Dealing with these kids has upset me. This younger generation has no respect. It's disgraceful."

"What do you mean? What's happened?"

"What's happened," Ed said, "is that with everything going on lately, I've been distracted."

She wanted to know what he meant, because it seemed at times as if nothing was going on, hence the big pile of ungraded papers, but she held back.

"In my distraction, I've made a few calculation errors. And they've raised a stink about it. That's all. These kids today feel entitled to everything instantly. You say you'll review the grade, and they say they can't wait until the next class. They go berserk! I like to take my time with things, give them an honest going-over. That's impossible with a crowd of people at your desk. Especially when they speak in such a fresh and disrespectful way."

So much of what he was saying was odd. He was one of the most popular professors in the department, a status made all the more remarkable by the fact that he was no pushover in the grading arena. They wanted to work for him, to impress him. His belief in them made them want to believe in themselves. It also made her want to kill him sometimes, because she didn't believe they deserved it.

After taking an old sheet from the linen closet, she went out to the driveway and picked up one of the cinderblocks holding down the good sheet. Beneath the sheet lay two-by-fours that had been sawn in an irregular fashion. Ed had been attempting to construct something. She couldn't tell if it was supposed to be ornamental or structural. What it resembled more than anything was a pile for a bonfire. There were none of the heavy tools she'd imagined Ed hadn't wanted to move several times, only this inert, enigmatic heap. She folded the good sheet up and replaced it with the old one in a way that would discourage his noticing she had done so. When she had finished, she hurried away as she sometimes did when she got spooked in the basement and felt something closing in on her.

She considered saying something to Ed on the way back in. Then she decided the time for checking things with him had passed. If he noticed it was a different sheet tomorrow—by no means a certainty—he would just have to deal with the fact that she had messed with his arrangement.

• • •

She awoke to find herself alone in bed. She stumbled out to the living room and saw Ed's light on in the study. He was hunched over, as if so many hours of sitting at the desk had sapped the energy in his back. His hair was wild. The desk lamp radiated tremendous heat. The smell of sweat mingled with the mushroom odor of old books to give the room a greenhouse quality.

"Come to bed," she said.

"I'm working."

"It's three in the morning. Come to bed."

"I have to finish this." His voice sounded weak, as if he'd fallen asleep in the chair, but his expression was oddly alert. His eyes were sunken and dark, like he'd reached the end of a long fast.

"Can you finish it tomorrow?"

"I can't."

"Let me see," she said.

She leaned over him. He shifted his body to block her view, but she could see the piles on either side of him on the desk, the calculator between them. She picked up the pile of tests and flipped through them. They all had grades on their first page, which surprised her, because what was Ed doing if not grading these things? She put the tests down and picked up the lab reports, over his protestations. The same was true of those: grades had been assigned, red numerals in distended circles emblazoning their upper right corners.

"These are all graded," she said. "Why don't you come to bed?"

"I'm still working."

"You have more to grade?"

"I do."

He covered a pad on the desk with his hands. She could see it was the set of names and numbers he had been working with earlier. Yet another pad lay next to it.

"What's that?" She pointed to the second pad.

"Will you leave me alone? Will you go back to sleep? I'll be in when I'm done."

She picked up the second pad, fending off Ed's hands. On it were written all the same names and numbers as on the first pad. They appeared to be identical.

"What is all this?"

She answered her own question by looking at the first test. Each number listed on the pad corresponded to the student's performance on a section of the exam. His grade book lay splayed open at the back of his desk. She picked it up to check her hunch; indeed, the grades weren't there. Was he that nervous about making a mistake? Just how fresh had the kids become that a teacher of his stature could be moved to such excessive scrutiny of his no-doubt flawless math well into the night? He should have been resting and quelling the psychic demons that were draining his confidence in the first place. All of this had become far bigger in his sleep-addled mind than it ever should have been allowed to be.

"Let me help you with this," she said, careful not to describe what "this" was. He surprised her by capitulating quickly. She gathered his things and led him to the kitchen table. "You keep the grade book," she said. "I'll tell you the number to enter."

He held his pen poised over the book. She took the first test off the pile. Edwin Alvarez had earned an 84. She flipped through the test, making sure the subsection grades added up to the indicated total. Eighty-four it was. This was probably the kind of kid Ed was proudest to see achieve, a kid from the neighborhood.

"All right," she said. "Edwin Alvarez."

"Wait!" Ed said, suddenly panicked. "Wait! Wait!"

He stood up and bolted out of the room. Before she could follow he reappeared holding a long ruler. He squared himself in the chair and lined the ruler up under Edwin Alvarez's row of boxes. She had to laugh at his intensity. He didn't share the laugh, though; he didn't look up at all, as though he had to stare unblinkingly at the name in front of him in order to prevent it from disappearing.

"Okay," he said. "Go."

"Edwin Alvarez."

"Edwin Alvarez," he said hesitantly, as if cross-referencing it with the names in the list, an odd thing considering it was the first.

"Eighty-four on the test. We're only dealing with the test right now."

"Yes," he said. "The test only."

"Okay? Can we move along?"

"Eighty-four?"

"That's correct," she said, biting her tongue. As disturbing as this drill was, now wasn't the time to discuss it. She had to get them both back to bed.

"Okay," she said. "Lucy Amato. Give me one second."

She flipped through the test, adding the numbers in her head. She saw how this could get to a person; late at night, numbers ran together. Ed had added them correctly again. She could see it would play out as an exercise in redundancy. It was the kind of thing you signed up for when you got married, idiosyncrasies that bordered on obsessions at times, quirks that became handicaps if allowed to thrive. It could have been worse: he could have had a wandering eye, a gambling habit.

He had located Ms. Amato's name; his ruler was brought to a sharp congruency with the line underscoring her performance for the semester.

"Seventy-three," she said.

"Seventy-three." The desperate edge had left his voice. Despite her tiredness, she was touched by the feeling of working together with her husband on a project; it beat being adversaries. Maybe she'd even be able to tell him about the house.

They went through the stack, she calling out the name, he orienting himself in the ledger, she checking his addition, which grew quicker the more she saw he'd been accurate in his math, she calling out the number like a bingo caller, he repeating the number before committing it to paper, he confirming it again with a rising intonation, she reconfirming it in a tone that made her feel uncomfortably like a teacher with a student. They got to the end without incident, Ed never wavering in his focus, his laser-like application of the ruler's metal edge. He was sweating; he paused to wipe his forehead while she did her quick math, but didn't look up from the page.

The last name, Arash Zahedani, also happened to be attached to the highest grade, ninety-seven, a happy coincidence that might send Ed to bed in a better mood. It was getting on four o'clock; she had to be up in a few hours. She knew she wouldn't be able to sleep; she was far too awake now to drift off again. Still, she could lie there and rest her muscles. To-

morrow was an important day at work. The Joint Commission was examining North Central Bronx Hospital, bringing with it the usual headaches.
Her people were well prepared, but she would have to dig deep to perform
well on little sleep. She was already exhausted from the previous week of
late nights getting ready for their arrival. She'd had ten nurses call in sick
Friday, and she was going to have to fire some of them, because they'd
known better than to do that at the start of the weekend. Since she'd been
understaffed, she'd had to struggle to handle a room full of gang members
who'd burst in after visiting hours, demanding access to the ICU to see
one of their own who'd been shot in the stomach. They pushed past the
security guard and through the double doors in front and were advancing
on the room. It could have been two dozen of them. She ran to block their
way. "You're not allowed in there," she said. "You can come back tomorrow." One of them asked, "Aren't you afraid of us, white lady?" She didn't
have the energy to be. Security backup arrived, two more guards, all three
of them black. If the gang members didn't stand down soon, the guards
might draw their guns, and who knew what would happen then? She was
the only white person in the room. The guards told the gang members to
leave. There was a young girl among their number; she must have been
the injured man's girlfriend. She held a baby in her arms. She gave Eileen
a pleading look. "I will let a few of you in, one at a time," Eileen said, "and
we will all be civil to each other. And then you can come back tomorrow.
And I promise you he will be in good hands, and we'll let it rest at that."
The guards relented. They had the gang members line up against the wall.
She could see the leader of the gang calming everyone down. He gave her
a look that said, *Lady, you are all right.* It had stuck with her, that look. It
had meant something to be recognized, even by this thug. She wanted that
young man to give her that look in front of her husband the next time Ed
was half-crazed about some absurd infraction. There was more to life than
Ed's petty grievances.

She wanted to end on a high note, but a spirit of excess caution had
crept into her own thinking. "Let's go through the numbers again," she
said, and from his look she got the feeling he hadn't planned for it to be
any other way.

"We'll switch," she said. "I'll read down the column. You call out the grades."

They proceeded through the tests, Ed dispatching his task with a new alacrity. Four tests from the bottom, La Shonda Washington, she asked Ed to repeat the grade he'd just read out.

"Eighty-six," he said.

But the number he'd entered for Ms. Washington was sixty-seven, which also happened to be the score received by Melvin Torres, the student above her in the grade book.

"One second." She rose to look at the test in his hands. The glow of the sun was filtering into the air outside. It felt more like the remnant light at dusk than the herald of dawn.

"What? What is it?"

"I just wanted to check something."

"I told you," he said. "I told you. Eighty-six."

"That's what I thought you said, honey." Her throat constricted. "I wanted to double-check."

"Is there a problem? A mistake?"

"I just need to change one thing," she said. "Give me a second."

She reached for the pencil and he slammed his hand down on it. "What is it?" He was seething. "What is it?"

"The number for the student directly above La Shonda Washington has been repeated," she said matter-of-factly. "That's all. I'm going to erase it and write in the correct number."

"Ah, Jesus!" He threw his hands up. "Jesus Christ! It's all wrong! It's all wrong!"

"Just hold on while I make this one change."

"Forget it," he said. "What's the use?"

"It was an honest mistake," she said. "You wrote the number above it. It's late."

"Yes, yes," he said dismissively. "That's it. Now let me finish this. I'll be in when I'm done."

He took the book away and closed it, then held his head and rubbed his eyes.

"We have three more to go," she said.

"It's *fine*," he said firmly. "We're finished."

She should have made the switch without saying anything. She should have come out and done it after he'd fallen asleep. Now she had to convince him to leave off his vigil.

"If we're done," she said, "then come to bed."

"I'll be in in a while."

"Come now."

"I said I'll be in. I'll be in."

"You need some sleep."

He slammed his fist on the table. "I'll be in when I'm in! What the hell else do I need to say to you? Will you leave me alone, God damn it?"

She snatched the book out of his hands. "Don't say a word to me," she said slowly, giving him an icy stare. "Not one word."

She opened to the page with the grades and looked at the last three numbers. Whitaker, seventy-three. Williams, fifty-eight. Zahedani, ninety-seven. She checked the tests and slammed the book shut.

"That's it," she said. "They're all correct. I'm going to bed. You can come, or you can stay here. I don't care either way."

She felt her hands making fists as she walked down the hall to the bedroom. She'd already wasted too much time on him. She imagined he'd spend the whole night out there, going over the numbers endlessly.

She lay in bed, counting sheep for the first time since she was a child. She bit the pillow in frustration. Then she heard him walking down the hall. She rolled over and he climbed in bed alongside her. She moved as close to the edge as she could. Even an accidental touch might enflame her so much that she'd have to go to the couch. There was no point in trying to sleep; she would lie there until it was time to get up and shower.

She felt the slight shaking of the bed but didn't register the sound as what it was until the shaking grew more forceful. Ed was doing a good job of keeping it in, but the springs of the bed gave him away. The sound of gasps followed. She had trouble identifying it at first because she had formed an image in her mind of Ed as a man who didn't cry. It wasn't macho posturing; he simply didn't shed tears, not even at his father's funeral.

She turned slowly in the bed. She was tentative with her body; there was no telling how he'd react if she touched him. It wasn't impossible that he'd get violent, like an animal in a cage. They were in a new territory, with new rules.

She shifted closer to him. When he didn't stir, she reached out to touch his shoulder, expecting him to slap her hand away; he let it rest there. She gave the shoulder a consoling rub; he sobbed a little harder. She pressed her whole body against his and he folded into its curve. She brought her other arm up against him so that she was hugging him fully. She found herself holding him to her as though he were a child. She'd always resisted cradling him in such a manner, fearing it would diminish her attraction to him, but attraction was the last thing on her mind at the moment. He sobbed as she held him, and she soothed him by making shushing sounds, long and slow and quiet, until he turned and sobbed into her nightgown.

She knew what it was about, even if he didn't. It was about getting old. She felt it too, but somehow she knew it was different for men. They got spooked when they lost their hair, when their backs gave out. Women were better prepared to deal with death and old age, especially mothers, who, having delivered children, saw how tenuous the line was between life and death. And as a nurse she had seen so many people die, people to whom she'd grown attached. Ed had taught anatomy and physiology. He'd been in the museum of death, not on its front lines. It was irrational for him to react this much to a bit of misentered data, but what was rational about a midlife crisis? Weren't they always a little absurd?

They were beginning the next phase of their lives together. She was not afraid of it. *Let it come*, she thought. *He'll be in good hands.*

Within minutes he was sound asleep, the crying having exhausted him. She lay awake until the alarm clock went off. He slept through her getting dressed. She made a neat stack of the papers on the table.

The Joint Commission sent eight people to do the inspection. She and the other administrators went into a conference room to make their presentations. She was glad she'd taken some extra time doing her hair and makeup that morning, and that she'd worn her gray skirt suit, which clung enough to give her some sex appeal while still looking professional, because the team was mostly male.

She was exhausted, but she felt confident about her staff's preparedness. She'd been readying the nurses for a year, training them in how to answer questions. They were up to date on all the standards: pharmacy, equipment, staff knowledge, patient care. It was the patient interviews that troubled her. Usually the patients were generous in their comments. Still, one disgruntled patient was all it took to get the commission sniffing around. "How is the service?" "Terrible." "How is your room?" "The place is filthy." "Are you getting the medicines you need in a timely fashion?" "I can never get anyone around here to answer my call."

She gave a rundown of the state of affairs in nursing and took a seat. She struggled to stay awake through the other administrators' presentations. Then they loosed the team.

She wasn't allowed to follow them around. It made her feel like a criminal. Accreditation was at stake; there were standards to uphold. Still, they were so damned humorless about it. They stalked the place like stormtroopers. They went through labs, making sure everything was cleaned and stored properly. They looked at every chart in the place. They pored over paperwork like district attorneys looking for a break in a prosecution. They grilled staff members. No one knew exactly how long they'd be there once they showed up. It could be three days; it could be the whole week.

Her staff could have withstood a press conference after all the paces she'd run them through. Still, things don't always go as planned. One inspector found an expired IV solution while interviewing a patient. That got the others digging. They found an expired medicine in one of the carts. The expirations killed you. You could have nurses trained to say all the right things, but if they found one bottle a couple of weeks past its prime in a lineup of fifty good ones, it negated weeks of coaching. A crash cart wasn't in the locked cabinet it was supposed to be in. They didn't tell her where it was, of course, only that it wasn't where it was supposed to be. That one hurt. She prided herself on running a tip-top ER. No one in her hospital was ever going to expire after cardiac arrest because the cart didn't

have the proper medications on it. If the cart wasn't where it was supposed to be, though, it didn't matter what was on it.

Before they left for the day, they gave her a list of citations. Too many and the accreditation could be compromised. They gave her a chance to follow up the next day. It was a simple matter of a few fixes—switching out the old medicine, changing the IV, putting the cart back where it belonged—but it also served to tell her that she was on notice. She'd get through it; North Central Bronx would retain its accreditation. Nothing about it promised to be easy, though. They seemed like the kind of crew that wouldn't give them a pass on anything. It was going to be a long week. In the meantime, life continued at the hospital. People didn't stop getting sick. People didn't stop having heart attacks. One kid came in having blown off his hand with a firecracker.

She dozed off at a red light on the way home. When she pulled into the driveway she saw the sheet still over the pile in the back. In the tumult of the day she'd forgotten about it. She walked over to it and lifted a corner. It was all there, untouched. She didn't have the energy to spare Ed's ego. She whipped the sheet off. If it was a bonfire he was after, he'd have to find another way to exorcise his demons. She gathered up the pieces of lumber and put them in the garbage can; they stuck out jagged and tall. She dragged the can to the curb for pickup the next day. Ed would flip out when he saw it; in fact, that was the point. Fatigue was hardening her toward him. His vulnerability last night, and her tenderness—it felt as if it had happened a year ago. She hardly remembered it at all; it could have been a dream. It was all so stupid; how could she have indulged him in it?

She marched inside and found him hunched over the stack of lab reports they hadn't gotten to the night before. She felt she'd fallen into a film loop.

"I took your wood to the curb," she said. "I'd appreciate it if you could keep the backyard from looking like a junk heap."

"Okay," he said without looking up.

"That's it? Just 'okay'? No rage? No telling me not to mess with your stuff?"

He kept working as though he hadn't heard her. She could smell a musky odor coming off him. He hadn't showered. He had changed his clothes, thank God, but he hadn't washed before he left for work. Ed hated not to shower. He felt a layer of grime sitting on him all day when he didn't.

"What were you trying to make, anyway?"

"I don't know what you're talking about," he said, swiveling in his chair. He gave her a look that said he was only trying to get an honest bit of work done. He was one of those aggrieved husbands who had to deal with the not-always-sensible ravings of wives who meant well but made things so difficult sometimes.

"I'm talking about the pile out back," she said pointedly. "Your little Stonehenge."

"I really have to focus," he said. "Whatever I did, I'm sorry."

"You don't remember the sheet you put over the pile of wood in the backyard?"

"Yes," he said. "Yes." She could see that he remembered it, possibly for the first time since he'd done it; he was that absorbed.

"Okay, fine," she said. "Just tell me something, and I'll let you work all night. What were you making?"

"What?"

She knew this gambit; he was pretending he hadn't heard her, stalling for time.

"What were you making?'"

"Oh, you know."

"I don't. That's why I'm asking."

"I was making something. I told you what I was doing. You know this."

"When I left on Saturday you told me you had some projects in mind. Home improvement projects."

"Yes! Yes. I was making something for the house."

His answers sounded like those given over the phone by kidnapped people being watched for signs of betrayal.

"What exactly?"

"Well, it was a surprise."

"I don't need any more surprises." She looked at him for a few moments. "How did it go today?"

"Fine."

"No problems?"

"No."

"No students complaining?"

"No."

She hesitated for a moment, then came out with it.

"Do you want some help with that other stack tonight?"

"Yes," he said in an instant.

She had no energy to cook, so they ordered pizza. At the end of the meal she took a long, hot shower. Afterward, she wanted to rest for an hour before she helped Ed with the lab reports. She didn't feel like drowsing in the musty air of the bedroom, so she availed herself of the couch. It was one of those times she wished they had a television in the living room. It had been a principled stance of theirs—of Ed's, mostly, though she went along with it. At the beginning of their marriage, Ed didn't hate television, precisely; he just didn't like what it was doing to American life. It wasn't always convenient to be without a set in their living room, but there were benefits. Actual conversations took place when people came over, unlike at Ed's sister Fiona's house, where the all-seeing eye made any exchange a series of distracted monologues. And when the three of them crawled into the big bed on Sundays to watch *Fawlty Towers*, it was an event. Recently, though, Ed had grown more severe about it, insisting she shut it off when she tried to watch Johnny Carson at night. It was part of a general trend in his thinking. He was becoming more reflexive, more reactionary. She was becoming the opposite. When they moved to the new house, she would get a big television for the den.

She went to the bedroom and wheeled the little television out to the living room. She wanted to shut her brain off. She didn't care if the noise bothered him. He couldn't be doing anything of consequence, and it was only a matter of time before she'd be sitting with him at the kitchen table, running through the grades.

She woke to Ed pounding on the television set.

"Keep that off," he said. "I'm trying to work."

She was too sleepy to take umbrage at what he was saying. She waited curiously for the next thing.

"Take it inside. Take it away."

"I happen to live here too," she said, her blood rising.

"Get it out of here! I can't concentrate."

She stood and fixed the pillows behind her. "We don't talk to each other like that in this household. I didn't let my father talk to me like that, and I'm not about to let you do so. You've been a complete jerk for I don't know how long. I've had it. I can't take another day of it. Either you stop this behavior right now, or I swear, Ed, I'm leaving. I won't make a big production of it. I'll just take our son and go. Do you have any idea how tired I am? How long my day was? Because I stayed up to help you. You want to do everything yourself, fine. Do it. It's easier for me to have nothing to do with you."

He dropped into the armchair and sat looking at her. It almost unnerved her how intent his look was. Against her will, she felt herself warming to him. There was something in his gaze that could make her embers catch fire, even when they were buried under layers of ash.

"I'm sorry," he said.

"You said that yesterday."

"I'm under so much stress at work."

"I am too," she said.

"I know."

"Since when are you under this kind of stress? I thought one of the perks of your job was how low-stress it was."

"Lately it's not."

"Your head's not in it," she said. "I think your mind's not right. But you won't talk to me. You won't let me in."

"I'm dealing with a new generation," he said. "I need to be perfect."

"You're having a midlife crisis," she said. "I don't mean to diminish it, but that's what it is."

"I just need to get through the next couple of weeks," he said. "Then I'll be fine. I need the summer to recuperate. I put a few things off, and now I'm dealing with them. I've tried to shield you from all this. I'm tired. I'm making mistakes. I haven't been sleeping well. I just need to recharge my batteries." He took off his glasses and rubbed his eyes.

"I know the feeling," she said as she yawned. "When do you need to return those lab reports?"

"Tomorrow is the last day of classes."

"Go get them and we'll check them together. Then we can both get some sleep."

She put on water for tea. She felt as if she was moving through a thick soup. She stood by the stove, watching the kettle boil. She fixed her tea and with languid movements joined Ed at the table. She wanted to insist on a little ceremony. She was going to sip her tea, not gulp it. But she needed Ed to calm down first. His knees were jackhammering up and down in that way that sometimes overcame him.

"Let me drink this before we start."

"Fine, fine."

She tried to let the warm liquid have a tonic effect, but she had put too much milk in it, and it wasn't a good cup. It was foolish to make tea in order to stay awake; all her years of drinking it before bed had turned it into a soporific.

"Let's get started," she said.

He focused on the open grade book with the unwavering attention of a runner about to start a race. She thought back to the chaos at the end of the previous night's efforts, the way a spirit of collaboration had devolved into a shouting match. If only there were a way to avoid the altercation that would ensue if—when—Ed made a mistake. She could feel it as a certainty for some reason, perhaps because of the barely contained mania in that pumping leg. He was in a place mentally where she couldn't follow, where an entry error was a harbinger of doom. She thought of the bum rap women got: as hormonal as she'd been after delivering Connell, she'd never been certifiably nuts.

An idea occurred to her and she saw right away that it was the correct one, the only one. It should have occurred to her last night, but she was on Ed's terms then, and tonight he was on hers. Still, she hesitated. Any deviation from the pattern, however short-lived that pattern happened to be, promised to unleash in Ed a disproportionate fury. She had a vision of his overturning the table like a card cheat before a shootout.

She cleared her throat. "I have an idea," she said tentatively, and he didn't respond. He was tossing aside, one by one, the gestures of nicety that accounted for much of conversation. "It can save us some time. Of course, if you want to do it another way, it's up to you."

He nodded to indicate he was listening—an improvement. She sipped her tea.

"I can just enter them directly into the book," she said. "You can check it over when I'm done."

"Yes," he said, lightning-quickly. At first she thought he hadn't heard her. Then he looked up and said it again. She felt her body relax. She hadn't realized it, but she had been bracing for a shock—a blow, even.

"Good," she said as she took the gradebook from him, but she didn't mean it. He was so quick to relinquish control of the project, it was as if he had been hoping all along that she would take it over.

She filled in the grades. It took no time at all. It almost made her laugh. She had let herself be convinced that this was a task that required the gravest concentration. In fact it would have been difficult to make a mistake once the first few were in place. They were already alphabetized. She shuddered to imagine how much time Ed had spent checking the alphabetization.

"Done," she said, closing the book. She hoped he wouldn't insist on checking it himself.

"Thank you," he said, to her surprise.

"Let's go to bed."

They made love; it was a frenetic affair. Ed seemed to take his stress out on her body, but she enjoyed it anyway. They hadn't made love with vigor like that in a while. There was something less than terrifying about his anger; it was that of a man in chains. He finished with a grunt; she climaxed along with him. As they lay in silence afterward, their bodies coated in sweat, Ed looking at her intently, she felt an invisible barrier between them had been breached. It would be easier now. She would be able to tell him about the house.

26

On Saturday she drove up to Bronxville to meet Gloria. No bids had been placed yet, and she wasn't interested in seeing any other houses. Still, she drove up. The clutter on Gloria's desk infused her with a feeling of unease.

"What do you say we walk and talk." Gloria gestured outside. "Take a look at the town."

Outside, Gloria extended the pack; Eileen demurred.

"You don't mind if I do, right?"

"Of course not."

"Good. 'Cause I have to anyway!"

Gloria laughed a raspy laugh and began to cough. She lit the cigarette and took a long drag.

"Talk to hubby yet? What's his name?"

She didn't know when it had happened precisely, but Gloria had dropped all pretense of formality with her. A hint of coarseness idled in her voice. At first their familiarity had been bracing. Now that Eileen was a step closer to living there, though, she felt conflicted about it. It meant a small diminution of her ideal. She thought of all the people Gloria probably knew in town. A real estate agent could wield a lot of power if she wanted to. She could control the narrative. She knew people's secrets no less than a psychiatrist or priest did.

"Ed. Ed's his name."

"Have you gotten the thumbs-up from him yet?"

"We haven't discussed it. He's been busy."

Gloria took a drag. Eileen could feel her gaze on her.

"You're afraid if you bring it up, you'll hear a no, and then there'll be no negotiating from there. I get it. I've been there—believe me."

Eileen bristled. It was far more complicated, and even if she had time to explain the subtleties of it in a way that did them justice, she wasn't sure Gloria was the kind of person who could appreciate such subtleties. She wondered how she had managed to let her guard down with this crude woman.

"I'm going to talk to him about it soon," Eileen said, "and I'm confident we'll be in a position to make an offer."

"You have a bit of time," Gloria said philosophically. "But I wouldn't wait forever. This house is under market. You can't afford to get into a bidding war."

She had been thinking of the house as protected by the invisible bubble of her interest in it, and she felt a seed of panic take root. They did a loop around the block, Gloria waving to owners and salespeople, a few of whom came out to chat. Eileen felt edgy and ill-equipped to win anyone over. It was safer when they were in the car; it was safer to walk around alone.

She didn't admit to herself where she was really heading until she had passed the on-ramp to the Bronx River Parkway. She kept driving until she came to the street with the two stone pillars at either side that Gloria had turned onto when she'd taken her there. She felt her way up a couple of turns until she saw the house. She didn't have a plan. She just knew she had to be near it, to confirm her feeling about it.

She parked in front, figuring the driveway was too conspicuous. She sat in the car for a while, looking at the stone wall that girdled the front yard, working up the courage to walk the grounds. She knew what she intended to do was technically trespassing, even though whoever was selling the house wouldn't have minded if it helped to firm up her resolve to buy it. She walked up the driveway to the back stairs. No table and chairs sat on the patio, but she saw them in her mind. Someone was being paid to care for the plants and shrubbery. She saw where she could add a few flowers. In a house like this she would be inspired to learn to keep them alive. A path of stone stairs led up the hill in the back. She followed it to a flat area halfway up that had been left untended. She could put another table there. It could be the aerie from which she looked down on her domain.

The property ran all the way up to a wall that abutted the yard of an Italian-style villa at the top of the hill. It dwarfed this house in grandeur and size, but there was no shame in being outstripped by a house that majestic.

After a little while she saw a worker turning over soil in the backyard of the house next door. He hadn't seen her, but all he had to do was look up. She hid behind a tree and watched till he disappeared inside. Then she scampered down the steps. The bush cover on the patio gave her courage to try the screen door to the den. It slid open, as did the glass door behind it, and in an instant she was in the house.

She didn't turn any lights on. Sounds echoed in the big empty spaces. She hesitated going deeper into the house, but a rustling of the leaves outside sent her scurrying into the living room.

She headed upstairs. The place smelled different than it had; she picked up a faint hint of mildew, perhaps wafting up from the basement. It might only have been the close air trapped in the house. She went to the bedroom where Connell had lain on the floor. The room felt imposingly empty with no one else there, and she couldn't stay in it long. She went to the guest bathroom and ran both taps. She looked at herself in the mirror, then looked away, afraid that something would appear behind her. In the quiet of the house every sound was magnified.

She went to the master bedroom and sat leaning against the wall, by the windows. The longer she sat, the more nervous she grew, but she couldn't bring herself to get up. She was waiting for external circumstances to dictate her next move. She felt like a mountain climber who had reached a longed-for summit and couldn't bear to return to normal life.

She didn't know how long she'd been sitting when she heard the voices. She shot to her feet and looked for a place to hide. She gave no thought to walking downstairs and forthrightly greeting them. She didn't know who they might be: the owner, other prospective buyers, a neighbor, the police. She thought to hide behind the shower curtain in the master bath, but there was no curtain, and even if there were one, how would it look if they pulled it back and found her there? They'd call the cops for certain. She thought of the attic stairs hidden in a ceiling panel in one of the closets, but she didn't know if she could pull them down quietly enough, and where was she going to hide up there?

She stood by the doorway to the bedroom. Lights were being flicked on downstairs. She heard enough to tell it was a couple looking at the house and a real estate agent who wasn't Gloria. She decided to stay in the bathroom until she had heard them start up the stairs. If she heard them go left at the top, she would slip out and head down. If they stopped her, she would burble something and keep moving. They weren't likely to follow her or keep interrogating her. And if they turned right and headed into the master bedroom suite, she would say she had stayed behind after looking at the house.

She listened to this foreign agent enumerating the house's virtues. Hearing them presented to another couple curdled the joy she took in their particulars. They were taking forever down there. Anxiety and impatience combined to produce an unexpected boldness in her. She flushed the toilet for a bit of theater, then thrust herself out on the landing and headed down the stairs.

"Oh!" the agent said. "I didn't know anyone was here."

"Pardon me. I stayed behind to use the bathroom."

"Not at all."

"Don't let me interrupt you," she said as the couple appeared from the kitchen. "It's a great house."

"It is," the husband said.

"Well, we know the toilet works!" she said, and felt instantly foolish. The agent looked as uncomfortable hearing it as Eileen felt saying it.

"Yes—ha!" the agent said, a little belatedly.

"Do you mind if I leave through the front door? Could you lock it after me? I'd like to get a look at the front porch."

"Not at all!" The agent looked relieved. "Please!"

Outside, Eileen's frenzy subsided. She caught her breath leaning against the railing, feeling its smooth but bumpy paint. She smelled the mown grass and the lavender scent of the lilacs in the tree, and she listened to the birds, the shuffling leaves in the branches. The manicured bushes shook mildly in the wind. No police or ambulance sirens battered her ears, nor any thunder from souped-up cars. A little girl rode by on a bicycle and offered her raised hand in a wave. Eileen waved back, completing the illusion of ownership. And then it hit her, the peace she had sought in going up there, the ineffable something she'd been chasing. Then she heard the agent and the couple enter the foyer and felt the peace slip away. Their voices were muffled through the door, but she knew they were speculating about the house, weighing it, considering it. In her mind it already belonged to her. She would do whatever she had to do.

27

Connell wasn't sure why he'd told his mother he wanted to move. Maybe it was because he'd seen how much she wanted him to want to. The truth was, he didn't want to go anywhere. It felt like leaving right now would be like quitting, like saying, *I really am the pussy you think I am.* And he was heading to a new school. He'd make friends there, but if he moved, he'd lose the ones he had now; he was pretty sure of that. Farshid, Hector, and Elbert had stuck with him through all the teasing he'd endured. Farshid was going to Brooklyn Tech, Hector to St. Francis Prep, Elbert to Molloy.

When they moved, he was going to leave part of himself behind. Even the ex-friends who gave him so much trouble were part of his life. Maybe they'd all look back on it and laugh when they were adults, drinking wine around each other's kitchen tables, throwing their heads back and remembering how they were as kids. You had to stay in the same town to get that kind of rich history with people. You had to have ties that ran pretty deep.

He wasn't going to have a home anymore, not in the same way. His mother didn't seem to mind that idea. But his mother had stayed in Woodside until she was in her twenties. Her best friends were people she'd known since first grade. He saw the way they enjoyed each other's company. She said it wasn't like that anymore, that people moved around, that there weren't neighborhoods anymore like there used to be, but he knew it could be like that. All you had to do was not go anywhere.

He was playing *Mike Tyson's Punch Out!!* at Farshid's. He tried twice to get past Piston Honda, but his heart wasn't in it. He handed the controls to

Farshid and watched him work his way through Soda Popinski and Bald Bull. Connell couldn't even get to the place Farshid started from. Farshid's fingers on the buttons looked like the beating of a hummingbird's wings.

Kids pretty much left Farshid alone. He'd come to St. Joan's in sixth grade, by which point everybody had settled into cliques. He was kind of a free agent.

"My mother's going to move us," Connell said.

"Yeah?" Farshid sounded like he'd heard him but not heard him. He was moving the controller around in the air as he slapped furiously at the buttons.

"She wants to get us out of here."

"Where to?"

"Westchester."

"Where's that?"

"The suburbs."

"That's cool." He cursed and threw the controller, though it landed softly on the rug, and he retracted it by the cord and restarted the game.

"I don't want to go."

"Why not?"

"I have my friends here," he said.

"You'd get a backyard. Maybe a pool."

"Yeah."

"I'd do it."

"What about your friends?"

"What about 'em?"

"You wouldn't care about leaving?"

"No offense," he said, "but yeah—no."

"I'd miss you and Hector. Even Elbert."

"You're not gonna see us anyway, even if you stay. You're gonna be in the big city with all your nerd friends. You're gonna jerk each other off in the locker room."

"Maybe you have me confused with yourself," Connell said.

"I'm going to have girls do that for me, thank you very much."

"Everything's going to change all at once."

Farshid finished the level and paused the game. "You just need to re-invent yourself. That's what my mother said to me, 'Reinvent yourself.' In Farsi, though: '*Khodeto az no dorostkon.*' I didn't want to come here, man. There was some political shit with my father. We had to leave fast. Talk about everything changing."

"You couldn't go to Brooklyn Tech if you moved."

"I don't give a shit where I go to high school, man! Here, there, I don't care. I care about what's after that. College! Living on my own." He slapped his hands together. "Beautiful girls in my dorm room! Hah!"

Connell knew why the other kids didn't tease Farshid. He wasn't vulnerable to them; he already had a plan.

"This is home," Connell said.

"Home?" Farshid said. "What does that even mean? I'm going to work on Wall Street. I'm going to have a hot wife like Alyssa Milano that I bang a lot in my big bed. I'm going to have a big house and a big pool. That's home."

Connell felt like a child; all he cared about was getting to hold a girl's hand someday, and Farshid was already thinking of what he would do with his wife.

"Sounds good," Connell said.

"Reinvent yourself!" Farshid said, handing him the joystick. "You can start by not sucking so bad at *Punch Out!!*"

"I have to invent myself before I can reinvent myself," Connell said.

"Aw, don't say that," Farshid said. "You're already somebody. You're the biggest nerd I ever met in my entire life."

28

It started in math class. Gustavo Cruz was tapping him on the back. Connell had been resisting all year, but Gustavo hadn't given up. It was the time of year when every point counted for some kids. Usually Connell just framed his test more tightly with his arms, leaned over it more to obscure it with his body. He didn't care if it made him look like a hopeless nerd; he wanted the teachers to know he had nothing to do with cheating.

Gustavo was slapping him on the neck now. Connell couldn't turn around to tell him to stop without risking looking like a conspirator.

He thought about what he must look like to the others—a stiff kid incapable of acting normal, a former fat kid still awkward in his body, a nerd with no style or balls who would never, ever kiss a girl. He'd been insulted and made fun of a thousand times, and he'd hung from the basketball hoop, desperate to shift his hand down to cover his privates but too afraid to fall, but he hadn't suffered the truest humiliation, because his parents always told him he was worth more than other kids could see. He wasn't sure he believed that anymore.

He sat up straighter, leaned to the side, and gave Gustavo full view of his paper—the top part, at least. It was a multiple-choice test with a couple of show-your-work problems at the bottom. The multiple-choice alone was enough to get Gustavo to pass. Connell was nervous. He would have been even more nervous if Miss Montero ever even looked his way during tests, but he'd put up such staunch resistance that it must have seemed to her as if the fight on that front had been permanently won.

In the lunchroom Gustavo exulted.

"Man, that was the *shit*. Cuh-*nell!*"

"Shh . . ." Connell tried to play it cool, but he felt exposed. "Keep it quiet."

"I get you, man."

A couple of days later, when they had a surprise quiz, Connell waited until he'd finished and then leaned to the side a little. This time Miss Montero snapped, "Eyes on your own paper!" but Gustavo had probably had enough time.

"Cuh-*nell!*" Gustavo said again, and Connell thought, *Con*-null. *Con*-null.

That afternoon, instead of hustling home, he found himself sitting on the rectory steps with them. Some cosmic sleight of hand had deposited him in their midst. He hoped none of them would notice he didn't belong.

They went to Shane's apartment to make prank calls. They called Gianni's and had a pie delivered to the address in the phone book for one of their teachers. They called Antigone Psillos, a good-hearted, untouchably homely girl who had been given the unimaginative nickname of An-*pig*-o-nee. Pete asked her out, and when she cautiously agreed, he said, "Psych!" and hung up the phone.

"What's that Chinese kid you hang out with?"

"Who?"

"Your friend," Shane said. "Elbert. Elbert Lim."

"He's not my friend."

"Whatever. What's his number?"

"I don't know," Connell said.

"Here," Shane said, passing him the phone. "You dial it. Order some Chinese food."

The guys were sniggling and slapping their knees. They were in Shane's living room. His mother worked late, and his father wasn't even in the country. He was a Marine who'd been in the Gulf War. He was supposed to have come back in March, when the war ended, but he'd been sent to Bangladesh to do relief work after a cyclone. There was a picture of him in his uniform on the wall right above the phone.

"I don't know the number," Connell said.

"Bullshit," Pete said. "You talk to that kid every day."

"Hang on," Shane said. "I had to call him once for homework."

Shane got his address book and dialed the number. He made excited faces as it rang.

"Hello?" he said into the phone. "Is this Chow-Chow Kitchen? I want to order some fried rice and spare ribs."

The other guys were hooting. Connell tried to smile. Shane had his hand over the receiver. *His father*, he mouthed.

"No, I said I want to order spare ribs. For delivery."

Shane slipped into laughter and hung up.

"Call back!" Pete said. He handed Connell the phone. "You call."

Connell pretended to look at the paper and picked up the receiver. He dialed slowly, made a mistake on purpose and started again. Then he made a genuine mistake, from nerves. Shane grabbed the sheet and dialed. Connell was still holding the receiver. It rang a few times and someone picked up. It wasn't Elbert's father. It was Elbert himself now.

"Hello?" the voice said.

Connell was too nervous to speak.

"Hello? Who is this? Can you stop calling, please?"

Elbert hung up.

"He slammed the phone down," Connell said, hoping that would be enough.

"Call back!"

"Don't you want to call someone else?"

"Call back!"

Connell took the sheet and dialed the number. The phone rang for a while. He was relieved to have been spared. Then the line clicked on. It was Elbert again.

"You assholes need to leave us alone now. Isn't your break over at McDonald's? Oh wait, I forgot. Even McDonald's wouldn't hire you. I bet they'd hire your mama, though. By the hour. I hear she comes pretty cheap."

He'd always appreciated Elbert's adult air, his razor-sharp intelligence. Now it made him feel ashamed. They were looking at him intently, his new, old friends.

"Say something," Shane urged.

"I want to order spare ribs and fried rice," Connell said in a fake voice deeper than his own.

"That's really funny," Elbert said. "Original. I've never heard that before. Not even once."

Connell didn't know what to say. He felt an idiot grin spread across his face. He could feel himself getting dumber. He saw the other faces looking back at him with—could it be?—appreciation. All he could think to do was order more food.

"And some egg rolls," he said in a fake Chinese accent that made his friends laugh even louder. "And wonton soup." It made him feel sick to do it—his father would have lost his mind if he knew—but it also felt good to be one of the guys.

"Shane Dunn? Is that you? Pete McCauley?"

He was praying Elbert wouldn't say his name.

"We're not even Chinese," Elbert said. "Not that you idiots would know the difference. We're Korean. I don't even like Chinese food. Why don't you ask for some kimchi? Maybe my mother would make some for your ignorant asses. I could come over and throw it in your face."

Elbert was like that: pugnacious. Usually it was awesome; now it just scared Connell. Elbert's mother's kimchi was delicious. The first time Connell had had it, he'd felt like his mouth was on fire; he'd never had anything so spicy at home.

"Come on, Connell!" Pete shouted. "Say something."

A hush fell over the guys at this transgression of protocol. They feigned shock and started cracking up.

"Connell? Is that you?"

Connell hung up before he could answer. He knew Elbert wasn't going to talk to him anymore, so when they told him to call Farshid, he just took the phone and dialed.

"Give me that," Shane said. "I want to talk to this sand nigger myself."

Standing beneath his father's stern portrait, Shane shouted a stream of insults into the phone. He didn't bother trying to disguise his voice.

• • •

When Donny went to the bathroom, Connell stood by the hall door and listened for the sound of a flush or footsteps. He grabbed handfuls of coins from the big bowl on the breakfront, filling his pockets. He had an allowance, but he took the money anyway. It made his stomach ache to do it.

He bought food, comics, baseball cards. At a store on Roosevelt Avenue, he watched some guys buy nunchuks and throwing stars. Then he bought a curved-bladed knife that snapped with a violent click into its protective handle. He brought the knife to school and unzipped his backpack to show his new friends.

"Put that shit away," Shane said. "How can you be a nerd and so stupid at the same time?"

He didn't have a game at Elmjack, so he went to the park. All his new friends played hockey. He didn't have any hockey gear, so he played catch with one of the older guys for a while and then sat and waited.

Afterward they walked up to Northern to Dance Dynamics to watch through the blinds while the girls danced. All the girls he'd ever had crushes on were in that class, and every guy there but him was dating one of them. The class took a break for a few minutes and some girls came outside. He was the only guy not in hockey gear. He tried to hold his glove behind his back. "Baseball's gay," he'd heard Shane say, and even though he'd seen how awful Shane was in the field whenever he played softball with the older guys, he still felt like a kid carrying that glove, while the others wore protective padding and towered over him on skates and rollerblades. The girls only glanced at him quizzically, as though waiting for one of the guys to explain why they'd let Connell follow them there.

They headed to the Optimo store to steal. It was coming on evening; he knew he was supposed to have gone shopping for his mother before dinner. He should have left a while ago, but he wanted to preserve his legitimacy by doing everything they did.

The plan was for each of them to take something while the rest distracted Andy the Korean guy behind the front counter and his mother back by the storeroom. They fanned out around the store. Connell stood up front, by the baseball card display case. It wasn't hard for him to pretend to be interested, because he went in there a lot for comic books and cards. He kept Andy busy by asking a lot of questions, but he didn't steal anything. He was sure he'd be congratulated anyway for helping the cause, but when they got down the block and showed each other their loot—candy, soda, a thermos—and his hands were empty, they called him a pussy.

They went to Pete's house a few blocks away. Pete got some liquor bottles out of his parents' closet and passed them around. Connell wouldn't take a sip.

"You are such a nerd," Pete said. "I can't believe what a nerd you are. What is he doing hanging out with us again?"

Pete looked to Gustavo, who shrugged his shoulders. "My man Connell is helping me out," Gustavo said, and then he shot Connell a look that said, *You have to help yourself out.*

They went back out to meet the girls after their dance class. He could imagine what it would feel like to be able to relax, to talk to them as if he had a right to. Once, in seventh grade, he'd called up Christin Taddei at Farshid's urging and asked her out. The call had ended in humiliation. Now Christin was standing right there. She said something he didn't understand. He felt like he could barely hear anything, the way the excited blood was coursing through his system.

"You reek," Christin said again.

"What?"

"You need to use deodorant. Or cologne. Or take a shower."

The other girls tittered. "I will," he said. In his embarrassment he could feel his toes curling.

"Damn, yo!" Shane said. "My girl just dissed you *hard.*"

Shane peeled off with Christin, Pete headed home, and Connell walked down Northern with Gustavo and Kevin. They neared the Optimo store.

"You should have taken something," Gustavo said. "Everybody else did."

Dusk was coming on. The store would be closing soon. Andy had his back to the window. He was in college; Connell had seen him wearing an NYU sweatshirt. Connell bought cards from him every day practically, and comics once a month at least. Andy put together a regular bag of comics for him. Sometimes he threw him a free baseball card pack, just for being such a good customer. He liked to watch Connell open packs and find rookie cards.

Gustavo was saying something, but Connell had stopped listening. He walked into the street to get a little distance, turned, and threw the ball he'd been carrying as hard as he could. The big pane shattered with a terrific crash. Sheets of glass fell like icicles.

Gustavo shouted "Holy shit!" and he and Kevin ran down the Boulevard. Connell ran across it into traffic and kept running until he stood in front of his house, alone, his chest pounding. The front door was unlocked. He stood in the vestibule looking out to see if anyone had followed him. He wanted to switch skins with someone else, switch bodies.

His father was on the couch, wearing his headphones, and his mother was in the kitchen cooking what smelled like broccoli and ziti, which was what she whipped up when there was nothing left in the fridge. He said he was home and didn't answer when she asked where he'd been. He headed to his room. He heard a cop siren outside and started biting his nails. He went into the bathroom and stripped naked and smelled his armpits.

She was right; he did smell. Maybe he was getting ready to stop being such a damned baby about everything. He got in the shower and turned the knob for hot water all the way, with only a little cold to balance it out. The water scalded his skin and he started turning red. Steam billowed out into the room, filling it up.

He couldn't stop thinking of that window breaking. He could see it happening over and over, the glass caving in, the one big piece dangling and falling off with a crash. They would find the baseball. They would have it dusted for fingerprints. They wouldn't need fingerprints, because he went in there every day carrying his glove and a baseball. Once, he'd even left his glove there and called in, and they'd held the store open late for him to come get it. He could see Andy shaking his head in wonderment at what the hell had come over this crazy kid. He'd always enjoyed Andy's sarcasm whenever somebody said something less than intelligent or acted like an ass. Andy was in college but he had to spend all his time entertaining these little kids. Connell could see him banging his fist on the counter. He could see him locking the door and consoling his mother, and then the two of them sweeping up the shards. He pictured him emptying the window display of cards, picking pieces of glass out of boxes of packs, pulling the gate down with a muttered curse. They deserved better than what he'd given them.

He scrubbed himself with punishing quickness, but he could not calm down. He kept thinking of Christin Taddei telling him he reeked. Christin used to date Gustavo before she dated Shane, and some people said she and Gustavo had had sex. She hiked her skirt higher than the other girls did, and her blouse was always a little tight. He had an erection. He grabbed it in that steamy cloud, and after a few quick strokes he brought himself off and watched the viscous stuff disappear down the drain. He rubbed at his hand, trying to get the gluey residue off. He felt even worse now, even more scared. He was guilty, guilty. He would have to get caught. It was only a matter of time. He wanted to get out, get away. High school couldn't come fast enough, but it would not be sufficient. He wanted to get far away. He never wanted to see Andy or Andy's mother again. They would carry around the truth about him wherever they went.

He heard a knock at the bathroom door. "Dinner," was all his mother said, but he felt like he'd been called up before a judge.

29

The night before he posted his final grades, Ed didn't even grunt when she asked what he wanted for dinner, or lift his head; he just put his hand up in an imperious dismissal.

She retreated and pounded her frustration into some hamburger meat. She chopped the carrots with savage thwacks, relishing the sound of the knife crashing into the cutting board.

After dinner, as she was cleaning up, he brought all his papers into the kitchen.

"Sit with me until I'm ready for you to enter the numbers," he said.

"I'll be reading in the living room," she said. "Come get me when you're ready."

"No," he said. "I want you here. I want you ready. I'll give you the signal."

He was acting like the head of an ER team waiting for an ambulance to arrive. It was absurd that she had to be on such high alert. She didn't raise a fuss, though. She made tea and got her book and sat at the table with him.

"No," he said, looking up. "No."

"What?"

"No reading," he said. "I need you ready."

"You can't be serious," she said, and returned to the book.

"No!" He grabbed the book out of her hands.

The testy ER doctors who took their nerves out on the nurses sometimes apologized later; with the ones who didn't, you learned not to take it personally. But these men were saving lives. Whose life was Ed trying to save?

"Honey," she said. "Is it really hurting anything if I just read here next to you while you work? What's the harm in it?"

He slammed his pen down on the stack of papers. "We have a system!" he shouted. "We have a system that works! We need to follow it! Just follow the system!"

She had already figured out that they had a "system," one of his doing whatever he wanted as she looked on his work silently, benignly, unblinkingly.

"Okay." She closed her book and looked at him. His hair was graying at the temples, but otherwise it retained its deep-black hue. His lashes were still long enough to be the envy of any woman, and his crystal-blue eyes softened the sharp impression his nose and strong jaw made. It still took her by surprise how handsome he was.

She sat and waited, sipped her tea slowly. It seemed that tea drinking was something he could tolerate as in-system. She reached for a pile he'd finished with, thinking to get a head start on it. He stopped her hand and told her to wait. She stood up, just to stand, and walked over to the sink. He told her to sit down. She could feel herself messing with him. She peppered him with questions at short intervals. He ignored them and kept his head down. Eventually he looked up at her, breathing through his teeth, his eyes flashing with hate.

"Be quiet," he growled. "Sit there and be quiet and wait till I'm done."

She wanted to say something acid, to humiliate him the way he'd humiliated her. The only thing that stopped her was the vague sensation that this was not the man she'd married, that some metempsychotic transfer had occurred. She sat in the chair with one hand on the table and one embracing the mug.

When he was done he slapped the pen down and took a deep breath, rubbing his eyes. He sat back in the chair pointedly, with as much presence as if he were studying her for the first time. She was surprised by his suddenly intense look and blushed. She wanted to touch him, to dispel her nerves. She took the pile of essays and began entering the grades in the book. She made short work of it. When she was done, he produced another sheet, with numbers on it and blanks next to them.

"Now this," he said.

"What is it?"

"The final grade sheet."

"What do I do?"

"You find the student number next to the names on this other sheet."

He had everything ready for her. Considering how organized he was about all the papers, how much he seemed to have the situation in hand, it was a wonder he was asking her to do this at all.

When she was done she closed the book with a thump. Ed clapped his hands together and raised them above his head exultantly. The gesture embarrassed her—seeing him celebrate so quotidian an accomplishment. She looked for signs of irony, but there were none.

They had another bout of lovemaking. He went at her purposefully, giving her deep kisses and holding her down by the wrists. It reminded her of the way he had made love to her during their brief attempts to conceive a second child: both of their bodies moving as one; the thrust of his hips compact, rhythmic, and deliberate. The only thing that kept it from feeling perfect was her nagging worry that Connell would hear the headboard knocking against the wall.

In the middle of the night—a groggy check of the clock revealed it to be four in the morning—Ed was shaking her awake. It took some effort to figure out what he was saying, but eventually she understood that he wanted her to follow him to the kitchen.

The sheet from earlier was laid out before her, along with another that appeared identical. She looked at him, confused. Her eyes were adjusting to the kitchen light, but she could see that the grades she'd written next to the numbers had been crossed out, with new grades written in their place.

"I need you to make these changes."

"I don't understand."

"I made some changes. I need you to transfer them to this clean sheet. I have to tape it to the wall outside my classroom."

"Why are you making changes? We were done."

She wanted to put her head down on the table. She felt that if she did, he would be standing there in the same position waiting when she woke up.

"Changes!" he barked. "I made some changes! I need you to transfer them."

She couldn't make sense of it. She would simply have to submit to the logic of this inquisition. The pattern in the grades became obvious quickly: Ed had taken every grade and kicked it up a full letter, irrespective of pluses and minuses. A C– became a B; a C+ became a B; a B became an A. Ed had long held the line against rising grades. He gave out As sparingly; getting an A from Ed still meant something.

"What's this about?"

"There were other things I had to factor in. Participation. Et cetera."

"You were very generous," she said sardonically.

"There's nothing wrong with being generous."

"Not at all." She smiled. "But you were *very* generous."

"I reconsidered a few grades. It's not your concern."

"Fine," she said. "I'm tired. I don't know why I said anything." She filled in the grades next to the corresponding numbers in the new sheet and put the pen down. "There. I'm going back to sleep."

In the morning she found him on the couch. On his desk the grade sheet had been revised upward again. Now there were only two categories, A and B. Below it was another blank grade sheet. She saw that it was her duty to transcribe these trumped-up scores to the final grade sheet. Or could there be another one in store, with all As?

Standing there, she remembered how, in the years after her father retired, when she was still living at home, she would slip cash in his pants pocket for him to find when he was out at the bar, to spare him the embarrassment of not having money to buy other people's drinks. If she did this, it would be to spare Ed embarrassment.

He was curled on the couch, which was too small for his frame. It was hard to be worried about him when he was sleeping. He looked like a child, like a larger version of Connell. His hands were folded up near his face, as though he had been arrested in the act of praying. It seemed that all men were the same in the few vulnerable instants after they'd been awakened, as though they'd been called back from some universal state into the particulars of their lives. For a moment she stepped out of time and all of existence made sense; then the moment passed, and Ed returned to being her husband.

30

She sat on the stoop, listening with a new equanimity to the sounds of the neighborhood. She heard the rumble of a plane in the distance and watched it course across the sky. As a car rushed past toward Northern Boulevard, she could hear music faintly thumping within it. The laugh track of a sitcom echoed in the little valley between the two houses. It was easier to tolerate the flaws of a place when the promise of release from it loomed. Whoever bought the house would know what they were getting and willingly embrace it. If she wasn't quite going to feel nostalgic for the neighborhood, she could at least imagine that once she'd signed the papers relinquishing the deed to the house, she'd feel the rage slip from her, and she'd be able to return to survey it with detachment. She could always come back to get her hair cut; no one tamed her cowlicks the way Curt did, and his price was reasonable. And she could imagine coming back to Arturo's, though the truth was, Arturo's was a good neighborhood place, the kind that made it bearable to live there, but it wasn't anything more than that. There would be other places, better places.

Connell did a dance to avoid the back-swinging car door, pinching a plastic-sheathed comic book carefully between uplifted fingers as if holding aloft a key piece of evidence. In his other hand was a shopping bag.

"Big day at the comic book store," she said dubiously to Ed.

"He did well this year. He's a good kid."

"Looks like he did well today too, big spender."

"It's an investment," Ed said. "He knows his stuff. He didn't get junk."

She went to Connell's room. He was slotting his new comics into his long boxes with the quiet gravity of a special-collections librarian.

"Did you take advantage of him?"

"No! Why?"

"He's happy to be done with the school year. You must have seen that."

"It wasn't my idea. He just came home and said, 'We're going up the block to the comics store.' I told him I didn't want to go. He kept insisting. I kept telling him I don't go to that store anymore. I don't like those people in there."

"Why?" she asked. "What did they do to you?"

"Nothing," he said. "They're just not nice. Anyway, I don't go there anymore. He said, 'Then let's go to that store near where your orthodontist's used to be.' He drove us all the way out to Bayside. I didn't want to get all this stuff. I mean, I wanted to, but I felt bad. He just kept saying, 'Get what you want.'"

"How much did he spend?"

"A bunch."

She moved closer to him. "How *much*?"

"Two hundred. Over two hundred."

"*How much* over two hundred?"

"Two forty-eight," he said. "And seventy-eight cents."

She couldn't believe the number. She would have thought it impossible to spend that much on comic books unless you brought a wheelbarrow into the store.

"You took advantage."

"I did not," he said, indignant. He was slipping cardboard backings into the comics' plastic sleeves and ferreting them into the archival boxes he kept his collection in. If it really was an investment, she couldn't accuse him of not tending to it. "He kept saying, 'I want you to feel like you can have anything you want.' He was telling me to fill up my basket. I didn't get any really expensive ones."

Eileen shuddered, as if a cold breeze had blown through the room. She sensed a sadness at the heart of Ed's largesse. The boy seemed to have sensed it too; it had tainted his happiness at his haul. She felt a powerful sympathy for her husband, like one of those synchronized pains experienced by people miles apart, even though he was in the other room.

With a dignified informality, the ancient maitre d' directed them to a table. Arturo's hadn't changed since it opened years ago: white aprons over black outfits; napkins draped over forearms; tinted, marble-patterned wall-length mirrors; mild music; steaming sliced loaves; a reliably robust house red. There were neighborhood Italian restaurants like it all over the city—strong in the specials, respectable otherwise—but she'd always felt this place represented a bit of refinement. Sandro, Arturo's son, ran it with a seemly reserve. Still, she was looking forward to putting it behind her for places of real distinction.

Ed smiled and looked benignly at his menu, as if written in its pages were the answers to diverting but trivial questions.

"Are you happy the year is over?" she asked.

"Very happy," he said.

She fidgeted with some sugar packets. "So, Ed," she said, after what seemed like an interminable pause. She tried out a smile. "We saw a nice house. One we liked a lot."

"You found a house?"

He was looking at her with a strangely blank expression.

"Well, we didn't find a house, exactly," she said. "We did see one. It may not be perfect. There's no saying we can even afford it."

"You want to move? We can move."

"What?"

She felt a little light-headed. She put both hands on the table to steady herself. His capitulation was so instantaneous that she had to think it was because the boy was there and they were in a public place; once home, he would give full vent to his displeasure. Another thought gave her greater pause, though: that she actually believed him. It was as if he'd never truly been opposed to the idea in the first place.

Ed turned to Connell. "This is what you want?"

She took a deep breath. Her stomach was in such a knot that she felt she might throw up.

"Very much," the boy said, with a strange gravity. "I'm ready to leave."

"You are?" Ed asked.

"Right away."

"Why?"

"Well," he said, "I've been thinking it over a lot." She wouldn't have guessed he'd thought about it once since the day they'd seen the house. "And what I've come up with is that I'm starting high school in the fall, and that's a fresh start for me, and I think we should all get a fresh start."

The boy had come to her aid. She had no idea where he was getting this poise. Perhaps her dream of having a politician in the family might come true after all. Ed looked to her. She shrugged her shoulders.

"Plus," Connell added, "the house we found is great. The driveway is wide enough for almost a half-court game."

She had no need to sell it to Ed when Connell was doing so much of the work for her.

"You want to move?" Ed asked again, as he shoved more bread into his mouth.

Connell nodded.

"Why not?" Ed said. "Let's move."

"We don't have to rush into anything," she said, disturbed by the quickness of his about-face.

"You found a house, you say?"

"Yes, but—"

"We can move."

"Really?" Connell asked.

"Yes."

"Well," she said, "I'm glad to see you're open to the idea. We'll discuss it more later."

"It's a fine idea." His grin was so wide as he buttered a slice of bread that Connell broke into a goofy one of his own.

"Someone's in a good mood," she said, but Ed didn't hear her. "I said, *someone's* in a good mood." The pair of them chomped lustily. Ed signaled for another bowl of bread. When the waiter brought it, Connell ordered another Coke. "Save some room for dinner," she said, unsure which of them she was addressing. She had ripped a sugar packet open without realizing it; its contents deposited into her lap. She rubbed the crystals until they formed a grainy film on her fingers, but she refused to get up to wash her hands.

"All right," she said. "Connell wants to move. You want to move. I want to move. Does that mean we're all in agreement?"

Ed nodded as he slathered butter on a new piece.

"You don't mind if I go ahead and get some plans in motion. You're on board."

"Sure," he said.

She felt herself growing angry. "Just back up a second," she said. "Do you not remember saying you didn't want to move? Do you not remember saying it wasn't the right time?"

"I know we talked about it," he said.

"And do you or do you not remember telling me in no uncertain terms that you didn't want to—you *couldn't*—move?"

He was nodding, but once again it wasn't clear he was actually listening.

"All of a sudden it makes perfect sense to you?"

Her voice had been rising without her permission. People at nearby tables picked up their heads.

"I'm sorry," he said. "I'm sorry." He wasn't just trying to quiet her down; there was a note of real contrition.

"Hey, Dad!" Connell said. "It's okay. This is a good thing!" The boy had moved over to put an arm around his father.

"I'm sorry," he said. "I just wanted to have some of this bread."

His apologies were making her uncomfortable. "Just tell me one thing," she said. "What changed your mind? What's so different today?"

"I just feel good today. I'm so happy to be done! I don't have to go in there for weeks—months!"

He was almost giddy. Maybe this thing wasn't depression. Maybe it was manic depression.

Now that the year was over, now that he could look forward to three uninterrupted months, he'd sign off on anything she wanted. It wasn't that he hadn't wanted to move; it was that he hadn't been able to deal with anything extraneous at all. He'd had to spend so much energy managing his depression, his midlife crisis, his students, his research, that formerly ordinary tasks like doing his grades had become insuperable burdens. The strain had caused him to short-circuit. He had lost his mind over a few calculations, some entry of data into a book, some transposition of that data onto a sheet to tape to the wall. He had falsified the record for it, lost sleep over it, screamed at her because of it, cried in her arms about it. All he'd wanted was to be alone to lick his wounds, and his job never let him be alone. As long as he lay on the couch with his eyes closed, shutting out his thoughts with music, the demon couldn't get to him.

Ed and Connell scarfed their meals. Eileen stared into her plate to avoid conversation and took her time eating. After the plates were cleared, Sandro approached grandly, the waiter behind him bearing a dessert platter.

"With my compliments," he said. "I'd like you to choose one each."

Sandro had chosen this of all moments to allow his circumspection to falter. "You don't have to do that," she said.

"We're celebrating tonight," he said. "Believe it or not, we've been here thirty years. You're one of our oldest customers."

He must have seen her stiffen.

"I don't mean oldest," he said. "Longest-standing."

"We don't need *three*."

Sandro turned to Ed. "You see?" he said, a hint of pique in his voice. "This is why she still has such a nice figure."

Ed smiled warmly, registering no tension, though Connell squirmed in his seat. Sandro left.

"Here's to the end of the year," Ed said, raising his glass and taking the little bit of wine left in it down in a gulp.

"Here's to finding a house," she said. Ed held out his empty glass. Connell raised his water and the three of them clinked.

"Here's to high school," Connell said. They clinked again.

Ed looked at her. "Good luck," he said.

"With what?"

"Finding the right house."

"I told you I found the right one."

He turned to Connell. "Good luck in high school."

"Thanks, Dad."

"Good luck to all of us."

31

His mother yelled for him to come outside. When he did, he saw her leaning on a shovel in the garden box, where she'd spent a lot of time lately. Anytime he left for a game on the weekend, she was hunched over a plant, flashing a spade in her gloved hand, or spreading enriched soil from a bottomless bag.

"I want you to bury this for me." She handed him a statue that looked like the ones on the breakfront in Lena's apartment. It depicted a man in a red gown holding a baby, probably Jesus, dressed in pink. She pointed to a space between rose bushes. "Put the hole here," she said.

"How far down?"

"Start digging. I'll tell you when to stop."

"Why are you burying this?"

"St. Joseph is supposed to help people sell houses," she said. "You have to bury him upside down, facing the street."

"Do you believe that?"

"It can't hurt," she said.

He felt the shovel strike something hard. He cleared some dirt away and saw a large rock. He trenched around it and pulled at it. It came up slowly, like a recalcitrant root. He took off his shirt, hung it on the railing, and kept digging. He was enjoying his new physique. He had grown about four or five inches that year. He watched his muscles tighten and release as he worked.

"This is the second one I got," his mother said as he dug. "The first one cost four dollars. It didn't feel right. It was white plastic. Just Joseph;

no Jesus. I brought it in to the girl at the religious store. I told her, 'I need a good one, not this chintzy one.' She showed me this. She said it wasn't intended for burial."

"How much was it?"

"Forty bucks."

It seemed like a lot of money to bury in the ground. When he had cleared the space of backsliding dirt, he dropped the statue in headfirst, covered it up, and stomped the mound to make it flat again.

"What if it doesn't work?" he asked.

"It'll work," his mother said.

32

She gave the listing to Cindy Coakley's sister Jen, who was with Century 21 in East Meadow. It might have been easier to go with someone local, but she wasn't about to leave any money in the neighborhood that she didn't have to.

The next thing she had to do was tell the Orlandos. She went up the back staircase to the second-floor landing and listened without knocking. She could hear them all in there—Gary and Lena too, from the third floor—watching *Wheel of Fortune* and laughing. Donny was good-naturedly yelling at the set, calling out answers and cursing the contestant.

Selling meant throwing them out on the street, or at least putting more burden on Donny, who wrote the checks for both apartments. Brenda didn't make much money at Pathmark; Gary's odd jobs never lasted; and Lena was past the point of being able to work.

She went back downstairs. The next day, after steeling herself, she headed up again. She heard some murmurs of conversation and knocked. Brenda opened the door onto the dining room, where Donny and Sharon were sitting at the table.

"This looks like a bad time."

"Not at all!" Donny gestured to an empty seat. "You want to join us? We have plenty."

She felt herself drift into the apartment. Brenda disappeared into the kitchen.

"Did you eat?" Donny asked.

"I don't want to trouble you."

"Sit down," Donny said. "I'll get you a plate."

The truth was, she was hungry. Ed and Connell were going to stop at a diner on the way home from Connell's game; she'd been planning to heat up leftovers. A big pasta bowl sat in the middle of the table with huge, gorgeous meatballs under a blanket of deep-red tomato sauce.

Sharon regarded Eileen with elfin eyes over a glass of soda. Brenda came in with steaming garlic bread wrapped in tin foil.

"Are you joining us?" Brenda asked.

Donny grabbed a big forkful of spaghetti and ladled out a few meatballs and poured a little lake of sauce around them. Before Eileen could answer, he handed her the plate.

"I guess I am," she said.

Sharon's plate was taken and the girl smiled silently across the table at Eileen. She had beautiful straight hair and striking features. She was nine years old, shy and gentle, the compensation for all the dead ends and suffering in the family, and remarkably unspoiled, though they all doted on her. Her radiance was like a recessive gene come to life after generations of hibernation in the bloodline.

Brenda said grace, a habit Eileen had abandoned at her own table after trying it out for a while after Connell was born. Her conscience rumbled as Brenda spoke the familiar words and added a makeshift prayer.

"This looks amazing," Eileen said nervously after everyone had crossed themselves.

"Thank you very much," Donny said, winking at her broadly. "I try."

"That's rich," Brenda said. "You can't even boil an egg."

Donny caught Eileen's gaze and gestured theatrically with his eyebrows as he spoke to his sister. "What do I need to boil an egg for," he said, "when I have you to do it?"

"Keep it up," Brenda said. "You'll find poison in your coffee one morning."

Donny smilingly bit his outstretched tongue and shivered in triumph at having provoked her. Sharon giggled through the whole exchange.

"Did you want to talk about something, Eileen?" Brenda asked. "I was trying to get everything on the table; I forgot why you came."

"Would you let the poor woman eat? Look, she has a mouthful of food, and you're asking her questions."

Eileen held a finger up while she chewed. Donny looked at her with placid interest. He had a kind, broad face with exaggeratedly fleshy features, like those of a prizefighter. He had a boxer's broad back and meaty hands. He could have become a depressive like his brother or a gambler like his father but he had sought to make a life for himself instead. He used to run with a tough crowd, the kind that in retrospect was almost wholesome in comparison to the drug gangs that roved the neighborhood now. She stopped seeing them around the house after Donny's best friend Greg from up the block wrapped his motorcycle around a streetlamp. Donny got a job as a sanitation worker through his father. He still worked on cars, but now only on his days off and more as a hobby than as a source of income. The Palumbos let him park whatever he was working on in the back of their driveway.

"What I really want to know," Eileen said, "is how you make this sauce. Mine never tastes this good."

"The key is to use fresh sausage. Spicy or sweet, whatever you like. Good stuff, nothing cheap. You have to burn it in the saucepan."

"On purpose?"

"When you have a nice charred coat, you put the tomatoes in. The acid eats the burnt part off the pan. It gets in the gravy. I'll show you sometime."

"Don't listen to her," Donny said. "Our mother's is better."

"For once this idiot is right," she said. "No one's is better than my mother's. I'm okay with that. I have time to perfect it."

"She's gotta perfect it," Donny said. "She needs something to bait the hook."

"That's enough out of you." Brenda smacked him on the head. It was impossible not to get caught up in the high spirits around the table. It was no wonder Connell didn't come right down when she came home from work, why she had to go up and fetch him.

"I've been hearing your car make some noises I don't like," Donny said as he pulled on his chin. "You know what I'm talking about?"

"I'm not sure."

"Let me take a look at it. Maybe I can catch something before it turns into a problem."

"You don't have to do that," she said. "I can take it to the shop."

"They're gonna charge you an arm and a leg. I'll do it for nothing, and I'll do a better job. I can keep that thing running forever."

"Thank you," she said guiltily. In her nervousness she had put her finger through one of the lace stitchings on the old tablecloth and broken it. This was going to be even harder than she'd thought. How could she tell him that the first chance she got she was going to buy a much nicer car? She placed her napkin in her lap and pushed herself back from the table.

"You okay?"

"I ate a bit quickly," she said.

"Brenda's cooking will do that," Donny said. "You want to get through it as fast as possible."

Sharon chuckled.

Eileen wanted to abandon the plan, go downstairs, and come back when she'd be more collected, but there were signs to put up, and she was going to need access to all the apartments.

"Who wants dessert and coffee?" Brenda said after the clinking of forks on plates had died down.

"I don't want to put you out any more."

"Nonsense. Have a seat inside. I'll make a pot."

Donny led her to the living room. She sat on the yellow floral couch, which had a pattern she'd always found garish and worn areas by the skirt and armrests. She'd considered it a telling detail that they'd bought a big new television and kept this sofa. Now, as she sank into it, she was taken by its softness. The room, which she'd always thought of as a model of how not to decorate, radiated the warmth of shared usage. In the corner sat a small, beaten piano that looked like it might have survived the ransacking of an old saloon. At times she could hear someone practicing up here, and she'd never realized until that moment that it gave her pleasure.

Donny sat on the opposite couch. Sharon came and sat next to Eileen. The television was on, muted; Donny glanced at it out of the corner of his eye.

"Are those yours?" she asked, pointing to the framed artworks on the wall. Sharon nodded.

"I don't know where she got it," Donny said. "Nobody in this family has any kind of talent like that. You should see how she does in school. Tell Mrs. Leary how you did on your last report card."

The girl demurred.

"Go ahead. Tell her."

"Straight As," she said in a quick burst.

"I didn't even graduate high school," Donny said. "Gotta be proud of this kid." He had a faraway look in his eye. "I try to help her at the table, but she don't need it. My little daughter is the same way. She's like a whip. Not even two years old and she can count to ten. She don't get it from me, that's for sure. I tell Sharon to watch you and Mr. Leary. You folks are on another plane. I tell her to be like you. I never knew what an education really meant. I tell her to look at me and just do the opposite."

"Don't say that," Eileen said. "I bet she's proud to have you as an uncle." As she spoke, she realized to her surprise that she believed what she was saying. "And you're going to be a great father to that girl."

He smiled wearily, accepting the verdict without objection. Brenda came in with a plate of Duplex cookies, followed by mugs of coffee. Eileen searched about for a coaster.

"Don't worry about it," Brenda said. "This table's older than me. It does the job."

Circular embossments emblazoned the table's surface like trophies from all-night conversations. They were suddenly so appealing that Eileen wondered for a moment why she'd always been concerned to preserve a pristine surface on her own table, which looked almost as new as the day she bought it, no history engraved on its face.

"I have to tell you something," she began, as Brenda settled into the couch next to Donny. "It's not easy to say."

Brenda, who seemed to have a radar for danger, shifted in her seat.

"Ed and I have decided to move. We're going to have to sell the house."

Donny's eyebrows rose. Brenda took a sip of coffee with two hands.

"That's great, Eileen," Donny said. "Where are you moving?"

"To Westchester," she said. "Bronxville."

"That's up by Yonkers, right? It's beautiful up there."

It unnerved her a little to hear Donny place it so quickly, though she wouldn't have been surprised to learn he knew every major road within a hundred-mile radius.

Brenda took out a cigarette and flapped the arm of her robe out to sit more comfortably, a gesture that made Eileen unaccountably uneasy. It was then that the smell of smoke, which ineluctably pervaded the apartment, came to her all at once. It was in everything; Connell came downstairs smelling of it. She hated to think of him sitting in it, or of Sharon sleeping in a cloud of the settling vapors. It also angered her that it might be a detracting factor in the minds of potential buyers.

"When is this happening?" Brenda leaked a small stream of smoke as she spoke. Her cigarette dangled at the end of her lip, just as Eileen's mother's had so often. She felt her heart hardening toward Brenda, and by extension Donny and Sharon. Brenda was making it easier on her without meaning to.

"Soon. I'm not sure."

"How soon?"

"I found a house. We're ready to make an offer."

"What happens to us?"

"I don't really know. The buyer can choose to let you stay. He can ask you to go. It's up to him."

"There's a *buyer*?"

"I'm just thinking out loud."

"I don't care if they raise the rent," Brenda said. "I'll make it work. I just don't want to move."

"You've been very kind to us." Donny stretched an arm out as if to hold his sister at bay. "We appreciate it."

They sat in silence, Brenda taking deep drags.

"It's going to be strange not having you around here," Donny said.

"It's going to be strange not *being* around here," Brenda said.

"What do you need us to do?" Donny asked. "How can we help?"

He was broad-shouldered and game, and the warm roundness of his face admitted no despair.

"I'm going to need to show the apartment, and the one upstairs. There'll be an open house. A few of them. I'll let you know when."

"Okay," he said.

"You can't be here during them. The Realtor asks that. The same is true for your mother and Gary."

"Got it."

"She might want to bring some things in. Candles, comforters, et cetera." She paused and then added, "She's doing the same thing in my apartment."

"Not a problem," he said.

"When is all this happening again?" Brenda asked, jabbing her cigarette out forcefully.

"Soon. We could start next week." Brenda called Sharon over. As the girl took a seat between her mother and uncle on the couch, the moral balance of the room seemed to shift. "I'm sorry it's so sudden. We just decided. I came to you as soon as I could."

"Don't get me wrong," Brenda said. "I'm happy for you. I don't blame you. I'd get out of here if I could."

Eileen looked down at her interlaced fingers.

"How much time do we have after you sell?"

"It depends," she said. "Thirty days. Sixty. Ninety. I don't know."

"Don't we have some kind of rights as tenants?"

"I'm not sure, since we've never worried about a lease. I can ask the Realtor."

"That's bullshit," Brenda said. "Put us on a lease. Buy us some time."

Donny stood up. "It's hot in here," he said. "Anyone else want a beer?" He left the room.

Eileen cleared her throat. "That might make it harder to sell the house. Especially because your rent is substantially below market."

"Then increase the rent. I don't care. Double it. Whatever it takes."

"Let's not worry about that right now," Eileen said. "Maybe I'll have a buyer who would prefer to have the house fully rented. I'll see what I can do when I know more."

"Maybe we'll buy it ourselves," Donny said as he returned with a glass of ice water. She saw that he had meant for the beer comment to lighten the mood. "It'd be nice to have a room for my daughter when she comes over." He checked his sister's face to see what she thought of the idea. Brenda's expression hardened, as if to say, *Who's got that kind of money?* Donny sighed. "Don't worry about us," he said. "I'm sure you have a lot on your mind. I'll see what we can come up with on our end. Whatever we can do to help, you let us know."

She thought about Lena. She knew Lena should hear the news from her, but she didn't know if she had it in her to go upstairs and go through it again. Lena was upright in everything she did; decency and morality were her default positions. She was one of those heroic old women who sat in church all day taking on the burden of saving the sinners around them.

"There is one more thing," she said.

"What is it?" said Donny. "Just ask."

"Will you tell your mother for me?"

A week later Jen had an open house. The thought of all those people gawking at her furniture, her possessions, her bathroom annoyed Eileen, but then she thought, *Let them come. Let them see the oasis we made.* Jen came an hour early to put duvets on the beds upstairs—where they'd all cleared out, as requested, despite Eileen's visions of them haunting the stoop, hangdog or angry looks on their faces—and decorative items on the tables and breakfront. She'd warmed pots of potpourri on the stovetop. It already felt like someone else's home.

She wondered who would show up. This was the time to leave the neighborhood, not discover it—but perhaps some intrepid breed of young person might fancy themselves enterprising and patient enough to secure an outpost in the neighborhood of tomorrow. It wasn't her responsibility to tell them that this neighborhood's best days were in the past.

Eileen left to get her hair done. When she returned, half an hour after the open house should have ended, she saw a tall Indian man on her stoop, talking with Jen. She stopped in front of the Palumbos' house and watched him for signs of interest. He was gesturing around and nodding at whatever Jen was saying. A woman who must have been his wife was standing on the sidewalk, along with their son and daughter, both of whom leaned against her. Eileen resisted the urge to introduce herself and feel them out. When they left, Jen told her she thought they might bid on the house. The man had said he would need it empty to make room for his extended family— brothers and sisters, nieces and nephews, grandparents. *So that's how they live*, Eileen thought.

A couple of days later, the Indian man offered the full asking price— $365,000, which Jen had originally thought a little high. Eileen called Gloria to find out whether the Bronxville house had sold. Then she called Donny to let him know there was an offer.

"How much?"

She told him. Donny whistled into the phone and there was a long pause. Did he know how much less she'd bought it from his father for?

"That's a lot," he said. "That's great, good for you."

"Thank you," she said.

He paused again. "How long do we have?"

She explained that it would be soon, a week or two at the most. She wanted to sell as soon as possible.

"Can you wait a little longer?" he asked. "I might have some options, but I could use more time."

She didn't know whom Donny was going to ask for the money, or what kind of trouble he would be exposing himself to in order to get it, but that was his concern.

"I'll see what I can do," she said, and as she hung up she understood that there was nothing she was willing to do. She had to get out while she could.

She called Gloria and told her to make an offer on the Bronxville house.

The next day—she forgave herself in advance for the lie—she told Donny there had been a competing bidder and the first bidder had gone above asking, but it was his final offer, and he needed an answer immediately.

He was no closer to having a down payment, he said.

"I'm sorry," she said. "I'm going to have to take it."

Eileen had bid below asking for the house in Bronxville, but they hadn't had another bid, so they took it without parrying.

The Indian buyer insisted on a thirty-day closing, but Eileen was able to extend it to sixty when she pled the case of her tenants. That was the most she could do for them.

Donny still fixed her car.

33

Connell woke up to his father screaming at him and wagging his finger in his face.

"*Christ!* Do you know what you've done? *Do* you?"

Connell's mind raced, but he could recall no hanging offenses.

"You left the jelly out all night!" his father said. "You left the cover off!" Connell stammered an apology, but his father waved him off. "How could you *do* such a thing?" He stamped his feet, one after the other, as though smashing grapes. Connell had never seen him make such a childish gesture, and it disconcerted him more than the yelling had.

Ten minutes later his father was back in his room, sitting on the bed. "I don't know what came over me," he said.

All that summer, he was on an energy crusade. He said they didn't need to shower every day, that every other day was sufficient. If you walked away from a stereo for a second, he hit the power button. If you ran the hot water too long for dishes, he reached across you and pressed the handle down. If you turned on the air conditioner in the car, he told you to open the window instead. When he turned off the air conditioning in the house, Connell's mother threatened to leave and turned it right back on. That got through to him; nothing else did. He let the air conditioner run, but unplugged the coffeemaker, the toaster, the stereo, the TV, the Apple IIe.

One night, while they were sitting at the kitchen table, his father howled in frustration after breaking the point off a pencil by pressing too hard. "This goddamned thing's no good," he said as he snapped it in half. "It's no good at all."

His mother took them on scenic drives in the area they were moving to, but when they parked and got out, his father just stood by the car with his arms crossed. They went peach-picking once, in Yorktown, and his father stuck his hands in his pockets and leaned against the enormous wheel of an idle tractor while his mother filled a basket with the most shapely peaches she could find. When they walked back to the barn to pay, his father reached into the basket in his mother's hands and began tossing peaches to the ground. "We don't need all these!" he said.

"What the hell is *wrong* with you?" He'd gotten about half of them out before she fended him off. She was looking around to see who had noticed the outburst. "Have you gone crazy?"

"We don't need this many!" he said, squashing them underfoot as he followed Connell's mother. "We can't eat this many!"

"I was just going to make some pies," she said to Connell, as though appealing to his fairness. The only thing he felt safe doing was shrugging.

"Not for me!" his father said. "I could go the rest of my life without another bite of your pie."

Then his mother herself turned the basket over, dumping out the remaining peaches. She dropped the basket and they walked to the car in silence. They drove home all the way like that, half an hour at least. Connell put his earphones in, but he didn't turn his Walkman on. He waited and waited to hear the silence end, but it never did, and a queasy feeling grew in his gut. The only thing he heard was a little quiet sniffling from his mother in the passenger seat when they were almost home. He hit play on his Walkman after that.

34

It was the end of August when they moved, as hot a day as she could remember, the kind of heat that made a person happy to escape the city. She had packed boxes for weeks, and the walls were lighter in color where the pictures had hung and the furniture had stood, as if a slow-exposure photograph had been taken of their lives. The ghostly outlines of their things, together with the austere emptiness of the space and the dirt and dust gathered in the corners and wedged under the molding, increased her eagerness to get out of there. The movers came and loaded up the truck.

"Do you want to do a last walk-through with me?" she asked Ed, who was sitting on the stoop with Connell.

"I've made my peace with it," he said.

She resented the private ceremony Ed's statement implied. She'd pictured them opening a nice bottle of wine when they started filling boxes, or a celebratory bottle of champagne on their last night, but they'd had neither.

"You don't want to take a final look at it?"

He didn't respond. Connell looked as if he preferred to sit there too. Rather than squeeze past them, she went around to the side door and up the back stairs to the second-floor landing. Peeking in, she was overcome by the emptiness of the place. A spasm of anxiety rooted her to the spot; she couldn't enter the apartment. She'd half expected to see Donny and Brenda and Sharon there, but the previous week, Donny had moved them to a three-bedroom apartment—Brenda and Sharon in one bedroom, he and Gary in another, Lena in the third—in a monolithic structure around the corner that possessed none of the charm of the garden co-ops, with a cramped, concrete common area instead of generous grass. She called "hello" in the echoing dining room and stepped inside. She stood where she'd sat and told the Orlandos of her plans—which was where she and Ed had eaten when it was just the two of them, and for the first few years after Connell was born—until she got spooked and left.

She hurried down the stairs to her own apartment. She could see it that way now, as an apartment. The whole time she'd been there, she'd preferred to think she lived in a house with floors she didn't use.

When Angelo Orlando sold her the house in 1982, he'd done so in distress. Just shy of a decade later, his heirs had had an opportunity to buy back their childhood home, and they'd failed to secure it. The story of their line in the house had come to an end. They were adrift in temporary shelters: someone else's apartment, someone else's building. The great churning never stopped. Spackle was placed in the holes where nails had held family portraits, paint covered the dirt marks of shoes left by the door, a coat of varnish leveled the worn hallways, and it was ready for a new family.

The family who'd bought her house was making a stand against obscurity. It would be their nail holes puncturing a fresh coat of paint, their cooking smells sinking into the upholstery, their shouts of laughter, pain, and joy bouncing off the plaster walls. They would use all three of the house's floors. In enough time they would forget the structure had ever belonged to anyone else. It was a thought that worked both ways: it would be as if she'd never lived anywhere but Bronxville.

At the closing, she'd met the Thomases. She was surprised to learn that the husband's first name was also Thomas—though the middle name listed on the contract was something closer to what she'd expected, a tangled thicket of consonants and vowels. When she couldn't stifle her surprise at such an odd name as Thomas Thomas, the husband, who was exceptionally tall and wore tinted glasses, explained to her that he wasn't even the only Thomas Thomas in his hometown, that the name was extremely popular there, due to the fact that St. Thomas had gone there in the middle of the first century to spread the faith among the Jewish diaspora. She dismissed this idea as ridiculous; St. Thomas might have visited India, but there was no way he or any other apostle had reached there before Western Europe or Ireland. Thomas Thomas seemed like an intelligent enough man, but his dates had to be incorrect.

The fact that Indians had bought her home and were going to fill it with their entire extended family, floor to ceiling, was another reminder that Jackson Heights was a big cauldron and that it was spitting her out in a bubble pushed up by heat. Supposedly it was the most ethnically diverse square mile in the world. Someone more poetically inclined might find inspiration in the polyphony of voices, but she just wanted to be surrounded by people who looked like her family.

The only thing left to do was walk through her own apartment for anything left behind. In the guest bedroom she spotted a solitary die on the floor and went to pick it up but pulled her hand away right before she touched it.

In the kitchen pantry she found a broom leaning against the wall like a forlorn suitor at a dance. Ed and Connell were waiting outside, but she couldn't resist the urge to sweep up the dust bunnies and bits of debris on the floor. She remembered sweeping the kitchen floor in Woodside as a girl, methodically, covering every inch of that fleur-de-lis-patterned linoleum in an invisible geometric march. Back then, she'd dreamed of a house like the one she was now leaving. Somewhere along the way, she'd adopted a higher standard. Her new house was large and full of light and made an imposing picture from the street, with a sloped driveway, slatted shutters, and stone pillars to mark the front walk. It was everything she wanted, and she tried not to wonder if the new house would one day feel as old and heavy as the one she was leaving.

She stared at the pile in the center of the floor. There was no dustpan, not even a scrap of cardboard to sweep it onto. It would be dispersed by the footsteps of movers, or the Thomas family themselves. It wasn't her responsibility anymore. This was another woman's kitchen now. There'd be a victory in leaving it there and heading outside, in allowing something niggling to go unattended to, but she'd been cleaning messes all her life.

She'd heard Ed tell Connell once that skin cells constituted the majority of dust. If that was true, then there were microscopic bits of her in that pile. She got down on her hands and knees, carefully because she was wearing stockings, and scooped the dirt with one hand into the cupped other. She dumped it in the sink. When she saw a little raised ridge of residue where her pinky finger had passed along the floor, she wet her hands to mop up the last remnants of her life in the house.

She went outside. Ed and Connell were already in Ed's Caprice. She had driven the Corsica up the previous night after work and parked it in the driveway. The house had been dark, and she'd started for the train in a hurry, not wanting to linger too long there alone.

Ed didn't look angry at having to wait. He looked simply blank. Blank was fine by her right then; she could map something onto a blank. There was a roiling complexity to Connell's expression, though, an untidiness that she wanted nothing to do with at the moment. She took a seat in the back. With their Caprice in the lead and the moving truck behind them, the caravan of their belongings set out for the Triborough Bridge.

It was a clear day, and as they headed toward Northern, the sun cast a warm eye on the block's houses. Connell waved to an old man who didn't look familiar to her. The neighborhood itself hardly looked familiar anymore; it was as if she were slowly stirring from a dream. The faces she saw through the window looked benign in the heat. Pairs and trios, even solitary amblers, were carried along by an unseen buoyancy. She was no longer afraid of these people; she'd cleared that infection from her bloodstream. The previous day, when she'd realized she'd never again have to attend one of Father Choudhary's Masses or walk on the Boulevard, she'd laughed in relief.

She spotted a clerk stacking cans in a bodega and leaned back against the headrest to stare at the ceiling foam. When she looked out again, they were a couple of blocks from the turnoff for the BQE. She knew the trip to Bronxville by heart; she could see one highway turn to another, then another, until they reached the surface streets and the house where they'd begin their second act as a family. There was still this short stretch left of her present life to go through, though. She felt no stirrings of nostalgia as she took in the Boulevard for what might be the last time. She shut her eyes to put it behind her the sooner. There was a blessed nothingness behind her eyelids; the darkness there could have been the peace of death. She'd spent her whole life working toward this moment, and she was exhausted. She felt she could sleep for years without waking.

The sounds of the streets, muffled by the air conditioning, grew less and less distinct, and the next thing she knew the car was pulling into the driveway. Her first thought as she took in the house through the window was that it didn't look the way she'd remembered it. It was smaller some- how, more ordinary. She thought to tell her husband to pull back out, that this was not their house, that they'd find their real house if they kept look- ing. Then she saw the truck with their belongings coming around the bend.

She stepped out and stretched her long limbs to shake off the drowsi- ness. Ed and Connell were standing looking aimless. She remembered that she had the only set of keys in her pocketbook.

The driveway, which had baked in the heat of a dry summer, was scored with cracks that would only expand as the weather got colder. The forecast called for clear skies for a couple of days. If Ed and the boy got started first thing in the morning, there would be time for a new layer of blacktop to dry. In a little while she would send Ed to the hardware store for push brooms and buckets of asphalt.

She let the three of them in. They drifted to different corners of the kitchen and stood looking at each other in silence, frozen by the unknown future awaiting them in other rooms. She opened a cabinet door held on by only the top hinge, and it swung like a pendulum in her hand. She had seen the chipped paint, the peeling paper, the old cabinets, the ugly lacquer, the Formica countertops missing edges and chunks, but somehow she had forgotten just how bad it all was. It struck her now that this kitchen was worse than the one she had left behind. She was beginning to understand how much work everything was going to be and how much it would cost.

She considered saying something to christen the house, but she didn't want to think about how inept her words would sound. Instead she just sent them out to unload the car. There would be time later to savor the re- ality of their altered lives, to appreciate having arrived where they'd arrived.

She opened the front doors and stepped out onto the porch, leaning cautiously into the rickety railing. She watched the couch sway slightly as it rose up the lawn, the heavy hickory dresser behind it undulating as the movers took their halting steps. For a moment the furniture seemed borne on invisible waves, like flotsam from a sunken vessel, and she imagined she'd been hauled up from the wreck of her old life to stand on the deck of a ship bound for an unfamiliar shore.

She stepped inside and made way for the wide arcing path the couch took through the expansive foyer. She examined the bricks. The finger-thick lacquer on them would have to go immediately. She felt she was coming out of a stupor.

The movers held the couch up in the living room and looked to her for instructions, but the simple question of where it should go baffled her utterly. She told them to put it down while she thought it over. She directed the men with the dresser upstairs. She wanted the next phase of her life to remain forever potential and the rest of her things to stay in the truck. When the movers were finished, they would drive off, leaving her and her family behind in the empty spaces she'd fought so hard to procure.

She told them to place the couch flush against the wall, under the windows. She didn't get the jolt of pleasure she'd expected from making her first decision in the house, because aside from the fact that nothing would have a home for a while, certainly not the kind of permanent home that could put her restless mind at ease, she also had a nagging feeling that it was only the first of many more decisions to come, that she was the ship's captain now.

The men with the couch were heading back to the truck, but she asked them to wait a second. They stood on the steps looking up at her. They were all, herself included, waiting for the next thing she would say. She tried to freeze the moment in her mind. She knew it would be one she'd want to come back to later. The future stretched out before her like a billowing fog, nothing about it distinct. All she had was her vision for the house and their lives in it. The house itself, as it was, was not what she wanted. It could be what she wanted, but it would take time and money, and she was afraid that both would soon run out. The reality of how their lives would be lived was waiting at the bottom of that hill, in the dark of that truck. These men, on the other hand, were clearly in focus. They pulled at their damp T-shirts, leaned on the railing. She would have to say something; there would have to be something to say. If only she had another minute, she could come up with the perfect thing. She could see them growing impatient. All they wanted to do was move her things from one location to another. They had no idea that everything they placed in a definite spot brought her one step closer to disappointment.

Part IV

Level, Solid, Square and True

1991–1995

35

Connell passed through a long, dark tunnel and emerged into an enclosed courtyard, where he joined a buzzing mob of boys waiting, as per mailed instructions, for someone to usher them in. There were no adults present, so they were exposed to each other without buffering—boys used to being at the top of their class, each now merely one of many. One head towered over the others, and Connell heard speculation about the big guy's basketball prowess, the city championships he might lead the team to by dunking on helpless opponents. It was thrilling to think of the havoc he'd wreak on their collective behalf, the revenge he'd enact for the years of slights and indignities they'd suffered as grammar school nerds. His size was a metaphor for the greatness promised to them. He would reveal the past to have been a prefatory period, a chrysalis of awkwardness.

In a sudden access of courage, Connell drifted across the courtyard toward the tall boy, who up close had a childlike face. When Connell introduced himself, a startlingly deep, though gentle, voice emanated from the boy, whose name was Rod Henni. He learned that Rod also rode in from Westchester, from a town called Dobbs Ferry. They were ushered into the auditorium, where they listened to speeches, filled out forms, and collected books, before heading to the cafeteria to continue buzzing through an excited lunch. At the end of the day, Connell and Rod took the 6 down to Grand Central together, steeped in the newness of everything they'd heard. They agreed to meet in the morning by the clock.

The next day, as Connell approached the clock, Rod waved to him and leaned his crane-like form down to pick up his backpack. Connell felt the nervous stirrings of new friendship, which offered the potential for mutual understanding but also for disappointment. He didn't want to start out on the wrong foot and be unable to recover.

"What's up, man," Connell said, looking away to affect casualness as they slapped five. He tried to drain his voice of any character whatsoever.

"I'm so excited to be heading to school!" Rod said. "I never thought I'd say that!"

As Rod looked to him for confirmation, Connell realized that this boy was not going to be his salvation. Rod's eyes were bright, his body hunched in an awkward question mark. Connell wanted him to stand up straight.

When they gathered in the gym that day for a free hour of play, Rod confirmed Connell's suspicions. He couldn't catch a pass or dribble. He certainly couldn't dunk. He could barely hold the ball and jump in the air at the same time. The only damage he could do on the basketball court was to himself.

That first week of school, Connell couldn't shake Rod, who came to the cross-country meeting with him. It was an open call; there weren't any tryouts. If you came to practice regularly, you were a member of the team.

Cross-country wasn't a cool sport. Waking early on weekend mornings to run for miles, running every day after school, and enduring the ribbing of "real" athletes kept people away. Connell prided himself on being a "real" athlete, a ballplayer, but no one would know it until spring came around. He joined the cross-country team to strengthen his legs for baseball, to increase his velocity and stamina. He learned to care about the sport and his performance at it, though, and to feel frustrated by his limitations. He had long, lean muscles and was trim and fit, and he was good enough to know what it felt like to hang with the really good runners for long stretches. As they pulled away, he could feel in his body what it would take to stay with them, to be great.

In practice, Rod was deadly serious, a grinder, Coach Amedure's example for everyone else. Coach always talked about how he was going to make a hurdler out of Rod come winter. It was obvious that Rod lacked the coordination necessary to leap over a single hurdle, let alone a series of them.

Rod's times in practice never fluctuated, no matter how hard he worked. He was always a minute behind the slow pack. He excoriated himself for his slowness. The source of this ruthless self-criticism became clear early in the season, when Rod's father came to a meet. As Rod crossed the finish line, Mr. Henni screamed at him in full view of everyone else. Connell and his teammates gathered around Rod, patting him on the back, but that week at practice they took up the charge themselves, sensing Rod's weakness. They made fun of Rod's gait, his heavy breathing, his profuse sweating, even his shorts. Connell didn't refrain from joining in. He knew it was wrong, and Rod knew it too. When he laughed at Rod's expense, Rod searched him silently with his eyes. A modicum of natural ability was all that separated Connell from Rod; that and maybe the fact that Mr. Henni was sort of insane. It wasn't easy to have a father like that, but Rod didn't help his cause by walking around with an innocent, vulnerable look on his face. That was the kind of look that made people nervous, made them want to do something to make it go away.

When Connell got home from practice, his father was on his hands and knees in the kitchen, scratching at the brick floor with a metal brush to strip away the dingy varnish. He was making his way from the kitchen to the den and into the foyer, one brick at a time. Connell changed into an old pair of jeans and joined him. Hunched and silent, they worked side by side. As Connell pushed his weight into the metal bristles, he felt the ache of the five-mile run descend into his muscles.

"At this rate, we'll be done in the year two thousand," he said.

"Keep working."

"The fumes are killing me." All the windows were open and there were fans set up on the kitchen counters, but it was a hot day in September, and the solvent-smelling air barely moved. "I have a headache." Connell sat up and rubbed at his hands, inspecting them for raw patches.

"You don't want to help, don't help."

"I'm helping."

"Then do it without commentary."

They dug at the crannies in the bricks. The solvent ate at the varnish, but he had to work hard at each brick. He thought there must be a machine to do this, but his father was determined to do it this way, his way. He refused to rest, as if he was trying to make some kind of point.

Connell scrubbed another half brick clean of varnish. "I have a Latin quiz tomorrow," he said.

His father waved him away without looking up. "Do your homework," he said.

"I can help," Connell said guiltily.

"Do your goddamned homework."

That weekend, his father took him to Van Cortlandt Park for a cross-country track meet. The sunny morning, the expanse of sky, and the brisk winds all filled Connell with a feeling of possibility dampened only by his dread of what would come once the gun went off: a mile-and-a-half run through hell; acid respiration and an agony of fatigue. A little distance away on the meadow, locals chased after a soccer ball, indifferent to the impending torture.

Parents and siblings stood around in a groggy pack. On the edge of the group, Rod was bent over double, palming the ground with his long planks of hands, as diffident a presence as a six-and-a-half-foot-tall boy could be. One of Connell's teammates, Stefan, who kept everyone on edge with sarcasm, snickered in Connell's direction at the spectacle of Rod's ungainly lankiness curled up in an awkward, striving stretch. The only one of Connell's teammates who didn't laugh was Todd Coughlin, whose natural dominance on the course allowed him to be generous.

Connell's father took pictures of the team as they stretched. Lately, his father had taken pictures of everything. In protest, Connell looked away from the camera, tunneling into his stretches, concentrating on the useful burn in his hamstrings and the territorial defensiveness he felt at the fact that another team had started stretching nearby. They were hopping and flapping their thigh muscles out with an aristocratic ease.

After the gun there was some rough jockeying for position—elbows, furtive shoves—as the mob converged on a point in the middle distance. The pack winnowed quickly into a grim line; a natural order emerged. A long, flat expanse led to grueling back hills, where, except for human trail markers stationed at bridges and overpasses, he was on his own, taunted by the leisurely scrawled graffiti on the rocks, dodging horse manure, and trying not to twist his ankle in the jagged ruts in the path. The hills culminated in a precipitous downhill, which he took at a breakneck clip to avoid giving away too much ground. At the bottom, near cars whizzing by on the Henry Hudson Parkway, came a quick turn and a shock of open space, a quarter-mile straightaway flanked by spectators and hollering coaches, where he wearily approximated his best sprint to the finish, his heart and lungs in pure revolt.

He saw the distant mob at the finish line as though through the wrong end of a telescope and wanted to step to the side and vomit. A large pack of runners passed him, calling on some mysterious reserve. He could hardly keep his head up.

He heard his father's voice before he saw him. "Come on, Connell," his father shouted gently through cupped hands. "Come on, son."

He took deep breaths and flung his legs out before him as though they didn't fit and he wanted to return them to their rightful owner. He gained on the pack a bit. A wall of cheers rose up as the finish line neared. He wanted to come through with the others. There wasn't much time left to catch them. It wasn't the first pack; those guys were resting already, turning over spray-painted gold in their hands. What it was was a little cluster of competitors. There may or may not have been medals left to fight for. They always gave out so many: thirty, fifty, God knew how many. The top quarter, the top third. Gold ones, silver ones. Then bronze. Then nothing. Coach Amedure got annoyed if anyone asked how many would be handed out that day. "Why do you care?" he'd say. "Why do you want to feed off the bottom?"

He caught up to the cluster, barely. They were funneled into the rope cordon. Plenty of medals remained. Hunching over, trying to catch his breath, he watched the officials hand them out. Each subsequent medal cheapened his own a little. When the medals ran out, runners came in to less fanfare. Individual voices could be heard in the din. The crowd at the finish line began to thin.

The laggards came trickling in. Among them was Rod, upright and stiff, like a totem pole come to life. Rod's reedy father screamed at him in frustration and the other voices around hushed at once. The harangue continued after Rod had crossed the finish line. People looked away, embarrassed for the boy, and Coach Amedure tapped his pen at his clipboard in impotent censure.

"What's that boy's name?" Connell's father asked.

"Who, him?" Connell said. "Rod."

"Stay here."

Connell nervously watched his father go over to where Rod and his father were standing.

"It's Rod, right?"

Rod nodded.

"What do you want?" Mr. Henni asked sharply. "I'm talking to my son."

"I was wondering, Rod," Connell's father said, ignoring him, "if you wouldn't mind posing for a picture with me."

Rod looked surprised but answered "Not at all!" while Mr. Henni was stunned into silence. Connell's father handed the camera to Stefan, who looked around in embarrassment before getting ready to take the picture. Connell couldn't believe what was happening, how much awkwardness could attach itself to a single moment. He rushed over and took the camera from Stefan and framed the shot as fast as he could. His father and Rod were smiling; you'd never know what had been going on moments before. Connell pressed the button once; then he went to Coach Amedure to find out what place he had finished in. The coach looked away in disdain as he showed Connell the clipboard.

A kid from Connell's grade, Declan Coyne, rode the train down from Bronxville with him. He started taking Connell around with him on the weekends.

"You look like a guido," Declan said. "You need to look like a prep."

"Okay."

"That mock turtleneck, for one. You need to wear a different shirt. Something with an actual collar. Rugby shirts are fine. Polo shirts. Buttondowns."

Declan had grown up in town and had gone to St. Joseph's. He knew all the Fordham Prep and Bronxville High kids in the area, and he fit in with them easily. They didn't care that he was a distinguished piano player; what they cared about was that he'd been the goalie on the Empire State Games soccer team during eighth grade. They probably also noticed the MG Declan's father parked in the driveway on sunny days.

"That spiky haircut—no way," Declan said. "All that hair gel. Let your hair grow. Part it on the side."

Declan's unruly curls peeked out from under his cap, which said U.S. Open. Even Connell's Mets cap didn't make the grade; it was the height of naïveté to wear a baseball cap that represented an actual baseball team.

"And those pants. You look like you're jumping out of a plane. Do you see anyone else around here wearing Z Cavaricci or Bugle Boy? You don't want all these pockets and loops. You could be a construction worker in that outfit. Just buy jeans, regular jeans, not those acid-washed atrocities."

Connell's mother had bought him the jeans Declan hated. Connell couldn't help noticing how Declan's mother seemed to get every detail right: pressing his school pants neatly; wrapping his sandwiches tightly in wax paper so that they resembled Christmas presents; lining up, alongside a bright bag of mini carrots that practically screamed good health, two perfectly round, homemade chocolate-chip oatmeal cookies. She even folded his napkins into neat triangles. And it wasn't just when Declan was at school that no seams were visible: Connell couldn't believe how neat and perfect-looking everything at Declan's house was. His own house had never looked like the Coyne house. Then again, his mother had always had a full-time job.

"And don't tight-roll the bottoms either. That's totally guido."

He imagined he looked to Declan like a member of an indigenous tribe that had just come into contact with civilization.

"Throw out those Reebok Pumps. Get some deck shoes. Bass is fine. And nobody wears tighty-whities. Boxer shorts. *Only* boxer shorts."

"Boxer shorts."

"No exceptions. I can't be emphatic enough about this."

"I'll get them."

"And get some soccer shoes. Adidas Sambas."

"I don't play soccer."

"That's because you don't know what's good for you," he said. "Everybody plays soccer. Get some soccer shoes."

"Won't I look like I'm trying too hard?"

"Would you rather look like you're not trying at all?"

The park ran alongside the Bronx River. Its western border was the Bronx River Parkway. Palmer Road lay to the south, Pondfield Road to the north. Trees lined its major path, and broad stretches of grass made up its main terrain. At night kids gathered in it to drink.

There wasn't much crime in town. The police were always driving up onto the lawn from the Parkway to take the kids by surprise, sending an under-aged exodus toward Palmer Road. He'd seen them leaving the park in a hurry and wondered how he would ever hang out with these kids.

Declan led him to a large group gathered a little ways from the path. Most of the guys, Declan said, went to Fordham Prep; a couple went to Iona; a few went to Bronxville High. The girls went to Ursuline, Holy Child, or Bronxville. There were older guys too: college students, dropouts, guys who had never gone to college and were working jobs.

One guy held a flashlight up to his own face as Declan introduced Connell, so that his features jumped out spookily. He had a fleshy face situated atop a pink-and-white-striped Oxford shirt. His eyes looked bloodshot. Declan said he was a senior at Fordham.

"Here," the guy said. "Have a beer."

He pulled a bottle out of a six-pack sleeve and handed it to Connell, who felt he couldn't refuse. He tried to twist off the top.

"Let me get that for you." The guy popped the cap off with an opener on his key chain. Declan waved over a guy who looked about Connell's age.

"Brewster, Connell," Declan said.

"So you go to school with this kid?" Brewster pointed to Declan.

"Yeah," Connell said, "but I'll probably fail out. I'll probably wind up at Fordham. I don't want to work all the time."

These kids didn't need to know that Connell was pulling good grades. He didn't want to start out in this town having everyone think he was just a nerd.

36

Because Ed's floor project had taken over most of the kitchen except for a narrow path between the refrigerator, sink, and stove, they ate their meals in the dining room. She was going to have to give up the dining room when Ed turned his attention to the rotted-out floor beneath it, but in the meantime she was determined to enjoy it. She had pinned up a bed sheet to separate it from the living room, which was packed not only with its own furniture but also with the pieces destined for the den and the foyer when Ed was done with the bricks. The dining room was her sanctuary. She had brought it to such a fastidious level of completion that it looked like a little theater in which a nightly drama was staged. The china leaned against the back of the cabinet, the polished candlesticks stood sentinel on the breakfront, the crystals sparkled in the chandelier after a chemical bath, and the white field of the lace tablecloth suggested a pristine altar.

Ed took a seat, rivulets of sweat still running from his head. He dropped his drenched forearms on the table and wiped his brow with the napkin she'd folded neatly.

When the kitchen floor was finished, the new cabinets and countertops could be installed.

"I don't know why you don't let me bring a contractor in for the floors," she said. "We have money for help."

"I'm doing a fine job," he said.

"I don't want to live like this. We didn't buy this house to live out of boxes. I want a real kitchen."

They had some money to work with. After they'd paid the deprecia-

"You want another one?" the older guy asked, taking the bottle from Connell's hands. Connell had drained it into the ground when no one was watching. With Declan looking at him with a slightly buzzed warmth, Connell felt the need to actually drink this one. He took a sip; it tasted bitter.

"You see that girl over there?" Declan was talking louder now. "The blonde? Her name's Rebecca. She'll suck your dick. You ever have your dick sucked?"

Connell hadn't ever even kissed a girl. "Nah," he said. "Not yet."

"She'll fool around with anyone."

He couldn't understand why a girl that pretty would fool around with just anyone.

"Did you ever fool around with her?" Connell asked.

Declan's face spread in a slow smile. "It was great," he said. "Feels awesome." He finished off his beer. "Why don't you go and talk to her?"

Declan pushed him in her direction. She was standing near the older guy who'd given him his first beer, and he chugged the bottle in his hand and went over and asked for another.

"My man," the guy said approvingly. "Plenty to go around."

He felt a burp coming up through his chest and let it out as the guy opened his beer for him. Rebecca had a cherubic face and a sweet smile. It was hard to imagine her being easy. Somebody made a joke and she laughed in a giggly way that made a wave of warmth pass over Connell's body. Declan came over and introduced him to a couple of nearly identically dressed guys, and Connell returned their desultory handshakes. He could feel the alcohol settling in. He felt a strange boldness steal into him.

"Is it always this dead around here?" he asked, and felt Rebecca look interestedly at him.

"Pretty much," one guy said.

"If I ever brought my boys from the city up here," he said, "these cops would shit their pants."

"Hard guy," one guy said derisively; Connell saw him look at another guy and smirk.

"I used to be in a gang," Connell said. He saw Declan shake his head. "I wonder what these cops would do if anything real ever happened here."

The guy made a remark Connell didn't hear, and the other guys started laughing. He wanted to say something witty, but nothing came to him. Rebecca walked off toward the trees by the river. Declan shifted his body, so he had his back to Connell as he talked to his friends. Connell couldn't hear them. When the others walked off, Declan stood there with him.

"Please tell me that was ironic," Declan said. "Please tell me you're not that corny."

Connell just drank his beer. When he was done, he went back to the flashlight guy for another.

People around him began to scatter before he realized what was going on. He was at the outskirts of the group closest to the cop car, and there was time to run and join the pack of kids leaving the park, but for some reason he just stood there. He was drunk, that was certain. He'd never been drunk before. The next thing he knew, an officer was removing the beer from his hand. "That's evidence now," the officer said. Another officer told him to stand against the car with his hands behind his back.

He'd played with handcuffs as a kid, but these were more substantial. They dug into his wrist bones. He felt himself being urged down into the car, and he sat back with a wince, the metal digging into his skin. The officers climbed in and they drove off. Through the grating he studied the impressive backs of their heads and felt strangely calm. The revolving lights illuminated the muddy grass outside. He knew he should probably be more upset, but something about this felt inevitable somehow. His parents were going to kill him.

They drove to the station house. One of the officers led him to a little room. "I'll bring you a glass of water," he said. "Have a seat."

Connell sat in the desk chair the officer pointed to, his head pounding. Above him, a framed print depicted a seafaring mission. The officer walked in with a glass, and Connell drained it.

"What I'm interested in hearing is where you got the alcohol. Did you purchase it yourself?"

Connell shook his head.

"I'm going to need verbal responses fro..."

"I don't know who gave it to me," he said.

The other officer stood. "This is going to be ... stand," he said. "Your school is going to hear abou... on their way here."

"They are?"

"What was the kid's name?"

"I just moved here, Officer," he said. "I don't know any...

"Do you remember anything about him?" the other offic...

"He was an older kid. A nice guy. He had on a collared shir...

"This kid is wasting our time."

"You're going to go to juvenile court," the first officer said. "W... this kind of thing seriously around here. You should know that right ... This isn't wherever you came from."

"Jackson Heights."

"Wherever the hell."

A little while later, his parents arrived. When his mother walked in, she smacked his face. His father looked more concerned than furious.

He was grounded from everything but cross-country practice. At the juvenile court in Eastchester, the DA offered a plea deal: thirty hours of community service. Connell had to stand before the judge. "If I ever see you in my courtroom again," the judge said, "you'd better have a toothbrush with you."

On the way out, his mother added her own threat. "If you ever disgrace me like that in this town again," she said, "don't come home. And don't even think of taking another drink until you turn twenty-one. You're not even close to man enough to handle it."

"Sorry, Mom."

"Not even close to man enough," she said again.

tion recapture tax (she regretted the low rents she'd charged the Orlandos all those years; the house had hardly generated "income" to speak of) and put 50 percent down on the new house, they'd pulled over forty thousand dollars out of the Jackson Heights house to make improvements with.

"You'll have your precious kitchen," Ed said. "The floor will be done soon enough."

"We're already two weeks from November, Ed. We could bring guys in and have this done in a day. They probably have machines that could do this in a couple of hours."

He grabbed her by the wrist, leaned into her.

"One guy touches that floor—one *single* guy that's not myself or Connell—and I've had it. Do you understand?"

She wrested herself free. "Have it your way," she said bitterly, rubbing at her wrist. "But don't expect any help from that boy. You're going to be the hero on this, be the hero. He's not helping you. He has too much work at school."

"I don't need his help."

She could almost taste the disgust she felt. A curd of sarcasm gathered in her mouth.

"*Good,*" she said. "This is just beautiful. This is everything I dreamed it would be."

37

At the gas station, when his father went inside to pay, Connell's mother whipped around to him in the backseat.

"I just want you to know," she said, "how much this means to your father. I would have preferred to stay in a nice bed-and-breakfast by the mountains and look at the foliage. But your father wanted to do this for you. You remember that, and be grateful. Do you hear me?"

"Fine," he said.

"And I have a bone to pick with you. What did you say to upset him before we left this morning? He said it was between the two of you, but I could tell he was bothered by it."

"Nothing," Connell said.

"I'm sure it wasn't nothing."

"He's right. It *is* between us."

"Don't get testy with me," his mother said. "You live under our roof. Don't you forget that."

He didn't want to tell his mother what he'd said. It would confirm that he was just the sort of brat she'd been implying he was. He didn't know why he'd said it; it had just come out. He and his father had been standing near the sink together. Connell was rinsing his dish before he put it in the dishwasher, and his father reached across him for a hand towel, and as he did so, Connell said, "You have bad breath." His father looked at him quizzically, and Connell said it again, a little differently this time: "Your breath stinks." His father put his hand up to his mouth to blow some air into his nose, and then he looked at him with a look that could have been hurt, confused, or grateful, Connell couldn't tell which. "Thanks," his father said, again inconclusively, and he left the room and headed to the bathroom. He didn't come out for almost an hour. Connell heard him brushing his teeth endlessly in there, the tap running while he brushed, and then silence, and then the tap running again.

His mother's mood brightened when they got to Cooperstown, which was full of nice little stores. They parked and walked to the Hall of Fame, a red brick structure that looked like a university building or a large post office. Outside, at his father's request, his mother took a picture of the two of them in front of one of the rounded doors. Then she left to go shopping. They arranged to meet back in front in two hours.

Inside, Connell and his father walked past the parade of plaques. His father pointed out players he'd loved in his day—Jackie Robinson, Duke Snider, Roy Campanella, Pee Wee Reese. He complained that Gil Hodges, his favorite player, hadn't been elected along with the others. He stopped at the plaques of players he'd admired for their personal characteristics who hadn't been Dodgers: Lou Gehrig, Stan Musial, Roberto Clemente. It was cool to read the plaques and see how the writers of these brief biographies condensed players' careers into a handful of statistics and a few pithy lines, but Connell would have liked it more when he was about twelve. He couldn't get enough of this stuff then.

After a little while it felt like they'd seen a lot, and Connell was thinking about lunch and wondering whether his mother might have had a point about the foliage, which, boring as it was, at least wouldn't have required him to spare his father's feelings by pretending to be as interested in this stuff as his father wanted him to be. They were passing through a big room with glass cases on all sides and people crossing in every direction when his father stopped short.

"The next time we come here," his father said, "they'll be inducting you."

Connell waited for an ironic chuckle, but it didn't come. "Sure, Dad," he said, rolling his eyes. "Okay."

He was good enough to make his high school team, but he wasn't going to get scouted; his father knew that as well as he did.

"I want you to listen to me," his father said. "I'm going to talk to you seriously for a minute."

A cute girl was standing with her parents and her little brother, looking at some old mitts in a case.

"Here?" Connell asked. "Does it have to be here?"

"I've noticed something in you that worries me," his father said. "Maybe because it reminds me of me at your age. I made life harder for myself than it needed to be. I see you hardening yourself. That isn't you. I see you closing your mind. You are open and beautiful."

"All right, Dad," he said, putting his hands up to stop him.

"Do you understand what I mean by that?"

"I don't know," he said. "I mean, I'm okay, Dad. I'm good. You don't have to worry."

"You *are* okay," his father said. "You're more than okay. You're wonderful. I know that, believe me. But there's something in you that is closing up."

"Dad," he said, "is this about me saying you had bad breath?"

His father laughed. "Listen. I'm going to ask you to do something you might find a little strange. Will you do it for me?"

"What is it?"

"You'll have to trust me."

"Is it going to be embarrassing?"

"Nobody but us will know about it."

"All right." Connell slapped his hands on his thighs in defeat. "Okay. Sure."

"Life is going to give you things to be angry at. I don't want you to be consumed by that anger or forget how much you're capable of. So we're going to do a little exercise right now."

"Are you okay? I mean, is everything all right?"

"I'm fine," his father said. "Are you ready?"

"Sure." Now Connell was genuinely curious.

"What I want you to do now is to feel in your bones that the next time we are here, they will be inducting you."

This was too much. "What does that even *mean*?" Connell asked as the cute girl passed him, meeting his gaze.

"Shh," his father said. "Close your eyes."

Connell closed them.

"I am telling you that we will be back here when they are inducting you. I want you to feel the reality of that for a moment."

"Okay," he said, relenting a bit. There was something sort of exciting in the way his father had said it. He sounded so sure. Connell wanted to believe his father could see the future or something.

"Feel it. Let yourself. You pitched for the Mets your whole career. You heard your name over the loudspeaker thousands of times. You heard the cheers. You heard the boos. You played on grass. You played on Astroturf. You killed your shoulder, you blew out your elbow, you mangled your knuckles, but it was worth it. You set aside seats at every home game. Your kids were in those seats. Your wife was. Now you're looking at a plaque with your face on it. You're thinking the portrait makes you look like someone else, but it's you—those are your numbers, under your name."

The way his father said it was like he'd been talking about more than baseball, more than the Hall of Fame. He meant it to mean whatever Connell wanted it to mean; he meant it to mean he believed in him.

And then, somehow, Connell did feel it: what it was like to have brought joy to people and done something extraordinary. He never let himself imagine outcomes like that. He didn't want to open his eyes.

"I want you to really feel it," his father said. "And I want you to remember that feeling, because it is as real as any experience you will have in your life. Will you remember?"

Connell nodded with his eyes closed.

"You have to use your imagination," his father said.

Connell could feel his mind opening like a flower in bloom. If he wasn't afraid to consider the impossible—that he would be a Major League ballplayer people would talk about for years—then in imagining it, he would not need to live it; he could have it, along with whatever else he wanted.

"Okay," Connell said. He could hear people passing by. He didn't peek, but he could see them going past, what they were wearing, the looks on their faces.

"Do you feel powerful?"

"Yes," he said, and he did; he had stepped outside time.

"Are you angry right now?"

"No."

"Are you afraid?"

"No."

"Do you know that I love you?"

"Yes," he said.

"Open your eyes," his father said, but Connell waited a bit, because something told him they would never be back where they were. "Let's go find your mother."

38

The kitchen cabinets were installed on a Friday. When Eileen came home from work after a week that had threatened never to end, and saw their pristine white surfaces, she stood leaning against the island she'd always coveted, looking around in frank amazement. Then she began opening doors and running her hand for pleasure over the sanded interiors. She couldn't wait to head to the Food Emporium. Ever since she'd emptied out the cabinets in preparation for their dismantling, she'd anticipated with great relish this restorative trip.

The next morning, she waited for the countertop man to arrive with his enormous slabs. She had settled on Corian, because granite was too expensive and she'd be damned if she'd live with Formica again. Then at the last minute she'd called and changed the order to granite.

She had thought she might like to watch them put the slabs down on the cabinets, but as the fabricator and his assistants hauled them up the back steps she realized she preferred that magical feeling of seeing the job complete, which she'd gotten as a child whenever she'd come home from school and seen the lines her mother had put in the carpet by vacuuming.

She snaked her way up and down the aisles of the supermarket, filling her cart with anything she could think she'd ever need. She hadn't even gotten through dry goods before the cart was so full that she had to check out, bring the bags to the car and start over. After this second round of shopping, not only was the trunk full, but also the back seat, the passenger seat, and the floor areas. She couldn't see in any direction except straight ahead and in the driver's side mirror. She felt the engine laboring to get her home.

She pulled into the driveway and honked for Connell to come down and carry the bags. She went upstairs and gaped at the glossy countertops. She walked their length, running her hands over their cool surfaces, amazed at how they kept going and going.

Connell came up with the first bags and lay them on the island. "What gives?" he asked.

"What?"

"You planning for a disaster?"

"I bought some things," she said defensively.

She started putting them away. Connell made an endless circuit from the garage to the kitchen. When he had nearly finished, and bags were arranged in a ring around the island, Ed walked into the kitchen and flew into a frenzy. He started grabbing items from the refrigerator and throwing them into the trash can.

"We eat too much!" he yelled. "This is too much food!"

"Would you please control yourself?"

"We need a new regime around here," he said. "We're getting fat. There are going to be changes. One meal a day! No more than one!"

"This should last us about a decade, then," Connell said.

"Get rid of it!" Ed shouted as he left the room. "All of it!"

Eileen followed him out. "You can throw it all out if you want," she called up the stairs, to his retreating back. "That's fine by me." She was trying to stay calm, not to sink to his level. "All it means is I'll have to spend more to replace it. I want every inch in that pantry filled." He disappeared into the bedroom. "I don't care if you starve to death, the rest of us in this house are going to eat." He didn't answer. "Like kings!" she shouted. "We'll eat like kings!"

39

In recent weeks, Ed had taken a hammer to places of rot in the drywall all through the basement, so that it looked like a target in a shooting range. In the minefield of the living room, he'd made a bigger mess, ripping up floorboards almost indiscriminately. The drainpipes were clogged. The garage door had stopped working. They'd suffered another flood in the basement after a heavy storm. And now that the cabinets and countertops were in, Ed refused to hire a single contractor to help.

He sat beside her at the wheel, seething in the mismatched outfit he'd passive-aggressively donned after she'd barked at him for half an hour to change out of his dirty undershirt and get a move on. They were going to the McGuires'. Ed was beset by distraction as he drove, drifting between lanes and slamming on the brakes to stop just short of stalled traffic.

"Would you pay attention? You're all over the road."

"I know how to drive," he said. "I've been driving for"—he paused—"since I was sixteen."

They'd left late and hit a bad jam, and by the time they arrived they were quite late indeed. Ed sat in the car after he'd shut it off. She stood outside the car, waving him out. Then she opened her door again.

"Are you coming?"

The light in the foyer went on; one of the McGuires would soon be at the door. She climbed back in the car. Maybe she had to try another approach. She drained the impatience from her voice. "What's wrong?"

"Just give me a minute," he said. "I can't think straight with you talking."

"Honey," she said as gently as she could, "we don't really *have* a minute."

"Who's going to be there again?"

"Just us. Us and Frank and Ruth."

"That's good," he said. "We see too many people."

They hadn't seen anyone since they'd moved, but this wasn't the time to argue. "You're right," she said. "I'll scale back. We'll just focus on the house for now."

"Thank God."

"Now, can we get inside?" She handed him the bottle of wine. Ruth opened the door and gave them both kisses. Ed's hand was shaking as he handed the bottle over; she saw Ruth notice it.

Dinner was ready and they took their seats right away as Ruth shuttled dishes in. Eileen tried to help her, but Ruth told her to sit. Frank opened the bottle to let it breathe. She felt herself begin to relax.

"How's the money pit?" Frank asked. "You find where they buried the bodies yet?"

This was where Ed would say something snappy and the two of them would be off.

"It's fine," Ed said flatly. "Coming along."

"Ed's been busy trying to get rid of the rot from the flood."

"Funny enough, I've been taking a continuing ed course in the history of water," Frank said. "Irrigation, water transport. We haven't gotten to floods yet. I'll let you know when we do. Maybe I can give you some tips."

Ed didn't say anything.

"It must be nice to get back in the classroom and learn something new," Eileen said.

"We're not getting any younger," Frank said. "We have to keep the brain going. Am I right?"

Again, Ed didn't speak. Ruth came in just in time with the platter of roast beef.

"Please," she said, gesturing to Ed. "Help yourself."

Eileen felt an instinct to serve him, but he was sitting between her and the platter. Ed stabbed at a piece with the serving fork. The tines didn't get a good purchase on the meat, which fell back to the platter with a juicy splash that sluiced grease onto the tablecloth. He went in again, stabbing with too much force, but managed to get one piece onto his plate, and then another. The third dropped into his lap. Ruth and Frank shot each other looks. Ed picked it up and put it on his plate. He didn't try to wipe the marinade from his pants. The three little strips huddled on his plate. He handed her the fork, though protocol called for him to serve her or pass her the platter. She had to stand up to reach the meat. When she was done filling her plate, she put two more pieces on his. She looked up and realized that both of her hosts were watching this transaction intently.

"You want me to serve you?" she asked Frank.

"That's fine, I'll do it myself."

"This all looks beautiful," she said, handing over the utensils. She stayed on her feet. "Let me have your plate," she said to Ruth. She felt like a chess player thinking several moves ahead. "I'll serve the potatoes." She spooned some out for Ruth; then she put some on her own plate, and then, as though it were a matter of course, on Ed's. She did the same with the vegetables.

Ed looked skeptically at his plate. After having trouble gathering food onto his fork, he started pushing it on with his finger. He transported a few bites successfully to his mouth before one dropped on his shirt.

This was a good time for Frank to make a joke about Ed being drunk. It was impossible for Ed to take offense at anything Frank said. They ribbed each other all the time, and nothing was sacred; they fell into hysterics while she and Ruth wondered what was wrong with them. Tonight, though, Frank just sat there, looking at Ed until he saw that Eileen saw him looking and looked away.

They got through the meal with some effort. "You sit with them," Ruth said, as Eileen tried to follow her into the kitchen to help clean up. "Sit in the living room and have a drink. Make sure they don't get into any trouble."

Eileen brought them drinks. There was less awkwardness in the living room. Frank helped by talking at length about the class he was taking. She was never more grateful for his long-windedness. Ed interjected here and there, and the exchange resembled an actual conversation. Ruth came in and they sat holding their glasses in the comfort that follows dining with old friends, the engine of one topic running down as the engine of another revved up.

"So how's Connell?" Frank asked.

"His grades are good, but he's struggling in biology, if you can believe it."

"I was a horrible student in high school," Frank said. "If it had mattered then the way it does now, I wouldn't have had a prayer."

"Me too," Ed said.

"It's a different world," Ruth agreed.

"He's in his second year already," Ed said. "He's got to settle down soon."

Eileen flinched.

"I thought he was a freshman," Ruth said. This was the danger of having friends like Ruth and Frank who paid attention when you talked about your kid.

"Yes, freshman," Ed said. "That's what I said."

"He likes English," Eileen said quickly.

"That's great," Frank said. "I love literature. I'm going to take a Shakespeare course next semester."

"Ed's disappointed," she said. "He wants him to love science. He wants him to go to medical school."

"Speak for yourself," Ed said. "I want him to follow his bliss."

"Maybe he'll come around," Frank said. "Listen, we were thinking of having him up for a weekend. Do you think he'd like that? Or would it be more of a drag for him?"

"He'd love it," Eileen said.

"Maybe while he's here you can talk some sense into him," Ed said. "He's having a hard time with biology, if you can believe that. He's not applying himself, is all."

"I don't know how much help I'll be," Frank said. "I failed bio the first time I took it."

"That sounds like Connell, I'm afraid. His biology grades aren't the greatest. He's focused on literature."

"Is there an echo in here?" Frank asked, laughing. "I might have to cut you off."

"Please do." Eileen tried to sound authentically relieved. "For all our sakes."

"Or maybe what he needs is not less but more." Frank stood up and took her glass, then Ed's, which was still full. He looked at it for a moment.

"Let me freshen this for you," he said.

The business of getting drinks occupied a few minutes, and Ruth re-filled the cheese and cracker plates.

"So tell Connell to think about what weekend he wants to come up," Frank said.

"You're having Connell over?" Ed asked.

"If he wants."

"Do me a favor and talk to him about giving more of his time to sci-ence," Ed said.

"Before I forget," Ruth said abruptly, "I have to tell you the funniest story." She embarked on a narrative about having had her car towed the last time she went into the city. It wasn't funny at all, and it wound up being far shorter than Eileen had hoped, but she felt her eyes well up in gratitude.

Soon it was pumpkin bundt cake and coffee. The rituals of meals had never been more of a comfort. Ed ate his cake without trouble and they sat in the pleasant ease of digestion. She could see the distance to departure beginning to narrow. They might very well escape without further incident.

Ruth gathered the coats, and they said their good-byes in the hallway.

"Remember," Frank said. "Ask Connell when would be good for him to come up."

"I will," Eileen said.

"Maybe you can talk some sense into him," Ed said. "He's slacking in science."

Frank's eyes widened. He broke into an awkward grin that looked more like a grimace. "Don't let this guy drive," he said.

Although she had had more to drink than Ed, she got behind the wheel. She felt exhausted, and more than once she had to blink away sleep. Ed snored the whole trip, like a child, oblivious of the danger he was in every time she let her mind wander.

40

The floors in the living room and dining room were still a mess. Not only hadn't he begun to lay down wood, he hadn't even bought any, and it was now the second week of December. He had put the floor job on hold to focus on the basement. It drove her crazy to have the most important rooms in the house be off-limits. She had given up on the dream of entertaining the first Christmas in the new house (when the Coakleys agreed to host, she was afraid she might have lost dibs on Christmas Eve to Cindy forever), but she wanted to be able to finally sit in her living room. He was kidding himself if he thought he was going to be able to handle it alone.

The noises of destruction and toil emanating from below made it sound as if he was overseeing a torture chamber. She never approached him when he was down there, and when he came up covered in plaster dust and dried concrete, he sat and ate in remorseless silence. When he was asleep she went down to check on his labor. The space was coming together somehow. A do-it-yourself home improvement book sat perpetually splayed on the floor, its dog-ears attesting to the concentration that had gone into making things flush and square.

She found a disposable razor on the coffee table in the den, sitting in a streak of shaving cream. She told herself that Ed had come downstairs to answer the phone while shaving and gotten distracted. When she picked the razor up, though, and saw that the book under it was his beloved fifth-edition copy of *The Origin of Species*, she let out a shriek. No one but Ed ever touched that precious volume, and it never left his study. The fact that it was on the coffee table at all was amazing enough, but for its front cover to be stained by a filmy dollop of Barbasol was simply unfathomable. Her first thought, her only thought, was to leave the razor alone so he could see he had ruined the book himself.

She'd written him notes lately—gentle reminders she would leave on his nightstand before bed, like a secretary laying out the next day's agenda for the executive she was secretly sleeping with. *We're going out with the Cudahys tonight,* or *Don't forget parent-teacher conferences at 6:00.* There had been something pleasant about writing the notes; whatever tension still hung in the air after a given evening's misunderstandings evaporated like a cup of water on a hot afternoon.

One note struck her as odd when she read it over. It grew more opaque the longer she looked at it, like one of those unfathomable koans. She couldn't escape the sensation that she'd written the note to tell herself something as much as to get a message to Ed. *Christmas is six days away, Edmund,* the note said. *Please don't forget to get Connell a new baseball glove. I've asked you three times now. I'd take care of it, but I don't know the first thing about them. It seems like the kind of thing a father should pick out. That is still you, right, a father?*

How had they gotten to the point where she could write him a note like this? She thought of the hours he spent grading papers every night, how he never came to bed before eleven anymore, how just recently she'd spent a night helping him tabulate the grades for a lab report, as she'd done during the crisis at the end of the last academic year. She thought again, as she couldn't help doing lately, of that inscrutable pile of wood with the sheet over it in the backyard in Jackson Heights. She recalled the scene with a strangely heightened clarity, as if it were an installation in a museum dedicated to preserving the unimportant details of her old life. She panned around it in her mind, studying it from every angle, attempting to understand why this nettlesome image hadn't receded into the ether of the past.

The dawning came all at once, though it felt as if it had been heading her way for a while, like a train she'd heard whistle from miles off that was now flying past and kicking up a terrible wind.

Still, she couldn't pronounce the sentence in her head, *Ed has . . .* , because it was impossible that he had it. He had a demanding job that kept him stimulated. Until recently, he had read constantly, done the crossword puzzle almost every day, exercised four times a week. He was still the fittest man in their circle.

Maybe it was a tumor. Maybe it was a glandular problem, a dietary deficiency, a failing organ.

Whatever it was, she would get him checked out.

It wasn't going to be easy to bring it up. He was going to tell her she didn't know what she was talking about, that if something was wrong with his brain he'd be the first to know, being a *brain expert*, she could hear him saying. And part of her wanted him to dismiss her fears with an imperious wave and tell her she was behaving hysterically. But she couldn't allow him to overpower her on this topic. She needed to find out if something was wrong with him.

She waited for an opening. She wanted him to forget something or say something demonstrably strange, but he just went to work and came home and started in on the basement like an indentured servant paying off his debt. He made runs to the hardware store and returned with Sheetrock, cinder blocks, and bags of cement that he hauled piece by piece from the car. She worried his body would give out on him.

When she called Ed's doctor and suggested worry about Ed's health, he told her she was crazy, that Ed was as healthy as a horse. "I just saw him, what is it, six months ago," he said. "He's got the lungs of a swimmer. Not a whisper when I put the stethoscope to him. Only thing is his blood pressure's a little high. Let him put his feet up on the weekend. Give him a glass of iced tea and put the game on for him. And his cholesterol could be lower. Maybe no cheeseburgers for a while. No more shrimp."

It sounded like an indictment of her, somehow. "We don't eat any shellfish," she said. "I'm allergic." She tried to rein in her annoyance. "Did he seem *fuzzy* to you at all?"

"Fuzzy?"

"In the head. Slower on the uptake."

"Maybe you're expecting too much of him. Men aren't perfect creatures. We get miles on the engine. We need repairs. The warranty runs out. Ed's got a good engine. He's got a lot of road left ahead of him."

She watched him and waited for the mishap, the big slipup. He continued to make incremental progress, continued to refuse outside help, but every day, as he beat himself harder and harder to finish the work, as she watched patiently, intently, she could feel the ground shifting in her favor, Ed's resilience weakening. As much as she needed to bring the work on the house to completion, as much as she couldn't wait to have a team of workers laying down boards in her living room and dining room, and as much as she was glad to see the ground ceded to her, she found herself rooting for Ed and feeling sorry for this man who spent every night hammering away. She saw him on his haunches, head in a manual, hammer poised, his back a rounded stone, and she willed him to brilliance, though she knew she was willing the impossible.

She watched Ed grow more weary at each dinner, look more disheveled, push away his plate after a few bites.

One night he didn't come when she called him to eat and she sent Connell to get him.

"He says he's not coming," the boy said when he returned.

"Tell him I said to get in here."

"Maybe you should go in, Mom."

"What is it?"

"He's just sitting there."

She went into the dining room and saw Ed surrounded by planks of wood. He had half a plank in his hands. Nails were sticking out of it, and its end was a comb of shards. She could see the other half nailed into the floor. He must have tried to rip it up in his hands.

"Get up, Ed."

"I'll be in when I'm done," he said. He was hunched over, breathing hard. He looked like he'd been whipped. He lifted himself up onto one knee in a vaguely supplicating manner, and the sight of him there put her uncomfortably in mind of the Stations of the Cross. She wasn't going to give him the chance to make some kind of poetical self-sacrifice, if that was what he was after. The only person who'd feel sorry for him if he did that would be himself. He'd had all the chances in the world to bring some-one in. They had enough money for at least the floors and the kitchen. He was too damned stubborn.

"You're done."

"I have to finish this section."

"You're done," she said. "Come and eat."

But he didn't follow. After she and Connell had finished, she brought a plate of cold sausage and beans in to him. She could barely stand to look at him as she left it on the floor by his feet. He hadn't moved in half an hour. He was in the same place in the middle of the room, a perfect vantage point from which to survey the mess he'd insisted on making.

She made the phone calls and settled on a general contractor who could finish the kitchen, do the floors, put in high-hats, and plaster and paint all the walls on the first floor.

The night before the workers were scheduled to start, she told Ed they were coming, and he didn't put up any kind of fight. She wondered whether she should have forced his hand sooner, but they gave out no manual when you got married, no emergency kit with a flashlight for when the power went out. You had to feel your way around in the dark for the box of matches.

he work began a couple of weeks after the new year, 1992. The
ustle in and out of her kitchen was exciting. She offered them
s and set out platters of cold cuts on the island, rolls, tubs
f potato chips.

e of six-packs for them one day. Ed took one
he cans landed with a thud and shot a
floor installer who had been using
way back to the living room.

vbe she'd never heard

e backed

stic

guys in

g room
for years.

y father's. I'd

basement would
down there were
f bath between the
he first floor from the
or that couldn't come
nted. She had pictured
She had flipped through
nd, white had seemed ap-
could deal with right now.
hite. She would have to deal
mauve. She thought that a lot
he path from kitchen to dining
hat company would travel—this

She felt a need to protect Ed. "It's just that he's losing his job," sh said, surprising herself with the lie. "Layoffs."

"I'm sorry to hear that."

"It's going to be fine. We're going to be fine."

He and the other worker looked at her as if they were waiting to se she'd make another revelation.

"Please drink these," she said, holding up the beers.

"You don't have to tell us twice," he said. "But we have to wait ur we're done for the day."

It reminded her of her father, to hear him responsibly defer havin drink. They returned to laying in the boards, and she went to the bre front to find the red velvet-lined box that held the set of crystal gla with "Schaefer" etched into them that her father had received upo retirement. She took them out and ran a cloth over them.

At the end of the day, when she laid the six-pack on the dinir table, she set out the glasses too, on a Schaefer bar tray she'd saved

"Please use these," she said.

"Oh, we don't need glasses, ma'am," he said politely.

"It would make me happy if you'd use them. They were n like to see them filled with beer for once."

The roof could wait for a couple of years. The rot in the have to remain for now. The tile floors she'd pictured a project for another time. So was renovating the ha kitchen and den. So was moving the laundry room to t basement. There was old wallpaper on the second fl down, and there were walls that needed to be pa fresh paint and white tiles wherever she looked. design magazines for elaborate ideas, but in the propriate, the cleanest option, the only one sh She would have to wait for everything to be with gray and yellow and brown and a sickl of her house looked like a waiting room. room to living room, though—the path

path was ready to go. She could keep them from going upstairs or downstairs. And as soon as she had a spare few thousand dollars, she was going to put a better half bath in for them and spruce up the den.

There was, on the other hand, the question of the furniture. She simply wouldn't be able to live with the things she'd brought from the old house, not if she couldn't fix this one up the way she wanted. Her furniture squatted shabbily and hardly filled the room. The scratched dining room table, the worn armrests on the chairs, the boxy end tables, the permanently depressed couch cushions: they were like placeholders for the real pieces to come. She saw now that she would need to replace nearly all of it. She would put it all on credit cards. Upstairs, she would create a sitting area, buy the desk she'd always lacked, and outfit each guest room with a stereo, an armchair, and a beautiful reading lamp. As soon as she got these bills paid off, she would replace Connell's childhood furniture.

She knew she lacked the aesthetic sense necessary to give the house the ambiance it deserved. She would bring in an interior decorator. There would have to be new art everywhere, and the little touches that put one in mind of real discernment. She could pay for that with credit cards too. Ed would veto these expenses if given the chance, but he was past the point of possessing veto power. He was simply going to have to place his fate in her hands. They would pay it off. Ed would get another grant. Their salaries would rise. Once everything was in place, they would live frugally, sensibly, like Boston Brahmins. They would even find a way to build their savings back up. There was always a little more money to be had every year.

f nothing's wrong with him," Eileen told her own doctor, when she went in about a shortness of breath she'd been experiencing, "I'm going to divorce him. I can't take it anymore."

Dr. Aitken told her to bring her husband in. She sold it to Ed as his annual checkup, that she'd like him to try her doctor, and when he didn't object in spite of having gone in for a checkup less than six months before, she knew she was doing the right thing. They sat in the discordant placidity of the waiting area before she led him into the examining room and went back out. She'd blustered about divorce, but now she saw that she would put up with anything in exchange for hearing that her husband had simply become an asshole.

After spending half an hour with Ed, Dr. Aitken came out to meet her.

"Don't divorce him yet," he said, handing her a referral to a neurology team he trusted.

She braced for the fit she expected Ed to throw once they got to Montefiore, but he sat docilely again on the papered, padded table, waiting for the doctor to arrive. His big, fleshy back looked like raw dough.

First came blood tests and a physical exam. Dr. Khalifa, the lead doctor, wanted to eliminate anything that might cause memory loss, so he checked Ed's thyroid levels, as thyroid problems had run in his family. They gave him a CT scan.

His thyroid was fine. The CT scan showed no sign of a tumor.

She took him back for diagnostic exams. Dr. Khalifa sat Ed at a table and took a seat opposite him. She sat in the extra chair and felt nervous for

Ed, as though she were about to watch his debut in a theatrical production that had limped toward opening night.

Dr. Khalifa told Ed to count backwards from one hundred. Ed got to ninety-seven before pausing. "Eighty-six," he said, then ran off a few other numbers in accurate succession, until he jumped another decile, at which point Dr. Khalifa stopped him.

The obstreperousness she'd anticipated was starting to seem like a fantasy. Ed looked vulnerable and small. He was smiling, trying to ingratiate himself with his examiner, perhaps in unconscious pursuit of mercy in the diagnosis.

Dr. Khalifa told him to draw three concentric circles, and Ed put a good one down on the page, then drew another that was ovoid and attached to the first like a chain link. The third, a shaky line meeting finally in something more like a quadrangle than a circle, sat apart from the first two.

"Great, that's great," Dr. Khalifa said dully when Ed was done. The doctor was a picture of imperviousness. She watched his eyes: he betrayed no sign of surprise, gave away no clues as to whether this was a normal result or not, the product of mere aging or something more sinister. She didn't know whether she herself would have been able to draw the concentric circles. Certainly it would be difficult under this kind of scrutiny. She had a sensation that she was watching a child take a test, and she felt a sympathy with Ed that made her question her decision to expose him to this. What right did she have to subject him in the quiddities of his middle age to a man who would be looking for any sign of deviation from a norm that was probably arbitrary in the first place? She wanted to whisk him back home and let him go at things in his own way. A category existed to describe men like him, a time-tested, venerated one at that: absentminded professor.

"I'm not an artist," Ed said, laughing. "You should see my drawings of the digestive system."

The doctor chuckled.

"This could be something abstract," Ed said.

Dr. Khalifa looked at it and shook his head. She didn't like his attitude. He was too glib, too detached. His hair was too perfect, his teeth gleamed too white. She had long wished Ed had pursued medical school, but now she felt she'd been too hard on him in her mind. She knew doctors like this at work; they thought they walked on water. The work Ed did might not have been as lucrative or flashy, but it laid the groundwork for guys like this to come to their conclusions. If Ed said nothing was wrong, then most likely nothing was wrong. She had insulted him by bringing him before this cipher who didn't deserve to carry his briefcase, let alone pass judgment on him.

"We're almost done with this part," Dr. Khalifa said. "One more question and then I'm going to have you do some physical things."

"Okay."

"Tell me something. Do you know who the current president is?"

If he wanted to insult him, this was a perfect way to do it. She almost wanted Ed to answer sarcastically or deliberately incorrectly, but she didn't want the doctor to have the satisfaction of writing it down on that little pad of his.

Ed sat with it; maybe he was coming up with a witty riposte.

"I know it's a Republican," he said. "I know that."

"Can you tell me his name?"

Ed pulled on his chin. "Reagan?" he asked. "Is it Reagan? I can see his face. It's not Reagan, is it? This is embarrassing."

"You know this, Ed," she said. The doctor gave her a look; she wanted to smack his face.

"I can see him," Ed said. "I just can't recall the name."

Dr. Khalifa wrote something down. She wanted to call the answer out. The whole thing was so stupid. She couldn't believe he was letting him dangle there like this. Ed looked ruined, as if he had failed a test not merely of memory but of character.

"Give it a second," Dr. Khalifa said. "Sometimes it's hard to think of a given thing when you have to. Think of something else. It might come to you."

"White elephants," Ed said.

"Something like that."

Ed rubbed the top of his head, as if to massage the answer from his scalp. He let out a deep sigh. "I can't remember," he said. "Who is it?"

"I'm not going to stop looking, and I'm not going to sell the house out from under you, Ed. I need your consent."

"I'm going to work on the house this summer," he said. "Maybe you'll want to stay after that."

"Do it if it makes you happy," she said. "But don't go thinking it'll make a difference. You can't put out a fire with a thimbleful of water."